THE PILLARS OF THE SEA

ZOË TAVARES BENNETT

THE PILLARS OF THE SEA

ZOË TAVARES BENNETT

MEDITERRA
PRESS

To Homer,
the best bard among all Helenes,

and to Odysseus and Penelope,
whose love crossed the very oceans of time.

The Realm of Emmeson
Cimmerians
Mysia
Cicones
Keteians
The Land of the Dead
Aeaea
Islands of the Sirens
Pillars of Hercules
Scylla
Charybdis
The Middle Sea
Cave of the Sibyl
The Mountains of Atlas
Island of Aeolus
Island of the Cyclopes
Laestrygonia
Scheria
The Enchanted Isles
Ogygia
Ithaca
The Inner Sea
The Eastern Edge
The Wandering Isle
City of Helena
Lotus-Eaters
The Golden Sea
Black River
Neilo
Weru
Hapy

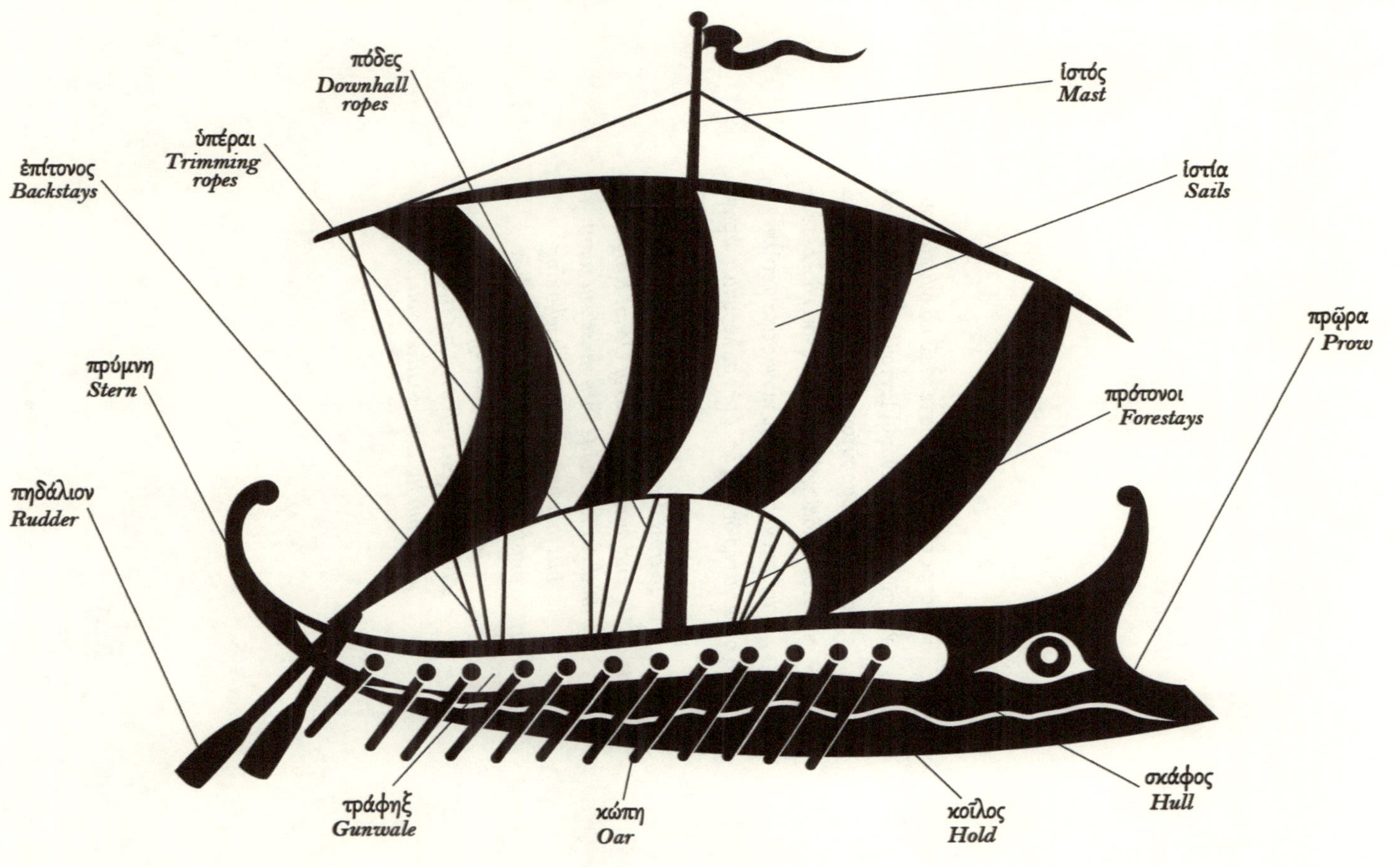

πόδες
Downhall ropes
ὑπέραι
Trimming ropes
ἐπίτονος
Backstays
πρύμνη
Stern
πηδάλιον
Rudder
ἱστός
Mast
ἱστία
Sails
πρῷρα
Prow
πρότονοι
Forestays
τράφηξ
Gunwale
κώπη
Oar
κοῖλος
Hold
σκάφος
Hull

οἴνοπος οἴκαδε μὴν ὥστε πλεῦσαι διά πόντου
καὶ μῆνιν καταπαῦσαι Ποντομέδοντος ἔπειτα ·
πλάγξαι καὶ τοσσοῦτον χρή καὶ εὐρύ τὸτ’ ἀλλά
πρῶτον ἀοιδαί κούρας δεῖ τε φέρειν δολόεσσας
τιν’ ἐπὶ νηὸς πόντου κίονας εἶτα μετῆλθε
οὖ θυγάτηρ οἰντῆς ἀπ’ ἀρῆς σὲ λύουσα τ’ ἀρήγοι

To cross the wine-dark sea back home
and quell the wrath of Ocean King
both far and wide then must you roam
but first beguiling maids who sing
must one aboard your ship endure
then seek the pillars of the sea
where daughter his may grant succor
and from his curse shall set you free.

οὐ μὲν γὰρ τοῦ γε κρεῖσσον καὶ ἄρειον,
ἢ ὅθ' ὁμοφρονέοντε νοήμασιν οἶκον ἔχητον
ἀνὴρ ἠδὲ γυνή: πόλλ' ἄλγεα δυσμενέεσσι,
χάρματα δ' εὐμενέτῃσι, μάλιστα δέ τ' ἔκλυον αὐτοί.

For there is truly nothing mightier nor better than
when two people who see eye to eye keep house
as man and wife: a great pain to their enemies,
a joy to their friends, but themselves know it best.

—*Odyssey*, Homer, Book 6.181-185

The Queen of Death

Then thus replied the prophetess divine:
"O goddess-born of great Anchises' line,
The gates of hell are open night and day;
Smooth the descent, and easy is the way:
But to return, and view the cheerful skies,
In this the task and mighty labor lies.
To few great Jupiter imparts this grace,
And those of shining worth and heav'nly race.
Betwixt those regions and our upper light,
Deep forests and impenetrable night
Possess the middle space: th' infernal bounds
Cocytus, with his sable waves, surrounds.
But if so dire a love your soul invades,
As twice below to view the trembling shades;
If you so hard a toil will undertake,
As twice to pass th' innavigable lake;
Receive my counsel. In the neighb'ring grove
There stands a tree; the queen of Stygian Jove
Claims it her own; thick woods and gloomy night
Conceal the happy plant from human sight.
One bough it bears; but (wondrous to behold!)
The ductile rind and leaves of radiant gold:
This from the vulgar branches must be torn,
And to fair Proserpine the present borne,
Ere leave be giv'n to tempt the nether skies.
The first thus rent a second will arise,
And the same metal the same room supplies.
Look round the wood, with lifted eyes, to see
The lurking gold upon the fatal tree:
Then rend it off, as holy rites command;
The willing metal will obey thy hand,
Following with ease, if favor'd by thy fate,
Thou art foredoom'd to view the Stygian state:
If not, no labor can the tree constrain;
And strength of stubborn arms and steel are vain.

—Aeneid, Vergil, Book 6.125-148, translation by John Dryden

1

THE SEA UNFURLED SMOOTH and clear before her like the surface of a polished gem, gleaming turquoise beneath the high sun. Penélope stood at the front of the ship. Sprays of mist gently kissed her face as the carved prow cut a path through the gently lapping waves.

"Penélope."

She turned, her heart beating clumsily at the voice. The tall figure of Prince Leandros came to stand beside her, but she ignored him, watching the city of Helena shrink on the horizon, the lofty Gate of the Moon seeming to hover between sky and sea, where only days ago she had watched Zeb disappear before her eyes, forever condemned to the Underworld. *Not forever,* she reminded herself, but the little hope she had quivered in the face of this vast, unknown world.

"Penélope," Leandros repeated firmly, and she was forced to look at him. He always spoke her name as if in Ancient Greek, a reminder of the impossibility of this world existing, as if it were another realm—or *road,* as Ari and Alexandria liked to call it, though she still had trouble believing in it. "What do you ponder in solitude?"

"Nothing," she said quickly, her cheeks already heating up. She was not normally so awkward around people, especially men, having grown up with brothers, but no other man had professed his undying love for her before, nor spoke so formally.

Leandros sensed her reserve and nodded slowly. He was younger than she had thought, only a few years older than her, she had learned, but somehow he seemed older, as if the storms he had weathered at sea had aged his spirit. "You doubt the success of our mission, perhaps? I, too, doubt whether we shall recover your friend from the Halls of the Dead, or whether we shall ever find the King."

"We will rescue Zeb," Penélope corrected tersely, then added, "and your father." She sighed. "I don't doubt the success of our mission. I just don't understand it. Sister Stella told us we can't go to the Underworld the same way as the last time, that the door had been sealed against us after we trespassed. So now we have to go to some island and capture a sea god? And he's gonna tell us how to go to the Land of the Dead because he only speaks the truth? I don't even believe in your gods."

"The Old Sea god," Leandros said wryly. His eyes glittered with amusement as he stood beside her near the prow, looking down at her with his warm brown eyes under long, straight lashes. "Then it is a question of faith?"

She turned away from the intensity of his gaze, looking out at the strange seas about them. While she had encountered gods and goddesses already—Dionysus after the revelry, Demeter in the desert, Osiris in the Underworld, and Zeus in the Great Library, not to mention the nymphs, satyrs, and magical beasts—now that the initial shock of being in the city had faded, Penélope was left with a hollow, anxious feeling that everything she had ever known was wrong.

"I'm just..." *Lost* was at the tip of her tongue, but she held the word back. "I'm unsure of the future."

"I understand," Leandros said softly, as if he had read her mind. "But that is when we must rely on faith, for amidst the darkest of tempests she may be the only light to guide our way."

She was silent. While she had been raised in a very typical Mexican-American Catholic family in rural California, she doubted whether Leandros was speaking of faith the same way she spoke of religion. His eyes roamed the wide seas about them as if he saw something there that she did not, as if the entire world was alive, as if the very air was filled with the breath of mythical beings and perilous monsters.

Before either of them could speak, Owen jumped past them and clung to the curved prow, grinning as he spread an arm out. "Can this thing go any faster?"

"Owen!" Penélope cried out, worried that he would fall over the side of the ship. "Get down from there."

Leandros said nothing, but Owen shrugged and hopped back on the deck. "So, how far away is this island?"

"No one can say," Leandros said unhelpfully.

"It *is* called the Wandering Isle, remember?" Penélope said pointedly. Sister Stella and the Queen of Helena had debriefed them on the journey they would have to take to rescue Zeb and find the King, but she had still left a lot of important details out. "But Owen has a point. If it keeps, you know, *wandering*, how do we know when we find it?"

Leandros smirked, leaning in closer to her and whispering, *"Faith."*

Then he turned and walked away, shouting orders to his men as they rowed them farther and farther away from the city, their muscles straining to pull the weight of the ship across the water. With about twenty-five rowers on each side, the ship seemed to fly across the water like a bird skimming the ocean's surface, while the dozen or so officers and steersmen patrolling the deck made sure the. ship ran like a well-oiled machine.

Owen surveyed the scene next to her, his face uncharacteristically grim. He had taken to being more serious since Zeb had died.

"We're really doing this, aren't we?" Owen said with a sigh. "How do we know this is going to work?"

Penélope knew she would have to be strong for both of them, even though she herself could hardly believe that Zeb was gone. She would never forget the moment she crossed the Gate of the Moon and realized that Zeb had remained trapped in the Underworld. The pain that had choked her breath away had been indescribable. Owen had also been distraught, but they had little time to grieve with the imposter King, who was really Brother Ezra, hot on their tails. They had barely escaped with their own lives after facing Zeus, while the power of the Emerald Stone that had burned inside Alexandria had left her too weak to accompany them.

In some ways, she was glad only she and Owen could come, that Chloe had decided to join the Seven Sages, that Ari had been appointed Headmaster of the Academy, and that Warren and Alexandria had returned home. Penélope knew deep down that this journey was meant for them to take alone, who had the most claim on Zeb's fate. Would she ever see him again? Or would he remain in the Underworld, trapped forever in a realm that wasn't even his?

She watched Leandros weave his way through the benches, speaking with different members of his crew before slipping inside his captain's cabin at the opposite end of the deck. Some of the men were the same they had encountered on Leandros' pirate ship, who had decided to follow their beloved Wanderer even after he was revealed to be the exiled Prince of Helena.

As if noticing her eyes on him, the peg-legged pirate, given the rank of

Helmsman and second in command to Captain Leandros, glanced at her with a slight sneer, though now his wild, sea-worn figure had become familiar and even welcoming to her.

"I trust Sister Stella," Penélope said finally. "She was Zeb's official guardian when his parents couldn't be. She wouldn't send us on this mission if she didn't believe there was a chance we could rescue him."

"She also said our journey would very likely end with our 'certain death,'" Owen countered, not without sarcasm, though his eyes betrayed his real fear. . "We barely know this Leandros guy either, and now we're trusting him with our lives on the open sea?"

Penélope cut him a glance. "Don't forget why we're doing this. Zeb is in the Underworld somewhere because of *us*. If we don't rescue him, then no one will. I would never be able to forgive myself if I left him there."

Owen didn't answer, staring hard at the ground. Penélope didn't quite understand his feelings toward Zeb, or how Zeb might feel about Owen, but she could tell *something* happened between them that made Owen feel responsible for Zeb's fate. She only wondered how long that feeling would last.

"What have you told your parents?" Owen asked suddenly, looking up at her.

Her stomach twisted at his words. She didn't like to think about her parents as she let a foreign ship, steered by a foreign man, carry her across foreign seas to even more foreign lands. "I told them the truth, more or less. I'm at an archaeological dig somewhere in Greece for the rest of the summer with Ari and Zeb, and Sister Stella would communicate with them for me because cell service isn't available there."

"Clever."

"Well, what did *you* tell your parents?"

"Nothing, really," Owen said, ignoring her glare. "They don't care what I do, so long as I stay out of trouble. They think I have an internship this summer, and I'm staying with Warren. But I told Harvard that I was taking the next year off for personal reasons."

"You don't think we'll be back by the end of the summer?" Penélope asked in surprise. She had never considered that their journey to rescue Zeb and find Leandros' father would exceed two months, and she had counted on all three of them—her, Zeb, and Ari—being back in the classroom at the New Academy come September.

Owen looked out at the strange, blue-green waters around them, the last sight of the city having already sunk below the horizon behind them. "We're sailing to the Land of the Dead, Penélope. We might not make it back at all."

2

PENÉLOPE TURNED FITFULLY ON her mat, her back aching from sleeping on the hard sand. The bright light of day pressed against her eyelids, seeping through the flimsy fabric of her tent.

She could already hear men shouting orders outside. For the last two days, they had sailed until dusk, before Leandros had them anchor the ship by the shore, which had been closer than she realized. It turned out that they had sailed due east from the city, and while they had the chance, would sleep on land, which they relied on for refilling their fresh water supplies and rations by hunting what wild animals they could find.

Despite it still being early June, the days felt hotter here near the desert, and the warm waters of the sea hardly helped alleviate the heat, instead shimmering with humidity as soon as the sun climbed up into the sky. Penélope, being the only woman amongst the crew, had already struggled alone amidst tall brush and parched trees to take care of her business, though it was worlds better than using the ship's latrines, even if she was allowed to use the captain's private latrine at the stern instead of the communal ones at the bow. She longed for the luxurious baths of the palace and wondered how soon they would find a river to bathe in—the last time already the night before last—and dreaded how the ship would smell in a few days.

"Penélope!" Owen's silhouette moved in front of her tent. "I've been commanded to tell you that it's time to go. The last rowboat is waiting for us."

She sighed, then crawled out of the tent, combing her fingers through her hair. While all the men slept in pairs or even in groups of three in the small tents, she had a tent to herself to give her privacy to change into fresh clothes when need be. The Queen had provided her with a small toilette as well, but there was no alternative to squatting in the wild, not to mention the lack of running water. But if this is what it would take to rescue Zeb, then she would not complain.

Sure enough, as Owen had said, a small rowboat was waiting on the shore, the high tide already kissing the rudder stuck in the sand. Leandros and the peg-legged helmsman stood beside it, though neither of them was looking her way. She knew that it was highly improper for a woman to be traveling with them as a common sailor, but sometimes it was annoying to be treated as a delicate flower that got the men blushing if she even raised her voice too high or wore a pair of pants. But sometimes their propriety had its perks.

"Tell the captain that they will need to wait a little longer," Penélope said, grabbing a small wooden chest in her tent containing her toilettes. "They can pack up my tent while I'm gone."

Then she hurried away in the opposite direction of the boat until she found a thick patch of reeds and bushes to relieve herself.

By the time she returned to the rowboat, her body cleaned with splashes of fresh water from her large canteen and perfumed with the scented oil flask the Queen had given her, Leandros and the helmsman seemed very annoyed.

"We cannot delay," Leandros said as she neared the rowboat. "Otherwise, we shall never reach the Wandering Isle."

"While I am sure you and your men don't mind doing your business behind your own tents and smelling like fish—and worse," she added with a glare at the helmsman, who frowned as if he understood what she said. "I, for one, want to keep up my personal hygiene."

Leandros blushed as if she had said something especially scandalous, holding out his hands to help her into the rowboat. "If you know what my men know about the journey ahead, how we might smell would certainly be the least of your cares."

"What do your men know that we don't?" Owen asked sharply as Leandros and the helmsman pushed the boat into the water. "Is there something you're not telling us?"

"Hands to the oars," Leandros ordered.

Owen scowled but picked up his oars, while the helmsman did the same behind him. Leandros took his seat beside Penélope on the small wooden bench. She ignored his lingering gaze on her and how close they were sitting in this small rowboat.

Once they were back on the deck of the ship, Leandros ordered the crew to lift the anchor. The ship took off across the water like stones skipping on a lake, the prow rising and falling rhythmically with the cresting waves. It was hard to imagine the calm, clear waters teeming and dark in a storm, but Penélope hoped she would never have to see it for herself.

Owen hurried to his seat on one of the benches, grabbing onto the long handle of the oar and rowing in unison with the rest of the crew. Leandros had quickly given him a rank and a job to do after the first day sailing, when Owen, with nothing to do, had explored every inch of the ship and distracted many of the crew members with his antics despite not speaking their language. He even looked like them now, his curls longer and more wild from the salty wind at sea, and dressed in a sailor's brown and leather tunic.

Penélope was the only one who truly had nothing to do. She took her usual place at the front of the ship near the prow despite the sun glaring down at them. The rowers were now covered with thick awnings on either side of the ship to protect them from the sun. She had been given a broad hat and shawl that she refused to wear, along with her own brown linen and leather dress to match the sailors. Before they reached the island, she would change into pants, despite the odd glances she received while wearing them.

Once the ship took off, she sensed the captain's now familiar presence approach.

"You should sit in the cabin. It was fitted for passengers," Leandros said. He stood beside her, his hands clasped behind his back. "It is not wise to stand for so long in the sun when out on the open sea."

She kept her eyes trained on the horizon. "I'm looking out for the island."

Leandros shook his head. "The Wandering Isle cannot be seen with the naked eye."

"Then how will we know where it is?"

"We will not," Leandros said simply.

"I don't understand." Penélope felt frustrated, but kept her voice level, trying to match Leandros' unwavering stoicism. She hated uncertainty and liked to be in control, but ever since she agreed to help Alexandria find her mother, everything had become uncertain and out of her control.

"Do you not?" Amusement was clear in his voice. "Close your eyes."

"What?"

"Follow the orders of your captain, Penélope."

She stared at him, surprised at his stern commanding voice that he had not used since the night he captured them on the Necropolis Island. "What are you going to do?"

Leandros met her gaze challengingly. "Have faith, Penélope."

He walked behind her and placed his hands over her eyes, forcing her to close them. She felt her heart hammer in her chest, the same as when she had been dragged and chained at the mast of this very ship, but this time there was anticipation rushing through her rather than dread.

"What do you see?" he asked in a low voice.

"Darkness."

"Look again."

"I can't *see* anything, Leandros."

"Πηνελόπη," he whispered. "Τῇ κραδίῃ."

She understood what he said, even though κραδίη could mean many things. *With the heart.* But how could she see with her heart? What did that mean? It wasn't tangible. It wasn't logical. But didn't she always long to live according to her heart? When she read her books, didn't she always wish to stop before the end and experience for herself the thrill of the unknown in real life, which could never be neatly explained and wrapped up in an epilogue?

Penélope longed for love, for adventure, to be swept off her feet, but was she willing to let the currents of the tide take her to an unplanned ending?

Here she was, at the prow of a strange ship, whose captain, a prince of a magical city, stood behind her, his hands covering her eyes and asking her to trust him. Penélope breathed in deeply, focusing her attention on the quick beat of her heart, the pulse fluttering in her neck. As the world narrowed to her breaths, the sounds of waves lapping against the hull of the ship filled her mind, until even the splash of oars and the wind puffing the sails ceased. A seagull's cry pierced the air, far, far away, and then again, closer, mingled with the crashing tide upon a distant shore, a melody that would never end so long as the ocean held sway over the earth.

"Open your eyes, Penélope," Leandros whispered.

His hands were no longer covering her face. She wondered how long ago he had moved them.

Penélope opened her eyes. The ship was not moving, the anchor having already been dropped. Even the sails had been rolled up, and she realized that was why she had not heard the sound of wind against the sheets. Before her lay the wide sea, and jutting out amidst the swirling tides was an island wrapped in a shifting fog, a dark, thin shoreline of large gray rocks dotted with seagulls.

"You have found the Wandering Isle."

3

Penélope blinked, staring at the island. There was no way to know that it was indeed the Wandering Isle, but there was some strange enchantment in the tendrils of white fog that clung to the rocky mass, so that the island appeared to be floating on the sea.

"So, who *is* Proteus? Is he a good god or an evil god?" Owen asked. He had abandoned his post at the oars and joined her and Leandros near the prow.

Leandros looked at Owen incredulously. "I do not know what you mean, son of Godfrey. But the Old Man of the Sea has long haunted the shores of the Wandering Isle. He is a shepherd of the seals, daughters of lovely Lady Brine. He knows the depths of the ocean and serves Poseidon, Shaker of the Earth."

"A shepherd of seals?" Owen repeated.

Penélope looked back at the island. Suddenly, one of the large gray rocks moved. Then another. She realized that they weren't rocks at all. They were *seals,* clumped together and spread so widely across the shore that they appeared to be rocks, the white dots of seagulls gingerly picking a path between their large, blubbery heaps and circling over the shallows in the hunt for fish.

"I don't get it," Penélope said. "How did I find the island?"

Leandros smiled. "There is a well-known song we sing of the Old Man of the Sea. It goes like this:

πωλεῖταί τις δεῦρο γέρων ἅλιος νημερτὴς
ἀθάνατος Πρωτεὺς πολυπλάγκτῳ ἐν νήσῳ
θηῆται ἢν ναύτης οὐ θρασὺς οὔτ᾽ ἄναξ ἀνδρῶν
γὰρ δὲ φιλεῖ φώκας νέποδας καλῆς ἁλοσύδνης

ἄλλα πέτηται νηῦς ἄν πνοιῆς ἀνέμοιο
παρθένος ἠΰκομος δ'ἐν νηΐ μιν οἴη θέλγει."

They all stared as the grave, imposing figure of their captain stood very still and softly chanted the words to a tune as lilting and quick as the waves in a light breeze, but in a voice as low and rolling as the depths of the ocean. Penélope wondered at the melting, melodic syllables of the Greek that she could hardly understand in song, and realized then that whatever she thought she knew of the epic poetry of Homer or the lyrics of Sappho was wrong.

"That was…" Owen shook his head, as if waking from a nap. "That was not English."

Penélope did not have the heart to berate him, not when she still heard the soft song drifting in the air, the notes as tender and ancient as the island before her.

Leandros was silent for a long moment, then, "I can try to translate the song in your language, though it shall not be as beautiful, nor tell so much of the story:

Here haunts the Old Man of the Sea who tells no lies,
the deathless Proteus, on the Wandering Isle,
Where no brave sailor nor lord of men may see,
For only seals, daughters of Lady Brine, loves he,
But if a ship by the wind's blowing flies
Only a lovely-haired maiden aboard will him beguile."

"You just made that up right now?" Owen asked in shock.

Leandros nodded his head as if that should not come as a surprise.

"Wait," Penélope said when she fully registered the words of the song, nearly laughing. "Does that mean *I'm* the lovely-haired maiden?"

"Yes," Leandros said, his face already growing red. "You are unmarried and…"

She smiled. "And…?"

"And lovely-haired," he muttered.

Her smile turned into a smirk. "So you think I have lovely hair?"

Leandros could not respond, his blush traveling down his neck.

"You're scandalizing him, Penélope," Owen drawled, and she was surprised to see the slight annoyance on his face. Perhaps he was jealous that he didn't have Zeb around to scandalize anymore. "We should focus on how we are going to find this Proteus bloke."

"Legend tells that when the sun rises above the Wandering Isle, the Old Man of the Sea shall lift his head above water, where the breath of Zephyr hides him in mist," Leandros spoke, clearly glad to shift his attention away from Penélope and her lovely hair. He pointed to the sun, which arced across the sky above the island. "When he leaves the sea to sleep in his cave, two of my men and I shall sneak upon his sleeping form, and pin him to the cave floor."

"And where will I be?" Penélope asked tersely. "Waiting on the ship? Absolutely not. I'm coming with you."

"Me too," Owen said, crossing his arms. "I can help pin him down."

Leandros sized up Owen from head to toe, then nodded slowly. "You may join me." Then he turned to Penélope. "But you are not strong enough. Gods are immortal, and their strength and cunning are great. You may accompany us, for gods often prefer to speak with women, but three men are needed to counter his strength—no more, lest we wake him before we attack. For our third man, then, I shall bring along Μονόπους."

"Who?" Owen asked.

But Penélope already knew. The name was surely a nickname, meaning *One-Foot,* used for the only man aboard who had a wooden peg in place of half his right leg. She turned to look at the helmsman, who was grinning back at her with his rotting teeth, a metal tooth flashing where some had fallen or been knocked out.

"Are you sure he can handle a god with just one leg?" Penélope asked, not keen on having his sneering face near her.

Leandros looked at her indignantly. "He has faced monsters of the deep more frightening and dangerous than all the shifting shapes of Proteus and has lived to tell the tale. There is no one I would rather have by my side, nor trust so readily with my life."

Penélope was silent, suddenly embarrassed to have judged the helmsman by his appearance alone. She wanted to apologize, but Owen interrupted.

"While those are admirable sentiments, it's almost midday, and we still have to row to the island. Come on, Mono, I'll help you get the boat ready."

Then Owen slung an arm around the helmsman's shoulders, who shrugged him off with an angry grunt and a muttered word in Greek, before stalking off toward the small rowboat attached to the side of the ship. Penélope looked at Leandros once more, who was staring at the dark, briny deck in a thoughtful silence.

"What monsters did he face?" she asked quietly.

He glanced up at her as if surprised she was still there, then smiled grimly. "That is a story he himself must tell you one day, if you are stout-hearted enough to hear it."

"Then they exist," Penélope said, her stomach dropping at the thought of the many monsters and beasts that Odysseus encountered wandering the wide seas.

"That," Leandros murmured, gazing out at the horizon, "you had best believe, Penélope."

"But *we* won't face them, right?" He didn't answer. "Right, Leandros?"

He turned away as he spoke. "For that, we can only hope."

4

The enchanted mist engulfed their rowboat so that soon their ship disappeared in the curling gray tendrils, and they could see neither the Wandering Isle nor the wide expanse of sea.

Leandros and Mono—as Owen and Penélope had come to call him—rowed them in an eerie silence. Penélope sat beside Leandros, across from Owen, whose smile had rapidly fallen away with tense anticipation for the encounter with another god. Before they had rowed away, Leandros had explained that when they pinned the god down, he would change into every beast on earth, then the core elements, water and holy fire.

"How can he change into holy fire?" Owen had asked. Leandros had simply leveled him with a look. They would find out soon enough.

Penélope thought she saw a bird circle in the mist, but she could hardly be sure. The only sound that cut through the fog was the waves gently rolling against the shore. They had to be close.

Leandros motioned with his head for Owen to jump out of the boat with him. Despite not being able to see anything in the mist, they both hopped over the side, and their feet splashed in shallow water as they hauled the boat onto shore.

Once the boat was moored, Mono hopped out with surprising ease, landing most of his weight on his left leg. Leandros helped her as she shakily stepped up on the bench and climbed down into the soft sand, a calm tide kissing her ankles. She had quickly changed into her pants before, and swore she caught Leandros sneaking a glance at her legs now as he guided them through the mist.

Once they left the water, shapes of seals lying in a spell-cast sleep cropped up here and there until they were forced to walk in single file, she and Owen walking in between Leandros and Mono. The deeper they tread into the island, the thinner the mist became, but the more crowded the shore with clumps of gray seals, their immobile forms like large bloated rocks washed up by the tide. A thick stench of salted fish weighed upon the air, until Penélope had to hold her breath.

Leandros seemed to know where he was going, carefully picking a path between the sleeping seals. Penélope wondered what would happen if they woke one up, and then decided she didn't want to know.

At last, they slowed to a stop. A low-roofed cave made of the island's rock was nestled amidst the gray seals that stretched across the island in all directions until they disappeared into fog. Penélope tried to calm her racing heart as they approached the dark mouth of the cave. There was no fire lit inside, but the little light that pierced through the mist from above alighted on more sleeping forms of seals, and at the center of the cave, the sleeping form of an old man.

Long, reedy, dark hair flowed around a wrinkled, pale-gray face, his body covered in water-logged rags as dark as the rock around him. Leandros held a hand out to prevent her from crossing the threshold of the cave, then pointed for Owen and Mono to approach him from the left and right.

Penélope clenched her hands into fists as they tiptoed near the sleeping old man. No sound stirred the silence save the ever-present tide, which was heard from far away. Leandros, Mono, and Owen circled the old man, pausing a foot away from him. She saw Leandros make the count with his fist. *Three, two, one—*

They leaped upon the sleeping figure, and suddenly a terrible roar pierced the air, and Penélope saw them grappling with a large, growling lion, his jaws snapping and his head tossing from side to side away from their strong grips. It was a terrible sight, the golden lion caught in their arms, but Penélope's breath caught when she blinked, and the lion was gone, in its place a white polar bear, rearing on its hind legs and swiping the air with its clawed paws. She saw its roaring jaws turn towards Leandros, who was looking to make sure she was still there.

"Watch out!" she cried, unthinking.

Suddenly the bear swiveled its red glare upon her and roared into the air, spit flying from its blood-red mouth. Penélope did not have time to scream as the bear tossed the arms holding him down as if they were fleas and charged at her.

She shuffled backwards, her heart in her throat, when her heels caught on something—a seal, still fast asleep despite the noise—and she fell to the ground as all the seals woke up at once and exploded into bleating cries. The bear jumped upon her, its sharp teeth a breath away from her neck when it stopped, looking down at her with knowing, nearly human eyes, its large form radiating heat in the chill murkiness, and she felt his snout sniffing her neck eagerly. It was her perfume, she realized belatedly, but before she could speak, the bear yelped as it was dragged backward by Leandros, Mono, and Owen once more, their tunics tattered but their faces grim with determination.

They grappled with a shark, Penélope saw in horror, but just as quickly the god morphed into an elephant, then an alligator, a hippo, a tiger, a gorilla, a camel, a hyena, until the changes were so quick Penélope could not make out the animal, though they still struggled to pin down the god's shifting figure, their heels digging into the sand to keep each animal pinned to the cave floor. The animals grew smaller and smaller, a bird cawing, a bat screeching, a snake rattling, until suddenly the small shifting form expanded into a swirling ball of water and then exploded into a burning flame of holy fire.

Penélope gasped, but the fire dissipated with a soft hiss, until standing before them was the old man once more, hunched and helpless in the hands that clutched his arms. She stood up on shaky legs, taking a deep breath before walking towards the old man.

Proteus glanced up at her with dark, soulful eyes and stared. She stuttered to a stop. Then he spoke, and his voice was rough, a soft echo of the crashing waves, spoken inside her head. *Many a century has passed since any mortal stepped foot upon the shores of my lonely isle, less still such a beautiful maiden as you.*

"You are Proteus, aren't you?"

What do you want from me, Πηνελόπη?

She was too startled that he knew her name to respond right away.

"Hearken, deathless Proteus!" Leandros growled before she could speak again, yanking on his arm and forcing the old man to look at him. "You speak infallibly, and you know everything, as all the deathless gods do. You know the way to the Halls of Death has been shut against us. Tell us how we might cross into the Land of the Dead!"

Proteus turned away resentfully. *Son of Leon! You have captured me against my will. Now you ask for the truth? Ever overbearing you mortals are. But if you wish to reach the Land of the Dead, you already know the quickest way that needs no help from me...*

"This one has a sense of humor!" Owen said through gritted teeth, as if he were still using all of his strength to keep the god still.

"Proteus," Penélope said, lifting her head and staring into his eyes as she had once done with the Lady of the Golden Blade. "My friend sacrificed himself for me. He remained body and soul in the Underworld, with no real death or proper burial. It is just and right that he be saved. But I must ask you to tell me how I can rescue him."

'Tis a shame so beautiful a maiden shall cast herself so willingly into the depths of despair, Proteus murmured. He waved a knobby, wrinkled hand in her direction. *In saving your friend, you shall lose more than you have bargained, my Lady.*

A chill ran down her spine. "Tell me how I can rescue Zeb Hades from the Underworld."

Proteus seemed to shudder at her words, then nodded warily. *The door to the Halls of Death has been shut against those who trespass. But there is another road open to Death, yes, one road is always open. Across the Middle Sea, as far as Poseidon rules, then farther still, to the edge of the world, there you shall enter the realm of the Dead, and save your friend from mortal peril.*

"But how do we save him?" Penélope pressed. "How do we get him out?"

You may save him, Proteus said, then his voice grew dark, *but when one traps their own body and soul in the Land of the Dead, only* he *can find the way out.*

5

The house was dark.

"*Mom?*"

Zeb tiptoed past the living room. The door to his mother's bedroom was open. He peered inside. A sliver of light from the window fell on the sleeping form curled up on the bed, her limp hand inches away from an empty glass stained red. His mother had been drinking again.

He sighed. This was not the first time. Nor would it be the last. Zeb gently shut the door to let her sleep and went to the kitchen to finish his homework, ignoring the stinging of his eyes until the difficult paradigms of Ancient Greek verbs drowned out the screaming in his head.

Suddenly he looked up. He was no longer in his kitchen, and half-forgot why he was on the verge of tears. There was Penélope, laughing at his joke, though he didn't smile back. He swore never to smile again. She sat at their usual desk, across from Ari.

Ari.

He glanced up at Zeb, under his dark lashes. Zeb died a little inside with every one of those looks. Penélope knew. Of course, she knew. She knew everything. But did she know what it felt like? To love someone who could never possibly love her back?

"What's happening under that blond head of yours, mate?"

At first, it was Ari speaking. But no, he would never speak like that. Too... British, but with a hint of something else, a lingering South African accent. Owen stood before him now. Zeb's hand was reaching for a book on the shelf, but it paused midair. The girls were off shopping for clothes, while Ari and that stiff Warren guy were somewhere else, searching for books about the ancient city of Alexandria. He was supposed to find a book on the Temple of Apollo, though why he needed to find it slipped away from him at the sight of Owen's face.

"What do you want?" he asked sharply. Owen unnerved him, those bright eyes always amused in his handsome face. But it was more than that. He was obviously flirting. Flirting with him, with Chloe, with Ari, just for the fun of it. Because it meant nothing to him. Unnerving, indeed.

Owen leaned against the bookshelf, a careless hand loosely holding a book. "You're a strange one, Zeb."

"Thanks."

He spoke viciously, but a small part of him was thrilled that Owen spoke to him like this, all alone in another corner of the library. And it seemed he spoke differently to him, less theatrical and more serious, curious about Zeb as he was never curious about Ari and his strong, tan arms. But then he pushed the thought away when he realized it resembled something like hope.

"What are you so afraid of?" Owen asked.

Zeb blinked. They were by the shore. Everyone else had already succumbed to the waves, but he couldn't do it. He couldn't do it. He wanted to tell Owen, to explain that feeling he had all those years ago, but before he could, the water surged around him, up his neck, around his head, and he was drowning, drowning in the deep end of a pool. It was a pool party. He was almost eleven years old. He shouldn't be drowning. He was too old to drown.

But his mother never taught him how to swim.

The edges of his vision blurred, then darkened. Was this how he would die? The thought was incredulous. Embarrassing. This was a birthday party. A celebration. He had been teased endlessly about not going in the water, only to be pushed in by his so-called friends. He wished Penélope had been invited. He hated the other boys.

Where was his mother?

He heard shouting. Something splashed near him, but he didn't care anymore. Now he just wanted to get it over with. To die quickly. But he was being pulled out, saved, and he opened his eyes, expecting his mother, wanting it to be his mother against his better judgment, only to see the mother of the boy who pushed him in, her clothes drenched and her chest heaving with the effort, while other parents scrambled over and draped towels over him, worry mingled with confusion in their eyes.

"Zeb, my baby!"

His mother had been in the kitchen pouring herself another drink. She rushed over to him, hugging him close to her chest. She apologized, murmured comforting words. The boys were all huddled together. A few sneered at him behind their parents' backs, but others stared. He's weird, they would tell people at school. Who doesn't know how to swim?

"Don't worry, baby," his mother cooed. He could smell the wine on her breath, and he wanted to vomit, shivering silently in her arms. "Mama's here. You're safe now."

But it was too late.

He wanted to tell her that, to tell that to Penélope and Ari and Owen whenever they gave him that questioning glance, wanting him to be whole, to be happy, to smile. The deep, rolling voice of the old woman living in the city echoed all around him.

"Ah, the boy who lives with one foot in the dark and one foot in the light."

She was right. Half of him was already dead.

Zeb opened his eyes. Darkness. But it was always dark in this place, the sky a gloomy haze that no light pierced, like the inside of a tomb turned inside out. He wondered at his strange dreams, reliving so clearly the different moments of his life. Sometimes he lived them simultaneously, as if Time had ceased to be linear in his memory.

Memory. He had no memory. If he tried to think about Life before Death, before this endless darkness, this bleak, weary place, if indeed it was a place at all, he could never get farther than slipping down into the black abyss of the Halls of Osiris, Alexandria's outstretched hand trying in vain to pull him back to the world of the living, and Penélope's scream, so very much like another scream, one that he heard often in the thick, unmoving air, an echo of a girl snatched untimely in a field of flowers...

He himself stood amidst a field of flowers, but these were white and wispy flowers, their gray, limp stalks eternally swaying in an empty breeze. The gray field speckled with dreary white petals stretched out for miles and miles without end around him. Where was he? What was this field? It was a sea of emptiness, of flowers that never died, but never grew, like a rose embalmed in a jar of fluid. But sometimes when he looked beyond the field into the horizon, he swore he caught a silvery glint as though a dark sea were in the distance.

Others were roaming the fields. Yes, many others, with pale, gaunt faces and haggard steps. Who were they? Why were they all in this field together? They never spoke with one another. Most were too busy grieving anyway. Weeping and wailing, their cries persistent in the darkness, though about what Zeb was not sure. He knew this was not where he was supposed to be, this bleak field under a sunless sky. While the others wafted across the fields, hardly noticing anything, occasionally Zeb's hand would graze the soft petals of a flower, or its long stem, and he would be painfully reminded of something, though of what he could not name. A place far away, perhaps, or another time, though even those words had lost meaning to him.

Only in his dreams did he relive his life. The dreams came on suddenly, for there was no sleeping or waking. They flooded his mind like an intoxicating fume, bombarding him with images and scenes, voices and feelings, most of which he would rather forget entirely. Often the dreams were false, twisting memory with his bitterest hopes and deadliest fears, kissing Ari in the library, his mother twisting a knife into his stomach, raging drunk, or Owen placing a hand on the back of his neck, only to shove his face into water, drowning him to death.

But very rarely, he would dream of impossible things, memories that felt real, but from so long ago that he sometimes thought they must be of someone else, though he knew that was not true. He would look up and smile at the handsome face of a young man, hardly older than Zeb had been the day he died, with warmer blond hair but the same icy blue eyes. The man would whisper his name, lovingly, and then carefully lower Zeb into his bed before the memory would disappear like smoke in the wind.

"Zeb Hades."

He heard his name spoken softly again, but this time by the voice of a woman. Zeb looked up and froze. Alexandria stood before him. She was dead too, then. But that was impossible. He looked closer and realized it was not Alexandria at all, but a woman who looked very much like her, older and with broader cheeks and longer hair, dressed in a loose white tunic and her bare feet upon the ground.

"Elena," he whispered.

6

The dusky night sky unfurled across the sky as the setting sun gave way to a rising crescent moon, the constellations peeking out one by one.

Penélope watched the waves crash ashore and recede in a hypnotizing rhythm, her feet sinking into the soft sand. They had left behind the Wandering Isle and sailed a full day west, back in the direction of the city, though they had no plans to stop there.

Once the sun had sunk below the horizon, Leandros had anchored them by the shore of the vast deserts, thankfully close to a river this time. But even after washing off the pungent, salty smell of the seals, Penélope could not rid herself of an ever-present worry that had settled in her stomach after speaking with Proteus and learning of the journey ahead.

"You should sleep, Penélope," Leandros said, appearing at her side. "We have a long road ahead of us."

"How long will it take us to reach the Land of the Dead?"

"Who can say?"

Penélope turned on him angrily. "How can you be so calm about this? Zeb is trapped in the Underworld, and now we are sailing to God knows where to rescue him. And we might all die in the end too. At the very least, I need to know how long it will take us and how we will get him out."

Leandros raised a brow. "A lady ought to be calm if she wishes to think clearly about the situation at hand."

"Calm? You're telling me to be *calm?*"

His eyes widened slightly, and Penélope realized she had taken a step forward and raised her voice so that a few nearby sailors glanced their way. She took a deep breath in and out before she spoke again.

"I'm sorry that I cannot be calmer, but you don't understand," she said steadily. "This is my best friend. No, like a *brother*. I'm all he has, and I let him sacrifice himself for me. Now I have to sail across a sea I don't even know to places that don't even exist where I'm from in order to save him, and even that is not guaranteed."

"If you wish to know where you are, then I will tell you," Leandros said, still infuriatingly calm. Then he pointed toward the horizon. "If you keep sailing that way across the Inner Sea, you would reach the Enchanted Isles, where they say ships that linger too long may lose their will to return home, and become ever stranded there. In the direction of the setting sun, you will come upon yet more dangerous islands, where witches and giants and violent mortals dwell, though they say a grand, fortified city with a palace made of bronze may be found among them. In the deep waters hide sirens and sea monsters, along with the rotting corpses of crews drowned in storms and shipwrecked. And far, far beyond the Middle Sea, past the sturdy, towering Mountains of Atlas, farther still than the land of Cimmerians, lies the Land of the Dead."

Penélope stared at him, then back at the suspiciously still waters of the ocean before her. "That didn't make me feel better."

"Knowing rarely does."

"What is there after the Enchanted Isles?" she asked, pointedly ignoring his comment.

"Hostile tribes of men. You would not wish to cross paths with them."

"And after that?"

He frowned. "No one knows. But if you follow the rising sun long enough, you shall reach the Eastern Edge."

"The Eastern Edge?" She tried not to sound skeptical.

"Legend tells that to go beyond it is to cross over into the land of the gods, where from the peak of the tallest mountain they reign over Emmeson."

"What is Emmeson?"

Leandros smiled and cast his arms wide at his sides. "Everything you see here between sky and sea. We have a saying amongst our people: οἱ ἄνθρωποι θνητοί ἐν μέσῳ οἰκείουσιν. *Mortal men dwell in the middle*. That is why we call all this the Middle Place, for above and below are reflected here as the heavens above and the depths below are reflected in the water of the sea."

The words struck her as familiar somehow, but before she could respond, someone called Leandros away. Darkness had swept across the earth quickly, and soon she wouldn't be able to find her way back to her tent in the dark.

Penélope took one last look at the wide expanse of sea before returning to her tent. Owen must have already fallen asleep, surely exhausted from wrestling the changing shapes of Proteus and rowing for an entire day with little rest. She herself hardly laid her head on her pillow before she fell fast asleep, rising when the first light of day shone through the thick cloth of her tent.

She gathered her chest and clothes and set off for the river, hoping to bathe once more before dawn rose and they would soon be off again. No other tents stirred as of yet, but she knew by the time she returned, they would be waiting for her.

The river was a wide, calmly flowing current that would be difficult to ford due to the thickness of the reeds and mud in the middle, but here and there it spilled into wide pools safe and deep enough to bathe in and even swim. Glancing around to make sure there was no one else nearby, Penélope stripped and gently waded in.

Despite the coldness of the water and the chill of the early morning, Penélope let out a contented sigh as the fresh water bathed her skin. She vowed never to take for granted running water, or even the heated baths at the palace, which seemed like pure luxury in comparison. She closed her eyes and pinched her nose before dunking her head under the water and resurfacing quickly.

When she opened her eyes, she saw a figure further down on the riverbank that had not been there before. She remained with her body submerged. It must've been one of the men who woke up early to bathe before departure like she had, which was unfortunately more rare than she'd wish. He had not noticed her yet, running a hand through his long hair. Penélope knew she should get out and dress quickly, but a part of her wished to remain still, watching the man lift his tunic over his shoulders in one swift motion, knowing in her heart to whom the strong stature and broad shoulders belonged.

Leandros took a few running steps across the river and then dove under the water. Then, to Penélope's horror, he began swimming. In her direction. She crouched, frozen, watching him approach and wondering if she should make a run for it.

But it was too late. Leandros paused, as if sensing her presence, then swiveled around until his eyes landed on hers, widening as he muttered in Greek what might have been a curse.

"My sincerest apologies, my Lady, I did not see you bathing," Leandros said, his face already turning red at his words alone, his eyes trained somewhere to her left. "Please forgive me."

"Penélope," she corrected automatically. "I'm not a *lady*. And I thought you didn't care about hygiene?"

Leandros looked even more miserable, as if he wished to drown himself right then and there. "This is most improper."

"Why?" she asked, feeling emboldened by his embarrassment. They had skirted the issue long enough, and they were rarely alone enough to speak openly about it. "Are we not allowed to talk in private?"

"It is not that," he muttered.

Penélope raised a brow, daring to wade a few inches in his direction, so that Leandros shut his eyes in self-defense. He suddenly appeared much younger, the scar that sliced his face a perfect white line when at rest. "You already declared your love for me. Isn't this what you wanted?"

"No," Leandros said sharply, then hung his head. "Or rather, yes, but not like...this. I would have you be my wife."

The words hung heavy between them once he spoke, oddly pained and regretful. Penélope's heart pounded at the word *wife*. She was so young, and in her world, she would not have to think about marriage for many years. Perhaps here it was different. But did she *want* to marry Leandros? The moment she asked herself the question, she ridiculed herself for it. What was she thinking? That she would marry Leandros and become a princess of some terrifying, magical city? That she would give up her life at home and remain here forever?

It was impossible. But was she willing to give up Leandros and the city for an equally unknown future just because she was afraid?

"Where I am from," Penélope said slowly, and Leandros opened his eyes, "when two people want to get married, the man usually gets down on one knee and proposes with a diamond ring."

Leandros raised a brow. "A ring of diamond? That is a queenly gift."

"Well, most people buy the ones made in laboratories, which can be less expensive."

"Your people *make* diamonds?" he asked in awe. "You must all be rich beyond compare!"

"Some people are," Penélope said with a laugh. "But not everyone."

"That is strange," he responded slowly, "though I suppose many would say the same of our city. Not all share in the wealth of the rich, nor do all live in palaces save those of royal lineage."

"But it seems like everyone in the city loves your family."

"Not everyone. We believe in the Old Faith. There are those who oppose it."

"You mean Brother Ezra?"

"And others. He has many followers."

"*Fear* has many followers," Penélope corrected. "He does not believe in anything except power. And power is fickle."

Leandros shook his head, a small smile on his face. "You are unlike any woman I have known, Penélope."

She didn't know what to say. In the silence, she heard the shouts of men and knew the camp would soon be packed and ready to sail. Leandros heard it too, turning away.

"I shall see you on the ship, Penélope."

Penélope watched as he dove under the water and swam back to where his tunic lay cast on the riverbank. She averted her eyes only when he stood up and walked to his clothes. After waiting for thirty seconds, she opened her eyes. He was gone.

With a sigh, Penélope sank back under the water until her heart returned to its normal beat.

7

THEY HAD BEEN SAILING for another four hours when Penélope had had enough.

She had already stood by the prow, then back by the rudder, stood by Owen and chatted with him before his usually welcome silence bored her, then sat inside the small cabin, even rummaging through Leandros' navigating trinkets and hand-drawn maps, before she decided to find something useful to do.

"I want to learn how to sail," Penélope said, standing before Leandros and crossing her arms.

He stood next to his cabin on the elevated deck, conversing in a low voice with Mono. They both looked up at her in surprise, then confusion.

"You wish to sail?" Leandros repeated slowly. "But a lady need not be concerned with such matters."

"First of all, *I* will decide what matters concern me," she said, finding herself fed up both with her boredom and Leandros' expectation that she remain idle at all hours of the day. "Second, if I don't have something to keep me occupied, I will go insane. You gave Owen a job! I can't row, but I'm smart and a quick learner. If you teach me how to work the ship, I can help out."

Leandros looked at her, contemplating. Then he nodded quickly, before turning to Mono and speaking in rapid Greek. Mono listened, and as Leandros went on, his frown grew more and more bitter. But he did not respond, instead, he stomped off toward the front of the ship. He paused halfway across the deck and turned to look at her.

"'Ἴθι!'"

Penélope turned to Leandros, who smiled at her.

"You ask and I provide, my dear Penélope," Leandros said, motioning to

Mono, who now stood at the prow grumbling. "My helmsman shall teach you how to sail."

"Mono?" she asked incredulously.

"I assure you, he is the best teacher. He taught me all I know when I was first exiled from home."

"But—"

"He doesn't like to be kept waiting," Leandros interrupted with a smirk, before returning to his cabin and shutting the door.

She hardly had time to think about Leandros calling her *dear* when Mono beckoned her again. With a deep breath, she made her way to the prow of the ship where Mono stood waiting impatiently. Up close, Penélope could see all too clearly his sun-weathered, sea-worn features, the wide, dark eyes, the scarred skin, the rotting, missing-toothed sneer, not to mention the wooden peg sticking out from the bottom of his stumpy right knee. He was not nice to look at, but perhaps the worst part of this would be having trouble communicating.

"Ἴθι, κούρη."

This was the first time he addressed her by any kind of name, even if it was only *girl.* Penélope followed him hesitantly to the very front of the ship, where the tall curved bow rose in front of them. She felt salty mist spray on her face this close to the ship's hull as it dipped below the water's surface and emerged with a hiss.

Mono pointed to the tip of the boat. "Πρῷρα."

She stared at him.

He pointed again insistently. "Πρῷρα."

Suddenly she understood. "The prow!"

"Πρῷρα," Mono repeated firmly, slapping the wooden prow. Then he pointed to the large mast at the center of the ship, which held up the sails. "Ἱστός."

Penélope pointed to the prow, then the mast. "Πρῷρα καὶ ἱστός."

Mono glanced at her in surprise, then nodded. "Καλῶς."

She nodded back with a suppressed smile at his approval.

He looked up at the sails, whose white sheets unfurled and puffed out with the wind's breath. "Ἱστία."

"Ἱστία," she repeated.

They continued like that from prow to stern, which was called the πρύμνη, including the rudder that steered the ship, or the πηδάλιον. He pointed out the top of the hull where the oars rested, which they called the τράφηξ, then the different ropes used to lower and raise the sails, like the ὑπέραι and πόδες, as well as the thicker ropes anchoring the mast to the front and back of the ship, such as the πρότονοι and ἐπίτονος. Lastly, he showed her the hold below deck, or the κοῖλος, where the crew members slept in hammocks and mats on the damp, dirty floor, though she quickly left due to the salty, pungent smells, not to mention the critical glances her way from a few lingering crewmen below.

Once she had memorized all the names, he taught her how the rudder worked to navigate them, as well as which ropes could be adjusted to tighten and loosen the sails according to the wind patterns, and even how to measure the shadows from the sun to gauge which direction they were going.

By the end of their lesson, the sun had begun creeping toward the horizon, and the sailors prepared to anchor the ship. Penélope was exhausted from standing beneath the sun and struggling to converse in Ancient Greek. But Leandros had been right. Mono was a good teacher and had named each part of the ship and how it worked with very clear, comprehensible Greek, waiting patiently until she could repeat it.

"Χάριν οἶδα," she had said once they finished. *I am grateful.* It was one of the phrases Ari had taught them before going to the city for the first time. Essentially, it meant *thank you.*

Mono had looked at her strangely, then bowed. "Χάριν δὴ οἶδα."

No, thank you.

It was as close to a compliment as she could get.

After the ship had anchored and they rowed to shore, Penélope found Owen standing among a group of sailors by the large roaring fire they had built in the middle of the camp, where a few men were roasting a spit of meat. She saw Leandros sitting on the other side next to Mono and a few other sailors, flasks of wine in their hands and laughing together. For the first time, Penélope felt truly left out of the male camaraderie, which she had never felt back home with her brothers or Zeb and Ari.

"So, how's our captain-in-training?" Owen asked as she approached. The sailors with him clapped his shoulders or shook his hand warmly before melting back into the crowds of men clumped around the fire, as though not willing to be caught conversing with the foreign girl.

"What are you talking about?" Penélope asked, unable to hide her annoyance.

Owen raised a brow. "That's what all the men are calling you. Κυβερνητίδιον.

Little captain. Leandros helped translate it for me."

"You're kidding."

"Nope. Some of these guys are a right laugh. They don't speak English but I'm picking up some useful words, like πυγή which means *ass* and πέος which means—"

"I know what it means," Penélope interrupted, trying to keep her cool when a few guys nearby pointed at Owen and began laughing. "You sound like a five-year-old boy learning bad words for the first time."

"Hey, don't be jealous that I'm mates with the boys."

"You're ridiculous." She sighed. "Just don't get too comfortable. We're here to save Zeb, remember? Not to make friends."

"Oh yeah?" Owen said dryly. "I'll remember that the next time I catch you and Prince Leandros bathing together."

Penélope felt her face flush, and she instinctively glanced at Leandros, who happened to be looking her way. They locked eyes, and she only managed to tear her gaze away when she caught Owen's triumphant smirk out of the corner of her eye.

"That was an accident," Penélope said, crossing her arms. "And for the record, I'm not jealous of you and *the boys.* But I won't let them make fun of me and then act all embarrassed when, God forbid, I wear a pair of pants."

Owen grinned. "Sounds like jealousy to me."

She stared at him for a beat, then before she could change her mind, she stalked off towards Leandros, whose eyes widened when he saw her approaching. All of the men fell silent once she stood in front of him.

"Is there something you need, Penélope?" Leandros asked, eyeing her warily.

"Yes," Penélope said, standing as tall as she could. "Tell your men that if they have a problem with me, they can say it to my face. I am tired of their judgment of me simply because I am a woman. Back home, I am valued for my intelligence and ambition, and my gender has nothing to do with it, and I can wear whatever I want too. Do you know how hard it is to be diminished to something I cannot control?"

Leandros winced with every word that she spoke. "My sincerest apologies, Penélope. It is only that my men are not used to seeing a woman walk freely aboard a ship, and do not know all that you have borne in life."

She looked at the men standing around and staring at her with a mixture of confusion and disapproval, surely judging how freely she confronted their beloved captain. But they did not know she had faced far more terrifying things than a crew full of boisterous boys.

Before she could change her mind, Penélope lifted her hands to show where the Golden Blade of Demeter had scorched her hands and left ugly, thick white scars, which she had not shown to anyone too closely, not even Owen.

"Εἰμί Πηνελόπη χρυσάωρ δρακοντολέτης."

I am Penélope of the Golden Blade, Slayer of the Dragon. She spoke loud enough for all to hear her, even to the edges of the camp. Somehow, she had remembered the epithets for Demeter and Apollo sung by Homer and hoped they understood what she was trying to say. It was the only thing she could think of to prove her worth among the crew.

Some of the men began murmuring amongst themselves. They were not entirely convinced. But Penélope did not know any more words that could explain herself. She turned to Leandros helplessly, but he was motionless, staring at her hands.

Then he stood up and pointed at her. "Πηνελόπη Ἀιδόσδε ἦλθε καὶ δράκων Ὀσείριδος ἔκτανε! Ἡ ἐν θανάτῳ οὐ μόνον ἔβησεν ἀλλὰ νεομένη κόσμον ἀρχαῖον ἀνένεικε! Σὺν ἦ τὸν βασιλῆα Λέοντα σώσομεν!"

And when he raised his flask in the air, the men cheered, and they began to chant. Penélope could not believe her ears. But then she smiled, and for the first time, the men looked upon her with a newfound respect, perhaps even admiration.

"Πηνελόπη! Πηνελόπη! Πηνελόπη!"

Leandros shouted above their cries, "βασιλεύς Λέον!"

"βασιλεύς Λέον! βασιλεύς Λέον! βασιλεύς Λέον!"

King Leon! King Leon! King Leon!

They all lifted their flasks and drank before returning to their conversations and feasting. Penélope took a step closer to Leandros, only realizing a moment too late that Leandros had taken a step towards her too. She ignored how close they stood together.

"What did you tell them?" she asked, speaking loudly to be heard over the cheer and song that had erupted after they toasted.

Leandros leaned down near her ear and said, "The truth."

"And what did you really tell them?"

He smiled. "I told them you had gone to Hades and slayed the dragon of Osiris, that you had not only walked through death but returned home and restored the Old Order, and that with your help we would find and rescue King

Leon."

Penélope's face burned, but she felt a rush of pride nonetheless. His words made her sound like a brave heroine from one of her favorite fantasy novels. But even if he had bent the truth, omitting the help of her friends, only she had held the burning Golden Blade and killed the serpent of Osiris. No man on earth, let alone among this crew, could say the same.

"Alexandria was the one to restore the Old Order," Penélope corrected anyway.

Leandros took her hands and gently turned them over to the palms. "But you, Penélope, have the scars to prove it."

8

THE NEXT DAY ON the ship, Penélope was allowed to shadow Mono as he went about his duties, learning by example when to order the sail to be tightened or loosened and to help the steersman adjust the rudder when the ship drifted off the mark.

Even though the men now seemed to embrace her as one of the crew thanks to Leandros' speech, nodding their heads as she passed or even murmuring her name as if she were some goddess, she sensed a new tension in their glancing eyes and hunched shoulders.

She found Leandros in the cabin, scrutinizing a map. Mono had dismissed her for a quick break before she would be expected to shadow him until sunset.

The cabin was cramped, only wide enough for two people to comfortably stand in. Yet it was still fitted with a small wooden table and a few cupboards for the captain's food and personal belongings. Leandros stood over the desk, his fingertip tracing a path across the carefully drawn ocean.

He glanced up briefly in surprise when she entered. "Penélope."

"Leandros," she said. "Is everything okay?"

"Why would it not be?"

"I was hoping you would tell me. The men seem..."

"Nervous?" Leandros offered.

Penélope nodded. The shift in mood had been imperceptible at first, but by the time the sun had reached the middle of the sky, the crew had ceased to shout across the rows at each other and joke around, remaining silent and apprehensive even when the wind had picked up and they hardly needed to row.

Leandros turned the large map on his desk towards her. He pointed at a small star on the northern coast of what was labeled ἡ χρυσέα θάλασσα, or *The Golden Sea*. "There is the City of Helena, close to Neila, one of the three daughters of the Black River and surrounded by a vast, uncrossable desert. We passed it on our left just a few hours ago. You may not have noticed yet, with the sun still above us, but we have begun changing course. We are now sailing toward the open sea."

"Why is that a bad thing?" Penélope asked. "I thought we wanted to sail toward the open sea?'"

"Because we may not have land close by to anchor nearby at night," Leandros said, then circled the vast area labeled ἡ μέσση θάλασσα, or *The Middle Sea*. "If we wish to replenish our supplies on land, we shall have to rely on whatever islands we come across, be they hostile or not, else risk starvation or thirst. And not all islands have been charted, and those enchanted elude even our best navigators."

"So the men fear we will land on a hostile island," Penélope said, her heart beating faster at the thought.

Leandros smiled grimly. "Among other things."

But he refused to elaborate when Penélope demanded more of an explanation, and soon she was beckoned back to her post by Mono's insistent, grumbling voice outside the cabin. The sun had begun slipping to the western horizon, while their ship now clearly veered slightly towards the north. But after Mono put her to work managing the sails under his close supervision, she forgot all about the direction they were sailing in, and even the men seemed sufficiently distracted as they rowed harder without a strong wind at their backs.

As twilight fell, Mono took over the sails and allowed Penélope to rest for the night. A third of the rowers would take shifts sleeping until they spotted dry land and could anchor safely. Penélope knocked on the cabin door.

Leandros opened it, and when he saw it was her, raised a brow. "My helmsman has kept his word, it seems. You have hardly rested all day."

"I asked for it, I guess," Penélope joked. "I was told I might be able to sleep in the cabin?"

"Yes." Leandros stepped out and motioned with his hand. "Your sleeping arrangements have already been readied."

Penélope peeked inside the small room and saw a hammock pinned from the wooden beams on the ceiling, with just enough space for her to curl up and close her eyes. She turned to Leandros when a thought occurred to her. "But where will you sleep?"

Inexplicably, they both blushed.

"I shall not sleep this night," Leandros said quietly. He glanced up at the stars now smattering a bruising sky. "But you should rest while you can. It may be many nights before we make landfall."

Without another word, Penélope entered the cabin, Leandros shutting the door softly behind her. She crawled into the hammock and was surprised to find a soft wool blanket awaiting her, which she wrapped around herself as she lay her head down. She did not realize how exhausted she was until sleep rushed upon her like a wave crashing on the shore, pulling her under its lulling tide.

It felt like mere minutes when the door opened again, but she could just glimpse the earliest rays of dawn filtering across the sky. Owen stood in the doorway.

"I've been sent to wake you up," he said in a low voice, and Penélope's heart skipped a beat at his grave countenance. "We've anchored."

Penélope scrambled to her feet. "So soon? Where?"

Owen shook his head, leading her across the deck. "We don't know. No one does, not even Leandros. The island seems deserted, but it's too big to be sure. We'll have to scout the area."

"Isn't that dangerous? Maybe we should stop at another island." She was trying to pat down her hair and adjust her dress while following Owen to the prow of the ship, where Leandros and Mono stood as the rest of the crew prepared the rowboats.

"It's dangerous," Owen said slowly, "but the closest island we know is an eight-day journey away. We either risk danger or dying on the open sea without water. Personally, I'd take the danger."

Leandros clapped a strong hand on Owen's shoulder. "You say that now, my friend. But sometimes even thirst may seem better than the horrors beyond the Inner Sea."

Penélope looked out across the water at the shore of the island stretching widely before them, disappearing into misty horizons on both ends. They had no way to know how big the island was or if it was inhabited until they set foot upon the sand.

"We won't survive long without water," Penélope said pointedly. "I say we scout the island."

Leandros nodded his head. "You, however, ought to stay on the ship this time."

She only laughed and patted his arm, earning her a shocked look from both Leandros and Mono. "Not a chance, captain. I'm Πηνελόπη χρυσάωρ, remember?"

Then, before he could argue, she joined the line of crew members preparing to disembark. Owen shrugged and joined her. They waited for their turn to climb into a rowboat and soon landed ashore the strange isle. Beyond the white beaches, Penélope could see nothing but green, rolling plains only broken up by sun-bleached rocks fading into the distance of a foggy morning.

Instead of setting up camp and risking a surprise attack if the island was indeed inhabited, Leandros split the crew into two parties, each just shy of thirty men. Leandros and Mono headed one, joined by Penélope and Owen, while the third and fourth officers in command headed the other. They set off in opposite directions, Leandros leading them towards the rising sun.

At first, the walk was easy enough, pleasurable even, passing green fields peppered with delicate flowers, the ocean still visible as a receding strip of glassy blue between sky and land. But as they treaded deeper into the island, the ground grew steadily steeper, the hills rising suddenly into intimidating heights where miles before they appeared so small. Penélope had a more difficult time matching the pace that Leandros set for them, eventually falling behind the crew despite the large packs weighing down their backs. Owen kept his place by her side, but as the hours wore on, even his breath grew labored. The craggy landscape she had glimpsed from the beaches was more dramatic up close, boulders breaking out of the soft green earth and piercing the sky like chipped teeth.

"How much farther will we go?" Owen called out suddenly from beside her. She looked up and was surprised to see the sun nearing the western end of the island, where yet more endlessly rolling hills stretched before them. Her legs ached, and she desperately wished they had more chances to rest.

Leandros did not break his strong stride and spoke loudly over his shoulder, pointing up ahead to what looked like a small mountain peak in the distance. "We shall stop for the night up there!"

"It'll take us days to get there," Penélope exclaimed. But Leandros either did not hear her or ignored her complaint, trudging onward with a silent and grim Mono in tow.

So they continued walking in the direction of the mountain peak. The sun was hovering above the darkening horizon when Penélope realized they were much closer to the mountain peak than she had thought, and, in fact, that it was not a mountain peak at all. It was another outcropping of rock, built so high and large as to make the illusion of a mountain from afar.

"Strange," Leandros said as they stopped, and Penélope and Owen joined him at the head of the group. He looked up at the towering height of the rocks. "Some of those stones were not always there."

Penélope followed his gaze, and her stomach twisted. He was right. Some of the boulders on top appeared to have been placed there. But how? It was impossible for someone to reach that high. Unless…

She turned to Leandros. "We should be careful—"

"I found something!" Owen's voice floated from the side of the boulders. Penélope and Leandros shared an alarmed look, then quickly followed his voice around the bend, where they came to a sudden stop before a tall, black cave entrance. "Maybe we can sleep in this cave tonight."

"I would not sleep here if my life depended upon it," Leandros said darkly. The men who had followed them began murmuring, and even Mono was shaking his head. "This is no cave. It is a home."

"A home?" Owen asked, blanching. "Of who?"

"Κύκλωψ," Mono hissed, backing away with a hand on the hilt of his short sword that all the men had strapped to their waist.

Penélope could not believe her ears. "A *cyclops* lives here?"

"It is the only explanation," Leandros said. He pointed at the left side of the opening to the cave. "Do you see those stone indents? Door hinges, though the door might be pushed inside. And there is even a front porch made from stone."

Once he mentioned it, Penélope could not unsee the large divots in the door frame, nor the rather tidy square stone pushed into the earth before it. But that could also be coincidental, cherry-picking the dents and shapes in the boulders that merely looked like a doorway, like imagining shapes from clouds.

Penélope took a hesitating step towards the opening when a hand circled her arm. She looked down at the hand, then up at Leandros, who did not release her.

"It is too dangerous," he urged. "This could very well be a trap."

"If this is really the home of a cyclops, we might find supplies inside," Penélope said, trying not to sound as nervous as she felt. She shrugged Leandros' grasp away. "But if all you men are too scared, I can go inside myself."

Then she turned and walked confidently towards the opening. At first, she was plunged into darkness the moment she stepped over the threshold. Her eyes slowly adjusted to the large, dark shapes around the cave, her blood running cold as the cave sharpened into a room, crude but unmistakable stone shelves on one wall overflowing with meat, fruit, and vegetables, while on the other side wooden wine barrels were stacked up to the high, curved ceiling. Across from her was a massive stone slab jutting out from the cave wall, draped with a massive quilt of various animal hides.

A flame flashed beside her, and she jumped before seeing Mono's face in the eerie, flickering light of a torch. Leandros and Owen were right behind him, a few of the men brave enough to face the darkness of the cave tiptoeing inside.

"No one is home," Leandros said, before motioning with his hand. "Let us gather supplies while we can."

The men who had entered hurried over to the stores of food, while Owen and a few others wandered over to the barrels, which were a foot taller than them and five times as wide.

"This is a ton of wine, quite literally," Owen said, whistling softly. "Can we take one?"

Penélope rolled her eyes. "They're too heavy. Besides, whoever lives here might be coming home soon. We should get going, Leandros."

But no one seemed to hear her, too enraptured by the size of the cave, the gigantic wine barrels, and the overflowing pantry, whose food they shoved into their sacks as quickly as they could.

Penélope heard the wind whistling inside the cave. The sun must have set already. She heard the whistle again, as if it were Owen whistling a tune. She nearly snapped at him to stop being so loud when a shape darted past her, and her stomach dropped, the scream in her throat dying as she saw a fluffy white sheep trot inside the cave, past the weak torchlights of the men without a care, as if it were meant to be here. As if this were its home.

She turned, her heart pounding, as she saw another sheep and then two wander inside the cave. The whistling returned, but this time she knew it was not the wind. Towering at the top of the hill and looking down at the rest of the men crowded outside the cave entrance was a man, as thick and large as the stone boulders around her, his arms and legs like tree trunks, and bulging out of his face, above a wide, growling mouth, was a singular, bloodshot eye.

A single word tore from deep within her. "Run!"

9

For a split second, everything was still. Then chaos erupted among the men, and they began running in every direction, some inside the cave, others back to the ship. But it was too late. In three great bounds, the cyclops had charged at the cave entrance and scooped up two sailors, one in each hand, and lifted them in the air with a roar. Penélope realized the roar was, in fact, a word.

"Κλέπται!"

Thieves.

Suddenly she was yanked backwards. Leandros pulled her behind the large wine barrels where the rest of the men were hiding, including Owen, whose pale face was tensed in determination, his hands gripping a serrated plank of wood that had been torn from one of the barrels.

"Stay here," Leandros whispered. He turned to Mono, and with their heads bent together, they murmured in Greek.

Penélope wished she understood them enough to help formulate a plan. Instead, all she could do was lean against the wall, helpless, waiting for the cyclops to kill them one by one. She heard the heavy footsteps and low growl as the cyclops entered the cave. Her hands were trembling, the scars on her palms white and quivering. She recalled the Golden Blade's cool metal kissing her skin, the terrible wrath of the goddess as she stood and gazed into those blazing eyes. *Your courage, daughter, is admirable, but it shall be your doom.*

Had the goddess meant her slaying the serpent of Osiris? Or something else?

She glanced at Leandros, his face grim as he and Mono argued with hissing whispers. Beside him loomed one of the wine barrels, though this one was empty, the wooden planks rotten and leaving a gap wide enough for someone to squeeze inside.

"Τίς ἐνταῦθά που ἔρχεται;"

His booming voice echoed inside the cave, shuddering the walls. Penélope grabbed Leandros' arm and pointed to the gap in the wine barrel.

"Hide there, swords at the ready," she said quickly. He stared at her wildly. "I will distract him. You will know when to attack."

"He will kill you."

"I am a woman, remember? He won't kill me right away." She pleaded with her eyes. "Trust me, Leandros."

"Τίς εἶς;"

Leandros flinched at the deep, menacing voice, then he motioned for Mono and the rest of the men to follow him inside the barrel. Owen was the final crewmember to enter, giving Penélope one last worried look before they were hidden inside.

"Τίς ἀνήρ θαρσεῖ μιν προκαλεῖσθαι;"

He spoke slowly and loud enough that Penélope understood the first few words, and the meaning was clear enough. *What man dares to face me?*

"Οὐ ἀνήρ," Penélope said loudly, forcing the words out despite the slightest tremor in her throat.

"Οὖτις? Πῶς δή;"

No one? How can this be?

She emerged from her hiding place behind the wine barrels. The cyclops stood in the middle of the cave, peering around suspiciously. He held no weapon in his hands, but Penélope thought she saw the limp bodies of two men tossed on the ground behind him.

The cyclops peered down at her, his one furious eye widening. "Ἡ γυνή?"

Then he began to laugh. He laughed so loud the ground seemed to tremble from the force of it, and even his flock of sheep began bleating nervously. Penélope stood her ground and took a deep breath to calm her hands, which had not stopped shaking the moment she saw the cyclops and his impossibly large, bulging eye. She needed to focus if she wanted to remember enough Greek to execute her plan correctly.

"Ξένη," Penélope said. She could only hope the word, meaning *guest friend* as well as *stranger,* would call upon the ancient laws of hospitality.

The cyclops looked around cautiously, though the cave now appeared empty.

"Καὶ σοὶ ἑταῖροι?"

And your comrades?

She gestured to the dead sailors behind him, as if to indicate they were her only companions. "Εἰμί μούνη."

I am alone.

"Μούνη?"

His bloodshot eye seemed to fixate on her more eagerly, his gaze raking down her dress. She suppressed a shiver, lowering her head to hide the disgust in her face.

"Οἶνος?" she asked with a quivering voice, gesturing meekly to the wine barrels. "Ἱμείρεαι οἴνου?"

Penélope remained silent, pointing again to the wine barrels. The cyclops seemed to contemplate her, then nodded his head, his mouth widening into a sly grin.

"Οἶνος πρῶτον, φίλη Μούνη," he said with a chuckle. *First wine, dear Alone.* Then with one large hand he grasped a wine barrel, tearing off the top effortlessly and pouring the dark wine into his mouth, large splashes dribbling down his throat. He then looked around and picked up a small drinking bowl, pouring some wine from the barrel into it and setting it before her. She realized it only looked small in his large hand because the bowl resting on the ground before her was almost as big as a serving platter. Penélope needed two hands to lift the drinking bowl and take a sip.

The wine was surprisingly sweet, chilled from its long sleep in the cave. She wondered how the wine was cultivated, if the cyclops had vineyards somewhere that they hadn't seen. Penélope drank the rest of the platter as the cyclops belched loudly, watching her with a satisfied smile. She set down the drinking bowl, the movement making her head light. The wine was abnormally strong, as if it were enchanted. But it was the only way to keep him distracted.

"Πλείων οἶνος," she said, bowing her head. *More wine.*

The cyclops chuckled and grabbed another barrel. He ripped the wooden top off and drank greedily. Then he splashed a few drops into her drinking bowl. She lifted it and drank as he lifted the barrel with both hands and chugged the rest of the wine.

He grinned once they were both finished, his eyes lingering on her bare arms. She fingered the pin on her shoulder, then glanced at the barrel nearest to her, where Leandros, Mono, Owen, and the others were packed inside.

"Πλείων οἶνος?" she asked innocently.

Annoyance curled the cyclops' smile, but he obeyed her, his movements slow. Despite his massive stature, the amount of wine he had consumed in such a brief period must've gotten him drunk already. He clumsily grasped the barrel, then, after a moment's hesitation, shook it, as if to feel what was inside. Penélope held her breath.

The cyclops lifted the barrel close to his face to inspect it, then struggled to tear off the sealed top, revealing the gleaming swords of Leandros and his men.

"Now!" she shouted.

Before the cyclops could react, Leandros cried out and leaped out of the barrel, plunging his sword into the cyclops' eye. Blood and gore burst from the eye upon the blade, marring the cyclops' raging face.

Leandros twisted the blade into the bloody eye as the cyclops careened back on the stone floor, the barrel with all the men collapsing on top of him.

"Βάλλετε!" Mono cried out, lifting his sword, leading the men to the cyclops.

But they hardly moved a step when the cyclops let out a deafening roar, sweeping his arms out blindly and striking Leandros off his chest and to the ground while his strong legs kicked the other men away.

"Κλέπται! Φονῆς! Ἀρκεῖτε!"

As though in response, a few beats later there was a rumbling, but it came from far away, as if a stampede of horses were charging toward them. Penélope's breath caught. Not *horses*, she realized in horror. They were the cyclops' friends, come to help him against thieves and murderers.

"Leandros!" she shouted. "We have to go!"

The cyclops struggled to his feet, staggering to the left and right, though whether from the wine or his blind eye, Penélope could not tell. Either way, he was still dangerous. Leandros led his men toward the cave entrance, while Owen grabbed Penélope and together they ran to catch up with them, dodging the cyclops' swipes at thin air.

As they rushed out of the cave, one of the men shouted, pointing at the top of the hill, and they all came to a stop. Little red flames dotted the horizon, drawing closer at a terrifying speed. The rumbling felt more like an earthquake now.

"Watch out!" Owen cried.

Penélope swiveled and jumped backward, barely missing the cyclops' bloody grasp. Suddenly Mono jumped in front of her, his sword gleaming as it sliced the cyclops' thick wrist. The cyclops hissed, but with the same wounded hand, he ascertained Mono's location, grabbing him by his wooden leg and pulling him back toward the cave. Mono's sword clattered to the ground as the pirate let out a shout.

She didn't think, running toward him and picking up his sword. The cyclops didn't hear her coming above the shouts of the men and the distant rumbling. Penélope lifted the sword and, with all her might, brought it down upon Mono's wooden leg above the cyclops' fingers and chopping the peg clean in two.

Mono scrambled onto his good foot while she helped him hobble away, the cyclops shrieking behind them. Leandros saw them over his shoulder, and his eyes widened. He double-backed and carried Mono's weight on his shoulder, ordering the others to get back to the ship. Penélope tried her best to carry Mono on his other side, her arms burning.

Then they ran back the way they came without resting, the cyclops' angry shouts fading into the night sky behind them.

10

By the time they reached the ship, the eastern skies had already lightened ever so faintly with the oncoming dawn. Penélope's legs were numb and shaking with the effort of running the many miles they had walked only a few hours before, though the fear of death had spurred her on.

The other scouting group had already returned, having found nothing save a vast stretch of rocky plains with only a few rabbits and birds for hunting. Leandros quickly explained the discovery of the cave, their encounter with the cyclops, Penélope's successful diversion, and their narrow escape. Some of the men wanted to return and take revenge for their two fallen comrades, whose bodies they had to leave behind unburied, but Leandros refused. It was too dangerous, and they didn't know how many cyclopes there were. Besides, they had already scavenged a good amount from the cyclops' pantry before he arrived.

Once they were on the ship, Penélope retired to the captain's cabin, exhausted and hardly able to move. She curled up in the hammock and fell fast asleep to the familiar rocking of the ship as they rowed against a strong headwind.

By the time she woke up, a bright midday sun shone through the thin slats of wood. She still felt exhausted, her legs aching, but the fear and panic lacing her limbs had melted away with sleep, as well as any lingering intoxication from the cyclops' wine.

Right on cue, a knock resounded from the other side of the door.

"Who is it?"

"Leandros."

She ignored the way her heart suddenly raced at his name. "Come in."

The door opened a sliver, then fully, and Leandros stepped inside. He avoided looking directly at her, and Penélope realized that in sleep her dress had tangled and one sleeve had fallen down her shoulder. She quickly adjusted herself, lightly combing her hair with her fingers.

"Is there something wrong?" she asked worriedly when Leandros did not speak right away.

He cleared his throat, his face red. "No, nothing is wrong."

Penélope raised a brow. "Then what?"

"You put yourself in much danger last night," Leandros said suddenly, shaking his head. "You could've gotten yourself killed, or worse. Simply because you are a woman does not mean there are not men or monsters out there who would gladly do their worst."

He spoke almost angrily, but Penélope thought she could hear another edge to his voice. "I know," she said tightly, and Leandros looked up at her. "I was counting on it. If the cyclops had not wanted anything from me, he would have killed me right away."

Leandros' jaw tightened at her words. "It was reckless."

"My plan saved our *lives,*" Penélope snapped. "If it were up to you, we might never have made it out alive. The least you can say is thank you."

He flinched, his face lowering. "Please forgive me, Penélope. I meant no offense. I simply...I feared for your life. You are clever, no one can deny that, but cleverness can kill."

She shivered. His words felt like a bad omen.

"But I did not come here to tell you this," Leandros said. "There is someone who would like to speak with you. May I admit Monopous?"

"Oh? I mean, yes, of course."

He opened the door, then side-stepped to allow Mono to enter inside with a slight limp. Leandros remained at the door and hid a smile as Mono dropped to his knees, grasping Penélope's hands in his tanned, wrinkled ones.

"Ἐμή ἤρως," he said reverently, resting his forehead against her knuckles. "Τὸν ἐμόν βίον σοί ὀφέλλω."

"He called you a hero," Leandros translated. "And that he owes you his life."

Penélope looked down, startled at Mono's grave face as he showed her the wooden peg beneath his leg, the bottom half roughly severed. She squeezed his hands, and he looked up at her. "Εἰμί οὐ ἤρως. Μόνως ἡ γύνη." *I am not a hero. I am only a woman.*

Despite her halting Greek, Mono understood and shook his head vehemently. "Ἀμείνων πολέων ἀνδρῶν καὶ ἀρίστη γυναικῶν εἷς."

Penélope looked at Leandros helplessly. "What did he say?"

Leandros gazed fondly at Mono. "He says you are braver than many men and bravest of women."

She felt her throat constrict. "Χαῖρε, Μονόπους." She turned to Leandros. "Can you tell him that I'm sorry about his wooden leg?"

Leandros translated, then Mono laughed hoarsely, speaking in such rapid, passionate Greek that Penélope could not follow, waiting for Leandros to translate. "He says it was a clever decision that saved him from the jaws of a monster. He himself is not sorry that you did so. Besides, losing a wooden leg is a far cry from losing a real one."

"Can you ask him how he lost his real leg?" Penélope asked without thinking.

Leandros paled ever so slightly, but nodded, and translated. Mono's face darkened, before he closed his eyes tightly, as if reliving the day in his memory, before he began to speak, his words a near chant. Despite the sunlight peeking through the crack of the open doorway, the small cabin felt darker, filled with his low, pained voice.

"He says that they had been sailing for months on end," Leandros translated once Mono finished, avoiding Penélope's eyes. "A storm hit, and they were lost. Up ahead, there seemed to be a small, rocky island. Hope of food and water blinded them to signs of danger. Their ship was drawn in as by enchantment into a narrow passage between a powerful whirlpool and jagged rocks, and that it was too late once they realized what was lurking in the trap to which they had fallen prey. Poised between them like a spider above her net was a terrifying monster of the deep, six serpent heads with rows of razor-sharp teeth ready to eat a man whole. He was lucky to escape with only one leg missing. We lost many a comrade that day. He hopes you never meet such a foe, for she shows no mercy to men or women alike."

"Scylla," Penélope whispered, more to herself, but Mono heard and nodded. She eyed Leandros knowingly, a thought forming in her mind. "He said they were sailing for months on end. You were with them, weren't you? That's how you got those scars."

Leandros did not speak, staring hard at the floor, while with her eyes Penélope followed the thick white scars running down his face, splitting his mouth, snaking around his neck, and disappearing beneath his tunic. She wondered if the scars covered his whole body.

"You were searching for your father," she said when he still did not answer. "βασιλεύς Λέων."

Mono nodded sadly.

She sat up straighter, her chest filling with determination, the way she always felt when facing what seemed an impossible challenge. "Μιν σώσομεν." *We will save him.*

Leandros looked up at her with an unreadable expression.

Then Mono kissed her knuckles and reverently whispered, "Γύναι ἐμή," *my Lady,* and withdrew from the cabin. Leandros lingered at the door. Penélope still felt stunned from the interaction. Mono had always been kind, respecting her decision to be taught and showing her the ropes, quite literally at times. But he had also been stern, calling her *girl,* and otherwise treating her as one of the crew. This was the first time he had formally honored her, as if she were a princess instead of a near-useless stranger.

"He's right, you know," Leandros said, taking a step closer to her, then paused. She glanced at him in surprise. "You are braver than many men I have known."

"I thought you considered me reckless, not brave."

"In our language, they are often the same thing."

She stood up and dared to take a step toward him. The cabin was small enough that they were now very close to one another and entirely alone. Leandros went still at their proximity, but did not move away. As if in a dream, she reached up her hand and gently touched one of the scars running down his cheek as she had longed to do since the moment she had seen him. He closed his eyes, his body tense.

"You are the bravest man I have ever known," she said quietly, the words leaving her mouth without meaning to, and the moment they were said, she took a hasty step back, not knowing what had possessed her to touch him. Leandros' eyes fluttered open and landed on her cautiously. "But I hope the next island we land on isn't filled with man-eating monsters, because I don't know if I can be that brave again."

"Then you need not worry," Leandros said grimly, already turning to leave.

Penélope's heart sank, though at his words or his departure she did not know. "Why?"

"We have enough supplies now for the rest of our journey." He opened the door, then paused. "Our next stop is the Land of the Dead."

11

"Elena," Zeb whispered.

But if she heard him, the woman did not indicate it. She turned without movement, then began walking away. Zeb could only follow, his steps halting as they struggled to find their footing amidst the thick stalks of flowers and grass.

They walked for what felt like an eternity, and Zeb was not sure that it wasn't. This place *was* eternity, timelessness, where nothing lived but nothing died, because Life and Death were two sides of the same coin, inextricably bound as shadow was to light. Elena seemed unbothered by the strange, dark field, the cavernous, gray skies, or the pale, limp flowers unmoving in the stale air.

"Where are we?" he asked suddenly.

A light laugh tinkled in the air. "I thought you would never ask."

Elena was looking at him, and though her face remained calm and still, amusement lurked in her brown eyes. They had stopped for a long time, but Zeb hadn't noticed until now. Or had they never left? It all looked the same to him.

"We are in the Fields of Asphodel," Elena said. "Where the souls of the dead linger until the unmaking of the world."

Zeb glanced around at the pale shadows of other dead souls floating aimlessly around them, paying them no mind. "But I didn't die."

"No, you did not." He suddenly felt alert at her words. She almost smiled, though it was a mere twitch of her mouth. "Your body and soul have been trapped in the Land of the Dead. You did not die, but you have ceased to live."

"I don't understand," he said, the weight of his doom settling heavily on his shoulders.

"Much you do not understand."

She sounded so very like Alexandria, then, infuriatingly direct with a hint of condescension, that Zeb bristled. "Where are my friends?"

"Friends? What do you know of friendship?"

"Penélope is my friend," Zeb countered harshly. "She's…she's my best friend."

Elena peered at him curiously. "What lengths would you go for your friends, I wonder?"

"I would die for Penélope." *I did die for Penélope*, he corrected in his head. But now he wondered if that was even true. "Would you die for love? You left your only daughter and husband, probably for another man. What have you ever sacrificed for them?"

For the first time, Zeb saw a flash of emotion pass across Elena's face. "You do not know of what you speak. You do not know *love,* nor *sacrifice,* nor *motherhood.* Your words are merely a child's insecurities."

"My mother never sacrificed for me," Zeb said sullenly, then frowned. He did sound like a child. "Mothers are supposed to love their children, sacrifice for them, and make sure they feel safe. My mother almost let me drown."

"You drown still, with no help from your mother," Elena said, as if she knew something he didn't.

"And what about my father? He abandoned us when I was a baby." Zeb looked away from Elena's piercing brown eyes. They saw too much in him. "If he hadn't messed around with the wrong crowds and gotten himself locked up, then maybe my mom would've never started drinking." She continued staring at him, unmoving, and Zeb felt the words shut up in his heart come bubbling to the surface, as if Elena compelled him to remember. "And love? I have loved for as long as I can remember. I loved my parents, and they threw it away. I loved—"

Elena tilted her head when he paused. She already knew. This only made Zeb angrier.

"I loved Ari from the moment I met him. He was the only boy ever to be kind to me. I loved him for *years,* silently, painfully, without any hope that he would return it, knowing I would die still loving him, alone and miserable forever. And look where I am! What do *you* know of that kind of love?"

It took him a long moment to realize that all of the shades sulking about the fields had gathered around him, staring in silent awe. He looked down at himself and saw that his skin had ceased to be ghostly and gray, the skin glowing with light, so that even his pale skin had a pink flush. The gathered souls looked at him hungrily, creeping closer, like moths to a flame.

Elena slowly swept her hands in the air as if she were parting water, and the pale faces dispersed, suddenly uninterested in them. Zeb looked down. He had returned to the ghostly shadow of himself. He wondered sluggishly, like coming out of a dream, why he had been so angry. When he looked up, Elena was much closer to him, and now he could see the pain etched eternally in her eyes, the sorrow lingering around her mouth.

"To be is to suffer the living," Elena said quietly. "But to die is to forget their joys. The flowers of asphodel are here because they, too, mourn both life and death, for they have forgotten the joys of a late summer breeze as their petals begin to fall."

A thought struck him suddenly, and he looked at Elena anew. "Why did you come find me? You don't belong here either."

Elena smiled, and in that simple movement, Zeb glimpsed a wide land of green grass and pure light, laughter and joy and peace. "I have been sent to guide you."

"Guide me? Where?" He nearly took a step, wanting to reach that land of light, but her smile fell, and the vision disappeared, so that the Fields of Asphodel never seemed so dark.

"The choice has befallen you, Zeb Hades," she said, her voice stern and deeper than before, as if another voice spoke through her, the voice of a world as old as the cosmos as it emerged from chaos. "Shall you remain in the dark? Or shall you step into the light?"

Ah, the boy who lives with one foot in the dark and one foot in the light.

Had the old woman always known this would happen to him? Had Zeb always been destined to fall into this darkness, as if it were his own making?

"Are you telling me that I can return to the world of the living?" he asked, and as though in a dream, he felt his heart beating fast, before the feeling disappeared. "Are my friends coming to rescue me?"

"Much has been set in motion that cannot now be undone," Elena said, her eyes suddenly seeing elsewhere, far away. "The gods keep their own counsel, after all. I have done what I can to warn of His coming."

"His coming? Who is He?" Zeb demanded.

"My daughter was brave, so very brave." Elena's face took on a dreamy look, and her skin glowed ever so slightly, before she fixed her stare upon Zeb once more. "Retribution shall be swift and deadly. The fate of many rests on the decisions of a few. Who shall restore the balance before it is too late?"

Zeb's mind whirled at her words. "I-I don't know what you mean."

Her mouth twitched with that hidden smile. He suddenly recalled that Alexandria did the same thing. "Neither do I. My sight only reaches so far, and not for many an age has the world hung in the balance. Your friends near the jaws of death. War hovers on the horizon, a dark and deadly storm. Old enemies and new. But who can say how the Fates shall weave their threads? You, Zeb Hades, must choose to suffer—or forget."

"I want to go back," Zeb said hurriedly. "Tell me how to go back."

"There is no going back," Elena countered, before she turned and began walking away. "Only onward."

Zeb walked after her, only to realize that she was already gone, or perhaps she had never been there. He looked around wildly, the dark fields mockingly still and empty save the flickering shades of dead souls forever grieving. He thought he heard a faint scream in the air, a young girl caught and dragged under the gaping depths of the earth.

Zeb, can you hear me?

He froze. The voice was achingly familiar, but spoken as if in a dream.

If you can hear me, Zeb, please hold on. We're coming for you.

A ship rocked under him. Blue waves crashed against the hull. Bright green eyes glanced at him. Dark brown hair swished ahead. Was this a memory? The future? Or just another false dream?

Answer me, Zeb!

He turned, saw the roaring, fanged mouth of a monster above him.

Zeb—!

12

"Penélope. Penélope? *Penélope.*"

She turned, startled out of her thoughts. Mono had given her a longer break now that there were fewer rowers to command, and they wouldn't change course from due west. Penélope could barely focus on the tasks of the ship with their impending arrival in the Land of the Dead.

Owen stood behind her, arms crossed. The ship had switched rowing shifts for the night, so it must've been Owen's turn to sleep. He looked tired, worn out from days on end of rowing, but he hadn't complained about joining the crew's strict regimen and picked up on Ancient Greek phrases faster than her, so that he already had some friends among the other sailors. In fact, he seemed to like the exercise, often asking Penélope or Leandros to feel his biceps and judge if they had grown over the last few days.

"What were you thinking about?" he asked.

"I was praying."

He looked surprised, then skeptical. "Really?"

"Yes. Well, sort of. Not really. I guess I was only praying to Zeb, just in case he can hear me in, you know, the Underworld." She shrugged her shoulders, trying to appear nonchalant, but the thought burned her eyes, so she stubbornly looked out at the sea. Owen came to stand next to her.

"I never really believed in that kind of stuff," Owen said quietly.

"But now?"

He glanced at her sharply. "Now I don't know what I believe in. That cyclopes exist? That gods and goddesses can take human form and speak with us? If all that stuff only happens here and not in our world, does it mean it's all real?"

"Isn't this a part of our world?"

Owen threw his hands up at the wide expanse of a strange sea. "I don't know. Alexandria always called it a road. But a road to what? *The realm of the gods?* We aren't gods, Penélope. We're humans. And as we saw with Zeb, we can die here just the same as we can die in our world. Except here, monsters exist."

"Monsters exist in our world, too," Penélope challenged. "They just take on a different form."

"Maybe." But he sounded unconvinced. "But what is there in this world to even like?"

"How about magic?" she countered. "The Golden Blade? The Seven-Stringed Lyre? Hermes' Wand? I've never seen those back home."

"Exactly, Penélope," he said passionately. "Back *home.* This isn't our home. It's some kind of fairytale come to life, but much closer to the Grimm kind. And for the record, I found driving in my 718 Boxster to be more magical than anything in this damned place."

"Your Porsche?" Penélope deadpanned.

"Yes. And I won't even mention the modern utilities or our phones, all of which we left behind. And for what? A more dangerous, unsanitary world that speaks in languages that have been dead for thousands of years in ours?"

Penélope rolled her eyes. "I get it. Nothing here is like home. But for me, this place is all the stories I study come to life. This is Homer and Hesiod and Sappho. Whether it's part of our world or not, I want to see this through. I want to know what's waiting for us at the end of the road."

"It's death, Penélope," Owen said, his face hardening. "If we had never come here, Zeb would never have died. And we wouldn't be risking our own lives trying to rescue him. If Alexandria had never found her mother's diary and left her entire life behind, then I'd still be at Harvard, going to clubs and having a grand old time not worrying about any of this."

"If all that didn't happen, then you would never have met Zeb," Penélope argued.

"No, I wouldn't have."

She turned on him in frustration. "What's your problem, Owen? You act like you want to save Zeb one minute, and the next you pretend you hardly know him! I thought you two were...friends." The last word she spoke hesitantly, second-guessing her interference. If Zeb found out she was talking about him with

Owen, he would kill her and only rescue her from the Underworld out of spite.

"We are friends," Owen said reluctantly, not meeting her eyes. "Though I'm not sure how Zeb feels about me. We never…He seems quite reserved about… things like that."

Penélope heard the unspoken words and felt the need to defend Zeb. "And you're not?"

"Me?" Owen smirked. "I have no problems with telling the world how I feel."

"Attraction and emotion are not the same thing," Penélope said pointedly. "Just because you flirt with everyone and their mother doesn't mean you know how to express your feelings. Zeb might be reserved, but he feels very deeply. I don't want him to get hurt if you're just looking for a good time."

"What's wrong with a good time?" Owen asked, sounding offended. "I've always taken that to be a compliment."

Penélope rolled her eyes for the second time. "You know what I mean."

For the first time, Owen was stone-faced and silent.

She sighed, sensing his retreat. "Zeb should know what you want from him, that's all."

He let out a cold laugh. "What *I* want? *Zeb* doesn't even know what *he* wants. I won't make promises to a boy still in love with his childhood crush. And a bit of advice: you don't need to act like Zeb's mother. The more you baby him, the less prepared he'll be for the real world."

Despite his obvious attempt to hurt her as she did him, the words still stung. Penélope felt the guilt climb up her throat in a nauseating wave. She had let Zeb sacrifice himself for her. She had failed to protect him when she had always sworn to be there for the sad, sarcastic boy who befriended her when no one else would. But Owen didn't understand how difficult Zeb's life had been at home. His mother was an alcoholic, his father was in and out of prison, and he grew up in poverty with no friends besides her. Owen, on the other hand, had it all: a life of luxury, traveling to different continents, effortlessly attractive and charming. Penélope only worried that this situation would turn into another disappointment for Zeb if he got his hopes up too high.

"Zeb has seen more of the real world than you know," Penélope said coldly. "And I might ask the same of you. What about Chloe? You actually *had* a relationship, unlike Zeb."

Owen scoffed. "That meant nothing."

"Exactly, Owen." She saw his eyes narrow, but not before glimpsing a flicker of doubt. "That's what I'm worried about. That this is *nothing* to you."

He opened his mouth to speak when another voice called his name. Leandros had approached them, and Penélope had been too engrossed in their argument to notice. Owen straightened up like a soldier standing at attention.

"Captain," he said. Ever since the cyclops incident and witnessing Leandros fight, Owen had assumed an uncharacteristically respectful attitude toward him.

"You should sleep, son of Godfrey," Leandros said, though his eyes flickered to her, betraying the real reason for his interruption. "The next rotation will be in a few hours."

Owen nodded, then after a quick, regretful glance at Penélope, walked off to the ladder that led down to the hold, where the rest of the sailors on their break had already retreated. Leandros took Owen's place beside her, gazing out at the sea with his usual thoughtfulness. Since their last tense conversation after they escaped the cyclops and their brief moment of intimacy, almost a week had come and gone without their paths crossing for more than a few awkward pleasantries. Penélope wondered why he was choosing to speak with her now.

"Look ahead," Leandros said, nodding toward the sea unfurling beyond the steady prow of the ship. "Do you see that floating dot on the horizon?"

Penélope squinted past the foaming waves and endless, choppy waters, and sure enough, a little black dot sat on the line between sea and sky. "What is it?"

"The last known island before we sail to the Land of the Dead."

A thrill rushed over her, then cold dread, as if a rogue wave had rushed over the side of the hull and doused her in its chill water. "How will we know we've reached it?"

Leandros smiled wryly. "I thought I had already told you the answer to that, Penélope."

She closed her eyes briefly, forgetting how much she loved hearing the way he said her name. "Faith."

Instead of answering her, Leandros closed his eyes and gently began to murmur a tune under his breath:

> "πρὸς ζόφον ἠερόεντ' ἀνέμῳ δε φέροντ' ἔπευ ἄκρον
> τοῦ μέσσου ἁλὸς εἶτ' ἔπευ Ἡελίῳ τε δύνοντι
> ἢ ἵνα ἀσφοδελὸς λειμών ἐστ' ἀείμνηστος..."

"That was beautiful," Penélope said once his voice trailed off, as if he forgot the rest of the song.

Leandros shook his head. "It's the beginning of an old sailor's song. For many months, I heard Mono sing it to himself when all the men had fallen asleep and the fire blazed hottest in the night. But I never thought one day I would heed its command."

"What does it say?"

He was silent, thinking over the verses, then spoke:

> *"Follow the wind as it blows West*
> *To the edge of the Middle Sea*
> *Then follow the Sun as it sets*
> *To where the undying fields be..."*

"I thought I heard the word ἀσφοδελὸς," Penélope said. "The Fields of Asphodel are in the Underworld, aren't they? That's the undying field?"

"Perhaps I did not translate well enough, or my language does not need so many words as yours to say more than one thing." Leandros grew thoughtful. "When I said *undying,* perhaps I should have said *ever-memorable.* That is what ἀείμνηστος might literally mean. And I said *West* when ζόφον ἠερόεντα more nearly means the *dark gloom,* for my people believe where the sun is last to touch is the Underworld, and before Helios can rise again, he must travel below through the darkness."

Penélope could not help a smile. "You could be a poet, you know."

He blushed, but his eyes lowered sadly. "That is very kind of you, but I am no better a singer than any other palace-trained princeling. In my youth, if ever, I may have fancied myself a poet, but exile and battle have hardened my hands against such a life."

"You can still be a poet after this is all over," Penélope said. "You're a prince. You can be whoever you want to be."

"I am first in line for my father's throne, Penélope," he replied, almost bitterly. "My duty is to my people and my family, not to the whims of Poesy."

"I understand." But inwardly, the guilt rose again, knowing she was abandoning her family and a place in their world for a new one here. What did she know of duty? Her family expected her to be a lawyer, to lift them out of the working class and cushion their retirement, and all this time, she had squandered her potential by studying Classics, and now she was one step away from risking that too. Even if she managed to balance a double life, a part of her would always harbor that guilt, the truth of her life concealed from those she loved most.

"I know," he said, as if hearing her thoughts. She glanced at him in surprise. "You have left your family and your home to come to the city, just as my mother had."

"If I stay here," Penélope whispered, suddenly feeling tears press against her throat, "I might never be able to see my family again."

He stared at her, sensing the double meaning in her words, his offer of a life together, and what that would mean for her. She wanted to say more, to explain, but there was no way to explain how she had entered through a doorway from her world to a magical city, this road between the realms of gods and mortals. Leandros was a part of that world, just like the monsters and the magic. And yet, sometimes, he seemed to understand her. There was a part of her that wished to give in to him entirely, abandon herself to the whirling chaos in her heart whenever he said her name in a language that no longer existed.

But she never got a chance to speak. Leandros' eyes wandered back to the horizon, and he grew very still.

Then he spoke in a rough voice. "We have arrived."

13

Penélope whirled around, her heart beating furiously. But everything was the same as a moment ago. She scanned the horizon. The island that had been a faraway black dot had drawn closer, except that it wasn't an island, not exactly, but two towering rocks jutting out of the water like two pillars of a gate, the sea surging gray and dark against their sheer, slick surfaces.

"Ἡράκλειαι Στῆλαι," Leandros said grimly.

The Pillars of Hercules.

As they neared, the sky darkened, as though the sun had been left behind and they were moments from careening off the face of the earth. As Penélope squinted harder into the murky fog in the distance, she saw that beyond the pillars the sea dropped off into darkness, as if they had truly come to the edge of the world, though Penélope knew that was impossible. Or was it?

Mono was shouting orders, steering the ship so that its prow pointed directly between the Pillars of Hercules. Penélope held her breath as they neared the narrow gap, wide enough for five widths of the ship to sail through, but close enough that their intimidating masses towered over them, threatening to crush them if they strayed but a little.

The ship broke past the pillars, heading directly toward the edge, where murky darkness stretched endlessly before them, the sliver of gloom caught between a night sky and the black sea mirrored below. A few more strokes of the oars and their ship would tip over the edge.

Penélope gasped as they pitched into the dark, instinctively reaching out with her hand. "Leandros!"

But they never fell.

She was still grasping Leandros' arm tightly, her eyes closed, when she felt an arm gently cover her shoulders.

"Open your eyes, Penélope."

With a long, shaky exhale, she opened her eyes, realizing that their ship had continued sailing into the darkness. There was water below their ship, for the rowers strenuously pulled at their oars, working even harder now that the wind had ceased and Mono ordered the sails to be rolled up.

Penélope stepped away, her face burning when she saw Leandros' blush, his arm falling back by his side. "Where are we?"

"We have crossed into the Land of the Dead," Leandros said, though she detected a hint of a waver in his firm voice. "This water shall gather into the river Acheron, where lies the boundary between the living and the dead. But we shall have no need of the Ferry this time."

In the darkness, she glimpsed fathomless gloom—there was no better word for it—unfolding on either side of the dark waters. While there seemed to be no end to the murky skies above them, the darkness nonetheless clung all around, sucking the warmth out of their bodies. Penélope shivered, but resisted the urge to inch closer to Leandros.

"Where will we go?"

The currents of the water had slowed to an imperceptible movement, as if they were sailing in a thick marsh. A gray shore was unveiled as their ship pierced through the gloom, curling around them and fading into the distance, and she saw they had entered a wide bay. The still and sludgy water pooled black and slow before the shore, mingling with the mouth of a black river pouring out from somewhere deep inland, slithering between two separated shores and out into the sea like a large snake.

"We will anchor on the other side of the river," Leandros said, pointing to the left bank, where a dark forest hugged the shore. "We will avoid the forest. By the shores of the River Styx, we will perform the ritual to speak with the dead. Hopefully we find Tiresias and learn of my father's fate. Then we rescue your friend."

Penélope did not argue with the plan this time. The ship anchored close to the left bank, where a few trees cropped up sparsely by the gray sand. On the other bank, bordered by frail, white poplar trees, Penélope thought she saw a slim black figure gliding across the river as it stood atop a raft, but then she blinked and it was gone.

Leandros led her to the small rowboat they would use to reach the shore. Only Owen, Mono, and a handful of other sailors would join them; the rest were happy to remain on the ship and be able to sail back to the land of the living if anything were to go wrong.

"Are you okay?" Owen asked as they climbed inside the boat.

Penélope nodded, though the movement made her head light. "I'm fine." She glanced down at her hands, as though expecting to find them holding the Golden Blade of Demeter. Its presence had calmed her the last time they ventured to the Underworld, even if it had scarred her hands. She recalled telling her parents that she had accidentally picked up a pot filled with boiling water when they had seen the scars, the day she had briefly returned to the New Academy and packed up her bags, pretending to be leaving for Greece.

"Be careful," her mother said, holding her hands, her eyes sad, as if she knew exactly where Penélope was heading. "You are my only daughter, Pepa. I can't lose you."

Her eyes stung as she hugged her mom.

Then she blinked, pulled out of the memory. It had felt so real, as if she were reliving that moment, to the point that tears had welled in her eyes.

Owen eyed her worriedly. "Penélope, we're going to rescue him. I promise."

She nodded, hastily wiping at her tears. "I'm sorry. This place is strange, that's all. I don't like it."

"Welcome to the Land of the Dead," Leandros said darkly between strong pulls at the oar. "No living man wanders here willingly, for he cannot leave it so easily as he has come, if he can leave at all."

"But we're going to leave, aren't we?" Owen asked pointedly.

"If the gods will it, then we may."

Penélope shivered. "And if they don't?"

Leandros glanced at her with a wry smile. "Then you may need to hold a sword once more, Πηνελόπη χρυσάωρ."

Penelope of the Golden Blade. But was she still that girl? The same girl who had so willingly wandered into the Halls of Death and defeated the Serpent of Osiris? The same girl who had believed that with enough wit and courage, she could do anything? What did she know, in the end? All of her knowledge, all faith in herself, had crumbled as she knelt before the Gate of the Moon, where Zeb had fallen into the depths of the earth, swallowed up and gone forever.

No, not *forever*. Penélope had to save him, if it was the last thing she did. If it weren't for her, if she had never agreed to help Alexandria find her mother in a magical city, Zeb would never have followed her. Or was *that* even true? She glanced at Owen, his serious frown as he helped row them to shore. He had returned to the Underworld too, for the same reason as her. Why would someone like Owen, who had almost everything in life handed to him on a silver platter, risk it all for someone he hardly knew?

"Penélope."

She glanced up, heart pounding. Leandros stood outside the boat. Everyone had already gotten out, but all she could think about was Leandros throwing her an apple, his earnest eyes as he declared his love to her. *I knew the moment I laid eyes on you.*

Was it possible?

She held out her hand. He took it, his palm warm and comforting as it enclosed around her cold one. Her feet sank into the damp sand. It would seem like any other place if it were not for the lack of the sun in the gray sky or the ghostly whispering in the chilled air. The forest beside them was thick and dark, tendrils of mist curling around the gnarled trunks.

Leandros shouldered his pack filled with provisions, and his hand tightened around the hilt of his sword strapped at the waist. "We make for the river Styx."

Then they were off, walking away from the shore and their only means of escape. Penélope was able to keep up better this time as the landscape here was more level, but her legs still burned with the effort, unused to walking more than the length of the ship for the past week.

Their route swung them away from the forest's edge along the river Acheron, whose banks were bordered by more white poplar trees, until they could no longer see the shore behind them. The river Styx was supposedly a branch of the river Acheron, so they hoped to find it by following the latter until it forked.

"Why the river Styx again?" Owen asked, slightly out of breath. Leandros had picked up the pace as the ground sloped steadily down, as if they were heading toward a valley, though it was difficult to make out anything more than endless gray in the gloom.

"Because the gods call the river ὅρκος δεινός," Leandros said.

"*The Dread Oath,*" Penélope whispered.

Leandros nodded. "The gods swear their most terrible oaths on this water.

While the river Acheron lies between the land of the living and the Land of the Dead, the river Styx lies at its heart, most bound to the power of Death. If we wish to speak with the spirits of the dead, we must offer our sacrifices there."

"That sounds…dangerous," Owen said slowly. "What's the catch?"

"The catch?"

"Yeah, what's in the fine print?" Then Owen sighed irritably. "What is the risk? The last time we went to the Underworld, we had to make a deal with Death and sacrifice one of our own to leave."

"Ah, I see," Leandros said, then shook his head. "No deals with Death can be made this time, for you have already trespassed his Halls once. We must hope rather that our departure from this land is not prevented…"

"Prevented?" Owen repeated, glaring at the back of Leandros' head as he marched ceaselessly ahead. "Penélope, did you hear that? *Prevented?* By whom?"

"Or what?" Penélope muttered, but when Owen turned his glare on her, she threw up her hands. "I know as much as you do. Leandros will help us get out of here. All we have to focus on is rescuing Zeb."

Owen grew sullen and silent, falling into step beside Penélope. Their route along the river Acheron suddenly veered left. Leandros paused, squinting hard into the mist, but it was difficult to see past the shifting fog to the other side of the river. Suddenly a sliver of fog cleared, and Penélope saw a deserted bank on the other side, where the river Acheron split in two.

"This must be the river Styx," Penélope said, hoping her voice sounded firm. All eyes turned to her. "I saw the river split up ahead, the Acheron going right, the Styx going left this way. We should follow this river until we find a good place to perform the ritual. Besides, there would be no way to follow the other river unless we crossed it…by the Ferry."

Owen blanched at this. "There is no way in Hell that I'm getting on any Ferry, in this world or the next."

Leandros looked at Owen warily, then at her, before relaying her words to the others. Mono bowed low, then immediately joined her, murmuring her name reverently. Once the others agreed, Leandros led them along the steep bank of the new river.

Penélope and the rest followed him silently, as if it took too much effort to talk. Besides, the eerie emptiness of the land, the deadness of the grass, and the black, slow current of the river made talking feel like an unwelcome intrusion, a faculty of the living, not of the dead. Up ahead, she glimpsed a blond head running on the other side of the river, then heard her name called as if from far away.

"Penélope, catch up!"

"Zeb, come back here!"

He was too fast, but she was smiling. It was the most fun they'd had in a while. Summer made the dirt bake, but they didn't care. Zeb glanced back, almost happy, his lips nearly curling into a smile, when suddenly she saw a car flying out of the corner of her eyes, driving wildly on the same street Zeb was about to cross, and she cried out, too late to save him as the car slammed into—

She stumbled, nearly falling to the ground, shaking her head to rid herself of the strange memory she had, even though the ending had gone all wrong.

"Penélope, catch up," Owen said irritably, hands on his hips. The rest of the group had already walked several paces ahead and waited impatiently for her.

"It is best not to linger on the past here," Leandros said grimly, glancing around as if he, too, were having his own visions. "They are only false dreams."

Then he turned, Mono the only one to linger a worried glance on her, before they all continued the march. This time, Penélope ignored the whispers in her mind, as if someone were murmuring spells in her ear, snatches of phrases belonging to memory, or to her most terrifying nightmares. Owen appeared unaffected, but every once in a while she caught his face grow ashen, before he closed his eyes briefly and opened them with a hardened determination, willing himself not to give in to his own meandering thoughts.

Meanwhile, the river Styx wound in slow, sweeping curves away from the river Acheron and into a wide valley dotted with pale white like a sky full of bleak stars. Not stars, Penélope saw, but flowers, fragile white petals hanging limply from reedy, gray stalks. They paused to survey the expanse of undying flowers, frozen in time, beautiful and yet terrible, until it hit her all at once, the words from the song lingering in her mind as if Leandros were singing them now.

Then follow the Sun as it sets
To where the undying fields be...

"The Fields of Asphodel," Penélope whispered.

14

Leandros nodded, looking out at the Fields of Asphodel in barely hidden wonder. "We are close now."

They followed the river as it shrank to a trickling stream deeper into the valley. The forest had neared ever closer until it now loomed dark and ominous on their left, stretching endlessly under the gloomy skies. Penélope tried not to look too long at the shifting mist among the tree trunks, knowing somehow that terrors lurked inside those woods. She thought she heard a faint scream in the air, but when she strained her ears, all was silent once more.

When the stream slowed to a marshy pool at the heart of the valley, Leandros stopped. From there, the stream then curved and gathered more water, bending toward the forest and disappearing in a swifter current beyond the mist.

"First, we shall make the sacrifice," Leandros said, then motioned to his comrades. "Μηρία καιεσθε."

One of the sailors brought forth wood and dry brush, expertly applying friction to the branches until a fire began to burn, the sweet smell of burnt olive wood filling the air. Then another brought out the thigh bones of a pig wrapped in fat, which they had stolen from the cyclops' stores and prepared for the sacrifice.

Leandros motioned to Mono. "Αἷμα ἐμοί δίδωθι."

"Wait," Penélope said, stepping forward. Leandros glanced at her. "I want to help. I want to be a part of the sacrifice."

"Are you certain? If you take part in the ritual, you shall be able to hear them speak."

Penélope nodded firmly. "I'm sure. I want to hear them."

He looked at her for another long moment, then said, "Very well."

She took a deep breath and stood by his side. Mono handed them an amphora filled with a sharp-smelling liquid as two sailors dug a small trench before the fire, where the pig thighs had blackened, the fat dripping like wax onto the wood and burning hotter. Leandros held the amphora, then motioned for her to grasp the handles. She placed her hands over his and swore she saw him stiffen.

"What's in here?" she asked, sniffing the opening of the amphora and cringing.

Leandros raised a brow. "Blood."

She paused, her stomach heaving at the thought of the pig's blood sloshing in the amphora. Leandros watched her carefully as she breathed in and out, hoping the burning smell of meat would clear her nostrils of the tangy blood which seemed to settle in her throat as if she had taken a sip.

"Now we shall pour," Leandros said softly, and together they tipped the amphora forward until the bright red blood poured out in a thick stream inside the trench, coating the soft, churned soil and gathering in a sticky pool. "Then we offer milk-honey, wine, and water."

As he spoke, Mono and two other men came forward and placed three small bowls of liquid around the fire, one with clear water, the other with dark wine, and the last with the milk sweetened by honey. Once they placed the bowls down, they walked a few paces back, leaving her and Leandros alone by the fire, their hands still joined around the amphora of blood.

"What happens now?" she asked, her voice trembling.

His weight shifted imperceptibly toward her. "Now we wait."

Now we wait for the dead, were the words he did not speak, but Penélope heard them anyway, and she shivered, tightening her hold on his hands. Leandros stood still beside her, his chest rising and falling against her shoulder. Nothing stirred, nothing sounded amidst the fields save the crackling of the wood, the fire eating away at the charred bones.

Suddenly she heard Leandros suck in a breath. She looked up from the fire. *People.* The entire valley was filled with them, staring directly at her and Leandros, then at the trench of blood with greedy, dark eyes. She wanted to speak, to say something to Leandros or the crowd of the dead, but the words stuck painfully in her throat.

"Ποῦ Τειρεσίας ἐστι?" Leandros asked, his voice rough.

They stared back mutely. There were so many of them, shoulder to shoulder, unmoving, still in the pale light of the sky, like the asphodels hanging limply from their stalks. Penélope craned her neck to try and find Zeb's face among the crowd, but she only saw unfamiliar pale bodies, some bloodied from battle or disease-riddled, others still in rosy youth, many old and hunched. But they all seemed hollow and insubstantial, their mortality and warmth gone forever, their spirits, like an imprint of memory, were all that remained.

One old woman hobbled forward towards the blood, but before she could reach it, Leandros brandished his sword and pointed it before the trench. The old woman stopped, eyeing the sword ruefully.

Leandros raised his voice, firmer now with a sword in hand. "Ἄξεσθε Τειρεσίαν!"

All was eerily quiet. The vast throngs of the dead remained still, their dark, sorrowful eyes staring at them in faraway contempt. Penélope had half a mind to beg, when a rustling swept through them like wind among dead leaves, raising the hairs on Penélope's neck, before the sea of spirits parted like water around a rock and a figure emerged from the crowd.

He was an elderly man with a long, scraggly beard, and his eyes, blind but still round and searching, fixed on Penélope and then Leandros with a knowing gleam.

"Tiresias," Penélope whispered.

Leandros lowered his sword as Tiresias walked forward, aided by a glowing, golden staff. The seer stooped low and drank from the trench, then stood up and gazed at them anew, a flush returning to his pale cheeks so that he appeared almost living.

"Τειρεσίη," Leandros said, bowing his head.

He raised a brow. "Son of Leon, sprung from Helenus, the young Prince Leandros, why have you left the light of the sun and come hither to behold the dead? And you, daughter of Estela, Penélope of the Golden Blade, why have you forsaken the land of the living yet again?"

His shade spoke the words out loud in the thick silence, his voice gravelly and ancient and laden with wisdom. Though Penélope knew he spoke in Ancient Greek to Leandros, she still understood the words in her mother tongue.

"Ποῦ πατὴρ ἐμός ἐστι?" Leandros asked, his voice breaking as he spoke.

Tiresias' eyes saddened. "You ask of your father, and yet what shall I tell you that will not pain your heart more? Nay, the endless toils on the open sea he has faced all these years shall be his story to tell, not mine. But I may counsel you on where you might seek more news of your father. Sail to the island of Ogygia, in the middle of the Middle Sea. There you might learn more of his fate."

Leandros' face darkened. "Καλυψώ."

Calypso.

Penélope glanced at him, surprised to hear the anger in his voice, before returning her attention to the seer. He was already looking at her. "Tiresias, where can I find my friend, Zeb? Please, I've come all this way."

"Your friend? Why, he has never left your side," Tiresias said, an amused glint in his eyes. His gaze wandered over to the space next to Penélope. "Is that not so, Zeb Hades?"

Penélope turned, her heart thudding in her chest, the movement making her head go light. Zeb stood beside her, staring at her with his dark eyes, though never before had she seen such unfathomable sorrow pooled in their depths.

"Hello *Pepa*," Zeb said quietly.

At the sound of his voice, so low and familiar and sad, her stomach dropped as a coldness washed over her, and she heard Leandros call her name distantly as her vision tunneled to black, as if Death had snatched her from a field of flowers like Persephone herself, falling and falling below the earth.

15

"Penélope."

Zeb stood before her, nervously playing with his backpack straps on his shoulders. She was surprised he had approached, being so serious and quiet, mostly keeping to himself in the back of the classroom. Penélope didn't have any friends either, but she preferred to sit at the front of the class to better answer the teacher's questions.

"You're Penélope, right?"

"Yes," she said. He stuck out his hand and she shook it, amused at the formality but not daring to show it. "Zeb, right?"

He didn't smile, but his eyes lit up, as if surprised but reluctantly pleased that she remembered his name. "Do you want to sit with me at lunch?"

"Penélope."

She turned. Zeb was older, but still so young. Too young for his pains, the rings of gray around his eyes, the sheer exhaustion in his thin frame. Panic seized her when she glimpsed a tear fall down his pale cheek. "What is it?"

"My dad—" His voice broke. Penélope hugged him so that he wouldn't have to speak. His voice mumbled into her hair. "He's out of prison. I don't want to see him, Penélope, I don't—"

"You won't have to," Penélope interrupted firmly, a fierce protectiveness rising in her. "You don't owe him anything, Zeb. Nothing. No matter what your mom says. This is your *life."*

"I just—I hate him," Zeb said viciously. "I hate him for ruining our lives. I hate him for making my mom sick, for leaving us with nothing. I hate him. I hate him!"

She wanted to comfort him, but he stepped away forcibly. His hands were balled in fists at his sides, and his chest struggled for breath. There was nothing she could do for his pain. Never before had she felt so helpless. His eyes squeezed shut, and his lips trembled as if he were about to break down, even though she knew how much he hated to cry in front of other people.

"I hate him. I can't, Penélope, I can't live like this. It makes me want to scream—"

"Scream, then," Penélope said.

He looked up at her. "What?"

"Scream." She took his hands, squeezing them. "I'll scream with you."

Zeb looked at her dubiously, then glanced around, but there was no one there to stop them. The town always felt deserted this late at night. Then he screamed, a strangled shout clawing its way out of his chest, and then she screamed too, letting their cries of anger and pain dissipate in the night sky.

"Penélope."

She blinked her eyes open. Zeb stood over her. He did not look worried or angry, just vaguely sad. Penélope scrambled to her feet, looking around. Leandros was behind her, one hand on her arm to steady her and the other on the hilt of his sword, as if he were ready to protect her at any moment. Tiresias and the crowds of dead souls were gone, the fire all charred, encircled in unmoving smoke.

"What happened?" she asked, her voice weak.

"You fainted," Zeb said flatly.

It was so much like the Zeb she knew that Penélope began to laugh, and then she threw her arms around him, her laughter mingled with sobs as his arms circled familiarly around her. She took a deep breath and stepped away.

"I can't believe it's you." She wiped her tears, trying to compose herself. She saw Owen staring at Zeb in shock out of the corner of her eye, but she didn't want to draw Zeb's attention away. "What happened to you?"

His pale brows knitted together, though the movement was slow, as if his mind were elsewhere. "I died."

"I'm so sorry," she choked. "I'm sorry I couldn't save you."

"Never make a deal with Death." He spoke to her, but his eyes wandered off to the Fields of Asphodel.

"Zeb," she said quietly. He didn't seem to hear her. "Zeb."

His eyes snapped back to her, then widened in surprise, as if he were seeing her for the first time. Then they filled with a terrible sadness. "I have been so alone."

"We're going to rescue you," Penélope said through her tears. "I'll never leave you again."

"Don't make promises you can't keep." He spoke coldly, and Penélope flinched, any response dying in her throat as the tears spilled down her face.

"Hey, we sailed to the ends of the earth to save you, mate." Owen had stepped forward, his arms crossed and his face drawn in anger. "I'm not expecting any thank you's, but at the very least you could show Penélope some gratitude."

Zeb turned towards Owen with the same cold, dead eyes. "You shouldn't have come."

"Don't worry," Owen retorted. "The more you speak, the more I regret ever coming here."

Penélope battled her annoyance. "Let's not fight, guys. We need to get out of here, remember?"

For the first time, Zeb laughed, but it was mirthless and chilling to the bone. "There is no escaping Death."

Owen met Penélope's eyes, mirroring her fear, before he turned and began to walk in the direction they came, Mono and the other sailors eagerly following. A hand came down on Penélope's shoulder, and she nearly jumped. Leandros stood behind her.

"We cannot linger here," he said, glancing around worriedly.

She nodded. "Let's go."

They turned to leave. Zeb stared vacantly at the ground, but reluctantly followed after them. She wanted to speak with him, to ask what happened to him, to say *something*, but she was scared of his answer. While Zeb had always been sarcastic and borderline rude, he had never been so pitiless. She wondered if it was a product of the Underworld, if, surrounded by the dead, a part of him had died too.

"Penélope, run!"

Owen was sprinting back towards them, his face frozen in terror, eyes wide. She looked past him and saw a looming figure on the lip of the next hill. Mono and the other sailors had their swords out as they slowly back-stepped away from three massive, snarling hounds that stood between them and their escape back to the ship. Except that there weren't three hounds but one, its black fur matted with blood, three growling mouths armed with sharp fangs hanging out of its thick, veined neck.

"You've got to be joking," Penélope muttered to herself.

"Κέρβερος, hound of Hades. He guards the way against those who wish to leave." Leandros unsheathed his sword, the sharp edge glinting. "Get back." At the sight of his sword, the monster roared, spit flying from his jaws, the ground shaking beneath them. Leandros paled. "Run. Run! Φεύγετε!"

Zeb stood rooted to the spot, staring at the hound in horror mingled with awe. Penélope grabbed his arm and dragged him after her. *I won't leave you here again.*

They ran as fast as they could, not looking back to see if the monster was chasing them; his heavy, lumbering footsteps sounding behind them were proof enough. Penélope kept a tight grip on Zeb's arm as they ran blindly away from the hound of Hades towards the Styx river that bordered the Fields of Asphodel.

"We cannot cross," Leandros shouted back, his chest heaving, eyes glancing back in terror at the approaching hound.

Penélope looked to the forest hugging the Acheron. If they could lose the hound among the trees, they would reach the shore on the other side.

"Follow me!" she shouted, then dragged Zeb with her toward the forest. He followed with stumbling steps, his eyes glazed in fear, as if he were witnessing a nightmare come to life.

The first trees cropped up around them, ancient yew trees with their twisting, gnarled trunks covered in evergreen leaves. They wove a path between the white poplars and weeping willow trees as the edge of the forest neared. She heard the growls of the hound approaching closer, spurring her to run faster.

Suddenly, Zeb yanked her to a stop. "We can't go in there."

"It's the only way," Penélope said, pushing down a wave of anger. "You have to trust me, Zeb. You have to let me save you."

Zeb shook his head adamantly. "We can't go in there."

Owen reached them, panting. "What's going on? Why did you stop?"

Penélope looked back helplessly, watching as the hound of Hades ripped a tree out of the ground with one of its jaws, clearing a path directly toward them. Leandros and Mono shouted at them to continue running.

"It's *Her*," Zeb said, staring at the wispy tendrils of mist that the forest seemed to breathe in and out. "The Queen."

The hound had ripped the last tree in its way. They were running out of time. Leandros and Mono rushed towards them, stopping before the thicker tree line and peering into the forest. All of the men stuttered to a stop, their faces paling in the face of the forest.

"Who is She?" Penélope demanded, looking around at all of their terrified eyes. "Who is the Queen?"

Mono narrowed his eyes, clutching his sword tightly. "Φορεύς φόνου."

The Bringer of Death.

Penélope shivered, instinctively pulling Zeb closer to her. Then another roar from the hound of Hell brought Penélope back to the present moment. She saw the hound running towards them, though with a hesitating step as it neared the forest, its growl turning into a whine. Between certain Death and an unknown Death, she could only see one option.

Without another word, Penélope ran into the forest, dragging Zeb in with her.

16

Once they were in the forest, the hound of Hades hesitated, but Penélope didn't dare wait to make sure, running with all the strength she had left, her hand still holding Zeb's arm.

Leandros and Mono were a step behind them, Owen breathing hard to her left. She could hardly see where she was going, the mist growing thicker around the tree trunks the deeper they treaded inside the forest. Zeb ran reluctantly, his eyes wide and fearful as he looked around.

Suddenly he tried to drag her back. "Penélope, wait!"

But she ignored him, pulling him forward with all her might, only to take another step and catch her foot on a thick root jutting out from a nearby tree, her grasp on Zeb's arm slipping away as she tumbled to the ground.

She groaned, staggering to her feet. No one said anything. She whirled around, expecting Leandros or Owen's concerned faces to appear. No one was there.

She was alone.

"Leandros! Owen! Zeb! I'm here!" But her voice echoed faintly and died in the stale, thick air of the forest.

Penélope struggled to breathe, panic rising in her chest. She looked wildly at the tendrils of mist tenderly embracing the tree trunks, as if they had a mind of their own, or as if something—or someone—were commanding them. She felt eyes upon her, watching, and she knew then that she wasn't alone.

The Bringer of Death.

A faint rustling ahead of her caught her ear. The mist parted, and from thin air emerged the shape of a woman as tall as the first branches of the yew tree, her blood red gown brushing the forest floor where her bare feet tread, and her curls crowned with a glowing gold disk encircled by two horns. In her right hand, she held what appeared to be a rattle, and in her left a long, leather leash with three collars.

"You," Penélope whispered. "You sent the hound after us."

The woman glanced keenly at her, eyes dark and soulful in the smooth planes of her face. Then Penélope heard her voice, melodic and terrible, like a beautiful song sung by the grave. *My hound guards the way back to the land of the living.*

Penélope lowered her head respectfully, unable to bear her weighty gaze. "We have to go back, my Lady. We don't belong in the Land of the Dead."

You are mortals, she said with a light laugh that sent a chill down Penélope's spine. *Your lot in life is Death.*

"Where are my friends?" Penélope demanded, fearing that they would be stuck here forever, once more failing to rescue Zeb. "What did you do to them?"

You and your friends wandered willingly into my halls.

Penélope had already begun to understand, but a part of her did not want to believe it. She snuck another glance at the tall, queenly figure before her, the red dress and crown reminiscent of another goddess of Death they had encountered. Or were they one and the same?

"This is the Grove of Persephone. So that makes you...the Queen of Death."

Clever girl.

"What do you want from me?"

The Queen of Death laughed again. *No, the question is, what do you want from me?*

Penélope stared at the Queen, her dark tumbling curls, those eyes as black as the waters of the Styx. Unlike her mother, Demeter, this goddess harbored another kind of power, not the seed of the crop nor the fertility of the earth but its decay and destruction, the corpse as it decomposes in the soil, plants and flowers plucked at their prime and the constant companion of the living, like a shadow that never changes with the movements of the sun.

"I want to rescue my friend," Penélope said slowly, compelled to answer her more than she was willing. "And I want to return to the world of the living. Unharmed."

The Queen walked slowly around the nearest willow tree, her fingers gently brushing the hanging leaves. *This is my kingdom, shared by my husband, and I hold dominion over all the souls of the dead. You cannot leave if I forbid it. The hound of*

Hell answers to me. How shall you defeat such a monster without the Golden Sword?

Penélope watched transfixed as the Queen of Death walked over to her, tall and menacing and yet delicate, like a poisonous flower whose mere touch could kill. "Your mother gave me that sword."

And by its blade, you slayed the Serpent of the Underworld.

"I have already paid that price," Penélope said, her voice shaking with anger and fear. "Zeb already paid the price. His death may be your right, but his life is not, and he deserves to live it fully. Please let us go."

Clever that you are, there is much you do not know. By giving you that blade, my mother has helped set in motion a war that shall shake the very foundations of the cosmos. Your descent into the Land of the Dead was no mere chance, and neither was your journey to the ends of the earth. Nay, not even our crossing here was left up to chance, though it may seem that way to you. The Fates have brought you to me so that I may once and for all have my revenge.

At the last word, her eyes burned like the sacrifice's blackened wood. She stood now before Penélope, looking down on her with the unbearable judgment of the swaying scales, weighing the worth of her heart in one brutal glance.

"Revenge for what, my Lady?" Penélope asked, trembling under that stare, the shadowy power lancing through her very limbs.

For my father's crime against me. In the flower of my youth, I was stolen, plucked from a field of flowers by the Lord of the Dead. Severed from my mother, ever-grieving and gray-cloaked, never to return to her arms. So I rule the halls of Death by my husband's side. For to eat the fruit of Love is to eat the fruit of Death. None may return once the first bite is taken.

Penélope lowered her eyes, and the anger and hatred in the Queen's words echoed in the gathering shadow around her figure. "What can I do? I am only human."

She felt an ice-cold touch under her chin. Penélope looked up. The Queen's anger had left her, leaving an eternal chill behind. *You must save the exiled King of Helena. His restoration to power is the only hope your people may have in defeating my father.*

"But...but I thought Zeus was defeated," Penélope said, her mind spinning. "Alexandria fulfilled the prophecy. She wielded the Emerald Stone. I saw it happen."

The Old Order has been restored, but my father still holds sway over some. He shall use what power he still has to regain the throne, just as he once did against his own father, and in revenge, his retribution shall be swiftest upon the City of Helena.

"I need to warn my friends, the people of Helena. I need to get back to the city! I need to—" The cold touch brushed her lips, and they froze shut, as if they had turned to ice.

First, you must save the King of Helena. His life shall perhaps save another, but at great cost. Are you willing to pay it?

"I don't understand," Penélope said in frustration the moment her lips could move again. "What cost? Why do I have to pay it?"

Who else? Who shall you condemn to your fate?

Penélope was silent. She had never thought of it like that before, and immediately felt guilty for wanting to punish another with her own lot, the fate clearly assigned to her. After all, it was *she* who had wielded the Golden Blade of Demeter, *she* who had summoned the goddess Persephone in her grove, not Zeb, not Owen, not Leandros, but *her*, Penélope. If she condemned another to her fate, she would never forgive herself.

"I will do it," she said. "But I don't know how."

Follow the counsel of wise Tiresias and sail to the Daughter of Atlas. There, more shall be revealed. I cannot guide you on your path, but the road has been placed beneath your feet. When the time comes, you must sacrifice a love you have not yet known. It is the only way to ensure the King returns to the City.

Penélope nodded, even though the words jumbled in her mind, making less sense the more she labored over them. "And how do we get back to our ship?"

The Queen merely shook her right hand, the rattle sounding clear metallic notes in the air. Suddenly her left hand tightened on the leash as if reigning in a wild animal, before Penélope saw that sitting docile before her was the hound of Hades, appearing much smaller beside the tall stature of the goddess. Then she spoke:

Golden bough on Elm of Dreams
Falsely sent by iv'ry means.
If the dead can claim its coin,
May he cross the Acheron.

Her words were chanted like a spell, the weight of her power descending on Penélope's shoulders like earth packed heavily upon a grave, slowly forcing her eyes shut. Then she fell, her legs hitting the ground clumsily, the heels of her hands scraping the forest floor.

"Penélope!" Leandros was there, exactly where she left him, lifting her onto her feet as if she had never met with the Queen of Death. "Are you hurt?"

She ignored him, turning around wildly until she saw Zeb, letting out a long breath of relief. He looked at her strangely, almost fearfully, as if he could sense with whom she had just spoken, even though it appeared that no time had passed at all.

"I know how to get us out of here."

The Daughter of Atlas

Large was the grot, in which the nymph he found
(The fair-hair'd nymph with every beauty crown'd).
The cave was brighten'd with a rising blaze;
Cedar and frankincense, an odorous pile,
Flamed on the hearth, and wide perfumed the isle;
While she with work and song the time divides,
And through the loom the golden shuttle guides.
Without the grot a various sylvan scene
Appear'd around, and groves of living green;
Poplars and alders ever quivering play'd,
And nodding cypress form'd a fragrant shade:
On whose high branches, waving with the storm,
The birds of broadest wing their mansions form,—
The chough, the sea-mew, the loquacious crow,—
and scream aloft, and skim the deeps below.
Depending vines the shelving cavern screen.
With purple clusters blushing through the green.
Four limpid fountains from the clefts distil:
And every fountain pours a several rill,
In mazy windings wandering down the hill:
Where bloomy meads with vivid greens were crown'd,
And glowing violets threw odours round.
A scene, where, if a god should cast his sight,
A god might gaze, and wander with delight!

—*Odyssey*, Book 5.57-74, translation by Alexander Pope

17

"You spoke with the Queen," Zeb said. Everyone turned to him, and he hated it because they looked at him with a terrible pity.

Penélope nodded slowly. "Yes."

"Is this true?" a tall, muscular man with an oddly familiar scarred face asked doubtfully from beside Penélope. "You spoke with the Queen of Death?"

"Can you not tell?" Zeb asked. "Death has left her mark."

She lifted her fingertips subconsciously to her lips, where Zeb had noticed the touch of Death, much like how a kiss can leave a faint bruise, unseen to the eyes but felt all the same. "The Queen told me how to escape. She has called off her hound, but it's up to us to cross the Acheron. Actually," she paused, glancing at Zeb, "it's up to you."

"Me?" He heard the word from far away and did not know if he fully understood its meaning anymore.

Penélope nodded anxiously. "She told me. It was a poem, or a riddle of some kind. It says that if the dead can break off the golden bough from the Elm of False Dreams, we will be able to cross the river Acheron and return to the world of the living. It has to be Zeb."

"Proteus said the same," the scar-faced man said grimly. "It shall be up to you, my friend, whether you remain in the Underworld forever, or return with us."

"Who are you?" Zeb asked.

Penélope glanced anxiously between the man and Zeb. "It's a long story. We'll explain later."

"What are we waiting for?" Owen asked from behind him. He turned, and suddenly they were not in the forest at all.

He stood upon the shore of a strange beach, Owen standing beside him. All the others had already dove under the waves, fearlessly facing death. "What are we waiting for?"

Zeb's mouth went dry. He felt the water claw inside his throat, the helplessness as he drowned, the desire for death more terrifying than anything else. Owen watched him carefully.

"What are you so afraid of?" Owen asked softly.

"I can't–I don't—"

Owen took his hand. Zeb looked down at the strong brown hand in his pale one. "We do it together."

Zeb's heart beat faster, whether because of what they were about to do or Owen's hand in his, Zeb didn't know. Owen took one step forward, then another, waiting as Zeb took a hesitant step with him, then another, until they walked in unison toward the crashing waves.

"I won't let go," Owen said firmly once the water climbed up their chests. His green eyes, the same color as the sea around them, were unusually serious. "I promise."

Then he pulled them underneath the next wave before Zeb could stop him.

"Zeb." A hand brushed his. He glanced down at the familiar hand in his, then up. Owen looked at him with those same eyes, but their sea-green color was dimmed by the death surrounding them. "You have to do this."

His hand slipped out of Owen's grasp like wind between the trees. "Follow me."

"How do you know where it is?" Owen asked before he could take a step, sounding slightly stung at the rejection.

Zeb cocked his head. "Can you not feel it?"

No one challenged him after that, so he led them deeper into the forest, Owen and Penélope's eyes burning into the back of his head. The scar-faced man trailed after Penélope, his quick, unseen glances toward her filled with a painful longing. Zeb wondered how she didn't notice.

The trees grew denser as they passed the heart of the forest, so that they had to squeeze between trunks and duck under branches, thick, gnarled roots shooting out and tripping them without warning. Just when he heard the soft lapping of water against a shore, he saw it. A tall, ancient elm amid a small clearing, its trees flowering black, glossy leaves, as if the roots dug deep and drank greedily from the poisonous waters of the Acheron.

"This is it," Zeb said, pushing away the whispering voices trying to wriggle into his mind like worms in soil.

Penélope stared at the tree, then shook her head, as though shaking off an unwelcome thought. "Where is the golden bough?"

As she spoke, Zeb caught a bright glint at the top of the tree. A single branch swayed amidst the rest, unmistakably golden and impossibly out of reach. Penélope saw it next and sucked in a breath.

She glanced at Zeb and then set her shoulders. "I'll climb."

"No." Zeb shook his head, though his stomach dropped in dread. "I will."

Fear filled Penélope's eyes, but Owen placed a hand on her shoulder, holding her back. Zeb faced the Elm, knowing, somehow, what would happen once he began to climb. Owen nodded at him to continue.

Zeb turned away, then took a step forward. *Zeb, my baby!* He shook away the memory, reaching the bottom of the tree, its gnarled trunk staring back at him, the bark rough and peeling. But there were divots and small branches in the trunk where he could pick a path up to the top. Zeb recalled distantly that he was not the first who had to climb up this tree and break off the golden bough.

He grasped the nearest branch and hauled himself up, only to be pushed back—

Owen was kissing him in the alleyway. His back ached where it pressed against the rough wall, but he didn't care. Owen's mouth on his was addictive, wiping his mind of any doubts or criticism. This was a dream. Too good to be true.

The city was quiet at this time of night. None of the others knew they were here. None of them knew that Owen flirted with everyone and anyone during the day, but by night, he was kissing Zeb, his fingers trembling as they caressed his back, as if he, too, could hardly believe he was kissing him.

"You're so beautiful, did you know that?" Ari said in a rough voice he had never heard before.

Zeb pulled away, breathless, confused, staring at Ari as his hands traveled down the front of Zeb's chest as he had always dreamed he would. Then he was kissing him, and Zeb couldn't help twisting his hands through his thick curls, even if he knew it was just a dream.

Just a dream. Zeb pulled back, shoving Ari away, whose face twisted with hurt. "Zeb, what are you—"

"Stop."

Zeb gasped, pulling himself up to the next branch as the false dream fell away like rain parting against his brow. He grabbed the next branch. He thought he heard his name from far away, but he willed himself not to listen. *Zeb, listen to me.*

It was his mother's voice, clear as day. Zeb shut his eyes to block out the voice, but he heard it even more clearly this time.

"Zeb, listen to me," his mother said, taking his hands. He opened his eyes reluctantly. His mother crouched in front of him. She had that crazed look in her eyes, as if she had a thirst that could not be quenched. "I need you to go down to the store and get something for me."

"No, mom, not again..." He had promised himself he would never buy her more again.

"Just this once, baby, then I'll stop." She squeezed his hands, then kissed his knuckles. "Please. Mr. Abel will let you buy a bottle. Give him this." She slipped a fifty-dollar bill into his fist.

He wanted to say yes. He knew *he said yes. He said yes every time. But what if this time he said no? Her eyes pleaded with him, but Zeb remembered the glaze that settled over them when she was too far gone to reason with, when the alcohol diluted her blood.*

"Mom, you need help."

Her eyes narrowed angrily right before she slapped him clean across the face. "You ungrateful brat!"

"Mom, stop!"

She hit him again, clipping the side of his head so that his vision blurred.

"Stop!"

He surged to the next branch, ignoring the shouts of his mother that still lingered in his mind, climbing the next branch and the next. While his mother had never laid a hand on him, even at her worst, he still felt the tingling of her slap on his cheek as if it had really happened. His head swam with memories mingled with his darkest fears and most secret desires until suddenly his head cleared the treetop, his hand reaching out for the golden bough.

"Take it, buddy."

His hands grasped the plastic handle of the bat clumsily. He got in a ready stance, his dad fixing the position of his legs before taking a few steps back. Was this a dream? Or was it real?

"Okay, now on three, I'll throw the ball and you swing, okay? One, two, three—"

Zeb hesitated, a hair's breadth away. He was surprised to feel tears fall down his face, the image of his dad fading from his mind, the false dream somehow more painful than the fact that it didn't happen. But that was in the past, false or not, and the only way out of Hell lay in a future. *There is no going back. Only onward.*

From somewhere below, he heard his name, a reminder of what he had to lose if he failed to take the branch. *I won't leave you here again.* She had never spoken those words to him, but he heard them nonetheless, as if Penélope's will battled that of the Elm, both struggling to pull him in two different directions.

Ah, the boy who lives with one foot in the dark and one foot in the light.

He knew what he had to choose. Zeb grasped the branch, and it sprang into his hands easily, golden and heavy in his palm. The solid weight of it seemed to ward off the Elm's powerful visions. He shakily climbed down the tree, grateful when his feet landed upon solid earth.

Then Penélope was there, engulfing him in a hug, the faint perfume of lavender and honey clearing his mind of any lingering enchantment.

She leaned back and smiled through her tears, then said, "Let's get the Hell out of here."

18

Zeb sat shivering on the deck of the ship, even with the blankets they had wrapped him in. Penélope paced the raised platform near the captain's cabin, wishing things would go back to normal, though she knew they never would.

Once they had made it back to the ship—to the shock of many of their comrades, who had fully expected them to never return—Zeb had stood at the prow of the ship with his golden bough, silent and still as a statue while the sailors used all their strength to row the ship as fast from the Land of the Dead as possible.

As the ship broke past the Pillars of Hercules, the sunlight burst forth from the sky, and the golden bough dulled to a brown, though Zeb continued to clutch it in his hands. Penélope had tried to speak with him, but he had answered in brief, cutting remarks that he wanted to be left alone, that he didn't need her hovering around him. The words hurt, reminding her of what Owen had told her, but she decided it was a consequence of his time in the Underworld.

But he *had* changed, whether it was because of the Underworld or not. Penélope could tell in the pensive, unseeing gaze occasionally passing across his face, or his shaky grasp of the side of the ship as if he needed to know it was real. It seemed he had returned to the land of the living only half-alive, his skin ice cold to the touch, and a newfound emptiness etched into his dark eyes. But he was here. He was *alive*. That was all that mattered. And with time, Penélope could only hope he would return to his usual, snarky, but fully *living* self.

Owen had taken a different approach. The moment they reached the ship, he had clapped Zeb on the back as if they were good mates and then returned to his oar without another word. Zeb had stared after him with a vacant look before he turned away, his mouth twisted into a bitter frown. Penélope wondered why Owen acted as if nothing strange had occurred since their time in the New Academy, but wondered even more why Zeb accepted it without a fight.

The door to the cabin opened behind her, interrupting her thoughts. Leandros stepped out. He caught her line of sight on Zeb and sighed. "You cannot expect him to be the same."

Penélope could not help the spiraling worry from escaping her. "What if a part of him really did die? What if he'll never fully recover and I've lost my best friend forever? And it's all my fault."

She furiously blinked tears away. Leandros' hand stirred at his side as if he wished to comfort her, then thought better of it.

"You are not at fault for your friend's death," Leandros said. "The death of all mortals is allotted by the gods. Perhaps it was not simple chance that led him to the Land of the Dead."

His words reminded her of the encounter with the Queen of Death, her chilled, eerie laugh, the shadowy power gathered in her form, the dark depths of her eyes that burned with the anger of the dead. *The Fates have brought you to me so that I may once and for all have my revenge.*

"Penélope?" Leandros was looking at her strangely. "Is there something you are not telling me?"

"What?"

Leandros took a step closer to her, lowering his voice. "What did the Queen of Death say to you?"

Penélope's heart leaped in her chest at his sudden proximity, then she registered his question and recalled the dread she felt staring up at the tall goddess, the memory of it making her head go light. *When the time comes, you must sacrifice a love you have not yet known.* She stepped away, wondering if it was selfish of her to raise Leandros' hopes if they were only to be ripped apart.

"She told me how to escape, that's all," she said, avoiding his sharp gaze on her. "And she mentioned that we would learn more from the Daughter of Atlas."

Leandros' face darkened. "Καλυψώ."

"Do you think your father was...detained by her?" she asked hesitantly.

"I do not know, though I suppose we shall discover the truth soon enough." He closed his eyes briefly, his fists clenching at his sides, and when he opened them again, his eyes were filled with pain. "My mother will be heartbroken."

"She loved him, then?"

"She loves him still," Leandros said, sounding offended. "And my father deemed her the loveliest of all women. I never thought anything—or anyone— would change that."

"Maybe it hasn't," Penélope suggested. "Calypso is a goddess. Your father might not have had a choice."

Leandros shook his head angrily. "Love may not be a choice, but who you lie with certainly is." Then his cheeks colored. "I apologize for my frankness, Penélope. This is no subject for a lady to hear."

Penélope raised a brow. "Where I come from, women are allowed to talk about sex. In fact, they are allowed to *have* sex with whoever—"

"Penélope."

She turned. Zeb stood there, looking at her expectantly. "Is everything okay?" she asked hurriedly, trying to calm the quick beat of her heart.

"I need to speak with you." Zeb glanced at Leandros briefly, who stood red-faced and silent. "Alone."

Penélope nodded, following Zeb back to the prow of the ship with one last look back at Leandros, who quickly disappeared into the captain's cabin. Once they were far enough away from everyone, Zeb spoke, his hands twisting the once-golden bough.

"There is something you should know," he said, his dark eyes steady on hers. Where once there was a bitter amusement, now there was only emptiness. Would anything return that liveliness, that spark, to him?

"What is it?" She tried not to sound alarmed, in case he decided against telling her.

Zeb hesitated, then, "I spoke to someone. In the Fields of Asphodel."

It was the first time he had mentioned anything explicit about the Underworld. Her mind raced ahead, and she struggled not to press him with a million questions. "Who?"

"Elena de la Fuente."

"Alexandria's mother?" she asked in surprise. Zeb nodded. "What did she say?"

"I-I can't remember exactly," he said, his face tensing with the effort of remembering, brows furrowed. "She said something about old enemies returning. And new ones. That there was a war on the horizon. She was there to guide me. I didn't understand."

Penélope realized that Zeb did not know anything about the events that happened after he had been trapped in the Underworld. "We should sit down. There's a lot you missed since...since you died."

Zeb blinked at her, then nodded. They sat down at an unoccupied rowing bench, since half the crew were asleep in the hull below, letting the wind carry them eastward. She took a deep breath in, and then recounted what happened after they left the Underworld, how they discovered that Brother Ezra was actually pretending to be the King and an agent of Zeus' will, that the real King had fled for his life and his son had gone looking for him when he never came back, and that Alexandria found the Emerald Stone in the Great Library and had defeated Zeus, burning alive with the force of its Song.

She then told him how the Old Order was restored, Brother Ezra exiled, Chloe made an apprentice to the Seven Sages, Ari the Headmaster of the Academy, and Prince Leandros—who was the Wanderer on the pirate ship that had kidnapped them—returned to the palace, where he offered to help Penélope rescue Zeb from the Underworld as long as they also rescued King Leon along the way.

After she was done, Zeb sat back, stunned. He didn't speak for a long time. Then he turned, saw Leandros exit the captain's cabin and speak with Mono by the rudder. Zeb shook his head. "I knew he looked familiar. So he's the pirate who declared his love to you?"

Penélope's face burned. "That was a long time ago. He's Prince Leandros now. Actually, he's our captain. Mono, the one-legged pirate, is his helmsman. Well, his real name is Μονόπους, but Owen gave him that nickname."

"Of course he did," Zeb muttered, and for the first time, she saw a flicker of reluctant amusement in his eyes. He caught her staring and frowned. "So if the impostor King has been exiled, why doesn't King Leon just come back? Why do we have to find him?"

"No one knows where he is. The Queen of Helena allowed her son to help us rescue you on the condition that we ask Tiresias where to find King Leon. I have a feeling that wherever we find him, we'll learn that there's more to the story than meets the eye."

Zeb nodded pensively. "Old enemies...Elena said that a war hovers on the horizon like a storm, with old enemies—and new ones. Do you think she meant Zeus? Brother Ezra? Or someone else?"

"I don't know," Penélope said honestly. She recalled the revenge in the Queen of Death's face as she spoke of her father, the plan set in motion by the gods long before Penélope or Zeb or even Alexandria had anything to do with it. "The Queen of Death told me the same thing, that war was coming to the City, and that we need to bring back King Leon if we wished to defeat Zeus."

"Then you think it's possible?" Zeb asked. "You think *He* will come back?"

"Whatever is going on is much bigger than us," Penélope said decisively. "Like with the Trojan War, the gods have their own stake in it. We just have to hope we're on the winning side."

Zeb contemplated this while gazing out at the ocean. Once she had explained all that had happened, he seemed to come just a bit more alive, his eyes taking in his surroundings more fully rather than glossing over the world like in a dream. Perhaps Leandros was right. She couldn't expect him to be the same as before, because nothing was the same anymore. Not even *she* had remained the same after losing Zeb and witnessing the power of Zeus and the Emerald Stone.

She laid a hand on his. He looked at her, startled, but with a hint of softness that wasn't there before. "I know things won't go back to normal. How could they when we're in a different world, where people speak ancient languages and gods and monsters exist? And I can't promise that we'll both make it out of this alive. But I just want you to know that no matter how much our lives change, no matter how much *we* change, I will always be your best friend."

For the first time, Zeb half-smiled, squeezing her hand back. "I know."

Your friend? Why, he has never left your side.

Penélope searched his face, wondering if he had heard her praying to him. "Tiresias...he said you had never left my side. Is that true?"

Zeb's gaze clouded over, and she instantly regretted asking it. But then he shook his head slowly. "Not exactly. It was...strange, wandering the fields. Nothing grew, but nothing died, because nothing was living either. I saw the dead spirits grieving, but I wasn't like any of them. My body had been trapped along with my spirit. Sometimes, though, I had dreams. False dreams, maybe. About you, my mom, Ari, Owen, even my dad." His eyes flickered to hers, then away. "It was like I was living through the memories of every moment of my life at the same time, and every moment that could've been but had never actually happened. Sometimes I could hear your voice, telling me to wait, or I was on a ship, and there was a terrible monster. But I was not *physically* with you, not until you crossed the river Acheron and performed the ritual. Then..." He trailed off, looking at her once more, a terrible sadness in his eyes. "I thought you had died and were joining me. It was the first time I felt any spark of happiness, a reminder of what it felt like to be alive, even if it meant you had to die. But when I realized you were still living, that you came to rescue me...then I *wanted* to be alive, to leave the Underworld together. I think that's why I was able to leave."

Tears rolled down Penélope's face as he finished speaking. She had no words, all of the planned speeches she had rehearsed before rescuing Zeb flying out of her mind. Instead, all she could do was throw her arms around him and hug him like it would be the last time. Zeb hesitantly wrapped his arms around her before allowing himself to relax fully in her arms.

"I missed you so much," she said as they pulled apart, sniffling and wiping her tears. "I've been miserable without you. Ari too. Besides, someone needs to be here to keep Owen in check. He's been insufferable."

Zeb rolled his eyes, and the movement was so familiar that Penélope nearly burst into tears again. "Let's just rescue King Leon and warn the city of Helena about Zeus. Then we can go home and forget any of this ever happened."

Penélope nodded, forcing a smile, unwilling to voice her doubts, that she could never forget any of this, not the prophecy and the Emerald Stone, not the descent to the Underworld and the scars of the Golden Blade, nor the love shining in Leandros' eyes whenever he said her name. Of all the things she no longer knew, the world she did not recognize, the language she did not speak, the love she was terrified to feel, there was one truth that rang as loud and clear as the church bells of the Lighthouse back in Tierra del Sol.

She may never return home at all.

19

Penélope stood at the prow of the ship, shielding her eyes from the glaring sun above, her forehead beaded with sweat from the late summer heat. Since they had left the city, June and July had slipped past, August swiftly following. They had spent a fair amount of time in the Land of the Dead, according to their calculations of the constellations, though it hardly felt like more than a day had passed.

A slight wind was kicking up headlong as they steered toward the northeast. Penélope turned and called out, ""Ελκεσθε ἰστία! Πλέεσθε κώπαισι!"

Immediately, crewmen gathered to the ropes and pulled, drawing up the sails so that the wind would not hinder the ship, before they took their places at the oars and in unison rowed with extra strength. Penélope caught Mono's approving glance, and they nodded at each other.

After leaving the Underworld, Penélope had excelled under Mono's supervision to the point that he allowed her to take more command, as if she were his apprentice, which in some ways was true. Almost two weeks had passed as they sailed day and night to the island of Ogygia, whose location on their map was more of an estimate, since mortal men avoided landing there. It was a risk not to stop at the few islands they crossed paths with to replenish their resources, though there was also great risk in landing ashore, a lesson she did not care to learn again.

Yet their rations were severely depleted. Leandros hoped they would last them until they reached Calypso's island, but there was no guarantee that she would help them in their plight, let alone provide them with food and water. She was a goddess, after all. But Penélope hoped at the very least they could find a river where she could bathe in, desperate to clean the grime from her skin. Luckily, she had become rather nose blind to the smell of the crew.

She looked around the deck. Zeb was nowhere to be found. He must've gone down to the hold to sleep, since there was not much for him to do up here. Owen was busy rowing most of the time, and even when he was occasionally off duty, they hardly exchanged more than a few terse words. Penélope knew it was only a matter of time before their careful tiptoeing around each other blew up into a fight. She only hoped it happened *after* they got off the small quarters of the ship.

Suddenly she heard a shout. Mono pointed at the horizon. Penélope turned, eagerly scanning the blue waves, hearing distantly the cabin door open and shut.

"Χέρσον εὑρίσκω!"

She knew this phrase well now, though back home they would say it differently. *Land ahoy!*

Indeed, there was a small island hovering upon the horizon, below gloomy clouds that had rolled in with the early afternoon. Could the daughter of Atlas truly dwell there in the middle of the Middle Sea?

"Ὠγυγία," Leandros said, standing beside her. She secretly loved it when he found her by the prow of the ship, the two of them facing the unknown together. A warmth settled in her chest like the last rays of the setting sun, glowing hot in her heart. Would that be how it feels if she were his wife? The two of them together facing the world as one? But she pushed the thought away, forcing herself to focus.

"How do we know it's the right island?" she asked, eyeing the approaching green island suspiciously.

"If my calculations are correct, this must be the island of Ogygia, as you call it," he said in her English pronunciation, giving her a wry smile. "But we shall know for certain by night, when the stars take their place in the sky."

He said no more, insisting that they wait for nightfall before deciding whether to change course or not. So the ship sailed swiftly at the hands of the oars, making for the strange isle. The warmth of the sun waned as it slipped to the west, the blue of the sky purpling and fading as Night drew her dark skirts around the circle of the world.

Leandros found her once more by the prow of the ship as the last light of the sun departed from the sky and dusk ringed the horizon in a hazy gray. The only sound to be heard was the splashing of the water against the hull and the soft grunts of the rowers, drawing the island ever nearer. She held her breath when she felt Leandros stand behind her, pointing to the sky in her line of vision.

"Look there," Leandros murmured. Her cheeks warmed as she looked up at the sky, following his finger as he traced a constellation from the crowded tapestry of stars hanging directly above the island. "Ἄρκτος, we call it. *The Bear.* She is the only constellation never to sink below the sea, only bathe in its waters. If you are ever lost at sea, she shall guide you."

"Ursa Major," Penélope whispered, then catching Leandros' confused glance, added, "The constellation that points north. I remember learning about that in school."

Leandros nodded with a pleased smile. "Clever indeed, Πηνελόπη. But they say that in the middle of the Middle Sea, there floats an island where the Bear visits during the night, for the goddess, Καλυψώ, has tamed her. Now keep your eyes upon the stars."

Penélope watched the island loom in size steadily with each minute that passed, the stars shining like pinpricks poked in a velvet blanket pulled taut across the sky. She fixed her gaze on the Bear, hardly noticing that the constellation had already half-dipped below the island's rocky terrain, each star winking out of sight as if it were truly disappearing inside a cave on the island.

Distantly, she heard Mono call out the order for the rowers to ease up on their oars and the anchor to be at the ready. Leandros stood close to her, unmoving despite the obvious duties he would need to perform shortly. If Penélope only turned her head, she could kiss him, and the moment the thought occurred, she could not think of anything else, the ship and the island and the crew fading into the distance.

"Ἄναξ Λέανδρος."

He turned away at Mono's beckoning. Once he was gone from her side, Penélope could breathe again. Zeb emerged from the hold, looking more energized, especially when she told him they were heading ashore.

"This is the island where Calypso lives, don't forget," she warned.

Zeb looked at the island in real fear. He had read the same stories as her, after all, and none of them boded well. But they had no choice if they wanted to rescue the King.

"We can try to find a river and wash up," Penélope added. At this, Zeb's eyes brightened.

Owen found them waiting for the next rowboat after he finished his crew duties. He and Zeb shared an awkward nod. Leandros prepared their boat, helping Penélope and Zeb inside. Owen winked at Leandros before hopping over the side of the hull, a gesture Zeb noticed with a frown.

Unlike the island of the cyclopes, this one was devoid of rocks and hills, instead abounding with lush vegetation and trees embraced in soft, sloping meadows. Flowers grew by the shore, delicate white lilies growing out of the sand and opened to the soft moonlight from above, a sweet fragrance wafting from their pale petals. It looked like they had stumbled upon a paradise after their sojourn to the barren, gloomy lands of the Underworld below.

"Will we sleep here for the night?" Owen asked hopefully. He had been rowing for the last eight hours at the least, and despite his outward cheerfulness, he looked weary.

But Leandros shook his head. "Nay, it would be unwise to sleep on the shore so near to a goddess' dwelling. We must scout for her cave and seek her first, before she finds us."

Penélope shivered, tightening her shawl around her shoulders, even though it was not cold, the warmth from the hot summer's day lingering into the night. "Should we split up?"

"No." Leandros tightened the strap of his sword around his hips, revealing the outline of a narrow, muscled waist. Penélope tracked the movement, turning her head to hide a blush when Zeb caught her, raising a brow. "The island is small enough to cover in a few hours. I will take some men with me to confront the goddess. If we should succeed in finding out the King's whereabouts, then we camp for the night." Then he added, "With the goddess' permission."

"Hopefully she can spare some food," Owen said with a yawn. "I am *famished*."

Zeb and Penélope stifled a laugh. Leandros eyed them, wondering.

Owen flashed a grin at Zeb. "Miss my accent, did you?"

"Not a chance," Zeb replied, mimicking a horrible British accent. But when he saw everyone looking at him, he crossed his arms and scowled, ignoring Owen's eyes on him.

Leandros' brows lifted higher, before shaking his head. "We had best get moving." He whistled, motioning with a hand. "Μονόπους, Ἀκάκιος, Νικόστρατος, ἴτε!" He turned to Penélope. "I suppose you shall want to accompany us?"

"Did you even have to ask?" With a smirk, Penélope linked her arm with Zeb's, who now refused to speak, a slight scowl still on his face. "We'll follow your lead, Captain."

Once Mono and the two junior steersmen joined them, Leandros led them inland, the only light in the dark coming from the moon high above and the four torches carried by Leandros and the others. Penélope noticed that he followed a winding path already made in the soft meadow, as if someone walked often to and from the shore. Zeb noticed, too, and frowned.

Penélope looked back. She could no longer see the shore. Then she heard it. A lovely voice floated faintly upon the air, a tune sung to a melody as ancient as the trees and as beautiful as the flowers peppering the meadow. Their path led them closer and closer to the song as the earth climbed ever so slightly uphill, grass-covered mountains emerging on the horizon.

Suddenly they stumbled upon a green glade before the foot of the mountains, where a low-hanging cave could be glimpsed in its moss-covered rock, hidden by hanging ivy like a curtain before a threshold. The singing voice was louder here, coming from the cave. Leandros paused, his hand at the hilt of his sword.

Then Penélope heard the words begin again, surprised to find them familiar.

"ἄνδρα μοι ἔννεπε, μοῦσα, πολύτροπον, ὃς μάλα πολλὰ
πλάγχθη, ἐπεὶ Τροίης ἱερὸν πτολίεθρον ἔπερσεν…"

Her voice was rich like honey, light like the warmth of the sun, but laden with power, so that Penélope realized belatedly she had already begun walking towards the entrance of the cave, breaking off from the group, a burning desire in her breast to see the face who was singing.

Leandros followed after her warily, his hand still at the hilt of his sword. The others staggered forward too as the singing grew louder and louder, filling their minds like a summer haze.

Penélope's hand reached the curtain of ivy. Her fingers pushed the strings of leaves slowly aside as if in a dream, a humid, honey-sweet air embracing her the moment she stepped across the threshold.

Inside the cave was surprisingly spacious, the floor covered in plush rugs, carved shelves in the wall crowded with fresh fruit and vegetables. Lamps glowed around the room, illuminating a wide, pillowed couch at the far end of the cave, and sitting beside it, expertly threading a golden shuttle across a large loom of colorful threads, was the most beautiful woman Penélope had ever seen.

The woman glanced their way, her rose-red lips lifting in a smile. Her eyes met Penélope's, dark and flashing like a sky filled with stars. "Ah, welcome, Πηνελόπη. I have been expecting you."

20

PENÉLOPE STOOD ROOTED TO the spot, staring at the goddess. For a goddess she was, there was no denying it. "Calypso," Penélope whispered, the name escaping her lips.

Calypso stood up, her long robe of silver pooling around her sandaled feet. Around her waist was wrapped a golden belt, and her thick, dark braids were veiled with a glittering mesh. Penélope thought she heard Owen suck in a breath of wonder. The goddess took a few steps forward, then stopped, sweeping her gaze down the length of Leandros' body before lifting her eyes, where they lingered on his face. Penélope fought down a rush of jealousy.

"By Zeus, you look just like your father," she said. Leandros stiffened. "But you have brought friends. King Leon came alone."

Penélope saw Leandros flush red out of the corner of her eyes. He spoke harshly through gritted teeth. "Tell me where the King has gone."

Calypso raised a brow, walking to a wooden table made of two massive tree trunks sawed in half. "Well, well, is that any way to speak with your host?"

There she began laying out fruit and loaves of fresh bread. The scent of the food filled Penélope's nostrils, and she suddenly did not care if Calypso kissed Leandros right then and there. Owen and Zeb appeared equally starving, ogling the food, all thoughts of the goddess forgotten.

"Apologies, my Lady," Leandros said forcibly, bowing his head. "My men and I have not eaten fresh food for nigh on a fortnight. We have escaped from the Land of the Dead, where we were instructed to find you here."

Calypso handed out the cut fruit and bread on platters. Without thinking, Penélope bit into a pear, and her eyes widened at the burst of sugary juices in her

103

mouth. She marveled at the abundance of apples, cherries, plums, figs, oranges, and pomegranates laid out on the table and hoped she would be able to try each one.

The goddess noticed her gaze traveling across the table and laughed, a sound like the plucked strings of a lyre. "And what of your lady? She must be hungry too?"

Penélope and Leandros met eyes, and she stumbled a response. "No, no, I'm not his lady. I'm one of the crew members."

"Is that so?" Calypso handed her a small drinking bowl filled with mulled wine, still warm to the touch. Penélope took a sip and had to close her eyes, the warmth of the wine spreading throughout her limbs like a cozy blanket.

"As kindly as your welcome has been," Leandros said, tearing his gaze from the fruit and bread, "we have come on urgent business. Tiresias—"

"Business?" Calypso interrupted with a teasing smile. "You mortals are always in such a hurry. No wonder, I suppose, given your time is fleeting. But must you leave so soon? Ἄγε, Ἄναξ Λεάνδρος, μένε σύν ἐμοί."

Penélope understood the words well enough, and she stood rooted to the spot, watching the goddess approach Leandros and brush a delicate hand against his arm, beckoning. *Come, Prince Leandros, stay with me.* It took her a moment to realize that this goddess spoke as they did, not in their minds, and knew their languages, as if by taking the form of a mortal woman for so long, she had learned to speak like one.

Leandros' face grew red under his beard. He did not look at Penélope as he spoke, and the words were said too quickly for her to understand. "'Ην σὺν σοὶ μένω, σῖτον καὶ οἶνον ἑταίροις πέμψεις. Αὐτίκα ἔργον λεγώμεθα."

A flicker of annoyance passed over her face, twisting the beautiful features, but then she smiled, and the moment passed like a small ripple in a glassy lake. "Please, my friends, take as much food as you wish. Εἰ δοκεῖ, ἐμοὶ ξεῖνοι, λαμβάνετε ὅσον σῖτον βούλει. I shall send more down to the rest of your weary comrades. They are safe to sleep upon my shores; no harm will befall them here."

Then they were ushered out of the cave, their arms carrying woven baskets full of fruit, bread, and mulled wine. Penélope was the last to slip through the curtain of ivy. She glanced back one last time to see Calypso take Leandros' hand and pull him toward the coach.

She ignored the heat that bloomed across her cheeks, or the nausea that curled in her belly as she breathed the fresh air and truly grasped what had happened. Owen, Mono, and the other two sailors looked similarly disgruntled, like children when forced to wake up from a particularly sweet dream. Only Zeb appeared unbothered by the goddess' enchantments, though he kept sneaking furtive, angry looks at Owen.

When they made it back to the shore, the rest of the crew had already begun a large fire, roasting freshly caught meat. Baskets overflowing with more food than they could possibly eat and large barrels of wine had magically found their way among the crew, each sailor gleefully accepting a generous portion.

Owen laughed as one of the men began singing a drinking song in a deep, belting voice. "Oh, *this* is a party, alright."

Penélope found seats for her and Zeb on a blanket spread out near the fire, while Owen quickly joined his crewmates by the barrels of wine, jostling one of them when he skimped on the pour. Zeb watched the interaction with a thunderous look that he quickly schooled into nonchalance when he saw that she had noticed.

"What?" he asked.

Penélope sighed. "Are you two ever going to talk it out?"

"Talk what out?" Zeb huffed a laugh. "And I could ask you the same question. I saw your face when the goddess asked Leandros to stay."

"You understood that?" Penélope asked, her brows hitching up.

Zeb rolled his eyes. "My Greek isn't *that* bad. And you didn't need to understand what she said to know what she wanted. Her eyes said it all."

"Okay, that's enough." She had begun to forget about Leandros and Calypso with the commotion by the fire and the singing, but Zeb was painfully reminding her of it all again. "Don't change the subject. I was talking about you and Owen. Clearly, something happened between you guys."

"I assure you, *nothing* happened," Zeb said coldly. He watched Owen clink bowls with another sailor and drink, then tore his gaze away angrily. "We're barely friends. I don't know why he bothered coming to rescue me."

"Maybe he cares more than he lets on," Penélope suggested, though she withheld her doubts. It was time she stopped trying to protect him. "I don't know how Owen feels about you, but if you always keep your defenses up, then you'll never give others a chance to show you."

Zeb continued staring at the ground, his cheeks red, but he looked more alive than she had ever seen him since leaving the Underworld. Whether it was from true, genuine feeling or annoyance, she supposed it was better for him to feel something than nothing at all. Before either of them could speak again, a figure stood before them, holding out two drinking bowls filled with wine.

Mono bowed his head. "Γύναι ἐμή." He turned to Zeb. "Ξεῖνε. Πίετε!"

Penélope took her bowl gratefully. "Χαῖρε, Μονόπους."

Zeb hesitated before accepting his bowl. He took a sip, then his brows hitched up. "It's sweet." He paused, then translated, "Ἡδύς ἐστίν."

"Εὖγε, παῖδε," Mono said with a metal-toothed grin. He called out a rapid order to a nearby crewman, and Penélope thought she heard the word for *food* and something that sounded like Leandros' name. She scanned the tree line instinctively, but there was no sign of him.

"Τί οὐ πίνεις, γύναι ἐμή?"

Penélope looked up at him in surprise. He had spoken slowly so that she would understand. *Why do you not drink, my Lady?*

She shook her head. "Ὑπνώσσω." *I'm sleepy.* She had learned the phrase from Owen, who said it loudly and often after a long shift of rowing.

Mono glanced back at the tree line, which she had been hopefully scanning a moment ago, then smiled sadly. "Οἶδα, φίλη κούρη. Ἀλλὰ νοστήσει."

I know, dear girl. But he will return.

Her cheeks burned at his allusion to Leandros. She wanted to deny the accusation, that she didn't care if he came back, or that she hadn't been thinking about him at all, but she didn't know the words in Greek, and her throat had closed up with the ridiculous urge to cry, made worse by Mono's sad, weathered face gazing down upon her.

"Ἐρᾶν ἐστὶ πάσχειν."

To love is to suffer.

Penélope heard the warning echo the words she had heard in the Grove of Persephone.

For to eat the fruit of Love is to eat the fruit of Death. None may return once the first bite is taken...

Would she take the risk? Would she eat from the fruit of Love if it meant paying a price?

Or was it already too late?

21

THE EARLY LIGHT OF dawn slowly drew Penélope from her dream. Someone stirred beside her, then grunted.

"Pepa, get off me," Zeb grumbled, gently pushing her away. "You cuddled me all night."

Penélope laughed, hugging Zeb tighter as he squirmed in her arms. "Stop resisting! You know you love it when I cuddle you."

Zeb rolled over with a groan, like a kid not wanting to be told to get up. "And you snore. Couldn't I get a tent to myself?"

"Well, you can always ask Owen to sleep in his tent, if you don't mind sharing with two other sailors," Penélope said, suggestively lifting her brows. "I bet you wouldn't mind *him* cuddling you."

Zeb narrowed his eyes, about to respond, when a familiar voice outside the tent interrupted them.

"Oi! Time to get moving, sleepyheads!" Owen said, pretending to knock on the tent flap. "Leandros is back and wants to have a meeting."

Penélope sat up at this, ignoring Zeb's eye roll. "We're coming!"

They quickly got ready, Zeb jostling her to the side when she invaded his space, though she was quick to remind him that this was *her* tent before she so generously offered to share. Once she had brushed her hair and dabbed scented olive oil on her wrists—which Zeb eyed critically as he merely ran a hand through his hair—they were ready to join the others.

Owen was already sitting by the ashes of their fire next to Leandros and Mono, who were discussing something in Greek. When they approached, Leandros looked up at her and paused, before turning to Mono with a self-conscious flush and continuing his conversation. Penélope ignored the pang of disappointment that he hardly addressed her after his night alone with Calypso. Perhaps he realized that she would never live up to a goddess, let alone some princess from a distant land that he was surely bound to marry. Yet again, perhaps it was for the best, Penélope reminded herself, since she had no plans on accepting his proposal.

"Now that everyone's here," Owen said, cutting off Mono mid-sentence and earning a withering glare from the pirate, "can you tell us what happened with the sexy goddess?"

"Owen," Penélope berated, hoping she didn't sound too scandalized. Leandros' face blushed a deeper red, and she pitied him despite herself. "Her name is Calypso, and I don't think she'd appreciate you sexualizing her."

"Oh, I wouldn't be so sure," Owen said with a sly grin, then winked at Leandros. "Isn't that right, captain?"

Leandros bore the taunt as stoically as he could, though Penélope's heart sank, her stomach turning once more at the thought of Calypso seducing Leandros in her cave. "We must discuss more important matters," he said with an effort. "Such as the whereabouts of the King."

"Then you know where he is?" Penélope asked, forcing Leandros to look at her, though he did so reluctantly. "He also met Calypso here?"

"Yes," Leandros said coldly. "He did. The goddess told me that he arrived alone, after a storm had drowned his ship and washed him ashore. She provided him with food and shelter—"

"And more, I'd wager," Owen joked.

"Quiet," Zeb said sharply, earning him an offended glance from Owen.

"—and he told her of his harrowing journey from the city of Helena after the false king took power," Leandros continued, ignoring Owen's jibe. "In their flight, they chanced upon the Land of Lotus Eaters and the island of Cyclopes, where they lost many men. Their ship was caught in a storm as they barely escaped with their lives, sending their crew to the waves. The King swam as far as his strength could carry him before the waves bore him to this island. The goddess found him, healed him, and then heard his story, though it was told over many months, for she did not wish him to leave, and his tale was too sorrowful at times to tell in full."

"If Calypso didn't let him leave, why is he not here anymore?" Penélope asked.

"That is the same question I asked her," Leandros said, a hint of anger escaping his calm voice. "She replied that one day Hermes was sent on behalf of Mother

Gaia, urging the goddess to provide him with a ship, for the time had come for him to leave her island. However, his bad luck was not mere chance; nay, a curse had been uttered against him by Poseidon, the King of the Seas, who sent a huge wave as the King set out from Ogygia, throwing him off course."

"Poseidon?" Zeb repeated. "I thought it was Zeus we had to worry about."

"What Zeb means," Penélope amended quickly, flashing Zeb a look not to reveal any more of what they knew, "is that the whole conflict at the time was between Zeus and Gaia. What did Poseidon have to do with it?"

"Calypso did not say," Leandros said.

Owen scoffed. "Of course she didn't."

"Perhaps the king offended him, or he killed a cyclops who was dear to Poseidon," Penélope suggested, recalling the story of Odysseus and his taunt to Polyphemus, a cyclops and son of Poseidon.

"Perhaps." Leandros stroked his beard thoughtfully. "All we do know for certain is that his ship landed on the shores of a strange land, where he encountered the Laestrygonians, violent giants who know no mercy or pity. Though they invited him as a guest, once they learned he was the King of Helena, they traded him to the Phaeacians, whose enmity towards my people has been great for as long as my father has been alive."

"The Phaeacians?" Penélope asked, recalling what she knew of them in the *Odyssey*. "Why would they hate your people so much?"

"It is a long story," Leandros said darkly. "And I have not been told all of it, for my father considered me too young to know it fully. But he did say that the feud began with my grandfather, King Philoxenos, who had been shipwrecked on the island of Scheria during his many travels to distant lands. The Phaeacians had long been forbidden by Poseidon to help strangers, so they refused to aid his return home. However, the princess of the Phaeacians, first and only daughter of the King of Scheria, had fallen in love with my grandfather and helped him escape. They returned to Helena, where they were married and she bore him two sons, but their love brought the wrath of the Phaeacians upon them, and much war was waged between them and us Helenes. Though my people were able to defend themselves, my grandfather and my uncle, Alexandros, died in battle, leaving my father the throne."

Everyone was silent once he finished. Penélope, Zeb, and Owen shared shocked glances at the name Alexandros. Could it be the same person whom Elena had fallen in love with in the city? Would that make Alexandria…his daughter?

"What happened to the princess?" Zeb asked suddenly.

Leandros looked at him in confusion. "Who?"

"Your grandmother," Zeb clarified with a raised brow. "The one who helped your grandfather escape the Phaeacians."

"No one knows," Leandros said, shaking his head sadly. "She disappeared the night my grandfather died. They say she took her own life once she learned of his death, casting her body into the sea."

"Romantic," Owen muttered with a wince. "That explains the Phaeacians' anger at your father, I suppose. But if he was traded to the Phaeacians, how do we plan on rescuing him?"

"We go to the island of Scheria," Penélope said. "He must still be there."

"That is not certain, and even if it were, the people of Scheria are not friendly to strangers," Leandros warned. "And least of all to my people. We shall not be welcome there if we land on their shores."

"What other choice do we have?" Penélope asked, her frustration visible in her voice, not least because of the words of the Queen of Death. *First, you must save the King of Helena.* "We have to find him, and this is the best lead we have on where to start looking. Maybe he's hiding among the inhabitants, or the Phaeacians had a change of heart. Either way, we will need to go to Scheria, and you know it."

"And what will we do when they discover who I am? What if they have already killed the King, and will kill me the moment I step foot upon their shores?" Leandros asked pointedly.

"Then we pretend to be merchants or from somewhere else."

"This plan will not work."

Penélope stood up, the anger in her heart that had been festering there since the night before rising to the surface. "You know what I think? I think you don't really want to find your father at all."

Leandros shot to his feet, his eyes seething as they looked at her in anger and something that almost seemed like betrayal. "That is a lie."

"You constantly shy away from your relationship with him," she continued. "Maybe you blame him for allowing Brother Ezra to take power, or for abandoning the city, or for sleeping with Calypso and betraying your mother. Either way, you can't escape the fact that he is your father, no matter how many times you call him *king*."

Everyone stared at her in shock at her brutal honesty, save Mono, who, despite not having understood a word of their conversation, eyed Penélope with a thoughtful air. Leandros stood still, his mouth hardened into a line.

"We're going to Scheria, with or without you, and bringing *your* father back home," Penélope said after a long silence. "Now I'm going to find a river to bathe in before we leave, because I don't want to stop until we find that island."

Then she turned on her heel and began walking into the forest, ignoring the instinct to look behind her shoulder and see if anyone was following her. If *he* was following her, she corrected, knowing that she had only taken her anger out on him because he had slept with Calypso. Why was she so jealous anyway? No one had ever made her feel this way, not even her older brother's friends, who often flirted with her only to embarrass her by sleeping with some pretty girl at the New Academy the next day.

Penélope hardly knew where she was going, eager as she had been to escape before she said something more damning. While what she had said was true, perhaps Leandros didn't deserve her criticism. Who was she to judge, after all? She, who had contemplated abandoning her loving parents for a life in this city?

Her feet stumbled on a slippery slope, and she realized her meandering path had led her to a wide, clear river of gentle currents, as if some god had been directing her there. Penélope didn't care, however, after so many days without bathing.

She stripped off her clothes, kicking them away, then practically ran into the water, diving underneath and swimming a few kicks back and forth, unable to stop a smile, which felt good after so many days of tense discussion. Then she realized in her rush to leave that she had left behind her toiletry chest. Just as she decided to leave and get it, she heard a soft splash behind her and swiveled around, her breath leaving her when she saw who it was.

The goddess Calypso had entered the river, stopping once the water hit her thighs. She was startlingly naked, her dark braids undone so that her hair flowed down the length of her back in thick curls, but once again Penélope was awed by the effortless beauty, not so much from specific features or the shapes of her limbs, but rather how the goddess seemed to embody womanliness in its eternal nature, like a ripe fruit hanging heavily on a tree branch forever just out of reach, its imagined richness, softness, and sweetness more tantalizing and real than if she actually bit into it.

"I'm sorry," Penélope said automatically, as if she had been the one to chance upon Calypso bathing.

Calypso smiled. "Why? You would not be bathing here if it were not my will." She took a few steps forward and held out a small object. "Here, take it. I filled it from my very own stores."

Penélope took it and saw that it was a thin, colored glass phial filled with liquid, a cork stopper on top. She opened it and brought the flask to her nose, smelling a strong scent as sweet as honey or mulled wine, but with a hint of something else she could not place.

"You may bathe yourself with it, if you like," Calypso said. "No other mortal woman has been cleansed by my ambrosia, though I suppose no woman has yet stepped foot upon my shores to use it." She paused, her gaze lingering on Penélope's face, then trailing down her body. "Until you."

"Thank you," Penélope said in wonder, her skin already warm from the goddess' gaze alone. She poured some of the liquid into her palm. The sweet scent wafted from the shimmery golden ambrosia, and she quickly poured some on her hair and skin, scrubbing at the dirt and grime until all that remained was a glimmering sheen.

Calypso took the phial and poured some of the ambrosia on her own hair, scrubbing the golden liquid into her curls and down her arms, so that her skin seemed to glow from within. "Come."

She beckoned with a hand. Penélope took a hesitant step forward, then another, until Calypso reached out and turned her around. Then she gently massaged Penélope's head, rubbing the ambrosia into her hair in sweeping circles that made her irresistibly relaxed. The hands stopped, and Penélope turned around.

They were silent as Calypso studied her, a silence that seemed to last an eternity and a few seconds at the same time. The goddess traced a fingertip down the side of Penélope's face, contemplating her as if she were a new creature that she had found all alone in the woods. "Love is strange, is it not?"

Penélope stood still, wondering what she meant. Was she talking of Leandros? Or someone else?

"And we women pull the shortest straw," Calypso said, and Penélope was surprised to hear the bitterness in her voice. "I suppose that is the way it goes. The gods have always resented my affairs with men, then sow their seeds in thrice as many fields."

Penélope could not help but wince at the heavy-handed metaphor.

"What? Are you ashamed that I speak so?" Calypso asked, arching a brow. She swept Penélope's long, wet hair from her shoulders as if they had been hiding something of importance underneath. Even though she was fully naked before her, Penélope did not feel self-conscious in the slightest, simply in awe that the goddess beheld her so. "Do not be ashamed, my dear girl, for it is your greatest weapon. It is your *only* weapon, really, that might conquer a man. For any woman may have the intelligence, wit, or daring to match those of men, but there is no wile in the world that can defeat the charms of a woman."

"I'm not like you," Penélope said defensively, wary of what this goddess was suggesting and not liking it one bit.

Calypso smiled sadly at her. "Μοῖρα σὴ ἐρᾶν, Πηνελόπη."

Your fate is to love, Penélope.

She was silent, her heart aching at the words. What did it mean? The goddess gave no explanation, turning with an elegant swish of her hair and walking away from the river. The soft, rich curves of her body disappeared between the thin, white trunks of birch trees clinging to the riverbank, the sweet scent of ambrosia fading in her wake like a field's last flowery breath before winter.

Once she was gone, Penélope lowered herself into the water one last time, then stepped out of the river. Beside her dirty pile of clothes was a neatly folded, woven blanket and a dark blue dress that had not been there before. More gifts of the goddess, but this time Penélope was glad for them. Just as she slipped the soft fabric of the dress over her body—which fit perfectly, she found to her delight—she heard her name across the forest floor.

"Penélope! Penélope!" It was Leandros, panic lacing his voice.

"I'm here!" She lifted a hand so that he would find her.

When he saw her, his shoulders sagged at the same time as his eyes widened, passing over her new clothes. Her heart beat faster at his approach, and she wondered if something had gone terribly wrong, her thoughts immediately jumping to the worst conclusions, that Zeb had magically returned to the Underworld, or they were stuck on the island forever.

"Did something happen?" Penélope asked.

"No," Leandros said quickly, then blushed. "Rather, after you did not return, we had thought you were lost, or some ill-fate had befallen you in the forest."

"I said I wanted to bathe." She crossed her arms, then saw Leandros' gaze involuntarily dip to her chest, where the dress swept dangerously low. *It is your* only *weapon, really, that might conquer a man.* A rush of nausea choked her at the thought of Calypso conquering Leandros, her glowing skin against his, kissing those scars that ran hidden beneath his tunic. "Why do you care anyway?"

She moved to pass him, but his hand shot out and grasped her arm. "You could have been attacked. Animals prowl this forest, and we do not know who else might inhabit the island."

"Calypso said no harm would come to us on her shores," Penélope said, ignoring the heat that rose to her cheeks at their proximity and trying to shake him off.

Leandros pulled her closer instead. "Gods may lie to us mortals if they are not bound by a dread oath to tell the truth."

Penélope looked up at him fiercely. "Then maybe she lied about your father, too. Or did you believe her then because she had sex with you?"

Shock at her words and then anger once he registered their meaning passed across his face in quick succession before he spoke. "I did not lie with her."

His words jumbled inside her mind. "But you stayed in the cave."

"Why would I lie with the goddess?" he asked, his voice softening despite the thunderous look on his face. "I told you once before, I shall never seek the arms of another woman unless that woman is you."

She could scarcely breathe, his eyes flickering down to her mouth. "I don't...I'm not..."

"I swore an oath, Πηνελόπη," he whispered, the space between them narrowing. His other hand shakily brushed her damp hair, then skimmed the tender curve of her neck, landing gently on the blue pinned straps of her dress. "By Zeus, you look like a goddess."

Suddenly she heard the crunching of footsteps and voices close by. She stepped away from Leandros just in time before Zeb and Owen burst out of the tree line, slowing down when they spotted them standing by the river.

"There you are," Owen said with a grin. He elbowed Zeb, who scowled in annoyance. "See? Told you she was alright."

"What took you so long?" Zeb asked sharply. He saw her new clothes and his mouth fell open. "And what are you wearing?"

"And what's that amazing smell?" Owen wondered aloud.

Penélope glanced back at the river, as if she would see Calypso wading in the water right then and there. She saw Leandros' gaze land hopelessly on her and smirked. Perhaps Calypso had the right idea after all.

"Come on, boys, back to the ships," she said, picking up her belongings. "A woman can't tell all her secrets, and we have a long day ahead of us."

Then she turned and walked away, leaving them staring open-mouthed after her as if she truly were a goddess.

22

ONCE THE SHORE SHRANK behind them, it was already well into the night. Penélope was surprised to find herself regretful of their departure. The lush meadows and dells among the flowering woods had been a paradise compared to the harrowing escapes from the cyclops and the Land of the Dead.

Their ship hardly needed to row with a southwesterly wind at their backs, making Penélope wonder if the goddess had something to do with it. Calypso had instructed them to sail north first, but to trust the Ἄρκτος to guide them to Scheria if they kept the Bear constellation over their left shoulder, which they could not yet see due to the heavy layer of clouds that had rolled in overhead.

She also missed Zeb's solemn presence near the prow of the ship, despite the improvement in his mood. Unlike Owen, who had immediately jumped on the possibility of rowing with the rest of the crew, Zeb refused to commit to that kind of labor. Leandros instead had him work in his cabin, redrawing maps to include the islands and sights they had seen on their journey.

Penélope heard the telltale, heavy footsteps of the captain behind her and blushed involuntarily. *I swore an oath, Πηνελόπη.*

She still could not rid herself of that moment which replayed over and over in her mind, the hand on her arm tight and protective, the other trailing down her neck, his rough voice as he spoke, and his gaze flickering to her lips.

Calypso had also scrutinized her face, her hair, her body, and Penélope, nearly drugged as she had been on the goddess' ambrosia, had not thought much of her attention. *Love is strange, is it not?*

For the first time, Penélope wondered if the goddess had been jealous of her. Now that she knew Leandros had not slept with her, Calypso's words could be seen in an entirely new light, and the bitterness in her voice a hint of envy or even regret.

Leandros began chanting softly as he came to stand beside her, his eyes scanning the horizon thoughtfully.

> "παῦροι γάρ τοι παῖδες ὁμοῖοι πατρὶ πέλονται,
> οἱ πλέονες κακίους, παῦροι δέ τε πατρὸς ἀρείους."

He glanced at her, then, his gaze lingering on her blue dress gifted by Calypso, the same color as the depths of the sea at night, its folds soft and light as they cascaded down her legs.

"What is that from?" she asked.

"An ancient song from a different age, and a different land," Leandros said. "It sings of a man who has wandered much and seen many people and places. But none, I suppose, were so welcome to him as the arms of his wife."

Penélope avoided his eyes, the hope and love she saw lingering there. The last time they skirted the issue, they nearly kissed, and even the thought of it made her heart leap in her chest. But she forced herself to remain calm. "What do the verses say?"

Leandros, sensing her restraint, nodded, returning his gaze to the dark horizon. "In plain words, it says: *Few sons become like their fathers—most are worse, and few better.*"

"Do you believe that?" Penélope asked.

"I once did."

She turned to him, unable to resist the pull of his gaze on her. "And now?"

"Now I do not know what I believe in," Leandros said. He took a half-step closer to her, then thought better of it, his fists tightening at his sides. "Some days I think I shall become like him, wandering the seas forever, lost and yet never wishing to be found. Other days, I hate even the thought of him."

"Your father didn't have a choice," Penélope said gently. "Brother Ezra would have killed him if he remained in the city."

"Then he should have died," he replied harshly. "Or at the very least fought instead of fleeing at the first turn in the tide."

She did not know what to say to this. Perhaps he was right, that his father should have stayed to fight the impostor, even if it meant risking his own life. But her sensible side—the side that usually won over her heart—knew that the gods had decided he would play a very different part in the war to come, a knowledge she had yet to share with Leandros, though she couldn't quite explain why.

"My apologies," Leandros said after an extended silence. "I should not burden you with my troubles. After all, you must have your own share of sorrows, even if you do not give voice to them."

Penélope glanced back at the cabin as if in response. Leandros noticed and grinned wryly.

"Your friend is well taken care of, I assure you. His skill in drawing is impressive, and has been put to good use."

She sighed, recalling the brief glimpses of sketches in his notebook that he kept as private as his deepest secrets. "He has more gifts than he lets on, though I don't know why he's so afraid to show them."

"Strange is his reserve with such a tongue as his," Leandros mused, "often sharp enough to fell even the sturdiest trees."

"Ah, well, sometimes the sharpest swords hide the weakest metals," Penélope said, only half-joking.

Leandros' brows quirked. "Is that a common proverb among your people?"

She laughed. "No, I just made it up right now."

"Tell me," he said with a keen look, "do *you* hide something behind that cleverness of yours?"

Her laughter died on her lips as he continued to look at her all too knowingly. She had never thought about herself like that before, always taking some pride in what she thought was her greatest gift, the cleverness mirrored in her namesake. But maybe Leandros was right. Perhaps the very cleverness she liked to display was a cloak to hide her deepest secrets, the doubt that ate away at her heart when she faced the unanswered questions in her life.

Penélope looked up at the sky, where the clouds had begun clearing up while they spoke. She thought she glimpsed the stars of the Bear twinkling to their left. "We should make landfall soon," she said, eager to change the subject. "What is our plan once we arrive?"

Leandros noticed her evasion but only raised a brow. "I thought you already had it all planned out."

She crossed her arms at the reference to their argument back on Ogygia, before she stormed off and bathed in the river with Calypso. "I was only advising you to follow the advice we've been given. Your father was last known to be sold to the Phaeacians, so that's where we should go. The question is how we are going to find him."

"They cannot know who I am," Leandros said darkly.

"No, they can't," Penélope agreed, her mind running through the other possibilities they had. "We can pretend to be from another land. Royalty, even. We can say we're lost and found the island by accident."

"But they are bound by oath not to aid strangers. And it would be difficult to convince them of a royalty they do not know, for the Phaeacians are a seafaring people, and know these waters well. They are said to have even built ships with no need for oars."

"Then we don't ask for aid or pretend to be royalty," she said, then nearly gasped as inspiration struck her. "Maybe we don't go to them at all! We remain by the shore and wait for them to find us. Then we can pretend to be peaceful merchants. That way, we get access to the palace and can search for your father without threatening their oath."

Leandros considered this and then nodded. "It may be the best plan we have, though I would not trust the Phaeacians for hospitality. They are a cruel, violent people who have brought war to my city. If they show us any mercy, it shall be a miracle."

Penélope shivered at the coldness in his words. After their near-death experience with the cyclops, she knew not to trust people of foreign lands, but a part of her still hoped they would be kind to guests, at least as they were to Odysseus in the stories of old.

"Ah, there she is," Leandros said softly. "Ἄρκτος."

She followed his gaze to the night sky, where the stars shone forth brilliantly, a glittering mesh of countless constellations so that it was difficult to find just one. Then her eyes traveled down to the horizon, and there, glinting like sunlight on the edge of a sword, was an island, still distant enough to remain a mere dark smudge, but close enough to know that the island was already inhabited—and therefore dangerous.

"Scheria," she said.

Leandros stiffened at the name. "We'd best begin our plan now."

Then he turned and walked away, calling out sharp orders to the crew. Penélope saw a few of them lowering the banners that held aloft the colors of the city of Helena. If they were going to pretend to be merchants, they had to play the part.

Her pulse raced at their proximity to the island. She would have rather liked several days at sea to better hash out the plan and resign herself to the possible risks. Instead, they had to rush headlong to an island they hardly knew anything about, trusting to the designs of crafty gods and goddesses whose true purposes were so often shrouded in secrecy.

Once they had undressed the ship of her royalty, Leandros emerged from below deck in new clothes. They were not really *new,* but old and haggard, the same dirty tunic and leather vest he had worn as the Wanderer. Penélope stared at him, the scar across his face, the untrimmed beard, and wondered what he had looked like before his exile, whether she would have liked him half as much if he were a pampered prince, or if she might just prefer the rugged, sea-weathered pirate who had thrown her an apple the first day they met, bearing his heart to her as no man had ever done before.

"While that dress is..." he paused, his gaze reluctantly dipping to the blue folds of her dress, "...lovely, you should change into less conspicuous clothing. In fact, you ought not to be seen at all, for it is not customary for merchant ships to travel with women. That is, not *decent* women."

Penélope raised a brow. "You mean they're usually prostitutes?"

Leandros winced at her crude language. "I was suggesting dancers. Some merchant ships trade them to foreign cities. They are considered a luxury."

"Well, in that case, maybe I'm meant to look like royalty," she said, gesturing to her blue dress, which she had come to love too much not to resist the idea of abandoning it.

"Nay, dancers can never play royalty," Leandros said firmly. "Whether you condemn it or not, to be a dancer is beneath the dignity of a lady of our court and therefore an insult to be entertained by one in such a guise. That is custom in most places. Now, if you wish for our plan to succeed, you must stay out of sight. It would not be proper for you to be sold as any common good. I would not allow it either way, and then I could not guarantee your safety. Besides, the role would require you to be dressed...quite differently."

"And how might that be?" Penélope asked icily, her indignation rising at every word that came out of his mouth.

To her surprise, Leandros blushed. "That would be naked, you see."

"Oh." This time it was Penélope's turn to blush. She turned away, not wishing him to see her concede, because despite her desire to be treated with equal respect no matter how she dressed, she had no wish to walk naked all the way to the palace. "Fine. I'll stay on the ship and let you *men* do the talking. But you have to at least let me bathe first! And I refuse to be holed up in that stinky hull. I'll stay in the cabin with enough food and water for a few days, and only come out if I think you guys need rescuing."

Leandros laughed softly to himself. "Very well. You may bathe if there is a river nearby. But I cannot promise how long we shall remain in the palace, if they are so kind enough to host us. But if all goes as planned, we will discover the whereabouts of my father and leave with him as quickly as we are able."

When he put it simply like that and with his usual confidence of relaying orders, Penélope felt slightly more at ease, and they parted ways to begin preparing the ship for anchor. Zeb and Owen joined her by the rowboats when it was time to depart, and she relayed the plan to them quickly.

"That sounds like a good plan," Owen said with his typical careless confidence. "But I envy you, Penny. Alone in the captain's cabin with all the food and wine to yourself..."

Zeb cut a sharp glance at Owen's dreamy expression. "Actually, that plan sounds as bad as that nickname." He ignored Owen's offended noise of protest. "What will you do if something happens and all the crew gets imprisoned or killed? How would you be able to rescue us? Besides, it's not like you could row away by yourself if you had to escape."

"Now when you say it like that," Owen began in feigned agreement.

Penélope rolled her eyes. "This is the plan, whether you like it or not. But you have a point, Zeb. I'll tell Leandros to leave a squadron hiding with me here in case we have to leave quickly. But I need you two to go with Leandros and make sure he doesn't do something stupid like attack their king. All we have to do is find his father and get him back to the city so that we can—"

Owen raised a brow when she stopped suddenly, her face flushing as she shared a knowing glance with Zeb. "I sense you two know something that I don't about this whole thing, but from what I've come to learn, I rather think I'll remain blissful in ignorance."

It was their turn next to climb into their rowboat, saving Penélope from answering him. They were quickly rowed to shore, where she was delighted to spot a nearby wood cropped up around a river that spilled out into the ocean. The men went about setting up camp, though this time they were careful not to display their armor carved with the crest of Helena—a flaming sun at the heart of a laurel tree—and reluctantly bringing out baskets of food and barrels of wine that they would pretend to trade.

Leandros found them and nodded to Penélope. "It shall not take them long to discover our presence, if they have not already been alerted."

He was probably right. She also noticed that the sky had already begun to lighten in the east, and soon the daylight would rid them of any more cover under darkness.

"Then I'll be off," Penélope said, lifting her toiletries, which she thankfully remembered to bring this time. "Zeb, in the meantime, why don't you tell Leandros your addition to my plan? Be back soon!"

Then before he could protest, she sauntered off toward the river she had seen earlier, hoping there would be no wild animals or violent giants roaming the area.

The trek was longer than she had thought to find the mouth of the river, which she followed inside the small woody dell for some privacy. Once she was confident there was not a soul lurking nearby save for the few birds and small rodents scuttling around in the grass, she carefully slipped out of her dress and waded into the stream.

She hissed at the icy waters, so much colder than the river on Calypso's island, especially without the sunlight to warm it. But the cleansing currents were still welcome to her dirt-streaked skin, which was used to regular showers and strong, chemical-pumped soaps back home. Her scented olive oil did the trick, however, and soon her hair, face, and body were cleaned, and she dried off on the shore with a small towel she had brought.

"You are quite at ease for a lone woman in a foreign land."

Penélope whirled around, her heart lurching in her chest. A young man stood on the opposite side of the shore, and she struggled to cover her naked body with her small towel. The man was lean and muscular in a brown traveler's tunic, and his dark eyes roamed over her, sharp and knowing beneath warm brown curls.

"W-who are you?" she stammered, backing away a few steps. He didn't seem to be holding a weapon, but on second glance, she saw in his right hand a golden rod that looked startlingly familiar.

"I am many things," he said, his mouth curling into a slight, mischievous smile. "I have been sent to aid your quest."

Penélope felt as though the ground had fallen away beneath her, and she could barely speak the name. "Hermes."

The smile lifted into a smirk. "I have many names."

Now she realized that he was not speaking in Greek to her, though her momentary fear had blinded her mind from the possibility that he was a god. Still, the stories told about Hermes were like those of any other gods, and he posed a threat to a woman bathing alone in the woods, mortal or not. If she called for help, who would come? Who would answer to the injustice—the same injustice that Persephone bitterly repented—if not the gods?

Hermes cocked his head, watching her, as though he could read her thoughts.

"What do you want?" she asked, her voice shaky.

He seemed to hear something then, because he angled his ear towards the forest behind him. "A party of maidens from the palace is playing nearby. If they were to find you all alone, naked, and in need of aid, they may take pity on you."

Penélope's mind whirled with the implications of that statement. "Maidens? From the palace? But Leandros was supposed to..."

"If you wish to find the King of Helena, you must listen to what I tell you," Hermes said, the first cold authority creeping into his voice, reminding her that he was still a god, even if he seemed to be on her side.

"Okay," she agreed nervously. "Tell me what I need to do."

Hermes then lifted his wand and pointed it at her. She cringed, waiting for some enchantment to hit her, but nothing happened. He lowered his wand, his dark eyes glittering. "I have given you the gift of language, so that you may understand all those who speak and they you. But do not waste this precious gift. Among the maidens is the princess of the Phaeacians, whose heart shall be most moved by your distress. You must tell her how you came to live alone on the island, how your parents abandoned you in the woods when they had no more means to feed you, last of your siblings and unmarried, and you learned to eat leaves and berries, and trap small animals to eat meat. With her help, you shall succeed in your quest."

"I..." Penélope wanted to say, *I am not good at lying.* But that wasn't strictly true, was it? She had now lied many times, at least by omission. Besides, this was more like telling a story, and all stories held a kernel of truth.

"The choice is yours, Πηνελόπη."

She glanced up at Hermes to ask for more guidance, but he was gone, flashing before her like sunlight on water. A cold wind filtered through the trees, and then she heard young voices floating in the air. Even though she wanted to go back and tell the others what happened, she knew that by the time she returned to the camp and came back, the maidens would be gone.

Who else? Who shall you condemn to your fate?

With one last regretful glance at her blue dress and toiletries, she waded across the river and headed in the direction of the voices.

As soon as she passed a crowded thicket of trees, like a curtain drawing away from a stage, she saw the woods open upon a clearing in the rising dawn, where maidens pranced about a flower-speckled field, throwing a leather ball back and forth and twirling in long, colorful dresses. Amid the group was a woman dressed in a violet so dark it appeared black, her face veiled, standing beside a wagon harnessed to two mules.

"Come now," the veiled woman said to two girls who were wrestling for the ball. "No fighting, Sofia and Arete! Use your words, like proper ladies."

A cry rose up. One of the girls closest had seen her walking towards them and screamed, pointing her finger right at Penélope. The others all stopped, mouths agape, watching as Penélope came forward, naked and shivering.

"Who are you?" the veiled woman called out, the tremor in her stern voice betraying her worry. "Where have you come from?"

"I am Penélope," she said, standing before them, the words of Hermes circling in her mind. "That is all I know. Long have I lived alone in the woods, scavenging for food, abandoned by my family. Please, have pity on me."

One of the young girls took a step toward her, her raven dark hair tied into an elegant bun around the crown of her head, and her green eyes softening as she gazed at Penélope. "She looks harmless, Mother. Why don't we bring her to the palace?"

The veiled woman hesitated, looking at Penélope, who huddled against a sudden gust of wind. At last, she relented. "Very well, Korinna, we shall care for the girl. But do not tell the King anything yet! He would not approve, and it is best she supplicate him herself. Give the poor thing a blanket, my dear."

Korinna's eyes brightened, then she rushed over to their wagon and pulled out a woven blanket of red and purple thread. She quickly handed it to Penélope, who took it gratefully and draped it around her shoulders. No pretending was needed to show how cold she was standing naked in the early dawn. Meanwhile, the veiled woman had approached and stood before her, an older, weary face just faintly visible beneath her dark veil.

"Now, my friend," the veiled woman said gently, "you shall come with us to the palace, where we shall bathe you properly and give you food to eat."

Penélope was so overwhelmed with gratitude at their hospitality—when she had been expecting hostility if not outright violence—that all she could do was lower to the ground and grasp the woman's knees in supplication, which she knew was traditional in their world. "Thank you, my Lady."

"Please, call me Mother Gray, or simply Mother, as all those in the palace do." The woman took her by the hands and lifted her up. "Wipe your tears, child, there is no need to worry. You are safe now. You are *home*."

23

"How long does it take women to bathe?" Owen said with a sigh, stretched out on his back in the grass, one ankle hooked over the other.

Zeb remained stubbornly silent. He hated that Owen acted as if he were stuck with him when they had nothing to do, like he was his babysitter and not a friend, or whatever they were to each other. The word *acquaintances* was snidely spoken in his head, but he ignored it.

Meanwhile, Leandros kept himself busy, ordering the men around and discussing plans with Mono. Whenever Penélope wasn't nearby, he spoke more harshly and barely noticed the raised brows and knowing glances among the crew. After she left to bathe, Leandros had agreed to Zeb's suggestion with a distracted head nod, looking after Penélope's retreating figure with mingled regret and longing. Zeb had struggled not to roll his eyes.

Owen sat up. "Are you ever going to speak with me?"

Zeb continued to watch the men unload the ship of her wares in a single file. He wanted to answer Owen—he had so many things he could say, which he had rehearsed in his head as if they had been real conversations in the Underworld— that he didn't know where to start, the words trapped inside like the evils in Pandora's box. And worst of them all was hope, that little, poisonous deceit, which settles in the heart like a worm eating away at an apple.

"Zeb." He spoke softly. "Look at me, please."

"What do you want?" Zeb asked coldly, turning to look at him. He was surprised to see pain in Owen's green eyes, and a part of him resented it as much as another part was thrilled.

Owen hesitated, then said, "We're going to have to talk about it at some point."

"Actually, we really don't."

"Yes, we do." Owen sighed and sat up fully, a sign he was going to speak seriously when he usually only joked around. "Before you...left, I thought we had a fine thing going. Then ever since you came back, it's like that also..."

"Died?" Zeb asked sarcastically.

Owen flushed at his tone, but didn't back down. "Am I wrong?"

"It was never there to begin with," Zeb spoke harshly, then regretted it when Owen visibly flinched. "Yes, we had our fun, but that was before. Do you harass all your hook-ups like this? It was just a kiss."

"It wasn't just a kiss," Owen said quietly.

This time Zeb blushed, recalling all those nights together, Owen's hands roaming his body, leaving a flaming trail in its wake as he had never felt before in his life. Zeb would never forget the first time, the night they went out to *El Sol* for drinks, coming back to the dorms drunk and finding Owen there in the hall.

"You're a happy drunk, did you know?" Owen had said, sauntering up to Zeb's door, where Zeb had already inserted his key. "Usually you look like a dog ready to bite, but after a few shots of tequila..." He whistled. "Got you smiling like a puppy."

Hot anger had bubbled up inside, cut only by a sudden, intense desire to grab the front of Owen's shirt and kiss him senseless.

"Do I look like I'm smiling?" Zeb had asked in his usual bored sarcasm.

Owen placed a hand over his on the door handle, undaunted, any suggestive smile or amusement gone. But Zeb didn't need it to know exactly what words were going to come out of his mouth next.

"Not yet."

Then the next thing Zeb knew they were kissing and stumbling into Zeb's dorm room with no time for him to be embarrassed by the clothes he left unfolded on his chair or the mess of Greek homework on his desk, all thoughts in his mind wiped away by Owen's hands on him, his mouth firm and demanding, a sensation as startling and wonderful as a gust of wind on a hot day.

It had been his first kiss, but he didn't tell Owen that, and every night after that, they snuck into one of their dorm rooms or even the library when it had already closed, prying open one of the loose stained glass windows. They never openly discussed the new arrangement, but they did talk a lot, almost as much as they did anything else, lying in bed next to each other until the early hours of the morning. Owen teased him for his lifelong crush on Ari, though he understood the appeal, while Zeb teased him for his brief relationship with Chloe and his posh accent, though he secretly adored it. The only topics they skirted were their families, avoiding Owen's clearly fraught relationship with his absent parents or Zeb's alcoholic mom and deadbeat dad.

Zeb had hoped, despite all the warnings in his head about Owen's attitude towards love and relationships, that he would be the one Owen would fall helplessly in love with, when he should've known it was always going to be the other way around.

"You said it yourself," Zeb replied bitterly, shaking the memories from his mind. "We had a good thing going, but it's over now. What are we going to do, Owen? Keep hooking up in the hull when no one's around, like nothing's happened? Like I didn't just die? Like this world doesn't exist? And what about when we get back home? You go to Harvard and travel in private planes. My life is at the New Academy. I can't just run off to a new place whenever I feel like it."

"You could come with me," Owen said urgently, moving as if to take Zeb's hand before stopping himself. "I'll pay for everything, you wouldn't have to worry. And I could take you wherever you wanted to go—Thailand, Brazil, Greece—anywhere you'd like. What else could you want?"

"What about London or South Africa?" Zeb asked pointedly, and Owen's face fell, his shoulders sagging. "Would you introduce me to your parents? Your friends? Or is this all playing pretend? A fantasy you indulge in until you get bored with me?"

"What about you?" Owen countered. "You can barely tell Penélope. *You* wanted to keep it a secret from the others, not me. All because you're still in love with that Ari bloke—"

"I'm not in love with Ari," Zeb interrupted angrily. "And I wanted to keep it a secret because I knew you only wanted a–a distraction, something to keep you entertained while this shit show lasted. This isn't *real*, Owen."

Owen groaned in frustration. "Why must we be in a relationship for this to be real? Why ought we destroy something good and pure just for a label?"

"Because that's what people do when they're in love, Owen!" Zeb had stood up in his anger, then realized that some of the nearby sailors were looking over at them curiously. His face grew hot at both the attention and the words he had said, ignoring Owen's stunned face as he turned and walked away.

"Zeb, wait!" Owen scrambled to his feet and followed after him. Zeb didn't stop. "Zeb, where are you going?"

"I'm going to find Penélope," he answered harshly over his shoulder.

"Penélope?"

Zeb faltered in his step, then reluctantly stopped and turned around. Leandros was standing behind him expectantly, while Owen jogged to catch up. "She's taking a long time," Zeb said irritably. "I'm going to make sure she's okay, that's all."

Leandros looked towards the river, his hand tightening on the hilt of his sword. "I will come with you."

"Me too," Owen said, ignoring the glare Zeb cut him.

"Then we go together," Leandros said grimly, before taking off toward the cluster of trees on the horizon.

At the quick pace of Leandros and Owen, they reached the mouth of the river in no time, which they followed into the woods. Zeb wondered if he should've gone ahead and made sure she wasn't still undressed, but before he could say something, Leandros took off, running full speed ahead.

"What's he doing?" Owen asked incredulously.

Zeb couldn't answer, his heart beating in his throat. Leandros had knelt to the ground to pick something up, his head hanging down. When he turned, Zeb's stomach dropped, and Owen sucked in a breath beside him. In Leandros' hands was the unmistakable blue fabric of Penélope's new dress, her toiletry chest still opened a few paces from his feet.

"Penélope," Zeb whispered, but he knew in this world she would not be able to hear him anymore.

None of them moved, too shocked by the news, when suddenly, far-off shouts of a commotion among the crew reluctantly drew their attention away. Leandros listened carefully to the sharp sounds of metal on metal, then paled.

"What's going on?" Owen demanded.

Leandros stood very still, glancing between the blue dress and the distant noises. "The Phaeacians. They've found us. We must make haste."

"Then Penélope—" Zeb began.

But Leandros' crestfallen face said it all. "They have her too."

24

As the mules strained to pull the wagon up the hill, suddenly a massive palace rose above like an island at sea. Penélope's breath left her as she stared at the towering walls and curved domes made of bronze. The sun was now high above the sky, its light glinting off the polished metal. The young girls walking alongside the wagon began talking excitedly.

"It is beautiful, is it not?" Mother Gray asked knowingly from her seat behind the mules.

"Yes," Penélope whispered, hardly able to speak.

"Welcome to the palace of King Kleomachus, descended from King Poliporthes, whom legend tells was the son of Nausicaa and Telemachus. This shall be your new home for the time being."

"Telemachus…the son of Odysseus?" she asked in surprise.

Even though she could not see her face, she could sense the woman's smile in her voice. "So you have heard the old stories too, even raised by the trees and the birds as you have. Yes, the son of Odysseus, that wily, wandering hero, whose son was born far from battle. In those days, they say the men were greater warriors, the battles terrible to behold, and more men died upon the sword than in their own beds. Yet I do believe they were kinder, for they had fought for love, and knew it to be worth dying for."

Penélope wanted to ask more questions about that famed hero, but she needed to play her part, so she simply nodded and continued gazing at the palace. "I recall many stories my mother told me when I was a child. My favorite has always been the tale of Odysseus, when he returns home after years at sea and finds his wife still waiting for him. But I have not heard such a story since they left me to die in the woods."

"Ah, then you are in luck, my dear," Mother said over her shoulder. "Tomorrow we shall celebrate the end of the harvest. There will be much singing and dancing at the feast. Then you will supplicate the King and ask for his hospitality, and may the gods see to it that he grants it."

"Not today?"

Mother shook her head. "First you must rest. The King has many preparations to oversee today, and he shall be in a better mood after some food and drink."

The young girls gave excited shouts and raced ahead of the wagon, skipping inside the open gates of the palace grounds, where the palace now climbed high into the sky at the top of the large hill, surrounded by smaller houses, farms, and workshops. Their wagon rolled past the two guards flanking the gates, following a neatly paved stone road that wound up and up to the front doors of the palace.

The young girl, Korinna, raced back to the wagon, grinning and out of breath. "Mother, can we visit Farmer Eirenaios? Please, Mother?"

"If you return to the palace before sundown," Mother Gray relented.

With an excited laugh, Korinna ran back to her friends, and they took off down the grassy hillside to the vast stretches of plowed earth that extended far into the distance, where Penélope could just see the bronze wall encircling the land like a snake. Their wagon continued up and up the zigzagging road to the grand palace, where shining gold doors stood behind two pillars of silver rising from the bronze threshold. Sculptures of silver and gold dogs stood like sentinels on either side, watching their approach.

The wagon slowed to a stop amidst a manicured grove of apple trees. As Mother helped Penélope come down from the wagon bed, servants opened the doors to the palace, and two handmaidens in similar dark dresses and hair caps hurried out to meet them.

"Bring this poor girl to a room and bathe her," Mother said, handing Penélope off to one of the handmaidens, whose eyes widened at the blanket wrapped around her naked body. "Quickly. Speak of this to no one."

Penélope snuck one glance behind her shoulder, but she could no longer see the shore, and whatever her friends may think of her sudden absence, the gods controlled her fate now. So she quietly followed the handmaiden past the golden doors inside the palace.

"Right this way, my Lady," the handmaiden said, directing Penélope across a wide hallway where a blue painted frieze lined the top of the walls, illuminated by burning lamps held out by bronze servant statues.

The hall opened out onto a lush courtyard of pomegranate, lemon, and olive trees, dispersed with fountains and flower bushes. They turned left along a stone pathway, cutting through the trees until they reentered the palace. The handmaiden led her through maze-like passageways before stopping in front of a small wooden door. She fiddled with a metal lock and pushed open the door, allowing Penélope to walk inside first.

She entered cautiously, then saw the roaring fire at the other end of the room, beside a bronze tub already filled with water and a wide couch piled with fur blankets.

"Is this for me?" Penélope asked in wonder.

The handmaiden laughed. "But of course, my Lady! All of our guests are received hospitably by King Kleomachus."

She shushed Penélope's protests and guided her to the bath, drawing away the blanket from Penélope's shoulders and leaving her naked by the tub. Penélope hesitated in stepping in, but when her foot touched the water, she found it was delightfully warm. Firm hands lowered her into the bath, leaned her head back into the water, then massaged her scalp with surprising rigor. While the handmaiden was old enough to be her grandmother, she had strong arms that did not hold back as they scrubbed away.

Before she knew it, the handmaiden was pulling her out of the bath, wrapping her in one of the fur blankets, and then leaving her by the fire to dry. The warmth of the crackling fire heated her limbs from the inside out. Penélope snuggled deeper under the fur blanket, trying to remember when she had last felt so pampered.

By the time she was nearly dried, the handmaiden returned with a flask of watered-down wine and fresh loaves of bread and fruit, along with a beautiful dress made of soft linen, pinned at the shoulders with bronze fibulae. Penélope dressed and ate, relishing the taste of freshly baked goods and ripe fruit, but soon she began to grow restless.

When the handmaiden returned, Penélope asked, "Where is Mother Gray? May I speak with her?"

"She has other duties that she must attend to, as she runs all the household affairs of the palace. You are not to be seen until the ceremony tomorrow. Those were her exact orders, my Lady."

Penélope sighed irritably. The generous hospitality was starting to feel more like a prison, and her thoughts inevitably wandered to Zeb and Leandros. What did they think happened to her? If they went searching for her, what would they find? Her blue dress and abandoned toiletries on the river bank, but no signs of a struggle, and footsteps that ceased in a grassy meadow. Would they keep looking for her? Or would they sail away, accepting that she was as good as gone?

These thoughts circled in her mind as she paced the room. When she tried the door handle, she was shocked to find it locked, as if this truly were a prison. But unlike prison cells, her room exuded luxury in every corner, from the fur blankets of different exotic animals to the massive, gilded fireplace. Even the chamber pot in the corner of the room was made of silver and gold.

Penélope found it difficult to fight sleep as the sun lowered in the sky, lengthening the shadows in the room. The glow of the firelight flickered against the walls, its sweet smoke heavy in the air. She reluctantly curled up on the couch, sinking into the many cushions and blankets. Once the heaviness of the furs weighed her down, her eyelids drooped, then closed as she passed into a dream.

"You have to find the princess."

Sitting on her bed as if he had been there all along was Zeb. His dark, knowing eyes bore into her. Behind him, the fire had dwindled to embers, but she was still warm.

"Zeb, what are you doing here? I left you at the beach."

He scooted closer and placed an insistent hand on her arm. She winced at the tightness of his grip. "Tomorrow is the feast. Convince the King to grant you hospitality. Speak with the princess of the Phaeacians. She will lead you to King Leon."

"I don't know who the princess is yet," Penélope said in frustration. She had that peculiar sensation of time running out. Zeb had to give her more instructions.

"You have to find the princess," Zeb repeated, his voice smoother than usual and with a hint of something she could not place. "Find the princess and you find the lost King."

"Can you tell me where to find her?"

Zeb only tightened his grip on her arm. "Penélope."

"Zeb, tell me who she is!"

He shook her more forcibly, and she tried to wrench away from his grasp. "My Lady, it is time!"

Penélope gasped awake, her eyes opening to see her handmaiden shaking her by the shoulders. Sunlight streamed through the gaps around the door and from a slitted window in the wall. Her mind tried to grasp the details of the dream, but it was already fading. All she could remember was the command, the urgency in Zeb's voice, and those dark, knowing eyes. The words echoed in her mind as the handmaiden helped her out of bed.

You have to find the princess.

25

Her handmaiden, Penélope was surprised to learn, had been working at the palace since she was just twelve years old, and had practically raised half the servants and extended royal family in the palace. She was called Dora, which was short for Theodora, literally meaning *God's Gift*, for she had been born miraculously to her mother in her fiftieth year after they had lost hope of having children.

Just like the night before, Dora dropped her into the bathtub and began vigorously scrubbing, claiming that she had express instructions from Nausicala to dress her in their finest clothing so that she might impress the King at the feast.

"Now for the oil and strigil, my Lady," Dora said, helping her to her feet and immediately pouring a floral scented olive oil over her skin.

"Will it hurt?" Penélope asked fearfully, eyeing the curved bronze instrument that the handmaiden wielded in her hand more like a weapon than a cleaning tool, so unlike gentle Mother in the bathhouse.

"Have you never bathed at all before, my Lady?" Dora asked with one of her hearty laughs.

Penélope blushed. She couldn't mention the showers and soap she was used to washing with back home, even if it made her seem unclean. Besides, she had to stick to the story. "I have always bathed in rivers. My mother was the last who bathed me, and I hardly remember her."

Dora looked at her in shock. "My apologies, my Lady, if I have offended you. Mother Gray mentioned your story, but I could hardly believe it myself. Here, I will try to be gentle."

Then, with an expert stroke, Dora began scraping the oil from her skin, collecting dirt in its metal edge before she washed it away in the bathwater. Dora scraped all of her skin until Penélope looked as pink and tender as a newborn baby before declaring her cleaned, and she nearly lifted her out of the bath in a fur blanket, drying her quickly this time.

"We shall already be late as it is, since you did not wake up with the dawn," Dora explained, setting her down on a stool and beginning to brush her hair with as much strength as she had scrubbed, so that Penélope winced with every tug on a knot.

"What is the feast for, Dora?"

The old handmaiden spoke as she deftly braided her hair, pulling taut on the strands. "We are celebrating the Festival of the Mysteries. Every two years, after the harvest and before the winter, our people celebrate the Mother Goddess of Grain. Today shall be a feast with song and dance. Tomorrow will be the games. On the third and last day, the princess will be married and sent away in place of the sacrifices. Lords and ladies come from far and wide to celebrate our festival, especially with the marriage this year."

"Wait," Penélope said, trying to make sense of what Dora had said. "The princess? Who is that?"

"Why, she's only the kingdom's prized jewel!" Dora exclaimed, tightening the other braid with more force from her enthusiasm. "I believe you have met her already, for she was among the girls who first saw you in the woods."

Penélope racked her brain for the various names she had heard called out, recalling the unusual kindness displayed by one of them. "Korinna."

"Yes! That is the dear princess. Mother Gray has spent much time rearing her since the poor girl's mother died. She was very beautiful, her mother was, with hair as dark as the night and eyes as green as emerald. The King has never been the same, of course." Dora had finished pinning Penélope's braids in place around her head and turned her around. "There. You are nearly finished. Let us get you dressed, and then we will add the final touches."

Dora helped her slip into a plain linen slip, then draped her in a rich silk fabric dyed wheat-gold and embroidered with colorful flowers and blue waves. Her shoulders were pinned by gold fibulae inset with large sapphires. Then Dora took out a small, engraved chest of wood, lifting the lid to reveal various pots and flasks, along with wooden instruments.

"What's all this for?" Penélope asked curiously.

The handmaiden patted her cheek. "To enhance your lovely face. The King has a penchant for beautiful women, and besides, there will be many an unmarried lord in these halls. If I were in your situation, you may just find that your luck in life will turn."

Penélope laughed at her suggestion. "I'm not here to get married!"

For the first time, Dora looked at her seriously. "My dear, you are almost past the ripe years of your life. If you do not take a husband, be it a lord or no, where shall you go from here? The King will not allow strange guests to linger in his halls forever."

She struggled to think of a response that would not give her purpose away. "I suppose I could learn to work in the palace. Maybe you could teach me?"

Dora contemplated this. "Perhaps that could be arranged, though you will be late in your instruction. We would start with the grinding of the grain, then weaving. But I must warn you, this work is long and laborious, more than you knew even alone in the woods, where all you need to worry about is picking the right berries. Your beauty will be wasted in such a life."

While the possibility of marrying some lord to fulfill her quest was a risk she was not sure she wanted to take, on second thought, Penélope did not want to be stuck in the servants' quarters either when she was tasked with finding the princess. She had to speak with Korinna before she married and sailed away in three days.

"I will first try to find a husband," Penélope relented, her heart panging when Dora's face brightened. "If I fail—which I am sure I will—then you must promise to teach me all you know."

"Very well, my Lady," Dora said, her eyes twinkling with lighthearted mischief. "But once I have done my magic, every lord in the palace shall not help but fall at your feet."

As she spoke, the handmaiden took an oil flask and dabbed some drops on her fingers before rubbing them into Penélope's face. Then, with various rounded, wooden sticks dipped in oil, Dora drew a dark, powdery kohl around her eyes and along her brows. She also applied a red-tinted oil to her cheeks and lips, pinching the skin for further effect. Finally, Dora slid some small white and pink flowers into her hair and sprinkled a lavender rose-scented oil on her neck. Once she was done, Dora held up a small engraved mirror made of shining silver in front of her.

Penélope saw her reflection and almost gasped. Where she had expected to look as gaudy as a painted clown, the handmaiden's makeup was more akin to gloss brushed over a beautiful painting to brighten the colors and sharpen the lines. The kohl brought out her brown eyes beneath her brows and angled her face, while the red tint accentuated her cheekbones and the fullness of her lips. With the flowers framing her face, the sapphire jewels clasped to her dress, and the silk flowing down her body, cinched at the waist by a beautiful purple cord, Penélope had never felt more like royalty.

"I look…"

"Ready for the feast!" Dora declared, bringing Penélope toward the door, where she had her slip on leather sandals. "Now come with me, the feast is about to begin."

They walked hurriedly down the halls, back to the large courtyard they had passed on their way in. All around them bustled servants and guests, the latter adorned with jewelry and makeup in their dresses of silk, their hair done up in different braided styles. Penélope ignored the curious stares her way as Dora led her into a large royal hall not unlike the one back in Helena, where a throne of bronze stood before a long, circular array of couches. Servants around the room held silver and gold platters spilling with fruits, cooked meats, fish, soups, and wines, approaching the guests reclining and standing in the room.

She heard the whispers among them as she walked through the doors, their eyes following her across the room. Some openly pointed at her, and others' mouths fell open, staring at her in unveiled wonder, though whether at her appearance or her unplanned presence, Penélope couldn't tell.

Thankfully, Dora quickly directed her to a familiar figure near the throne that was still empty. Mother Gray seemed to be waiting for her, hands clasped tightly together. Just when Penélope reached her, drums and flutes began playing loudly by the door, and a deep voice bellowed over the silenced room from a soldier at the head of a small squadron.

"All Hail King Kleomachus!"

Everyone lowered their faces, so Penélope did the same, though she could not resist a discreet glance. The soldier stepped aside along with the others, allowing for an old man crowned with gold laurel leaves to hobble inside the room. His tunic was made of gold and silver thread that glimmered with the shifting light. Below a balding gray head were sharp, dark eyes and a long white beard. The soldiers escorted him to the front of the room, where he sat on his throne, overlooking the crowds.

"My honored guests!" said the King in a hoarse voice. "Thank you all for attending our Festival of the Mysteries. Please do the honor of welcoming the Princess of Scheria, my beautiful daughter, Korinna."

As he spoke, the same young girl from the day before entered the hall, dressed in a gold chiton, her cheeks rosy and full, her neck laden with emeralds to accentuate her green eyes, and her dark hair styled in elegant, thin braids around her head, with long curls spilling down her back like ink unfurling in water. A servant led her to the King, where she kissed his cheeks affectionately. Once she stood beside him, all of the guests looked up, and immediately the King's eyes fastened upon Penélope.

"Who might this be?" the King asked in surprise. Penélope's heart pounded in her chest. "I do not recall inviting strangers."

Mother Gray stepped forward with a low bow. "King Kleomachus, while my daughters and I were by the shore—"

The King held up a hand, silencing her. "I do not wish to hear from you."

A hand nudged Penélope's side. Mother whispered her name, indicating that she should go to him. Penélope walked forward hesitantly, her neck hot from the wide-eyed stares of the guests, dispersed with gasps when she lowered herself before his knees in supplication.

"Please, King Kleomachus, I beg you to have pity on me," Penélope said in a tremulous voice only half-feigned. "Long ago, my parents gave birth to me, the last of their children. When they could no longer feed me, unmarried as I was, they abandoned me in the woods, where I have been raised by the birds and trees, scavenging for berries and trapping what small animals I could. When I heard their lovely voices in a nearby meadow, I could not help but approach, wondering what could be making that sound. Your daughter, Korinna, had pity on me, and so Mother Gray brought me to the palace to aid me."

The King placed a gnarled finger beneath her chin and raised it, so that he gazed upon her face, his frown deepening. He turned his sharp eyes upon Mother Gray. "I am troubled by this, and the liberty with which you have brought this woman here, housing her as my guest. Long ago, my people vowed never again to aid strangers who wash upon our shores. Who is to say that she was not abandoned by barbarians passing our island?"

Before Penélope could respond, Princess Korinna placed a delicate hand on the King's shoulder. "But she speaks like one of us, *Papa*. I was there when this woman emerged from the woods, naked and shivering. Who could not pity such a helpless creature?"

"Please, King Kleomachus," Penélope said softly, her eyes filling with tears, though she was not sure if it was for the fear and uncertainty she had endured the last day or the guilt for leaving behind her friends. "For many long years, I have had no family, no loving mother or caring father. But I do remember being told a story as a child, the only one I remember now, that a soft voice sang to me at night, of a wandering hero lost at sea, his wife waiting and weaving at home."

The King looked down at her with saddened eyes. "That is a story any child of Emmeson would know. But how can I be certain my aid would not invoke the wrath of the gods?"

Suddenly, an unfamiliar voice spoke behind her. "Perhaps she is long-lost royalty, like Oedipus had been, exposed at birth, left to die as meat for the wolves and vultures."

Everyone turned toward the voice, including Penélope. Standing beside Mother Gray was a handsome young man, light brown hair falling in well-oiled curls around his face, framing olive skin, green eyes like Korinna's, and a charming smile.

The King laughed. "Lord Iason! My favorite nephew! I thought you would never come. Is your mother well? Your father?"

Lord Iason bowed his head. "All is well at home. A storm delayed my arrival. And I am only your favorite nephew because you have no others." The King laughed again. Lord Iason smiled at Princess Korinna, who blushed. Then his eyes flickered to Penélope. "If I may speak my thoughts, I believe we ought to house this poor woman, if the story she tells is true. For the gods will also punish us if we turn her away, if she is indeed one of our own. Is that not right, Princess Korinna?"

Korinna nodded her head eagerly. "Yes, it is, cousin. She is harmless and would make a pretty addition to the festivities. Her name is Penélope, like the wife in that old song."

"Penélope," the King murmured, still touching her face with his fingers. Both the princess' and his nephew's words seemed to have softened his resolve. "She *is* quite beautiful, is she not? Even after all those years in the wild. Who is to say she is not a nymph?" Laughter tittered in the room. He spread his arms wide. "I declare Penélope our guest and invite her to join our Festival of the Mysteries! Let us not delay any longer—begin the feast!"

At his words, the room erupted into cheers, and the servants came forward with the food, which the guests gleefully grabbed to pile on their plates. Penélope reclined beside Mother Gray, directly opposite Princess Korinna and Lord Iason. At the head of the circle between their pairs reclined the King, while the rest of the guests took up couches or mingled about the room, young girls dressed elegantly, handsome men and ugly ones, as well as anxious mothers introducing their daughters to unmarried lords and the rest discussing the upcoming games.

Penélope caught Iason looking at her and blushed. Korinna and the King were speaking animatedly about something and did not notice, but she swore Mother Gray stiffened beside her. She recalled the words of Dora as she dressed her this morning. *Once I have done my magic, every lord in the palace shall not help but fall at your feet.*

If she wished to speak with Korinna, Penélope had to remain relevant enough to be in the same room as her. What if she knew where King Leon had been sent? Iason's attention might be the only way to rescue him, even if it came at a steep cost. After all, is that not what the Queen of Death had warned her about? *When the time comes, you must sacrifice a love you have not yet known. It is the only way to ensure the King returns to the City.*

Despite her feelings towards Leandros, it was clear she would have to put them aside if she wished the city of Helena to have a fighting chance against the upcoming war. And at this point, even if she wished to take it all back and return to her home and the New Academy, she had entangled herself far too deeply in this world to find a way out of it now, much like Theseus wandering in the labyrinth if he never had a thread to guide him back.

To Penélope's surprise, Mother Gray remained silent and unmoving beside her. The King spoke to Korinna and Iason, even Penélope at times, to ask her questions about her life in the woods, but he never once addressed Mother Gray. She merely sat there, never once removing her veil, not even to eat.

"Will you not eat here?" Penélope asked Mother quietly once the trays had come and gone.

Mother Gray shook her head, but otherwise offered no explanations, so Penélope did not ask her any more questions, instead secretly listening to the King's conversation with Korinna and Iason while she pretended to watch the dancers at the center of the couches twirl and step in unison to the quick rhythm of a flute.

"Please, can we hear a song?" Korinna asked suddenly, interrupting the boring conversation between the King and Iason on the recent harvest. When the King hesitated, she pleaded with her round green eyes. "I am dreadfully sick of waiting. You know how much I love to hear Pyrrhos sing."

Iason laughed at her whining tone. "What song would you have him sing, cousin?"

"The song about Princess Nausicala!"

The King scowled. "Of all the many songs in this world, you choose the one whose tale pains me most."

"Oh, but the song is beautiful," Korinna said with a childish pout. "And shedding a few tears is never a bad thing, Father. We must remember the past, not hide from it, for only then can we preserve it."

"Very well, but only for you, my dear Korinna," the King said with a weary but fond sigh. "Pyrrhos, come forth!"

From the outskirts of the room, Penélope was surprised to see a young man break off from the crowd, holding a four-stringed instrument that looked like a lyre, but with a larger crescent bottom made of wood and wide-set animal horns strapped to it. The bard had flaming orange curls and pale, freckled skin, so different from the tan and dark-haired guests. But most shocking were his eyes, scratched with thick, red scars and sealed shut, rendering him blind. A servant led him to the center of the couches so that all the guests could see and hear him.

"Now sing for us, Pyrrhos, please, in your lovely voice," the King said. "The Princess Korinna would like to hear the song of Nausicala, which I am sure you know well, as we all do, even if in our grief we would rather forget."

Pyrrhos nodded his head obediently, setting up the instrument on his left thigh, his fingers arranged behind it on the strings, while with his right hand he gently plucked the strings in a slow, enchanting rhythm using a long pick made of bone. And then, in a deep reverberating voice, he began to sing, and though she knew Hermes had given her the gift of language, she was still surprised to understand it, hearing the song as though it were composed in her own tongue and meter:

> *"Of fair Nausicala please sing,*
> *O Muse, the daughter of the king,*
> *our princess with the lovely-hair*
> *Whose voice was heard in summer air*
> *by fields of flowers, meadows lush,*

her song as tender as a thrush,
and dancing lithe among the trees
would hum a tune just like the bees
from flowers sweet to rushing stream
her eyes like emeralds did gleam.

The jewel of King Kleomachus,
Nausicala, of her tell us,
when wandering by shores alone,
she found a man bereft of throne—
a king from distant lands had sailed,
until a storm his ship assailed.
For fond of strangers was the man,
to visit every tribe his plan;
his home he left before he wed,
against his mother's wish he fled
across the wine-dark Middle Sea.

For days he never saw a tree,
nor flower fair or meadow lush,
nor listened to a singing thrush,
until aboard his ship afar,
beneath the twinkling northern star
a rocky land seen midst the waves
where might be rivers, deer, or caves.
Then thirst and hunger found respite,
or enemies became a plight
those mortals cruel, unjust, and wild,
their temples bare and gods defiled,
upon his ships brought death and pain,
so none will there return again.

His troubles hence began anew
when wrathful winds against him blew,
his ship Poseidon drowned in ire,
alone he swam the ocean dire.

His body washed upon our shore,
where danced Nausicala before,
his heart with love did fill at sight
of princess fair who stared in fright
at princely face beneath brine hid,
though sweet his words when her he bid
to save his life from certain death.
Then stole he swift the maiden's breath,
so tenderly she washed his face
with cloth she ripped from dress of lace
and brought him back to royal hall
to supplicate the king of all.

But fury wrought the man in them
for fear that aid the gods condemn
to strangers given since the day
Odysseus there made his way.
When proud Kleomachus refused,
Nausicala her heart he bruised,
where love afore had grown between,
a curse the king had not foreseen.
In secret did his daughter plan
to sail away and save the man
from certain death away from home
or on the seas forever roam.

Her father grieved when morning came,
revenge inside his breast aflame,
bewailing loud his daughter's flight
with King Philoxenos at night.
So gathering his forces strong
he sailed to right the captor's wrong,
and after years of cities seen,
he found Nausicala the queen
in Helena, with their new king,
whose mother died alone last spring.

> *In fury Kleomachus fought*
> *against the Helenes and sought*
> *his daughter lovely-haired and fair*
> *beleaguered with her husband there,*
> *where children she had borne by him,*
> *two sons who fought in battle grim.*
>
> *When eldest Alexandros died,*
> *then bitter tears in bed she cried,*
> *but hearing of her husband's death,*
> *Nausicala, she lost her breath,*
> *and silently without a cry*
> *she climbed upon the palace high*
> *then jumped she straight into her doom*
> *to join her love in Hades' gloom.*
> *O woe! her father did bemoan,*
> *And sailed to Scheria alone,*
> *Bereft for life of daughter fair*
> *Nausicala with lovely hair."*

When the bard finished singing, the room burst into shouts of delight, though the King had listened in stony silence and merely nodded his head at Pyrrhos to show his approval. Penélope heard a stifled sob from somewhere in the room, but when she looked around everyone was already laughing and chatting excitedly amongst each other, complementing the bard's skills and exclaiming their readiness for another song.

She turned to Mother Gray, who still sat unmoving beside her. "Mother, who was Princess Nausicala?"

"My daughter," the King said tersely, overhearing her question. His aged face twitched in anger. "Or rather, she *was* my daughter. The moment that–that *thief* washed up on my shores, the daughter I knew had died."

Penélope pretended to be confused. "King Philoxenos?"

"Ah, yes, King Philoxenos was his name. The only comfort I had the day my daughter died was when that monster died too. Barbarians, that's what those men are who call themselves Helenes. But after many years, I will at long last end that line."

"I thought they were all dead?" Penélope dared to ask, hoping she would not raise his suspicion with too many questions.

But the King only smirked. "Not yet, but soon. I have for some time had his youngest son and heir to the throne in my captivity. But that is not all! Oh no. Just yesterday, my men discovered a ship anchored off our shores. They pretended to be merchants, but the truth quickly revealed itself when my men discovered hidden armor bearing the Sun and Laurel Tree. Soldiers they were from the city of Helena, seeking one of their own, no doubt. Among them is none other than the next in line for the throne, grandson of Philoxenos, whom they call Leandros."

He spat the name out at the end with bitter hatred, and Penélope flinched. She struggled to stop the tears that threatened to well in her eyes, her head growing faint at the sound of that name. Why did she ever leave them? What madness compelled her to listen to a trickster god's advice?

"And what are you planning to do with them, uncle?" Lord Iason asked the question that Penélope most needed to know, but didn't have the heart to ask.

"I have already thought of that," the King said viciously. "At the end of the festival, there shall be sacrifices. I do not suppose the gods will judge if those two barbarians are killed for the crime of my daughter's murder, will they?"

At his words, Princess Korinna's eyes widened, and Mother Gray stiffened beside her. Penélope struggled to breathe, her heart constricting in her chest as if the King had sunk a dagger there instead, and it took all of her not to cry out in protest.

"No," Iason said, his gaze settling upon Penélope curiously. "I don't suppose they will."

26

The feast lasted well into the afternoon with more song and dance until the guests all returned to their rooms to sleep off the wine and prepare themselves for more entertainment in the night.

Penélope struggled to walk back to her room without giving herself away either by crying or protesting. She wanted to sneak away and find the prison, but she had no idea where to start. Were the prisons in the palace or somewhere else on the island? If they were in the palace, where? And were they heavily guarded? Was Zeb with them or just Leandros?

She was too strung up to sleep. Once Dora deposited her in the room, Penélope waited a few minutes to try the door. This time it was unlocked, as if the King's approval of her stay meant she was allowed to wander the palace at will. She slipped out into the drowsy evening sun that filtered from the openings in the ceiling, the late summer heat heavy in the air.

The hallways were empty as she tiptoed down, trying to find the courtyard. Instead, she managed to stumble upon a doorway to a larger, unfamiliar courtyard, where a vast orchard of at least four acres in size, hedged around with tall bushes, stretched before her. In the waning sunlight, the fruit trees emitted an intoxicating, sweet fragrance which she paused to inhale, so that she did not see him walk out from behind a tree until he spoke her name.

Lord Iason smiled, and for a moment the pure beauty of his face stole her breath, before a more familiar scarred one flashed in her mind. "Lady Penélope. That *is* your name, is it not?"

She inclined her head, not wishing to engage in a conversation. There was still more of the palace she could explore in the time before the festivities to come.

"I must admit I was curious about you, Lady Penélope," he said, coming to stand across from her, his hands loosely linked behind him. "Life is strange, is it not? How can such a lovely maiden as yourself survive so many years in the wild? Why have the gods punished you so? Or have the gods sent you here to fulfill their plans?"

Penélope pretended not to be fearful of his questions, which were too close to the actual truth for comfort. "I have wondered so myself for many years after my parents abandoned me to my fate. But I suppose it is up to the gods, not us mortals, to answer those questions."

"Very strange indeed," Iason said, his eyes lit up by her words in fascination.

"If that will be all, my Lord…" Penélope began, hoping he would catch the hint and leave her alone.

"Have you seen the grounds of the palace yet?" he asked quickly, as if eager to keep her in his company. While a part of her was annoyed by this, another part of her found it rather endearing. Besides, she could use a guide for this maze-like palace if she wanted to discover where the prisoners were being kept without arousing too much suspicion.

"I have not since today been allowed outside my room," Penélope said, affecting a coy voice and lowering her face. "And now that I am free to wander, I have only become lost. In fact, I have found this orchard and you entirely by chance."

Iason held out his arm for her to take. "If chance it was."

Penélope rested her arm on his, and together they began walking through the orchard and away from the towering bronze palace behind them.

"The palace is like a labyrinth," she said. "I do not know how anyone finds their way."

"To those who do not know it well, it is difficult," Iason agreed with a chuckle. "I myself have been visiting King Kleomachus' palace for as long as I can remember. He is my uncle, and very fond of me, as I am of him."

"Yes, I could tell," Penélope said, then hesitated on how to phrase her next question. "Then that also makes you Princess Korinna's cousin?"

He grinned. "Yes, it does. She is as beautiful as her mother—my aunt." He faltered over the words. "As her mother *was,* I suppose. I still remember her, though she died when Korinna was just a babe and I in my early youth. She never did survive the loss of her first daughter."

"Nausicala," Penélope said softly.

"The Queen was horribly sick since learning of her death and died soon after Korinna was born. It was a terrible day for my family, since she was my mother's sister."

"Ah, I see." She glanced at Iason, noticing now more than ever the similar features between the cousins. "That explains the eyes."

"Her eyes like emeralds did gleam," Iason quoted, then shook his head. "But she has the lovely hair of our mothers, while I am more like my father in that regard, among other things."

"What other things?"

"My handsome face, I suppose," Iason said with a wry smile. "As well as my skill in hunting and riding horses. But I suppose you know all about that, don't you, my little huntress?"

His hand gently squeezed Penélope's at his words, sending her pulse racing when he did not let go. She cleared her throat and attempted to change the subject. "Where have you taken me? We must be at the end of the royal grounds."

They were nearing the hedges surrounding the orchard. "Did you know the fruit here grows all year round? Some say it was planted by the goddess Demeter herself, and watered with nectar and ambrosia."

Hidden inside the hedge was a small iron gate. Iason produced a ring of thick keys and deftly opened the gate, allowing Penélope to walk through first. The thought crossed her mind that he could be trying to take advantage of her, when her breath was well and truly stolen staring down at the vast, sloping countryside of vineyard after vineyard, growing all the way down to the shore, which she could see well from the top of the valley, the bright blue sea curling around a busy harbor of sleek ships.

Iason took her arm once more, this time linking them at the elbow so that she stood much closer to him than before. "It is beautiful, is it not? For so long, I have come to stand right where we are standing now, just to look upon this island's magnificence. Never before did I believe there could be something more beautiful in all of Emmeson." Then he turned towards her, his left hand brushing away a stray strand of hair that had fallen against her face. "That is, until I saw you, Lady Penélope."

She stared at him in surprise, unable to speak. But she didn't have to. Iason had already closed the gap between them and kissed her.

Immediately, she tore herself away from his grasp, her chest rising and falling rapidly.

"My apologies, my Lady," Iason said quickly, his face panicked, trying to come toward her again. She stopped him at arm's length. "Please forgive me, Lady Penélope. I was not thinking clearly. You make me lose all common sense, it seems."

Penélope felt a tinge of guilt for her reaction, but it was engulfed by the deeper guilt she felt for betraying Leandros. She also did not need to make enemies in the palace on the first day. "I was surprised, that is all. Your attention is very kind. But I have no intention of compromising my...honor."

"Then I suppose I will have to marry you," Iason said, grasping her hands in his, his green eyes earnest and filled with hope. "Not a day can go by when I may not lay my eyes upon you."

She remained silent as he lowered his face and kissed her hands. Then he held out his arm as before, and she rested hers on his elbow, and together they walked back inside the orchard and toward the palace. She hoped her face was not too flushed from the kiss, since the festivities would soon begin again.

Before she could return to her room to freshen up, the familiar veiled figure of Mother Gray turned the corner. She saw Penélope on the arm of Lord Iason, and her footsteps faltered. But instead of avoiding them as Penélope half expected, Mother Gray continued walking in their direction. Penélope quickly excused herself and left Iason standing there, meeting Mother Gray in the middle of the hall.

"Lady Penélope," the woman said in surprise. "I am surprised you are not in your room resting. It will be a long night with much food and drink."

"I was...given a tour of the grounds," Penélope said, carefully choosing her words.

Mother Gray paused, as if she were glancing behind Penélope where Iason had stood. "I see."

"Lord Iason was kind enough to show me the vineyards, though I hoped to learn more of the palace grounds so I do not lose my way." She felt the need to defend Iason's presence and also her own reason for wandering the palace.

"I may show you, if you like," Mother Gray said.

Penélope tried to hide her shock. "If that is not too much of an inconvenience."

"Not at all." She began walking away from Lord Iason, as though she wished to get Penélope far away from him as quickly as possible. "This way."

So Mother Gray led her down the hallways, pointing out the various guest rooms, offices, latrines, baths, courtyards, and dining halls with her usual calm, brief explanations. Penélope listened intently, waiting for her to let slip where the prisoners were held, but all too soon they were back in the same hallway near her guest room.

"Since Lord Iason has already shown you the orchard and vineyard, I hope this tour will suffice," Mother Gray said.

"I could not help but wonder after what the King said this morning…" Penélope began, her heart thudding in her chest. "Are the prisoners kept inside the palace?"

Mother Gray was silent for a moment, then in a terse voice said, "That does not concern you. For your own safety, I advise you to remain in your quarters and cease wandering the palace alone."

Penélope's face grew warm. "I was not alone. Lord Iason—"

"*Lord Iason,*" Mother Gray interrupted coldly, "just so happens to be promised in marriage to the Princess Korinna, and ought to know better than to be seen alone with a woman of your situation. If you have any hopes for a happy union with him, I suggest you rid yourself of them."

"Korinna?" Penélope repeated incredulously, her body flashing hot and then cold. "But I thought—they are cousins—"

"All the more reason for them to wed." Mother Gray glanced around to make sure they were alone, then leaned closer and said in a low voice. "The King has long ago arranged his late wife's sister's son to marry his daughter, for together they shall inherit the kingdom. If you do not wish to incur his anger, then do not encourage Lord Iason more than you already have."

"E-encourage?" Penélope spluttered indignantly. "*He* is the one who has made advances, not I. And if a man falls in love with me, it's not *my* fault, is it? Besides, I am not in a position to reject him. If I do not find a husband to take care of me, where will I go from here?" She paused, her breath shallow. Mother Gray stood silent. "I suppose you wouldn't understand."

She almost turned to enter her room when Mother Gray laughed, a soft laugh filled with pain, and when she spoke, her voice trembled. "If only I did not. But as it is, I have lost a love far greater than any you shall ever know. Husband and son forever severed from me, dead by an illness that almost killed me too. Some days I wish it had."

Penélope stared. She wondered if that was why she wore the veil, in mourning for her dead husband and son.

"But that is a story for another time," Mother Gray said quietly. Behind her, the guests had begun filtering out of their rooms to return to the main hall. "Dora is waiting for you to freshen your face. Go quickly, so you do not miss the feast."

Then with a slight bow, she hurried away, leaving Penélope standing in the hallway, stunned and silent.

27

"It is time to wake, Penélope!"

She looked bleary-eyed at Dora and groaned. "It is too early."

"Too much wine last night, perhaps?" Dora asked with a chuckle. She helped Penélope out of bed, undressing her quickly. "A cold bath will wake you right up. We must get you ready for the games."

After the festivities of last night, Penélope could hardly fathom how the men would compete in the games today. The feast in the morning had been a mere taste of what was to come. Never before had Penélope drunk more wine—even watered down—nor ate so much food, the meat tender, the fruit dripping with juice, the cakes sweet and savory at the same time. And it seemed she would never be full until she returned to her bed and fell fast asleep.

Thankfully, with the King and the Princess Korinna present, Lord Iason did not approach her, merely stealing glances at her that made her cheeks hot and Mother Gray grow still beside her. Penélope herself did not attempt conversation with anyone, and besides a few lords and ladies who were curious about her childhood growing up in the woods, no one seemed to care anymore about the strange guest, too preoccupied with the new gossip of potential marriage matches and the song and dance that played until dawn.

Once Penélope was dressed, this time in a bright red tunic bordered with gold that brought out the red tint on her lips and the rose petals woven into her braids, she gathered with the other guests in the hall and together they made their way out of the palace to a wide field, where a dusty, oval track stretched alongside large tents with tables full of more food and wine.

A group of strong, youthful lords stood wrapped in cloaks on the track where the guests flocked to have the best vantage point. Lord Iason was among them, smiling congenially and speaking to the other lords with his usual charm, though occasionally his eye would drift to her, and they would both blush. Only Mother Gray lingered on the outskirts of the crowd, solemn and veiled, but this time Penélope did not approach her, fearful of any more questions. The King stood frail beside his daughter, Korinna, whose dark, braided hair had been tied back into an elegant, modest bun.

"Today we celebrate games in honor of our harvest and the goddess Demeter!" the King proclaimed. He motioned to the lords on the track. "We shall begin with the foot race. The victor of each game will be crowned with a gold wreath, and during the banquet, each shall receive their victory song, composed by our very own Pyrrhos."

All the guests clapped, their eyes waiting eagerly for the competition to begin. Penélope discreetly shifted closer to Korinna, hoping that if the King ever left his spot by her side, she could speak with the princess privately.

"Athletes, prepare yourselves!" called out an older lord who was in charge of directing the games.

Once he spoke, the younger lords all dispelled their cloaks, causing Penélope to choke on her wine. The men stood naked on the track, their skin oiled and glistening beneath the sun, highlighting their toned muscles. Of them all, Lord Iason was most beautiful by far, his limbs proportionate, lean, and long, his skin bronzed and drawn in perfect curved lines like the sculptures she had always seen in museums, the sharp indents of his hips shifting as he stretched. Penélope could not help but flush, looking around furtively, though no one else appeared embarrassed.

Iason and the other lords began jogging to warm up their bodies, then jumping high in place, and it took all of Penélope's self-control not to laugh nervously. She snuck a glance at Korinna, who gazed upon the athletes curiously, the only sign of her thoughts the whitened knuckles of her hands, which she held together.

"Line up!"

The athletes took their places at the far end of the track, while the judges lined up at the finish line. Penélope took another small step toward Korinna, then another, hoping that neither the King nor Mother Gray would notice.

"Ready, boys—on your marks—run!"

Iason took off a hair's breadth early, but no one seemed to notice, loudly cheering the athletes on as they sprinted to the finish line, their arms and legs pumping so swiftly they seemed to hardly touch the ground. Penélope held her breath as Lord Iason broke ahead of the ranks and won.

"And the victor is Lord Iason!"

The crowds erupted into whistles and shouts, clearly having favored him to win. Penélope saw Korinna clap, smiling at her betrothed's win, though Penélope sensed a certain reluctance. She was close enough that if the King and the princess spoke, Penélope would be able to hear. But she realized her mistake when Iason approached, still breathing heavily and his skin flushed. She forced her gaze not to wander lower than his face.

"Ah, the victor!" the King said. "I knew you would outrun any of those lords. They've been too fattened up and pampered for my taste. But not you, Iason!"

He gestured to Iason's physique, who laughed. "Thank you, uncle. You are too kind. But I won only by two paces." His eyes flitted over to Penélope for the briefest moment, which the King noticed with a frown. Iason quickly addressed the princess. "And you, cousin, were you happy I won?"

"Of course, Lord Iason," Korinna said with a smile, but without her usual enthusiasm. "I suppose you shall win wrestling too?"

Iason narrowed his eyes at her question. "Ah, I doubt I can best Erasmos, descendant as he is of the great Euryalus, but I shall try my best just for you."

"I am sure you will," the King agreed rather curtly. Then suddenly he looked upon Penélope, who had the ill-luck of glancing over at the same exact moment. "And you, Penélope, our daughter of the woods, would you like to walk with me?"

She stuttered in surprise, "Of course, King Kleomachus."

As she walked by his side, she saw Mother Gray out of the corner of her eye and wondered if she had mentioned her questions to the King. They strode in silence, then the King turned to her with a forced smile.

"Mother Gray has mentioned to me that you seek a husband," the King said, eyeing her sharply.

"Well, I only meant—"

"Do not worry, my dear," the King interrupted, holding up a wrinkled hand. "It is perfectly natural that you wish to acquire a suitable situation. Your upbringing in the woods, though unfortunate, has brought you to my halls, and there is no better place to find a husband than here. In fact, several lords have mentioned their interest in you already."

Penélope winced. "That's very kind of you—"

"Under my guidance," the King interrupted again with a stern glance towards Iason, "you shall find yourself a respectable match."

She flushed at the implications in his words. "Of course, my Lord."

"Let me introduce you to Lord Erasmos, descendant of the great wrestler Euryalus, who as yet remains unmarried," the king said, leading her toward the track. "He has a sizable fortune, though bearing no formal title, and has won many victories in games."

They came to a stop.

"Ah, here he is! Lord Erasmos, allow me to introduce the Lady Penélope."

Penélope turned. She forced a smile at the lord before her. Even his cloak, which he was thankfully still dressed in, could not hide his well-built, muscled body made as though especially for wrestling. His crooked nose, certainly broken many times before, and the thick white scar swallowing half his upper lip graced a rough-hewn face framed by dark curling hair and set with a pair of thoughtful brown eyes. Despite his menacing physicality, he offered a kind smile that almost made him handsome and bowed before them.

"To what do I owe the pleasure of this introduction, my King?" Erasmos asked, his glance flickering to their left. Penélope saw out of the corner of her eye the Princess Korinna standing beside Lord Iason in conversation.

The King noticed too and sneered. "Many long years have you lived without a wife to grace your halls, my son. The Lady Penélope has much to recommend her despite a wild upbringing in the woods. And all can agree that her beauty has not been tarnished by savage ways. Is that not right, Lord Erasmos?"

Erasmos smiled forcibly and nodded. "Your beauty has been the talk of the festival, my Lady. I am honored by your introduction."

"It is a pleasure, Lord Erasmos," Penélope said, inclining her head. She turned to the King, hoping he would break the silence, but he had gone, leaving her alone with the wrestler. "Perhaps I shall go—"

"Lady Penélope," Erasmos interrupted, holding out his arm for her to take, and they began to walk along the edge of the track. "Have you ever seen a wrestling match before?"

"Not if you discount the wolves wrestling in the woods," Penélope said in complete seriousness, before slipping into a smile to betray her jest.

Erasmos blinked at her, then laughed. "Clever! I like you, Penélope. I can see why the King would wish to make you my wife."

"Me—your wife—" Penélope stuttered, struggling for the words.

"Have you not already agreed?" Erasmos asked in slight confusion. They stopped at the edge of the field where the crowds of people began to thin. Lord Iason and Princess Korinna had also taken a turn together, her delicate arm on his, several paces away from them but still in their line of sight.

Penélope's eyes met Iason's, and they both fought back a blush. She glanced at Erasmos to see if he had noticed, but his gaze was locked on Korinna's, their cheeks identically flushed. Korinna hid her pained face from Iason's keen eyes by directing his attention to a bird flying in the sky. Erasmos tore his gaze away with a troubled frown.

"I have not agreed, no," Penélope said quietly. "And I doubt you have either. But why would the King wish for you to marry so desperately?"

Erasmos' gaze strayed once more to Korinna's slim, youthful figure as she smiled in delight when the bird landed on the top of a nearby statue. "It is complicated."

"Love is rarely complicated," she said with a knowing smile. "It is people who complicate it."

His eyes narrowed. "I do not know what you mean."

"You do not need to tell me, because I can see it clearly." He opened his mouth to deny it, but she interrupted again. "Do not worry, my Lord, no one will know your secret. I myself do not wish to marry you for the same reason."

Erasmos smiled wryly. "Then you are also in love with the princess?"

Penélope laughed. "You are clever too, Lord Erasmos. The one I love is more forbidden than your dear princess. But tell me, why does the King wish for you to marry me if you are so in love with his daughter? I can tell you, Lord Iason does not care for her even half as much."

"That is precisely why," Erasmos said dryly. "He does not wish for me to love his daughter, but for her to marry Lord Iason, whose mother—sister to the King's late wife—is married to the King of the Keteians, a powerful people who live on the eastern edge of the Inner Sea, across from the enchanted isles. King Kleomachus hopes their marriage will cement a stronger alliance between them. I, on the other hand, come from more humble stock and bear no grand title despite my noble lineage."

"But love does not care for lineage," Penélope protested. "Does the Princess

Korinna share your love?"

Erasmos' cheeks reddened. "If her words are worth half as much as her father's wealth, then she would marry me tomorrow instead of Lord Iason. But she does not wish to incur her father's wrath." He shook his head. "But now that I have told you my forbidden love, can you trust me with yours?"

She glanced around to see if anyone important was nearby, a riddle-like answer ready on her lips, when she saw a movement out of the corner of her eye that pulled her attention away. Lord Iason had been escorted back to the track for the round of discus-throwing, and Princess Korinna had slipped away unseen in the commotion, the King busy speaking with the athletes and guests as they awaited the next competition.

"That's strange," she whispered to herself.

"You should follow her."

She turned in surprise. Erasmos was looking at her, but his eyes fixed on her sharply, with a knowing gleam that immediately rooted her to the ground. "What?"

"Quick!" he whispered in a familiar, ageless voice.

Penélope glanced back at the princess' retreating figure nearly lost between the trees surrounding the palace. She knew what she had to do. "I-I have to go."

Then she left the crowd, ignoring Erasmos calling her name out in confusion, once more in his usual voice, which now sounded more human than ever before. But she soon forgot all thoughts of the wrestler or the games as she followed Korinna around the palace to the front courtyard, where she cut a path through the trees and begun running excitedly down the sloping valley. There the farms and shops of the palace stretched out to the distant bronze walls encircling the royal grounds.

Korinna ducked into an inconspicuous doorway, disappearing inside one of the low-roofed shops. After looking over her shoulders to make sure no one had pursued them, Penélope followed Korinna inside.

She stopped when fifty pairs of eyes looked up at her in surprise. Inside the shop, fifty young girls stood at various wooden contraptions, some of them large looms like the one Calypso had used, others to spin the wool into colored balls, yet still others to embroider hems. Korinna stood next to a group of girls who looked familiar, and Penélope realized they had been with the princess that day, playing in the meadow.

When the girls looked her way, Korinna did too, then immediately her face fell. "Lady Penélope, what are you doing here?"

Penélope raised a brow. "I suppose I could ask you the same question, Princess. I doubt your father will be happy to learn you ran away from the games."

Korinna's cheeks turned red, and she mumbled, "I hate the games. I would much rather weave and play with my friends."

"What of Lord Iason?" Penélope asked. "You are betrothed to him, and you will marry tomorrow. *He* would want you to watch him compete."

The princess lifted her chin haughtily, making her seem younger than she normally did. "I do not care. *I* never wanted to get married to him, because then I would have to leave all my friends."

Penélope could sympathize with the poor girl on this, recalling the pain in Erasmos' voice when he spoke of the princess, and the possibility that she loved him just as much. But although she wished to comfort her, she knew how little time she had to save her friends. So she decided to play to her emotions, hoping in her vulnerable state the princess might let slip what she knew of the prisoners. "I know it is difficult to accept, but there is nothing in this life for young women like you and me save to marry."

"No!" Korinna protested, scooting closer to her friends, as if Penélope had threatened to drag her to the wedding right then. "I can weave! Like Sofia and Arete!"

"But you are a princess," Penélope began.

"I learned how to weave, just like they did." Korinna crossed her arms angrily. "But I suppose *you* never did because you grew up in the woods!"

Soft gasps rose from the girls at this accusation. Penélope could not deny it, nor mention her sewing skills learned from her grandmother, so she merely inclined her head and said, "You are right, Princess Korinna. I never had the privilege to learn once my parents abandoned me to my fate."

At this, Korinna's eyes softened as they had the day she first saw her. "My apologies, Lady Penélope, I did not think. Here, if it pleases you, I can teach you how to weave now. It shall only take a few minutes."

Penélope hesitated, wondering if she should return to the games before people noticed her absence and she risked her precarious position at the palace. But then she reminded herself that this was all part of the plan, and if she did not speak to the princess, there was no way for her to save her friends.

"I would love that," she said.

Korinna smiled brightly and prepared a station for them. Penélope joined her, sitting on a stool to watch as Korinna's nimble fingers took the shuttle and slid it expertly between the threads which hung from the wooden bar at the top of the loom, separated in two sections by a bar in the middle, and weighed down by ceramic circles at the bottom. Then with a flat paddle bar, she flattened the thread into the rest of the woven fabric, before moving the middle wooden bar inward and shifting the taut threads inversely, the ceramic weights clinking pleasantly together.

"I have always loved weaving," Korinna said, though she sounded sad. "When I am married, I suppose that is the only thing that will stay the same."

"I am certain Lord Iason will make a wonderful husband," Penélope said, though she wasn't so sure, recalling the kiss they had shared by the vineyards.

"My father loves him like his own." But she did not sound happy about it, focusing more on her weaving, moving the shuttle between the separated threads. "Ever since his first daughter, Nausicala, left him, they say the King has never been the same. I was born after he returned home many years later, when my mother was near her last birthing years. I was not supposed to be born, really, and he cherishes me as the last connection he has with her. He would never let me marry another if he could help it."

Korinna handed Penélope the shuttle so that she could practice weaving it between the threads, and then gave her the paddle bar to nudge the thread into place next to the rest of the pattern.

"But surely after capturing the rest of King Philoxenos' line, he will be more reasonable?" Penélope asked off-handedly, repositioning the middle bar and weaving the shuttle back between the threads.

"Here, you need to twist this now," Korinna said, momentarily distracted. She lifted the top bar holding up the already woven threads and twisted to bundle them up and make room for more of the pattern. "There, now continue." She nodded as Penélope swallowed her impatience and continued weaving. "You are a natural weaver. If I did not know better, I would think you had already been taught some kind of thread work."

"That is very kind of you, but it is only because I have a very good teacher," Penélope said, nudging Korinna's shoulder. "Your father wishes for me to marry Lord Erasmos, so it is a good thing I learn how to weave."

Korinna's smile quickly faded at the mention of her secret love, and a slight jealousy crept into her voice. "Lord Erasmos will be lucky to have you as his wife, for he is a gentle and kind man. As to your question, I doubt my father will ever rest his vengeance against the Helenes. Those men will be executed tomorrow, though I fear it will only stoke the flames of his fire."

"I see." Penélope racked her brain desperately for another question that might lead her to the prisoners' location. "It is strange to think such evil men have been inside the palace all this time. For they are being held in the palace, right?"

"Princess Korinna, what is the meaning of this?"

Penélope's heart jumped at the familiar, stern voice, and she looked up to see Mother Gray standing inside the room, the tense set of her shoulders clearly livid. Korinna froze beside her. "Mother Gray, I didn't hear—"

"Enough! You, princess, ought to be at the games. The King will withhold punishment if you return at once, given your *wedding* is tomorrow, might I remind you? And *you*, Lady Penélope." Penélope cringed under what must have been a withering glare beneath that dark veil. "You will come with me."

Korinna stood up, so Penélope did the same. They shared a regretful look before following Mother Gray out of the workshop in a heavy silence save for the quiet clinking of loom weights and the wooden clicks of the shuttle and paddle board against their frames.

When they exited the workshop, the sun had already begun lowering into the afternoon. Dora was waiting for them, avoiding Penélope's gaze. She took hold of Princess Korinna's arm and together they began to walk back up the hill to the track where the games were being held, Korinna's head hung low.

"Follow me," Mother Gray said tersely. Then she turned and began walking back towards the palace.

Penélope followed with a racing heart, wondering wildly if she was going to be put in prison. "Where are you taking me?"

"Silence."

She held her breath at the sharp tone, tears stinging her eyes. What had she done so wrong? Had she heard her probing questions and figured out the truth?

Mother Gray walked at a quick pace, glancing around furtively. They entered the palace and took a hallway that Penélope had never seen before, then another. Few lamps lit this way, so Penélope quickened her step to walk close by Mother's side.

At last, they stopped before a wooden door at the end of the dark hallway.

Mother produced an iron key and fitted it into a small slit in the door, then pushed it open. In the darkness, Penélope glimpsed dank stone steps disappearing below.

Mother Gray checked the hall one last time before taking Penélope by the wrist in a tight grip and dragging her down the steps. They seemed to last forever, when suddenly they landed on a dirt floor filled with stagnant puddles. They were in a hallway, but built into the walls were iron bars, lumps of people dressed in rags and chained to the floor scattered within each room.

It was the prison.

She followed numbly after Mother Gray, who led her down the hall, stopping short of the last cell and pushing Penélope forward. Who would find her here now? What about her parents, who would never know she had been left to rot in a prison of another realm? Distantly, another thought occurred to her, and the moment it dawned on her, she was standing before the final prison cell and looking inside.

There, sitting chained and looking haggard and dirty, were none other than Leandros, Mono, Zeb, and Owen.

28

Before anyone could speak, Mother Gray whispered, "Be quick. The guards will return soon." Then, after a last lingering look at the prisoners in the cell, she left, her long, dark dress swishing at her ankles and disappearing up the steps.

Penélope stood there in shock, staring at each of her friends in turn. Finally, Zeb leaped forward and grasped her through the bars.

"Penélope," he said in an oddly choked voice. "You're alive."

"I could say the same about you," she whispered through the tears. "When I heard the king had you all imprisoned, I thought I would never see you again."

"What are you wearing?" Zeb asked suddenly as he backed away to allow the others to see her, the initial shock fading.

"You don't look like a prisoner to me," Owen said, gesturing to their tattered rags they were forced into. "In fact, I dare say you look more like royalty than our dear prince over here."

Penélope was forced to look at Leandros, who stared at her with barely concealed wonder mingled with betrayal. "I am sorry I left you all without saying anything. But I didn't have a choice." At their blank faces, she muttered, "You wouldn't understand."

"Try us, darling," Owen drawled, rolling his eyes.

"When I was bathing in the woods, I-I heard voices of young girls nearby," Penélope said, hesitating. "I found a group of maidens playing in a meadow. They saw me, and so I had to beg them to help me. The princess took pity on me, and when I supplicated the King, she convinced her father to let me stay. I knew it was the best chance we had to find King Leon."

All of them stared at her blankly. Then Leandros asked, "And have you?"

His voice was tense. Penélope's cheeks burned. "Not exactly. I was...busy. They are celebrating the Festival of the Mysteries. When I heard that you guys were captured, I've been trying my hardest to sneak away and find where you were."

"If you wanted to find my father," Leandros said sharply, "you should not have wasted time on us."

"Well, I wasn't about to let you all die," Penélope shot back at the hidden accusation in his words. "I guess a thank you is too much to ask, though."

"What was that about letting us all die?" Owen asked, holding up a hand to interrupt them.

"Yeah, what are you talking about?" Zeb asked, his face pale. "Are we going to die?"

Penélope's voice shook as she forced herself to speak the words. "The King plans to execute you all tomorrow, along with King Leon, as the sacrifices for his daughter's wedding."

They were deathly silent, then Leandros asked, "How do you know this?"

"Yeah, are you fraternizing with the enemy now?" Owen demanded, though he didn't sound like he was joking.

"Mother Gray was kind enough to bring me to the palace," Penélope explained. "She was the woman who brought me here to see you. I told them that I grew up in the woods, abandoned there by my parents. It was the only way they would have let me stay here long enough to find King Leon."

"Then you have befriended King Kleomachus," Leandros said in a low voice. "My grandfather's murderer, who has taken my father and will murder us all!"

Penélope grasped the iron bars. "It was the only way. If I told them the truth, they would kill me too, and then who would've rescued us from here?"

"Speaking of rescuing us," Owen interrupted, "how the hell are you getting us out of here? You don't even have the key."

She hadn't thought that far ahead. Even if she managed to find the guard with the key, or convince Mother Gray or the princess to help her, how would she manage to escape the royal grounds without getting caught? It seemed impossible.

"She cannot rescue us," Leandros said darkly. "The gods have led us astray, it seems."

"Leandros, I'm sorry," she whispered, hot tears sliding down her face. She looked at Zeb, but he was staring at the ground, lost in thought as he had been the day they rescued him from the Underworld. "I will try to get you out of here.

I will not leave you here to die."

But none of them responded. Penélope struggled to find the words, but she had no idea how she would rescue them from the prison cell, let alone the island as a whole.

"That's the only way out," Zeb murmured to himself. He looked up and saw everyone staring at him expectantly. "We have to supplicate the King."

"He will not show us mercy," Leandros said harshly.

"Perhaps at the right price," Owen said, meeting Zeb's eyes with a growing smirk. "Men will do unthinkable things for a stash of coin, here as anywhere else."

"I don't know." Penélope hesitated, recalling the anger that shook the King's voice as he spoke of King Philoxenos. "I'm not sure money is what he wants. You don't understand how much hatred he still harbors towards King Philoxenos. He blames him for his daughter—Leandros' grandmother's—death, even if she left of her own will."

"Then we give him revenge, if that's what he wants, in some form other than death," Zeb argued. "Owen's right. Every man has his price. Even Leandros let us go after Alexandria told him about the prophecy."

Leandros scowled, clearly disliking this plan and offended at the insult to his honor. But Zeb and Owen had a point, whether Penélope or Leandros wished to admit it. Even the proudest, richest Kings could be convinced with the promise of something equally or more valuable in return.

"It's the only plan we have," Penélope said, trying to sound more convinced than she felt.

"And if it doesn't work?" Leandros asked.

Penélope looked at his familiar scarred face, the one she saw in her dreams at night. She couldn't help but smile. "Have faith, Λέανδρος."

The ghost of a smile flickered reluctantly across his face, but it quickly disappeared at the sound of footsteps on the stairs. The panic she felt was mirrored in his eyes as she stood frozen by their cell. Was it a guard? Or Mother Gray? She shouldn't have stayed for so long only to argue with them.

Before she could say goodbye or any last word, a cloaked figure emerged from the stairwell, entering the hall of the prison.

"Lord Iason?" she asked in surprise.

He was already back to his normal princely garb, his handsome face strangely glowing amid the crude torchlight. He looked at her and then at Leandros, his eyes widening in realization. "What are you doing here, Lady Penélope?"

She forced herself not to look at her friends. "I-I wanted to see the prisoners for myself. The song yesterday aroused my curiosity."

Iason continued to look at her suspiciously. "When Mother Gray escorted you to the palace, I had to follow. I stayed out of sight, but I saw her bring you here. I thought perhaps she had orders to imprison you, and came to rescue you." Then he glanced between Penélope and the prisoners. "But it seems I was wrong."

"Th-this is not what you think, Lord Iason," Penélope stuttered, her pulse thudding in her throat.

Lord Iason glanced behind him, as if to make sure no one was coming, then stood close to her and placed a hand on her arm, lowering his voice to a whisper. She fought back the hot shame climbing up her neck. "I warded off the guards on their last round, but we don't have much time before they grow suspicious. If you stay here, you *will* be caught. You had better come with me, Lady Penélope."

Penélope nodded silently, a lump in her throat. He held out his arm, and she rested hers on it, risking one last look back at the others. She almost regretted it. Her eyes met Leandros', his filled with pure agony—worse than any anger or betrayal could be—as if she had just ordered his execution herself.

Then Iason led her up the stairs, and together they left the prison in a tense silence.

29

ONCE PENÉLOPE LEFT WITH the strange lord, they sat in a terrible silence. Leandros looked absolutely heartbroken the moment Penélope placed her arm on that man's elbow. Owen appeared uncharacteristically serious, as if contemplating the real possibility of their death.

Even though they had been imprisoned after a brief skirmish on the beach—where they were greatly outnumbered and soon rounded up like sheep in a pen—the thought of being executed had not crossed Zeb's mind. Trapping his body and soul in the Underworld had been horrible, but he hadn't actually *died* in an irreversible way.

Owen rubbed his eyes wearily, as though he could hardly believe the situation they were in. At first, Zeb had been shocked when Owen had appeared in the Underworld to save him, then hopeful of what that might mean, and then angry when Owen had acted as if it meant nothing. Their argument before learning of Penélope's disappearance had been nothing more than confirmation of the truth.

But now they might die tomorrow, all the bad blood between them washed away by the cutting edge of death, whether they wanted it to or not. He could not rid himself of the memory of Penélope's panic-stricken face between the prison bars. Suddenly, he realized the nagging feeling he had since that handsome man appeared and spoke with Penélope.

"Is no one wondering how that Phaeacian lord understood what Penélope was saying?" Zeb asked aloud, his voice skittering across the damp stone so that even Leandros flinched.

An old voice in a thick accent spoke from the other side of their cell. "She was given the gift of language, my friend."

They all looked up in the direction of the voice, hoarse from disuse and illness. Sitting there hunched and shrouded in darkness was another prisoner, so still and silent that Zeb had wondered if the man was dead and no one had bothered to take him out. The prisoner remained at the edges of the cell where the torchlight from the hall did not reach.

"Who are you?" Leandros asked suspiciously. "And how do you speak in the strange tongue of my comrades here?"

The old man emitted a low chuckle that morphed into a cough. "Long ago, I learned to speak it. Once upon a time, it would not be so very uncommon to hear of that folk passing through Emmeson."

"What do you mean *she was given the gift of language?*" Zeb asked, wanting to know if this man knew more about Penélope somehow, however interesting it might be that people like them had found different doors to enter this realm.

"Can you not tell?" the old man said in amusement. "The enchantment of the gods is heavy upon her. I have seen enough of the gods at work to know when they have eyes on one of us mortals."

Zeb disliked the riddles this man seemed to speak in. "How long have you been imprisoned?"

"Too much time to count. Though I suspect the end has come."

"Are they going to execute you too?" Owen asked, not without a little sarcasm.

The old man paused, then, "Before you all came, every so often, a veiled woman visited me in my cell. She spoke to me about a young princess who fell in love with a wandering king, washed upon their shores."

"Princess Nausicala," Leandros murmured in surprise.

"That is she," he continued with a nod. "As the story goes, when King Kleomachus refused to help the stranger return home, Princess Nausicala helped him escape the island and sail back to the city of Helena. But when her father discovered that the man had kidnapped her daughter, he sailed far and wide to rescue her. He waged war against the Helenes, killing their king, Philoxenos, and his firstborn son, Alexandros, in battle. So hearing of her husband and son's death, the Queen Nausicala threw herself from the top of a tower and drowned in the depths of the Inner Sea."

"Yes, we've heard the story before," Zeb said impatiently.

"Ah, but that is not the *only* story," the old man said, with a low laugh at their surprised faces. "Oh yes, every story has two sides, as they say, and a third if you ask the seers. Another story is told by some who were at the palace of Helena that night, later imprisoned by King Kleomachus and brought back to Scheria. *They* told a very different story to anyone who would listen, that the Queen Nausicala had not jumped at all, but had been brought back in secret by her father, hidden in the darkest dungeon and fated never to see the light of day again in punishment for aiding a stranger against the will of the gods."

"That's impossible," Leandros said after a long, contemplative silence. "Even if it were true that she had not taken her own life, King Kleomachus would not imprison his own daughter. He may be a brute, but he is nonetheless her father. Whoever told you that story, old man, is mistaken."

"And if the one who told me was the Queen Nausicala herself?" the old man asked.

"How?" Zeb asked incredulously.

"I already told you, friends."

"Stop speaking in riddles," Leandros threatened in a growling voice. "How have you spoken with the Queen Nausicala?"

Owen sucked in a breath. "The veiled woman. You said a veiled woman came to speak with you. Is she Nausicala?"

The old man remained tellingly silent.

"The Queen Nausicala..." Leandros whispered, his face paling, before he narrowed his eyes at the prisoner. "If she is veiled, how can you be sure it was her?"

"Even after years of separation," the old man said gravely, "a son never forgets the voice of his own mother, though it appears the same cannot be said for a son and his father."

Zeb looked at the prisoner's shadow-covered face, glimpsing flashing eyes in a white-bearded face, his heart beating faster. "Who are you?"

The old man laughed, but did not answer, his laugh morphing into a wheezing cough.

Leandros leaped to his feet. "Show yourself, old man!"

Slowly, the prisoner stood up, taking a step into the glow of the torchlight. He had dark gray hair growing long and scraggly around his shoulders, a matted, curling white beard, and familiar brown eyes set below a strong brow. Even beneath his ragged prisoner's tunic, Zeb could see strong shoulders, and below the hem were thick, muscled legs. Despite his age, he looked more like a warrior than a common vagabond.

"Οὐ τὸν σεαυτοῦ πατέρα γιγνώσκεις, Λεάνδρε;"

Zeb didn't need to speak Greek to understand the question. Leandros took a small step closer, his eyes raking down the tattered prisoner's tunic and scraggly, graying hair.

"Πάτερ?" Leandros asked hesitantly.

Mono scrambled to his feet and bowed his head. "Χαῖρε βασιλεῦ Λέον."

"It's you," Zeb said in dawning realization. "King Leon. You're the one who left the city of Helena after Brother Ezra took power."

"I had no choice," King Leon said sharply. "There were questions that needed answering."

"You left Mother," Leandros said through gritted teeth. "She will never forgive you for what you did."

King Leon raised a brow. "Your mother was the one who told me to leave. *She* had tracked the movements of the heavens and consulted the priestess of Apollo. *She* had read the portents and deciphered the prophecies stored up in the Great Library. When she discovered one that spoke of the restoration of the Old Order, she knew what I had to do."

"What prophecy?" Zeb asked, though he already knew. "What did it say?"

"I shall tell you, though I long swore to speak its words to no other mortal save my wife," King Leon said. He was silent for what felt like an eternity, and Zeb wondered if he had changed his mind, before he suddenly began chanting in a low voice:

"κρύσταλλος γενόμην ἀδάμαντά τε καὶ τότε χαλκός

εἴς τε σίδηρον καὶ τότε τὸν χρυσόν τε μόλυβδος

πρῶτον μὲν μέλαν ἐστὶ δὲ λευκὸν δεύτερον ἐστί

μὲν χρυσὸν τρίτον ἐστὶ τελευταῖον τὸ δ' ἐρυθρόν

οὕτω τὸν δὲ παλαιὸν ἀνορθοῖ αὔτε νεαλής.

κρυπτὸν δ' ἄντροις τῆς βαθέσ' ἐν τοῖς σπέρμα ὀλέθρου

οἱ κεῖται δὲ ἀοιδὴ αἱ Μοῖραι ἀνέχουσιν

ἔνθε δ' ἄναξ πέπτωκε θεῶν ἀπὸ τῆς βασιλείας

τῆς πρὸς ἑαυτοῦ μούνης μορφῆς · Μοῖρα τε τέξει

ζωὴν καὶ ζωὴ Μοῖραν· προλέγει τέλος ὥς οἱ."

Zeb hardly understood all the words in Greek, but he didn't need to. The first line was enough to know that it was the same prophecy he had learned from

Penélope, Ari, and Alexandria when they tried to enter the Temple of Apollo, and Chloe had spoken the words in some kind of trance. He murmured aloud the verses:

> *"Quartz to diamond,*
> *Copper to iron,*
> *Lead to gold.*
>
> *First is black, second white,*
> *Third is gold, last is red,*
> *So the new restores the old.*
>
> *Hidden in her caverns deep*
> *Lies the seed of his defeat,*
> *A song the Fates uphold.*
>
> *The King of the Gods,*
> *Fallen from his throne,*
> *By one of his own mold.*
>
> *Death will birth life,*
> *Life will birth death,*
> *Thus his end has been foretold."*

"You have heard the prophecy," King Leon said in surprise once Zeb finished. He turned to Leandros. "Then you know now why I had no choice but to leave."

"Where did you go?" Leandros asked, still sounding unconvinced.

The King raised a brow. "The Sibyl of Apollo, of course. Your mother supposed the caverns spoke of her temple in the mountains by the edge of the Middle Sea. But I never reached her, waylaid by the wrath of Poseidon thanks to the curse by the Phaeacians upon my father, King Philoxenos. I have been imprisoned here for many dreadful months. But my quest is of the utmost importance if we wish to restore the Old Order."

"But the Old Order has already been restored," Zeb said in slight confusion. "My friend Alexandria used the Emerald Stone to defeat Zeus. *She* fulfilled the prophecy."

"That is not possible." Leon's gray brows furrowed as he thought this over.

"Only a descendant of Zeus may restore the Old Order, as it has been foretold."

"It is true what they say," Leandros said. "The Old Order has been restored, Father."

"We were sent to rescue you," Owen said slowly. "The Queen wants you to come back home."

Zeb recalled the conversation she had with Penélope after being rescued from the Underworld, about the return of Zeus and the war looming on the horizon, with enemies both old and new, and the Queen of Death's advice to rescue King Leon and bring him back to the city of Helena. Did this mean that the prophecy foretold more than just Zeus' defeat? Why did they need to rescue King Leon to fight the war? Penélope was right. The gods had set in motion something much bigger than them, and they could only hope they were on the right side of any upcoming war.

Leon hesitated, as if unwilling to abandon his initial quest on their word alone. "First, we must escape this dreaded island before discussing any further plans. Your friend in the red dress seems to be close to their King and court. Perhaps she may reason with him, or strike a deal to release us."

"Once the King knows where Penélope's loyalties lie, she shall be in the same danger as us," Leandros said tersely. "I fear there is no escaping this island without battle, if bargaining should fail. My helmsman, Mono, here tells me that the rest of the crew who survived fled into the woods, and our ship remains untouched by the shore. If a distraction can be caused and their forces split, we may have a chance to escape, though we cannot be sure our ship shall remain untouched for long."

"And what about Queen Nausicala?" Zeb asked. "If that's really her, shouldn't we bring her back to Helena?"

Leandros shook his head grimly. "If it is true that King Kleomachus has forced her to return, then Queen Nausicala is worse than dead. She is a prisoner too."

30

Lord Iason led Penélope quickly up the stairs, out of the prison, and down the hall. They began walking toward Penélope's room in silence, her heart beating loudly in her ears.

Soon they reached her room. He glanced around, but no one was wandering the corridors, still caught up in the festivities of the day. Penélope supposed they must all be feasting. Iason grasped her hands once they stood outside her door.

"Lady Penélope," Iason said quietly, his voice pained. "I wish to believe you were there by accident, but I heard you speak with them in their native tongue. Mother Gray shall be dealt with separately, for the King has no tolerance for treason."

"You cannot tell the King," Penélope said in panic, tears welling in her eyes. "Mother Gray is innocent. I'm the one who has been trying to meet with the prisoners. But please, Mother Gray had nothing to do with it."

Iason's eyes softened, his hand brushing a strand of hair from her face. "You are very kind, my Lady. That is why I wish to marry you, and to take you back to my home across the Inner Sea."

Penélope stared up at him in surprise just as he gently cradled her face in his hands and kissed her. She pulled away, her mind muddled by his kiss as if she had drunk a strong cup of wine. "But you are betrothed to the Princess Korinna."

His hands froze around her face. "Who told you?"

"Mother Gray," Penélope said.

"That meddling, foolish woman," Iason spat harshly. Then he caught her expectant look and sighed. "It is true, but I was promised to her against my will. The King had arranged our marriage before I was born, for I am heir to the Throne of Mysia, Land of the Keteians, and could unite our forces under one ruler. I have never dreamed of fighting against his wishes before. That is, until I met you."

Before she could protest, he leaned down and kissed her again, pushing her flat against the door, his hands running down her sides and squeezing her waist. Penélope stood frozen as he kissed her, while in her mind's eye, all she could see was the pain etched across Leandros' face.

Behind her, the lock to her door slid open with a click, and with the weight of Iason's body on hers, she stumbled backwards. Iason forcibly steered her to the couch, where she fell on her back as his hands bunched up the fabric of her dress.

"Iason," she said, and as though she had regained some wild will to fight, she placed her hands on his and pushed him away. He ignored her, continuing to lift her dress until his palms gripped her thighs. "Iason, stop."

He buried his face against her neck with a groan. His hands slid up her legs while trailing kisses down the low neckline of her dress. "Penélope, do not tease me."

"Th-this is not right," Penélope stuttered, this time pushing with more force. "You are still betrothed to Korinna."

Her words did not seem to register as he kissed her once more, his hands traveling higher up her thighs. Panic gripped her, and she shoved him away with all her might. Iason scowled, taking her wrists and pinning them by her sides. Penélope kicked out with her legs, and he groaned when her knee connected with his groin.

"Stop fighting me, Penélope," Iason grunted.

"I—don't—want—you," Penélope said between labored breaths as she freed her wrists and scrambled from underneath his strong arms, which struggled to pin her down again.

She ran to the door, but Iason overcame her and shoved her up against the wall. Her face slammed into the wood in a spasm of pain. A warmth trickled down her face and into her mouth, where she tasted the tang of blood.

Iason ran a hand down her side. "Are you certain you will not lie with me, Penélope?"

Penélope could not speak, so she shook her head, salty tears mingling with the blood. Her entire body felt numb, even her face, so that she no longer felt any pain.

"Then you leave me no choice," Iason said with an exaggerated sigh. "I must turn you in to the King for treason. Unless you will change your mind?"

She froze, her stomach dropping nauseatingly. If the King discovered that she had visited the prisoners, he might execute her along with Leandros and the others. But to submit to Iason unwillingly and out of wedlock could be just as damning for her fate on the island as treason itself, not to mention the nausea that rose violently in her throat at the thought of letting Iason touch her like that again.

"Very well," he said when she did not answer, before he took her by the arm.

He forced her out of the room and dragged her down the hall. Her hair had come undone in the struggle, and the blood from her nose had dripped down her chin. She wondered how she looked at that moment, bloodied and distraught, dragged carelessly down the hall like one of the prisoners, and then wondered if anyone would care.

They entered the great doors of the main hall, where the guests of the festival were feasting, and Pyrrhos sang in the center of the couches. The King was seated on his throne, Princess Korinna and Mother Gray on either side of him, an empty couch beside the princess where Iason usually reclined. When they saw Iason barge inside, the King immediately stood up, along with Mother Gray and Korinna, the King's eyes widening on Penélope. Pyrrhos ceased playing with a plucked note cut short as the hall descended into a tense silence.

"What is the meaning of this?" the King said angrily. "Lord Iason, explain yourself!"

Iason held up her arm. She could hardly face the scrutinizing eyes of the guests, the tears in her eyes falling down her face. "I found this woman in the dungeons speaking with the prisoners! Clearly, she is a spy of the enemy."

A gasp ran through the guests. Korinna stared at Penélope in shock, though whether at her bloodied face or Iason's accusations, Penélope could not tell.

The King turned his piercing gaze on her. "Is this true, Lady Penélope?"

"I am not an enemy or a spy!" Penélope argued, trying and failing to free herself from Iason's tight grip on her arms. "The real crime was done by Lord Iason, who tried to dishonor me by forcing himself on me when I was unwilling."

Korinna sucked in a breath. The King glanced between his daughter and Lord Iason, who yanked Penélope's arms behind her back to keep her from struggling. Penélope now noticed Lord Erasmos reclining a few couches from Korinna, eyeing Penélope worriedly.

"That is a lie!" Lord Iason shouted, spit flying from his mouth and hitting her cheek. "From the moment she saw me, this woman has thrown herself at me with the ferociousness of a wild beast, and was dissuaded only with violence."

"Crime, indeed!" the King exclaimed, his fury once more directed on Penélope. "As a guest in my court, your actions are worthy of death."

"No!" Korinna stepped toward her father, her face pale. "Lady Penélope would never have forced herself on Lord Iason. She knows we are betrothed. If anyone has committed a crime, it would be Lord Iason."

Another gasp rippled through the room at Princess Korinna's accusation. The King glanced between them in hesitation, as if reluctant to brush aside Lord Iason's claims but inclined to believe his daughter over anyone else.

"You do not know of what you speak, my dear cousin," Lord Iason said through gritted teeth. "I found this woman in the dungeons speaking with the prisoners in their own tongue. How could she do so if she had indeed been raised in the woods? It is her word against mine!"

The King contemplated for a moment before he raised his scepter and called out, "Bring the prisoners up! Only then shall we settle this dispute once and for all."

Penélope's stomach dropped at the thought of her friends chained and paraded in front of the King. Lord Iason dragged her toward the King, who eyed both of them in distaste, as though irritated at the spectacle interrupting their feast. Korinna's worried gaze traveled over Penélope's face, where the blood had already dried and cracked on her mouth and chin. Mother Gray stood off to the side, completely still and veiled.

Suddenly, the doors opened again. Held between pairs of soldiers were Leandros, Mono, Zeb, Owen, and a fifth prisoner with a white beard and gray hair, all their wrists and ankles bound in chains. Beside the four muscular bodies, Zeb appeared like a wraith, pale and thin, and Penélope's heart ached for him, though she tried not to show it on her face.

Leandros locked eyes with Penélope, and a spasm of shock and anger passed across his face as he saw the state she was in, before his jaw clenched and he kept his eyes on the ground. The guests pointed at the prisoners and stared openly, murmuring amongst themselves. The King smiled grimly, then gestured with a wide sweep of his arm.

"Please welcome our most dangerous criminals to our feast," King Kleomachus said with a sneer. "If you were not already familiar with their faces, you surely know their names, and the crimes they have committed against all of the Phaeacians. Here stands Leon, son of Philoxenos, King of Helena. Beside him is his son, Leandros, and three of his companions. The rest we have killed or put to flight."

Penélope stared at King Leon in shock, seeing the similarities between him and Leandros, the strong build, the square jaw, the long, curling hair, but then noticing the differences, the warmer brown of Leandros' eyes and his fuller mouth, like his mother. She wanted to speak with him about their mission, but there was no way they could risk it now.

"That one was speaking with her," Iason said suddenly, pointing at Zeb, who looked at him and then Penélope in confusion. She recalled that he and Owen would not understand what they were saying.

The King observed the two of them before nodding his head at the guards holding Zeb. One of them pulled out a dagger and held it at his throat. Zeb's eyes widened in fear.

"Stop!" Penélope cried out, tears springing to her eyes. "Don't hurt him!"

"Then Lord Iason speaks the truth," the King said viciously. "You are a spy of the enemy."

She shook her head, the tears spilling down her face. "I'm not a spy. I was sent here by a god to rescue King Leon without the knowledge of my companions. If you had known who I truly was, you would not have allowed me to stay."

"A god?" Owen muttered, wincing when one of the soldiers holding him shoved his back and muttered for him to be silent.

"So she has confessed to treason!" Iason exclaimed almost gleefully, then said to the King, "See, uncle? I would never lead you astray."

But the King ignored him, narrowing his eyes on Penélope. "A god, you say? Then I suppose it was not mere chance that you came upon my daughter in the woods that day?"

Penélope shook her head, desperate to have them believe her. "I happened to be bathing in a river when a young man approached and told me that if I were to be successful in rescuing King Leon, I must find and speak with the Princess of Scheria, so that she may pity me and lead me to the castle. I knew him to be the god Hermes."

Gasps and whispers rose up from the guests once more. Everyone stared at her, including Leandros and her friends. While they had known half the story, the other half she had kept a secret until now.

Lord Iason laughed derisively. "Do you hear how easily she lies? Why would a god send this woman here if they know we are bound by oath to Poseidon not to aid strangers?"

Some of the guests murmured their agreement. The King's brows furrowed as the murmuring rose in pitch until the room was filled with animated discussion and arguments. He closed his eyes, then suddenly opened them and shouted, "Silence!"

The room fell quiet. Penélope held her breath.

"Do you know these prisoners or not?" the King asked Penélope in a low, steady voice.

She lifted her chin defiantly. "I do."

"Penélope is innocent," Leandros cried out roughly. He spoke in the language of the Phaeacians, though Penélope understood every word. "It was I who forced her to accompany me on the quest to rescue King Leon. Her true purpose was to bring back her friend here from the Land of the Dead in exchange for aiding me in rescuing my father."

"Enough!" the King shouted, waving his scepter in the air. "You shall all be executed for treason, and your blood shall cleanse this island of any further pollution!"

"You have ventured to the Land of the Dead and lived to tell the tale?" King Leon said in barely hidden wonder, ignoring King Kleomachus and staring at his son as if he did not know him, then looking at Penélope anew. "Some god must be helping you indeed, my Lady, if this is true."

At this, the crowds burst into chaotic discussion again. Penélope heard snatches of conversation about the impossibility of returning from the Land of the Dead and guesses as to whether Penélope herself might not be a descendant of a god.

The King beat his scepter on the ground repeatedly. "Silence! Silence!"

"Uncle, did I not say—" Iason began.

"You as well, Iason," the King spat, and Iason flinched at his uncle's rebuke, his hands gripping Penélope's hands tighter. Leandros noticed, and defiance flickered in his eyes. "There is one part of this story that is missing, which I failed to realize at first." He paused, then looked at Penélope with barely contained wrath flashing in his eyes. "How did you enter my prison?"

Penélope stood frozen. Everyone waited, realizing that either Penélope had snuck into the prison by herself, or else someone had helped her and committed treason too. Iason began laughing bitterly, ready to reveal the truth, but before he did so, Mother Gray stepped forward before the crowd of guests.

"It was I, King Kleomachus," she said softly, but the silence in the room was so profound every word fell upon the tiled floor like a death sentence amid a courtroom of bated breath.

The King turned his furious gaze on her, a vein bulging in his forehead and his mouth trembling with rage, the words flying from his mouth in halted shouts. *"You—treacherous—witch!"*

Mother Gray tore the veil from her head as if in reply, ignoring the protesting cry of the King as he lunged toward her, held back by Korinna and Lord Erasmos, who had stood up just in time to help Korinna prevent the King from attacking Mother Gray with his swinging gold scepter.

Everyone stared at the face beneath the veil with their breaths held, and Penélope finally understood.

"Princess Nausicala," she whispered.

Mother Gray stood in front of the room, her hair still visibly raven black despite graying streaks, and her eyes as bright green as the Emerald Stone itself. Princess Korinna stared at the aged but undeniably beautiful face, so starkly similar to her own, before sagging against Lord Erasmos in a faint, who helped her sit on one of the couches. Even Lord Iason was silent, his grip on Penélope's arms slacking despite himself.

"I am Nausicala, daughter of King Kleomachus," said Mother Gray, looking around the room with the calm authority only true royalty could muster. "I am descended from King Poliporthes, son of Telemachus and Nausicaa, the son of Odysseus and the daughter of King Alcinous, and standing before you is my son Leon, whom I bore by my husband, King Philoxenos, who died to save me from our enemies in battle. If you wish to kill my son, you shall have to kill me first."

31

WHEN NAUSICALA FINISHED SPEAKING, the room erupted into shouts and cheers and clamoring voices at the sudden return of their princess, whom they had thought had perished in the battle at Helena many years ago. The King had sagged back down upon his throne, his wrinkled, bearded face appearing more old and haggard than ever. His deflated body only vindicated her claim more in the eyes of the people.

But her words had revived the Princess Korinna, who gazed upon Nausicala with new eyes. "Mother–I mean, are you truly Princess Nausicala?"

"She is." They all turned to King Leon, who had shrugged off the soldier's feeble attempts to restrain him. Now that Nausicala had claimed him as her son, the soldiers seemed less inclined to treat him as a common prisoner.

"My son," Nausicala whispered. "I did not think you would recognize me after so many years of separation."

Leon's weathered face hardened, though tears threatened to fall from his dark eyes. "Not if an eternity had passed would I forget the voice of my mother, whose soft singing lulled me to sleep as a babe, as sweet and tender as a thrush."

"Release these prisoners at once," Nausicala ordered the soldiers, ignoring the stifled gasps of the guests. "I shall be returning to my rightful place in Helena with them."

"Enough!" The King roared, leaping to his feet and swaying like a drunk before Lord Iason left Penélope's side to steady him. He shook his scepter at Nausicala. "I will not allow you to step even one foot outside of this palace!"

Nausicala smiled grimly. "You may not keep me locked up here forever, Father."

The King's face nearly spasmed as he gritted out, "I can and I shall."

180

"How could you do this, Papa?" Princess Korinna approached the King, the tremor in her voice a sign of the betrayal she felt. "Nausicala was a princess of our realm. She was the Queen of Helena. She...she is my sister."

A hush fell over the room, and the King blanched at his daughter's words. Suddenly, Penélope realized what she had missed all along, since the moment the god Hermes encountered her by the banks of the river and commanded her to find the princess of Scheria.

"It was you," she said, and Nausicala glanced at her in surprise. "You were the one Hermes told me to find."

Nausicala took a step closer to her. "A god spoke to you of me?"

"He told me to find the princess of the Phaeacians among the maidens, because her heart will be most moved by my distress. He said that with her help, I would be led to King Leon. But I thought the princess was Korinna, not..."

"Not *Mother Gray*," Nausicala finished, the name spoken coldly. "No one knew, of course. When my father forced me to return to Scheria after the battle, he would have kept me in the dungeons if my mother had not interceded on my behalf. But he would not allow me to live amongst the court as I once did, so he had me veiled and in charge of the women of the household. And once Princess Korinna was born and our mother dead soon after, I was to raise my sister as heir to the throne. My name was a reminder that a part of me had indeed died that day, when my husband and firstborn son perished by the Scherian sword."

"I knew you had not died that day, Mother," King Leon said roughly. "Though many had tried to convince me of it, I knew you would not leave the city to its fate after Father and Alexandros died defending it."

"Oh my sweet boy." Nausicala approached King Leon, their eyes shining with tears. She held his face between her hands and smiled. "I never once left your side, whether you knew it or not."

Then they embraced, Nausicala pressing her son's head against her chest as if he were still a boy, her eyes shut tightly as the tears slowly rolled down her cheeks. When they separated, Nausicala walked over to Leandros, who stiffened when her hand stroked a curling lock of hair beside his face.

"You have traveled far to come here, grandson, to the very ends of the world where no living soul dares to tread, and you have survived to tell the tale," Nausicala said, then paused. "Few mortals have done so, the only other I know of being one of our forefathers, Odysseus, son of Läertes. You have honored our name well, my dear."

Penélope nearly gasped. "The Queen of Death!" All eyes in the room turned to her. "In the Underworld, I spoke with the Queen of Death in the Grove by the borders of the Styx. She told me that first I must save the King of Helena, but that his life would save another. I think she meant you, Nausicala, because before this, we thought you were dead."

Her gaze grew troubled upon her. "Much has the world changed if gods speak openly with mortals like yourself, Lady Penélope. I sense that something much greater and more perilous moves the hands of the gods. We must release these men and wash and feed them, and then you must tell me all you know."

"This is preposterous!" Lord Iason left the King's side and suddenly grasped Penélope's arm again, raising it violently. Leandros nearly rushed forward, but Nausicala and Leon prevented him. "Is this how you punish treason, uncle? By rewarding them with food and warm beds to sleep in? I demand retribution! I wish to see blood spilled!"

The King slammed his scepter on the ground, though he did not rise from his throne. "Release the woman, Iason." Penélope stumbled when Lord Iason dropped her arm and pushed her away resentfully. "But you are right. These prisoners have committed treason against the kingdom of Scheria. Their fate shall be the same we allot to all those who betray the sacred laws of our realm." He rose shakily to his feet. "Tomorrow these prisoners shall be sacrificed to the god Poseidon, which we can only hope will stay his wrath."

"Papa—" Korinna entreated, her eyes wide and horrified.

"Be silent, girl," he spat. "These matters do not concern you. Justice falls upon the head of the King to dispense."

"Father, please," Nausicala whispered. "You cannot do this."

His face spasmed once more with pain, before hardening in his rage. "And *you*–you, Nausicala, shall be executed alongside them if you dare stand against me once more."

Everyone watched in shocked silence. The guests all glanced at each other hesitantly, as though reluctant to agree with the King's decision to execute Nausicala, who was beloved by the Phaeacians as their princess for many years, and whose death they had mourned for twice as long. But they did not openly show their disapproval of the King, and being fearful of the wrath of the gods, watched and waited instead to see how the events would unfold.

Penélope's eyes burned with tears. She did not know how to get them out of the mess she had made. Why did she listen to Hermes? Why did she follow the advice of the gods who always kept their own counsel? She wished one of them would come out of the sky right now and guide her. But had the Queen of Death not warned her of this? Who else, after all, would she condemn to her fate?

Penélope faced King Kleomachus, knowing in her heart what she had to do, even if the sacrifice would hurt someone she loved. But it was the only way to save him and his people. *Every man has his price.* "The Queen of Death has ordered me to rescue the King of Helena, and no one will stand in my way. But the oath of the Phaeacians to Poseidon still holds, which you unknowingly broke when you accepted my supplication. Therefore, we are in your debt, and only a sacrifice dear to the Helenes can clear your people of the offense they have committed in the name of hospitality. And I believe this sacrifice is great enough to clear the crimes of treason which began with the kidnapping of Nausicala by King Philoxenos all those years ago, and which have finally come upon King Leon, Leandros, and my friends."

"Penélope, no! Do not strike a deal with him," Leandros said harshly, but the King silenced him with a raised hand.

Then the King turned a curious gaze upon her. "And what do you suggest as this *great sacrifice*?"

She took a deep breath and lifted her chin. "To balance the theft of your firstborn daughter, Nausicala, I suggest that when the time comes, Leandros shall give up his firstborn daughter to the Phaeacians, where she will be married to one of your choosing."

"Penélope," Leandros whispered in shock, but Penélope ignored him, her heart aching.

The King was already grinning, his eyes flashing triumphantly at the thought of so perfect a revenge. "And how can I be sure of this sacrifice if the prince is not already wedded? Your oath will mean nothing if he never has a child to give."

At that exact moment, she heard a voice whisper in her mind, the terrible cold voice of Death, as if being so near to it meant she could hear her more clearly.

When the time comes, you must sacrifice a love you have not yet known.

She felt numb as she spoke her next words, the tears falling from her eyes as she realized the full extent of what the Queen of Death had meant when she said Penélope would sacrifice a love she had not yet known. She hadn't meant

Leandros at all. She had meant their *child*.

"He is not married," Penélope said slowly, "but he is betrothed. To me." Gasps rose up in the crowds. Leandros stared at her, silent and pale. "And I have accepted. His sacrifice will be mine as well. Our firstborn daughter will be given away in her first marriageable year. I swear by the dreaded waters of the Styx that this oath will not be broken."

Korinna stifled a gasp with her hand, and Nausicala turned her wide green eyes to Penélope. But it was too late. She had sworn on the Styx, and not even the gods could break such an oath. The King grinned, lifting his hands to address the room.

"It seems there shall be two weddings tomorrow, my friends!" the King cried out, immediately receiving an explosion of shouts and applause, though Penélope, Leandros, and the others near the throne remained quiet. "Lord Leandros with the Lady Penélope, and Lord Iason with my daughter, the Princess Korinna!"

Once the cheers subsided, Korinna placed a hand on her father's shoulder, and he lowered his arms, glancing at his daughter in surprise.

"I will not marry Lord Iason, Papa," Korinna said quietly.

Fury struck the King's face, while Iason froze beside him and stared at Korinna in shock. "That is not your decision—" the King began.

But the princess interrupted him. "No, it was not. It was never my decision. And I accepted because I did not wish to hurt you. But I shall not marry a man who has so willfully dishonored me."

"Dishonored?" Lord Iason repeated in disbelief, glancing angrily at Penélope. His handsome features, twisted in rage and panic, had never looked so ugly. "It was *she* who dishonored *me*. She forced herself upon me after I found her in the prison cells, hoping that if I lay with her, I would keep her crime a secret."

"That is a lie!" Leandros shouted roughly. "Penélope would never force herself upon any man, let alone on one so vile as you."

"Ah, it would seem I was not the first to be entrapped by her wiles!" Iason said with a sneer at Leandros. "But it is my word against hers. King Kleomachus, you have known me for my whole life. I would never betray my betrothal to Korinna."

"But you did." Korinna's voice shook as she faced Iason's seething glare. "I saw you kiss the Lady Penélope outside the orchard by the vineyards, where I happened to be walking among the vines to eat some of the grapes that were missed in the harvest. She pushed you away afterward. I truly believe that the

Lady Penélope would not compromise her honor or mine, but regardless of what happened today, it would not change your first betrayal."

Lord Iason blinked rapidly, as if he were about to cry, then threw himself at the feet of Korinna and the King. "Please, forgive me! You have no idea the power that woman holds! She is a viper! A siren! An enchantress!"

Penélope was suddenly reminded of what Calypso had told her when they had bathed together. *For any woman may have the intelligence, wit, or daring to match those of men, but there is no wile in the world that can defeat the charms of a woman.* She had the strange urge to laugh at the humbling state of Lord Iason, but quickly felt her humor dissipate when Lord Iason turned and lunged toward her.

She screamed as he attacked her, but his outstretched hands never made contact, and he fell to the ground, cradling his face where Mono had swung his fist into Iason's jaw. He shook out his hand and flashed his yellow grin.

"No man touches the Lady Penélope against her will," Mono said, bowing his head.

Penélope nearly gasped when she realized that the gift of language Hermes had bestowed upon her would allow her to understand the crew. She nearly hugged him when Iason stirred at their feet and tried to stand up, only to be pushed down by Mono's wooden leg against his chest.

"Thank you, Mono," Penélope said softly.

"It is an honor to serve you, my Lady."

Meanwhile, Lord Iason had crawled out from under Mono's wooden leg and back to the King's bejeweled sandals, who looked down upon his nephew with disdain. "Please, uncle, do not cast me away on the word of two women."

"But you see, Iason," the King said, "this is not just a woman. This is my daughter, and if she has deemed you unworthy of her hand, then so it is. Guards! Escort my nephew back to his quarters, and see to it that he returns to his mother with a full account of the proceedings here."

With that, a retinue of soldiers approached and dragged a protesting Lord Iason away from the hall. His green eyes fixed on Penélope, and he snarled, "Witch! Curse you, Penélope! This is your fault! You shall pay for your crime against me and mine!"

His shouts were cut off when the doors slammed shut on his twisting, raving figure. Once he was gone, Penélope felt that she could breathe again. She turned and saw that Korinna embraced her father and showered kisses on his balding head.

The King gently calmed her. "Now, now, my Korinna, you must still marry. You are of marriageable age, after all, and I cannot depart this world until I know my daughter's care has been passed onto better hands."

"Oh, do not speak so!" Korinna said, hugging the King's shoulders tightly. "I wish to stay in the palace with you, Papa, and carry on as I have with my weaving and my friends, and care for you in your old age. If I marry, I must leave all this for somewhere new. I must leave *you*. I would be miserable."

"If I may," Penélope said, stepping toward the throne hesitantly.

"You may not," the King replied coldly.

Korinna squeezed his arm. "Papa, let Lady Penélope speak. She has already righted her wrong and therefore must still be treated as a guest."

At her calm, wise words, the King's eyes softened, and he grudgingly nodded his head at Penélope. "Very well. Say what you must."

"If the Princess Korinna does not wish to leave the palace," Penélope said slowly, "then perhaps she may marry one whose situation does not require her to? Let us say, a lord of noble lineage who bears no grand title and may give up his home elsewhere to come and live here with the Princess and the King?"

The King hitched a brow. "And who might that be?"

Penélope smiled, and she swore Korinna's eyes filled with hope. "Lord Erasmos."

32

Clear water poured from the large vase and into the bath like a stream of silver. Penélope stood beside Korinna, both of them naked and shivering in the cold morning air filtering inside the princess' quarters. The pale light of dawn streamed across the marble floor covered in soft, woven rugs, where two identical bronze bathtubs sat waiting for them.

"Please, enter your baths," Dora said, stoppering the vase. She smiled at Korinna and Penélope. "This water shall prepare you for the sacred bond of marriage."

Penélope and Korinna hesitantly stepped inside their respective bathtubs, the princess reaching out to hold Penélope's hand to steady herself while they gently lowered themselves into the water. They both glanced at each other and laughed nervously.

"I cannot believe I am marrying today," Korinna said with a shake of her head. "I have wondered my whole life how it would be, but nothing could have prepared me. And I never thought I would marry anyone besides Lord Iason."

"I'm sorry," Penélope said automatically, feeling responsible for the new arrangements as well as putting an end to the old ones.

Korinna lightly slapped her arm. "Don't be! I am happy, for the first time in my life. Truly happy." She did look happy, her face glowing in the firelight still burning in the hearth and warming the bathwater.

"Lord Erasmos will be lucky to have you as his wife," Penélope said with a knowing smile, for it was what Korinna had told her when she thought the King had arranged Penélope and Erasmos to wed.

"Could you tell then?" Korinna asked, blushing.

"That you were jealous? Or that you were madly in love with Erasmos?"

"Penélope!" the princess cried, sounding scandalized, though she could not hide a smile. "Both, I suppose, if you must know. I can never thank you enough for convincing my father that Lord Erasmos would make a good husband for me."

"I am just glad that Lord Iason left," Penélope said, nearly shivering at the thought of what had almost happened yesterday.

Princess Korinna's gaze wandered sadly over Penélope's face, where a bruise had blossomed in the night around one of her eyes and across the bridge of her nose. After the wedding arrangements had been approved by the King, Penélope and her friends were pardoned for all crimes. Then, in keeping with wedding traditions, the men and women were separated and retired to different parts of the palace. Penélope and Korinna had slept in the royal quarters in preparation for the ceremonies today, when Dora had carefully washed the blood from her face and applied a healing salve.

"My cousin has always been prideful," Korinna said, then she shook her head angrily. "But I never thought he was capable of such violence against a woman so sweet and honorable as yourself."

Penélope remained silent, a strange mixture of anger, shame, and guilt weighing on her as the visions of that terrible night flashed through her mind, always returning to the agony on Leandros' face, the betrayal that she had caused by entertaining Lord Iason.

Korinna glanced at Penélope curiously. "And what of this Lord Leandros? You have already been betrothed to him all this time!"

It was Penélope's turn to blush, but she played it off with a smile and said cryptically, "I suppose you were not the only one to harbor a forbidden love after all."

"Ah, you shall keep this a secret too?" Korinna teased, then her brow grew thoughtful. "I knew when I taught you how to weave that you knew more than you were letting on. But I could never have imagined the full story behind the wild girl of the woods."

"Neither could I of the princesses of Scheria," Penélope said.

Korinna smiled sadly. "Ah, yes. It is a shame I discovered Mother Gray's true identity on the eve of her departure. I wish she could remain here and we could be reunited as sisters, and she could teach me all she knows of the palace and how to be queen one day."

Penélope rested a comforting hand on Korinna's slender arm. "You already know everything there is to know about the palace, and the rest you will learn in time. You will make a wonderful queen one day."

"And you as well, Lady Penélope," Korinna said with an encouraging smile, but the words hit Penélope so forcefully that she almost flinched. She had not fully digested the reality she had accepted, that by marrying Leandros, she had placed herself next in line for the throne of Helena.

Dora soon returned with several other attendants, lifting them out of the bath and drying them roughly with towels. They sat Penélope and Korinna down on cushions and began rubbing their skin with scented olive oil. Dora had braided their hair the night before and now unfurled them, their curls cascading down their shoulders. Then she wove flowers and jewels into the curls, pinning them in place.

"I will try to cover this," Dora said, lightly brushing the bridge of her nose.

Penélope reached out for Dora's arm. "There's no need."

"No?"

She shook her head. "We both have scars. I do not want to hide them from him."

"Very well." Dora rummaged in her chest for a wooden stick and lined her eyes with kohl, then dabbed red pigment on her cheeks and lips. "There. Now you can be dressed."

Both of them were slipped into white gowns of heavy, silky fabric, Korinna's dress dragging an elaborate train and a body with twice as many folds as Penélope's to distinguish her royalty. Then their handmaidens worked to sew jewels and flowers on the fabric, so that they glimmered as they moved in the growing light of the early morning.

Lastly, Dora lowered a saffron-yellow veil over Penélope's head, covering her face. Korinna and Penélope stared at each other, then burst into another fit of laughter.

"Nervous are we, girls?"

They both turned at the new voice. Nausicala stood in the doorway. She no longer wore her dark veil, but her gown was made of dark purple fabric, a reminder that she was still in mourning, and perhaps would always be. She beheld the two of them with a radiant smile, and for a moment, Penélope could glimpse a young Nausicala, in love with a handsome, wandering prince from across the seas, determined to follow him into the unknown. Penélope wondered how she had had the courage to leave her home and everything she knew behind for love.

Nausicala eyed Penélope as if she could read her thoughts. "This day marks the first step on your journey to becoming a woman. By tonight, you both shall be wedded, and your consummation of that marriage will bring life into this world."

Penélope's stomach twisted at the thought, and she glanced at Korinna, but the other girl merely blushed behind her veil and lowered her face to hide a pleased smile. She had momentarily forgotten that the most important aspect of marriage had traditionally been childbearing, and wondered if Leandros would force her to comply. After all, they did swear an oath to give their firstborn daughter over in marriage, so they would need to consummate the marriage at some point if they did not wish to enrage the gods in breaking it.

"But first," Nausicala said, "you shall offer sacrifices to the goddess of the hunt for protecting your maidenhead. Then we will feast in the hall, before the grooms carry you off to your new life."

Without further ceremony, Nausicala led them down the hall and across the palace, passing through the gold front doors, across the porch made of bronze, past the silver columns, then down the lane snaking around the warehouses of textiles and grain until they reached a large temple at the bottom of the hill, made from the same bronze as the palace.

Penélope followed Nausicala and Korinna up the stairs and inside the gleaming doors, where young priestesses dressed in robes the same saffron-yellow as their veils guided them inside to the inner sanctum. Behind the altar stood a towering bronze statue of Artemis, her hair crowned, bows strapped on her right shoulder, and deer prancing at her feet. In the dim, flickering firelight, her painted eyes seemed to settle on them as they approached.

The priestesses piled olive wood and bones wrapped in fat upon the altar before her, then lowered a torch to the wood, where a fire sparked to life a moment later. Sweet-smelling smoke rose from the fire as the fat melted and charred on the wood.

"Now is the time you must shed your girlhood by offering sacrifices to the virgin huntress," Nausicala said, then turned to Korinna. "What shall you offer the goddess, Princess Korinna?"

Korinna hesitated, looking down at her hands, where she held a small wooden figurine of a woman in a miniature cloth dress that seemed haphazardly woven by a young girl just learning to work the loom for the first time. She kissed the top of the doll's head, then dropped the doll in the fire, before taking a step back and hastily wiping tears from her eyes.

"And you, Lady Penélope?"

Penélope did not have anything from her childhood to give, but she had decided that there was one sacrifice which would substitute for it best. She nodded at Dora, who stood off to the side with the other handmaidens and women of the household. Dora came forward with a pair of scissors, while Penélope gently lifted the veil from the back of her head. With an expert twirl of her fingers, Dora twisted her hair into one thick lock and with the scissors sheared off half her length near her shoulders.

She instantly felt a weight leave from her, though she did not know if it was the weight of her hair that had once reached her lower back or of her past life that she was still holding onto.

Dora handed her the twist of hair, and with a shaky breath, Penélope walked forward to the fire, which already burned high in licking red flames. She threw the hair inside, which caught fire instantly, then stepped away.

Once their sacrifices had charred, the priestesses doused the fire with pitchers of water. The wood and sacrifices hissed, filling the room with steam. Then Nausicala stood before them and showered purified water over their heads with an olive branch.

"Now go forth, ready for your new lives," Nausicala said. "The wedding ceremony has just begun."

And as they bowed and turned, the women accompanying them began to sing, their voices lifted high and sweet in the warmth of the morning sun:

> *"I sing of Artemis with golden shaft,*
> *the loudly sounding august virgin maid,*
> *for deer she shoots and arrow-darts her craft,*
> *the sister to Apollo Golden-Blade,*
> *who over shadowed hills and windy peaks,*
> *delights in chase, her golden bow pulled taut,*
> *and sending darts she causes fearful shrieks,*
> *then tremble tops of mountains held aloft,*
> *grim cries of beasts in tangled woodland knoll,*
> *then quakes the earth and sea where fishes shoal!"*

33

THAT NIGHT, A GREAT feast was held outdoors on a grassy field beneath canvas tents, lit by many lamps held aloft by servants lining the perimeter. All of the women sat on couches separate from the men in large circles. Nausicala reclined between Korinna and Penélope, surrounded by the rest of the female household and distant relatives.

In the middle of their couches danced a group of young girls dressed as bear cubs, performing the ritual dance of maidenhood. Penélope watched mesmerized as they twirled and leaped in perfect unison, imitating wild bears frolicking in the woods. As the dance went on, they shed their bear costumes and returned to dancing as human girls, representing the transition from maidenhood to womanhood in marriage.

Two of the girls broke off from the group and approached Korinna and Penélope. The dancers took them by the hand and dragged them to the center of the couches, where the other girls surrounded them excitedly. Korinna and Penélope held hands as the dancers circled them in formation, singing the hymn to Artemis, goddess of the hunt and protector of childhood.

Slowly, they were led beyond the circle of couches where a group of young boys dressed as soldiers and dancing to a fighting song surrounded the tall, well-built figures of Erasmos and Leandros. All of the men and women rose from their couches and, at long last, mingled together as they followed the two groups of dancers to where the King sat on a bronze throne, observing the ceremony.

First Korinna was led by one dancer toward the King, while Erasmos emerged from the group of boy dancers, dressed in pristine white robes and decorated with a garland of different colored flowers. They stood in front of the King, facing each other. Then Nausicala came forward and lifted the yellow veil from Korinna's face. Erasmos beheld her with a blush, his eyes wandering over her face with loving tenderness. Penélope could not help but smile.

"May Hera and Hymen be my witness," the King Kleomachus spoke, his voice ringing out clear in the still night, "and invest in me the power to join this man and this woman into the sacred bond of marriage, with the promise to be of one flesh, to share one life together, and remain faithful until death renders their oaths fulfilled."

Then Nausicala brought forth two gold rings inset with emeralds. Erasmos slid the smaller ring on Korinna's left hand. The princess trembled and laughed nervously as she struggled to fit the other ring on his crooked finger, broken more than once from wrestling. They both smiled coyly at each other, then Erasmos took her hands in his and laid a gentle kiss on her lips.

All the guests applauded and cried out their blessings as Erasmos lifted the princess in his arms and carried her away. The handmaidens of Princess Korinna followed the newlyweds back towards the palace, where they disappeared inside, headed for Korinna's royal quarters. Penélope watched them go with a twisting feeling in her chest.

She hardly finished clapping for the princess when Nausicala led her forward to the throne, where Leandros already stood, his dark eyes lowered, the white robes upon his shoulders accentuating his tanned, muscular arms, and his brown hair and beard brushed into oiled curls. Her breath caught at his handsome face, cleaned of the dirt and grime of several nights in prison, the white scar running down his eye, nose, and lip only a contrast to the warmth in his brown eyes.

Nausicala walked behind Penélope and lifted her veil from her face. Leandros saw her shorter hair, and his eyes widened ever so slightly, but otherwise he showed no emotion on his face as he took her hands in his.

"Before we commence with the vows, first the agreed-upon oath shall be sworn," King Kleomachus said, his voice harboring a hint of a sneer. "By this unbreakable oath, your vows shall be forever bound with your promise to give away your firstborn daughter to the Phaeacians in her first marriageable year, as punishment for the crimes of your forefather, King Philoxenos, and the kidnapping of the Princess Nausicala."

Leandros' hands tightened on hers imperceptibly. She looked up at him and saw in surprise that his eyes were filled with sorrow. Distantly, she felt tears slide down her cheeks, but she locked eyes with Leandros and held her chin firm, determined not to appear daunted. The faintest smile hovered over his mouth as he gazed upon her, and in that moment, Penélope knew that whatever happened between them, or however the future unfolded, he would be there to protect her, loyal to the very end.

The King turned to Leandros. "Do you, Leandros, son of Leon, swear on the dreaded waters of the Styx never to break this oath?"

A muscle in his jaw flickered. "I swear it."

Then the King looked at Penélope. "And do you, Penélope, daughter of Estela, swear on the dreaded waters of the Styx never to break this oath?"

"I swear it," she whispered.

"Then may Hera and Hymen be my witness and invest in me the power to join this man and this woman into the sacred bond of marriage, with the promise to be of one flesh, to share one life together, and remain faithful until death renders their oaths fulfilled!"

King Leon stepped forward with the two gold rings, this time inset with glowing sapphires. She saw Mono, Zeb, and Owen behind him in the crowd of men, watching with silent, grave expressions. Penélope's hand shook as Leandros slid the ring on her finger, the weight of the solid metal settling like her doom, though his calloused hands were gentle around hers. She held his hand and slid the bigger ring on his finger.

They both looked up at each other. Penélope could not stop the tears from flowing down her face. She closed her eyes, wishing that they were not in front of a crowd of unfamiliar faces, wishing her parents were there to witness her marriage, instead of being another world away, ignorant of how much was about to change.

"Πηνελόπη," Leandros murmured. She opened her eyes and looked up. He tightened his hold on her hands. "Ἀμείνων πολέων ἀνδρῶν καὶ ἀρίστη γυναικῶν εἷς"

She stared at him. He said the words in Greek, but she knew right away what it meant, and not just because of the gift of language. *You are braver than many men and bravest of women.*

Those were the same words Mono had told her in the captain's cabin all those weeks ago, when she had saved him from the cyclops. And wasn't that more dangerous after all? If she could face a monstrous serpent, the wrath of the gods, and a murderous cyclops, could she not kiss the man she was about to marry?

But somehow, in the face of this, all of those monsters paled, like nightmares faded in the morning when reality came crashing down. Somehow, this was truly more terrifying.

"Your vows can only be sealed with a kiss," the King said, scarcely hiding his impatience.

Penélope nodded. Leandros hesitated, then leaned in. She closed her eyes. His mouth was on hers a moment later, a soft brush before it was gone. She opened her eyes, then let out a cry as Leandros scooped her up in his arms effortlessly without warning, leading her away from the tent and the applauding guests, who sang songs about love and marriage while Leandros carried her back to their new quarters, where a wide couch had been decked out in luscious fur blankets and pillows covered in woven cloth.

He set her down carefully, and she immediately turned away, wiping the tears from her face. She struggled to take the veil off her head, where it was pinned in place, and the tears fell thicker and faster when she could not take it off, blurring her vision.

"Here," Leandros said gently, moving her hands away from her veil. "Let me help you."

"I can do it," Penélope shot back, trying to shove him away, her hands still unable to remove the veil from her head without tearing her hair.

"Penélope, please, stop fighting me."

"Why?" Penélope demanded, whirling on him. "Because you're my husband now? And I have to do what you tell me?"

Leandros raised a brow. "No. Because I'm your husband now, and therefore it is my duty to help you when you need it."

"Well, maybe I didn't want a husband!"

The moment the words flew past her mouth, she began to cry, sinking to the ground with a shuddering sob. Leandros watched her with a pained, helpless look, the same look he had given her when he threw her an apple on the pirate ship and declared his love for her. And had she not fallen in love too? Had she not been resisting it from the moment she laid eyes upon him, convinced it was too good to be true, then terrified of actually losing herself to the feeling she had long dreamed of finding in every book she read?

"I regret that you find me so unsatisfactory as a husband, given the circumstances," Leandros said, sounding rather hurt. "I know you rejected my earlier advances, but I had thought, once or twice, when we spoke on Ogygia, that perhaps you felt the same." He broke off, shaking his head. "I suppose I was wrong."

"No, you weren't wrong," Penélope said, frustration lancing her voice. She caught the hope in his eyes and sighed. "You don't understand. I've wanted to fall in love since I knew what love was, when I saw my parents dancing in the kitchen together, still in love after all those years. I've wanted to fall in love since I read about Odysseus returning home and embracing his wife after twenty years at sea. But when it comes to marriage..."

"Do your people not marry?" Leandros asked dubiously.

"No, they do." Penélope felt the tears well in her eyes again, and she wiped at them angrily. "I don't know why I'm so sad. It's stupid, I know, but I've always imagined how it would be. Where I come from, if a man and a woman wish to be married, the man usually goes down on one knee and proposes. And when he asks her to marry, she can say yes or no. Then, among my people, there's a wedding in a church, where the bride walks down the aisle with her father, who gives her away to the groom in front of the altar. A priest usually officiates and the couple say their vows, exchange rings, and then seal their union with a kiss."

Leandros stared at her strangely. "A *church?*"

"It's like a temple, but different," Penélope said hesitantly, wondering how much of her world she should divulge to Leandros. "My religion only worships one god." At his shocked face, she continued hurriedly, "But it's not just about religion. My parents, my family—everyone would be present to witness it. There would be a huge party and then we would go on our honeymoon—"

"A *honey moon?*"

"It's like a vacation, but for newlyweds." She saw his helpless face and took a deep breath. "See? The point is that I was always imagining how my wedding day would go, and I guess it's hard to accept that I will never experience it as I had always dreamed it would be."

"Ah," Leandros said, nodding his head slowly. "I understand. You feel as though in leaving your old life behind, you have also left a part of yourself, or perhaps your entire self, and you are grieving for the life that you would have lived if you had stayed, but now will never know."

"Well, no—" Penélope paused. "Actually, yes, that's exactly how I feel. As if a version of myself died the moment I chose this life. But that's my fate, I suppose. The Queen of Death warned me that by saving King Leon's life, I might save another, but at great cost. I accepted my fate, knowing there would be consequences. Even Calypso told me so. *Your fate is to love.*"

Leandros stared at her in wonder. "There truly is no other woman on earth like you, Penélope. I apologize for dragging you into my life, which has only brought you danger and pain."

She shook her head, her eyes burning. "Don't be. It was my choice."

"You know, you need not feel ashamed to mourn your old life." He paused when she did not speak, the tears lodging any response in her throat. "Come. Let me help you with your veil."

Her shoulders sagged at his soft brown eyes and persistent, gentle voice. His strong arms remained still at his sides, waiting. She nodded her head silently and turned around. Leandros came up behind her, his fingers gingerly slipping the pins out of her hair and sliding the veil off her head, dropping it to the floor. She massaged her scalp where the pins had left her sore.

Leandros' knuckles brushed her neck as he sifted through her curls. "You cut your hair."

"Yes," Penélope said, sniffling. "I sacrificed it to the goddess of the hunt."

She turned around, surprised to find him so close to her, though a part of her did not mind. In fact, a part of her wanted him to grab her and bring her to the couch, though the rest of her recoiled from the mere thought of it. He reached out to her, and she flinched. His hand paused midair, ghosting her nose and eyes where the bruise showed stark against her skin.

"What did he do to you?" he asked, his voice hard.

"He tried to lie with me," Penélope said, surprised by her stark honesty but no longer caring, her exhaustion from the last few days seeping into her bones and making her feel careless.

Leandros' eyes flashed. "That bastard."

"When he caught me in the prison speaking with you, he brought me to my room and kissed me," Penélope confessed. "That wasn't the first time either. Like Korinna said, he tried another time, but I refused him. He said he wanted to marry me, but I knew he only wanted to take advantage of me. I played along because I didn't want to risk my position in the court. I did that in the end anyway, it seems."

"Do not blame yourself when a snake bites," Leandros said grimly. "It is in his nature, after all."

"When he brought me back to my room, he tried to lie with me. But when I pushed him away and ran to the door, he attacked me. That's when this happened."

She gently prodded her nose and winced at the tenderness. "The swelling will go down with time."

His lips quirked into a smile. "At least it shall not leave a scar."

Penélope lifted her hand and brushed her fingertips against his cheek. Her eyes filled with unwilling tears and his smile faded. "I'm sorry."

"Why?"

"For promising your firstborn daughter to the King without asking you first."

Leandros took her hand and gently reeled her in, then wrapped his strong arms around her. She sank into his embrace, her eyelids closing heavily, the weight of their combined fate settling on her. "You did what you had to do to save my father. We are forever in your debt."

Suddenly, a thought occurred to her, and she pulled back, her heart beating fast. "I don't mean to break our oath, but tonight..."

He avoided her gaze, his cheeks red. "You must rest tonight. There will be time to fulfill our oaths. First, we must focus on returning home and bringing King Leon and Princess Nausicala with us."

Penélope nodded in agreement, feeling lighter than she had for months. "First, we return home."

34

Penélope woke up alone and still in her wedding gown. She looked at the floor where the haphazardly made bed of fur rugs and pillows was empty. Leandros had refused to sleep in the bed with her, claiming that her rest was more important, and promptly fell asleep on the floor.

She froze at a knock at the door, then a familiar voice muffled through the wood. "It is Dora, my dear! Are you awake yet?"

Penélope hurriedly slipped out of her dress and dropped it on the floor. "Yes, come in!"

Her old handmaid scurried inside with her makeup chest and other toiletries. Behind her, two other female servants hauled in vases of water to the bronze tub by the hearth. Dora caught her confused expression and laughed.

"Today the King wishes to say goodbye with a feast before you depart these shores," Dora explained, gently helping Penélope out of bed, a small smile on her face when she saw the wedding dress cast carelessly on the ground. "You must be cleaned and dressed before the sun reaches midday. There will be song and dance and generally much merriment. The King has never been in such a festive mood."

"I wonder why," Penélope said dryly, recalling the glinting revenge in his eyes when she offered her firstborn daughter as compensation for the kidnapping of Nausicala.

Dora merely raised a brow and scrubbed her body in silence inside the bronze tub before pouring olive oil across her skin and scraping all her limbs with the bronze strigil.

Once Penélope was dried and dressed in her signature royal blue robes, Dora pinned up her hair in elaborate braids and adorned her face with kohl, colored

199

pigments, and jewelry—more gifts of sapphire and gold from the King and Princess Korinna. She was then led to the great hall, where she had attended the first feast of the festival. Zeb and Owen were already there, standing near the empty throne, where Nausicala stood with Korinna, who spoke with them excitedly.

"Ah, there she is!" Owen said, slinging an arm around her shoulder, before identical curious glances from Nausicala and Korinna caused him to drop it back by his side. "Sorry. Penélope is a good friend. That's all."

Penélope ignored the glances her way and hugged Owen properly, her eyes pricking with tears, though she did not feel as heavy with sorrow as she had yesterday. "I've missed you, Owen."

Zeb hugged her next. "How are you?"

She nodded with a deep sigh. "As good as I'll be given the circumstances." Then she glanced around, surprised to find herself automatically fidgeting with the gold ring on her left hand. She balled her hands in fists at her sides. "Where is Lord Leandros?"

"He is with the King, though they should be returning any moment now," Princess Korinna said happily. She had not stopped smiling since Penélope had seen her, and when Penélope raised a brow at her, she blushed. It seemed that, unlike for Penélope, the princess' wedding night had been more productive.

"It is customary after a royal wedding for the grooms to hunt with the King," Nausicala explained with a smile, reminding Penélope of her breathtaking, effortless beauty. It was no wonder King Philoxenos had fallen in love with her the moment he saw her. "Lord Erasmos is also with King Kleomachus and Lord Leandros."

As if they had been summoned by their names, the doors of the halls opened, and the King entered with a new energy in his step. Following him were Lord Leandros and Erasmos, along with a troop of lords—including King Leon and Mono—some of whom had competed in the festival games, all still dressed in their hunting gear, their cheeks red from exertion.

"Ladies and gentlemen!" the King called out to the guests mingling in murmuring clusters, though they all stood at attention and hailed their King. "Our hunt has been successful in providing for our feast. Lord Erasmos, as skilled with the bow as in wrestling, shot down a beautiful stag, while Lord Leandros trapped a wild boar and slayed it with his sword. Please, join me in congratulating the newlyweds, Lord Leandros and Lady Penélope, and Lord Erasmos with my lovely daughter, the Princess Korinna!"

Everyone burst into cheers and excited conversation, while the King led Leandros and Erasmos over to them. Penélope tried to catch Leandros' eye, but he hardly glanced her way, standing by her side in a stony silence.

"Please, sit, everyone!" The King took his place on the throne. "The feast is about to begin!"

Penélope dutifully took her place on the couch between Leandros and Zeb. The others all found a seat, and soon the servants brought in platters of cooked vegetables and seafood accompanied by glasses of wine, saving them from an awkward silence. She glanced at Leandros once more, but he did not seem to notice. Across the couches, Nausicala caught the interaction, and Penélope flushed in embarrassment. Was this how husbands treated their wives in Helena? Were all those words Leandros had spoken in private merely a lie to get her into bed with him? Or worse—was he in fact angry that they had *not* lain together after the ceremony?

"Now that we are all gathered here, I would like to discuss the matter of your departure," the King said after they had dug into their meals and Pyrrhos began singing a song about Helen's flight with Paris to Troy.

"You *shall* allow us to depart, will you not?" King Leon asked pointedly.

The King waved his hand. "Yes, yes, Lord Leon, you need not fret. Our deal will not be broken from my end. I only wish to provide your crew with enough resources for the return journey."

"That is very kind of you, King Kleomachus," Penélope said, inclining her head.

"If my daughter Nausicala is indeed to sail with you, then she shall require a small retinue of guards who shall protect her, and only her, as well as a handmaiden of her choice. That is my one contingency if my daughter shall once more depart these shores and leave her father."

"And these guards," King Leon said, eyeing the King suspiciously, "they will not be secretly plotting your revenge against me or my son?"

King Kleomachus leveled him with a dry look. "Your words wound me. But to ensure you of good faith, Nausicala may pick the guards herself, and choose those she knows are most loyal to her."

Nausicala lowered her head, and Penélope saw that she hid a glimmer of tears in her eyes. "Thank you, Father."

Once the feast was over, the guests followed Penélope and her friends back to their ship by the shore in a long procession of merriment and songs, though Korinna held Nausicala's arm and her eyes were red from crying. Penélope found herself walking alongside Lord Erasmos, who was perhaps the only one to look truly happy.

"I never thanked you, Lady Penélope," Lord Erasmos said with a bashful smile. "It is on account of you that I am a happily married man today."

"You don't need to thank me," Penélope said with a smile of her own. "After all, I did so for my own selfish reasons. I could not bear for the Princess Korinna to marry such a heartless, vile man as Lord Iason. And by chance, I knew of your situation, and the love you both hold for each other."

"By chance," Erasmos echoed with an amused shake of his head. "I do not believe any part of your time on this island has been left up to *chance*, Penélope."

Her smile faded as she recalled the oath she had sworn, which the Queen of Death had already known, the fate Calypso had seen written on her heart. "That may be so."

"But I suppose now you may be happy too?" Erasmos asked, raising a brow. "You told me you also harbored a secret love. I am not wrong in supposing it was the Prince of Helena?"

"No, you're not wrong." Penélope sighed. "But I did not expect to marry him, especially under these circumstances. My home is very far from here, but now I know I will never return there."

"I am sorry to hear it. But in my experience, home is not so much the place as the people we hold dear in our hearts. Perhaps one day you shall come to call Prince Leandros home too."

The words unexpectedly warmed her, and she shared a small smile with Erasmos before noticing Leandros looking back at them from further down the lane. Her smile faltered, but she forced herself to appear joyful as they reached their ship by the shore, where the rest of the crew had set up their camp with the few remaining supplies they had left.

Once their crew had reunited, with Owen greeting those he was closest to with hugs and playful kisses on the cheek—much to the annoyance of Zeb—they said their goodbyes to King Kleomachus and Princess Korinna.

Korinna threw her arms around Penélope and hugged her tightly. "I wish you would not leave, Lady Penélope. You must still learn to weave properly. You know, I consider you like a sister to me."

"I promise to visit as soon as I can," Penélope said, surprised to feel tears in her eyes. "And I will ask Dora to teach me how to weave, since I am told she will be Nausicala's handmaiden. Then, when I do visit, we can weave together."

After they said their final goodbye, Korinna approached Nausicala hesitantly. "If only I knew sooner that you were my true sister. I would have spoken with our father on your behalf."

"I know," Nausicala said with a smile, kissing Korinna's forehead. "That is why I held my peace. But we shall meet again, my dear Korinna, so do not shed more tears. Trust in the gods."

The King was helped down from his litter and hobbled to Nausicala. His eyes glistened with tears as they faced each other in silence. Then Nausicala kissed her father's cheek, where a single tear rolled down his aged face.

"Mother would be happy that you have let me go," Nausicala said.

"Your mother was always braver than I," the King said, his voice hoarse. "I suppose this is the goodbye I was cheated from all those years ago, yet I find it is even more painful to watch you leave with my own eyes, as if the gods have punished me once and for all with the very thing I feared most. May you forgive your father his selfishness and anger, and think kindly of me despite my faults."

"Oh, Father." Nausicala wrapped her arms around the King, her eyes shut tightly, her lashes beaded with tears. "I shall love you always. My heart's sorrow feels lighter knowing this time we part in love."

Once the last goodbyes were said, they boarded the ship, while Korinna, Erasmos, and the King waved from the shore, watching the ship lift anchor and sail away with the tide. Penélope stood at the stern and waited until their figures shrunk to small dots on the faraway shore, then retired to the small cabin that had been built larger and more roomy behind the captain's cabin for Penélope, Nausicala, and Dora to sleep.

She closed her eyes once she curled up in her hammock and slipped into a heavy, dreamless sleep, only waking when she heard a loud commotion outside, voices raising in angry discussion. Penélope quickly exited the cabin.

On the deck near the prow of the ship, Leandros and King Leon were arguing, with Nausicala standing between them as if trying to mediate, a silent Dora dutifully by her side. Zeb stood out of the way with Owen, both watching the argument unfold warily, not understanding their rapid-fire Greek.

Penélope approached, and everyone turned to her. "What's going on?"

Leandros' muscles flickered in his jaw. "The King does not wish to return to the city. I told him we had express instructions from my mother to restore him as King."

"I shall not return to the city without accomplishing my original quest," King Leon said sternly. "When I left Helena, I was to journey to the Atlas Mountains, where the Sibyl of Apollo presides over his oracle in the caverns deep inside the mountains. There I believed the Emerald Stone to be hidden, so this is news to my ears."

"What did the Sibyl say?" Penélope asked in surprise.

King Leon shook his head. "I never reached the mountains. My ship was waylaid thanks to the curse upon my family, fulfilled by the sea god Poseidon."

"Did you not say in the Great Hall that the Queen of Death herself commanded you to restore the King of Helena to the city?" Nausicala asked Penélope, giving her son a pointed look.

"The Queen of Death commanded me to return the King of Helena to the city," Penélope said, knowing with Hermes' gift of language everyone would now understand her, including Zeb and Owen. "But it was for another reason that I have kept secret from everyone, except Zeb, who was told the same by Elena, Alexandria's mother, when in the Fields of Asphodel."

"Penélope," Zeb warned, his eyes wide with understanding when he realized what she was about to divulge.

"Is that so?" King Leon asked sharply.

Penélope nodded. "Once you left the city of Helena, Brother Ezra took over as King."

"That wily snake," King Leon spat, more as a curse than in surprise.

"Yes, but he's more than a usurper," Penélope said urgently. "He follows the orders of Zeus, blinded in punishment for once trying to go against His will and cowed into loyalty. My friend Alexandria fulfilled an age-old prophecy that spoke of a descendant of Zeus who would find the Emerald Stone and use it to restore the Old Order. But when I spoke with the Queen of Death in the Underworld, she told me that Zeus would return to the city of Helena in revenge and that a great war was coming. Elena told Zeb the same thing. The goddess also told me that if we wished to defeat Zeus once more, we would need to bring King Leon home."

"If what you say is true," Nausicala said slowly, "then we must return as swiftly as possible."

Zeb stepped toward the group, Owen standing awkwardly by his side. "Penélope is saying the truth. Elena told me that enemies old and new would start a war with the city of Helena. There's no time to waste."

King Leon thoughtfully scratched his recently trimmed beard. "If the Old Order has been restored, then there would be no need for me to sail to the Sibyl."

"Why did you never tell me this?" Leandros asked, and for the first time since their wedding night, they both looked each other in the eye. He fought a flush from his neck while Penélope held his gaze.

"There was no time, *husband*," Penélope said, raising a brow. "I was saving all of you from execution, or did you already forget?"

Leandros' eyes narrowed at her new address but he remained silent.

"Then it is decided," Nausicala said, with the authority of a queen and a mother. "We sail directly for Helena, and hope we are not too late."

"Penélope," Zeb called out before she turned to walk away. "Penélope, we have to be careful. You said that when Alexandria revealed the location of the Emerald Stone, Zeus was able to find it. This war is much bigger than us. If we don't stay out of it, we'll have to pay the consequences too. The gods are watching us, Penélope."

"Stay out of it?" Penélope repeated incredulously, her frustration with Leandros and anger at their fate wearing her patience thin. "Zeb, don't you get it yet? I can't stay out of this war. My husband is the Prince of Helena. I'm bound by oath not only to bear his first daughter, but to stand by his side through life and death, and that means facing Zeus and finishing what Alexandria started."

Zeb flinched at her words as if she had slapped him. "You're not seriously considering *staying* here, right?"

Penélope glanced around warily at the side-eyes from the others at their discussion, then lowered her voice. "This is my life now, Zeb."

He stared at her, his jaw tightening, before he whirled around and stalked off to the ladder that descended into the hull of the ship. Owen jerked his head in Zeb's direction and gave Penélope a comforting smile.

"I'll speak with him," he said, then followed Zeb down into the hull.

Penélope covered her face with her hands. She had not expected Zeb to be so angry at her for marrying Leandros, but now she wondered why she had brushed aside her life with Zeb back home so easily. Did she not owe Zeb her friendship? Had she not promised herself to care for the helpless, scared boy who had no one to protect him?

"A storm hovers on the horizon."

She looked up. King Leon stood at the prow of the ship, Leandros by his side. They both gazed upon the horizon with similar expressions of hardened fear. Nausicala looked at the two of them standing there, the love and terror in her eyes speaking more than words.

Hovering on the horizon was indeed a storm, with dark and deadly clouds teeming, lightning and whirlwinds visible even from this distance away.

"That is no ordinary storm," Leandros said, a hand shielding his eyes to better see the churning clouds. "It flies too fast towards us against the wind. Surely some god has sent it to prevent our return to the city."

She recalled Zeb's warning that Zeus had found them only after Alexandria had revealed the location of the Emerald Stone. Could this be Zeus trying to prevent them from returning to the city? She remembered Elena's words to Zeb, of enemies old *and* new. What if that warning held a second meaning, unknown to them until now?

The wind from the storm had begun whipping their sails, and the waves beneath their ship rocked with more force. Soon, the storm would be upon them, threatening to drown them beneath the waves as King Leon had, and his father, King Philoxenos, before him.

"Only one god can muster such a storm upon the seas," King Leon said grimly.

Penélope suddenly understood, and she swore she glimpsed a flashing gleam of gold upon the waves beneath the storm, larger than life and glinting with three arrowheads as tall and sharp as mountains.

"Poseidon."

35

THE SHIP SWAYED DANGEROUSLY as Zeb angrily descended the ladder into the hull. Since all the crew members were on the deck manning the oars, the hull was empty save for the rolled-out sleeping mats and hammocks, the latter reserved for higher-ranked sailors. He found his sleeping mat near the side of the hull, resting his forehead against the cool planks of wood.

"Zeb?"

He sighed. "Go away, Owen."

"Are you alright, mate?"

Zeb looked at him, not bothering to hide the tears welling in his eyes or the tremor in his voice. "Do I look alright, *mate*?"

Owen grimaced. "Do you want to talk about it?"

"What is there to talk about?"

"Penélope is only trying to survive," Owen said with a sigh.

"Survive?" Zeb repeated angrily. "If she really wanted to survive, she would leave this damned place and forget about it. Instead, she's marrying some guy she barely knows and getting caught up in a war that isn't even hers to fight!"

"Some of that was to save us from execution, I might remind you. And that was after we rescued *you* from the Underworld."

"Because I paid the price of Osiris and *died* in the first place! And that wouldn't have happened if we hadn't helped Alexandria find her mother or had even ever come to the city! Sister Stella warned us that it was dangerous, but did we listen to her? No, we didn't."

"I get that you're upset—"

"No, you don't!" Zeb pushed Owen away when he tried to come close and place a hand on his arm. "You don't get it! You have everything! You have a family, a million friends, a million places you could call home. Penélope is everything to me. She *is* my home. I would have nothing without her. No family, no friends, *nothing.* And now she's choosing to stay here in this horrible place? Where I almost died? Where we *all* almost died multiple times? It's selfish."

He spoke the last word so harshly that it echoed in the silence of the hull. Owen stared at him in disbelief, but did not answer. Zeb wanted him to answer. He wanted to argue. He wanted to fight and fight until he forgot they were stuck in this miserable ship, on this miserable sea, an entire world away from home. How could everything he ever knew be uprooted and lost in a matter of months? Weeks?

"And you," Zeb said in a low, cold voice, colder due to the angry heat in his chest, taking a step closer to Owen, who stood still, watching him warily. "Penélope might be selfish and reckless, but you are a coward. You act all confident, like you don't care about anything or anyone, but it's all an act. You *do* care. You care about yourself, and only yourself—"

Owen shoved him away, and Zeb stumbled back in surprise. "Don't you dare call me selfish. I did not sail all the way to the Land of the Dead—"

"I never asked you to," Zeb interrupted, shoving him back until Owen grabbed hold of his wrists. He suddenly felt like he was eight years old, getting in a fight with one of Penélope's older brothers. "You just felt guilty—"

"Guilty? *Guilty?*"

"Yes!" Zeb struggled to shake off Owen's grip, and then suddenly Owen shoved him against the wall of the hull. "Let go of me!"

Owen shook his head, pinning him in place. "Not until you apologize."

"Me? Apologize to you?" Zeb wanted to laugh, but there was nothing funny about the situation. He twisted his body but couldn't get out from underneath Owen's persistent strength. "For what? Dying?"

"For being a fucking arsehole," Owen said, the last insult slipping out with a grunt when Zeb successfully shook off his tight grip, only for Owen to place both arms on either side of him, caging him against the hull.

They both breathed heavily against each other. Zeb couldn't help but notice Owen's strong biceps flexing around him. Owen studied his face, his jaw clenched as if it took all of his strength to keep Zeb there, even though he had to be three times as strong. He saw the smallest, reluctant smile on Owen's face and knew they had stopped fighting, or had never been fighting at all.

"I really want to kiss you," Owen muttered under his breath.

Zeb huffed a laugh. "You sick bas—"

Owen silenced him with a kiss, pressing his body against Zeb's, somehow spiking the anger in him even more. But instead of pushing him away, Zeb's traitorous arms grasped his shoulders and brought Owen closer, kissing him with the same force he had just used to push him away. The anger burned inside of him, mingling with the intense desire he had been suppressing since returning from the Land of the Dead.

"This isn't—an apology—" Zeb said breathlessly between kisses.

Owen laughed against his neck where he buried his face against his skin, wrapping Zeb in his arms and pressing him to his body with a contented sigh. "I wouldn't expect any less, Zeb Hades."

Zeb's hands ran down Owen's back, hoping he left scratches. "I'm still angry."

He kissed Zeb's neck, then his chest, glancing at the ladder leading up to the deck before sinking to his knees. "Not for long."

"Anyone can come," Zeb hissed, stopping his hands from lifting his tunic, nearly falling to the ground as the ship jerked to the side, a crash sounding from above while ocean currents drummed against the side of the hull with more violence than usual.

They shared a worried glance. Owen stood up, straining his ears. Voices filtered down from the deck. Zeb thought he heard Leandros shouting orders. A cold wind whipped through the hull, rifling their clothes, before water began dripping inside, as if it were raining, or a wave had run across the deck.

"Quick!" Owen grabbed Zeb by the hand and together they climbed out of the hull, ascending into what could only be the eye of a storm, rain pouring down and mingling with the waves crashing over the deck, lightning threatening to strike the masts, and wind swirling around their ship as strong as a hurricane.

Leandros shouted orders, squinting through the rain, his words swallowed in the wind. He saw Zeb and Owen across the deck and ran to them, King Leon trailing behind, fully soaked. Leandros pointed back to the prow, where three figures emerged from the sprays of waves slamming the sides of the ship. "Take Penélope and Nausicala to their cabin!"

Penélope, Nausicala, and Dora were already running towards them, hand in hand. "I'm not going anywhere," Penélope said firmly. "Owen, take Queen

Nausicala and Dora to our cabin."

Owen nodded and, without a word, escorted Nausicala and her trembling old handmaiden to her cabin, who watched with wide, helpless eyes as the storm raged around them. Leandros looked torn between fighting with Penélope to remain in the cabin and attending to his duties as captain.

Zeb took Penélope's arm. "I'm staying with her."

"Very well," Leandros said with effort. Then he was pulled away by a shout from the other side of the deck and ran in that direction.

"What's happening?" Zeb shouted over the roaring wind and rain.

Penélope looked after Leandros worriedly, then back at him. "You were right!"

"Obviously!" Zeb steadied Penélope as their ship sped down a steep wave and then nearly flew off the crest, the ship shuddering around them as it slammed back into the sea. "About what, exactly?"

"It's Poseidon!"

They ducked instinctively as one of the masts broke and swung around in the wind. The crew rallied together and threw ropes, lassoing the mast and straining to hold it in place. Penélope gasped, looking behind him, just before something slammed into Zeb's back, and he was shoved to the floor, doused in cold. He reached out blindly and found Penélope shivering on the floor next to him, both their clothes drenched from a rogue wave that had crashed over the deck.

"This ship is going to drown!" Zeb shouted.

Penélope stared at him, her eyes wide with fear. "We have to—"

A crash exploded in light and flame, and they both shielded their heads with their arms. Sailors shouted, the ship groaned, and the sails caught fire, smoke mingling with the rain. Then the mast, burnt and licking with flames, suddenly cracked and crumbled down, splitting the deck.

Waves poured inside the ship, filling the deck with swirling, sooty water. Zeb grabbed Penélope and helped them stand and move toward the end of the ship where the captain's cabin still stood, though the roof had been torn off. Zeb held Penélope, wondering if they would die at last, and regretted how he had argued with her earlier.

"Pepa, I'm—"

But he never finished, the ship groaning loudly, and Zeb turned to see a massive wave swelling beneath them, as if a force pushed the water from the fathomless deep and raised their ship to impossible heights. Zeb fell flat to the deck, Penélope slipping out of his hands as she skidded across the deck and fell into the ocean behind them. He cried out to her, but the wind billowed in chaos, whipping into his face and screaming against the ship.

Zeb slid across the deck and nearly toppled over the side like Penélope had, but he managed to grasp an oar bench, clinging for dear life. He cowered low, trembling as the ship careened across the sea, the storm blowing the ship away as if the wind was the wrath of Poseidon itself, tossing their ship about the sea like it weighed nothing at all. The ship screeched as the fallen mast finally cleaved through the hull entirely, and in the churning ocean ahead, Zeb could just see towering rocks jutting out of the water like jagged teeth, circling a small island.

They were going to crash.

Their ship tilted, ready to tumble into the ocean, speeding uncontrollably toward the rocks. Zeb braced himself for the impact, just before hands grabbed him, and he heard Owen call his name, dragging him to his feet.

"Jump!"

Before he could protest, Owen held him, and Zeb felt his body pitch forward into the air, his feet lifted from the deck. He gasped as they hit the water, his skin stinging from the slap, the icy cold currents swallowing him and pulling him beneath the waves. He couldn't fight the tide rolling him under the water, the salty water burning in his nose and throat, a tight grip still on his waist.

Suddenly his head broke through the surface, and his mouth gaped for air, his lungs on fire, and his eyes blurred from the constant churning waves around him. Owen bobbed beside him, struggling for breath, one of his arms still around Zeb. He felt his limbs suddenly seize up, fully realizing what had happened, the weight of his tunic threatening to sink him beneath the waves and drown him.

He couldn't swim, his head falling back, mouth gasping to the sky. He was going to drown. He was going to die.

Just as the water threatened to cover his face entirely, Owen grunted, and Zeb felt something sharp jab his ribs. He reached out and felt a slab of wood. Owen shoved him forward, and Zeb hauled himself onto the plank. Then Owen tightened something around Zeb's waist, his other hand holding the end of a rope.

The sea and sky had calmed as if by magic, but the waves still rocked from the aftermath of the massive wave and the crash of the ship against the jagged rocks. Zeb stared uncomprehendingly at the shards of the ship cast about the sea, where several bodies in their sailors' tunics floated, others swimming near it, having also jumped before the impact.

Zeb's stomach dropped nauseatingly. "Penélope."

"We—have—to—swim," Owen grunted with each word, wrapping the rope around his shoulders and tying it at the waist while kicking with his legs to keep himself from sinking below the water.

"I-I can't," Zeb stuttered, then realized it was his teeth chattering, though the water itself was not very cold.

Owen began kicking, and they inched forward. "Use—your—legs."

Then Owen turned and began swimming, kicking his legs and stroking with his arms. Zeb gripped the wooden plank for dear life and kicked with his legs. Slowly, they treaded across the water until they passed the jutting rocks and neared the island's shore.

By the time the tide rolled them to shallow waters, Zeb's muscles were cramped up with the effort, and soon even Owen floated on his back and allowed the waves to ebb them onto shore. At last he stood and helped Zeb shakily release the wooden plank and untie the rope around his waist.

They trudged to dry land and collapsed together. Zeb didn't care that the dry sand rubbed roughly against his wet skin. After what felt like hours—though it could have been mere minutes—shouting voices neared them. With an immense effort, Zeb sat up and squinted into the evening sun. Leandros approached, his tunic torn, shouldering a limping Mono whose wooden leg had been half torn off in the tumult. Behind him staggered King Leon, his tunic shredded so that his chest could be seen scraped raw and bloody, a distraught Queen Nausicala draped over his shoulder, her handmaiden Dora hobbling beside them, both their robes soaked and ripped at the hems.

Leandros saw Zeb on the sand and his eyes widened, before he left Mono with King Leon and ran towards them. "Penélope!"

Zeb staggered to his feet, then helped Owen stand as well. His head spun, and he blinked the black spots away from his vision, only to find Leandros standing in front of him, shaking his shoulders.

"Where is Penélope?" he shouted.

"She's gone," Zeb whispered, his voice hoarse. He felt numb, chilled to the bone. Leandros' hands on his shoulders were as strong as steel. "I lost her."

"You said you would stay with her!" Leandros shoved him, and Zeb stumbled backward, held up only by Owen. Leandros' eyes were red and wild, his face livid.

"Curse you! She was in your charge! If she's dead, I'll send you back to Hades myself!"

Zeb feebly held up his hands as Leandros advanced toward him, Owen standing between them, failing to calm Leandros. A cry drew their attention away. Nausicala had fainted against Dora, with King Leon and Mono struggling to hold up her body as it sank to the ground, her arm still pointing beyond them.

They followed her pointed finger across the beach, where something floated onto shore. No—some*one,* Zeb realized, recognizing the familiar dark curls, her body covered in a thin white slip. Then Zeb saw that a shining figure emerged from the white foam and swam with the body, gently guiding it to the dry bed of sand. She glanced their way, a beautiful, queenly face with white streaming hair, before the figure dove back inside the waves.

"Was that—?" Zeb asked breathlessly.

"Penélope," Leandros said, his eyes fixed on her unconscious form, before he took off across the sand in her direction.

As he ran to her, Zeb's vision darkened. He took a step forward, then stumbled. Owen called his name, but he heard it distantly, and the last thing he saw were Owen's sea-green eyes wide and worried before he drowned in darkness like a shell sinking to the bottom of the ocean where sunlight fails to kiss.

36

THE CURRENT DRAGGED HER *by the thick folds of her dress, the sea pulling her down and down and down. Zeb's terrified blue eyes were the last memory she had before they were swallowed in darkness with a loud crack of lightning, the ship splitting and yawning open beneath her like the tomb of Osiris in Hell.*

As the black of the sea gradually engulfed her, a distant pinpoint of white light shined like a single star in the night sky, growing bigger and bigger until before her floated a woman with silky white hair and skin, her body encrusted with shining, pearlescent shells. She swam toward her effortlessly, then carried Penélope in her arms and lifted her to the surface of the ocean.

"Unhappy Penélope," said the woman in a tender voice, looking down upon her with pale eyes, where the dark blue waves of the sea were reflected in the watery pupils. "How come Poseidon the Earth-Shaker has conceived such furious wrath against you? What outrageous act have you committed to offend him? Yet for all his rage, he shall not destroy you. Nay, I have been sent by our Great Mother to rescue you from the depths of despair. Heed me now and strip off these garments!"

Penélope only had to shrug down the dress from her shoulders for the heavy fabric to slip off her body easily, quickly carried away by the currents and swirling down into oblivion.

"Who are you?" she asked, sure that she was dreaming.

"I am Leucothea, White Goddess of the Foam, though once my spirit bore an earthly form as Ino, daughter of Cadmus. Here, take this and cover yourself!"

Her white arm dragged off her gauzy silk veil from her streaming white hair. Penélope took the veil hesitantly, the fabric as soft as seaweed in her hands.

"That veil is immortal," Leucothea said. "Do not fear, for now you shall neither

suffer nor perish. When you wake, do not cast it away, for you have reached the island of Aeaea, where dwells a dangerous sorceress. Wear the veil beneath a sailor's dress, but tell no one of this, nor of the island's name. Only alone shall the witch take pity on you and reveal what she knows. When you sail from the island, cast the veil into the wine-dark sea."

Penélope wrapped the veil around her body and felt the fabric cling to her like a slip. Then her vision turned hazy as the white light faded back into darkness. Her body rocked with the waves, floating aimlessly. She gave herself up to the sea, her vision fading to black as if she had been dreaming all along. After what felt like hours had passed in a dreamless sleep, she heard the soft, sweet voice of Leucothea.

"Open your eyes, Penélope." Hands shook her shoulders. "Penélope!"

Her eyes flew open, and she gasped for breath. Leandros crouched above her, shaking her shoulders.

"Penélope!" When he saw she was alive, he hugged her to his chest, his face buried in her hair. "I thought you were lost."

She hesitantly lifted her arms and threaded her fingers through his hair, the touch of his soft curls like the feeling of grass beneath her feet after sailing the ocean for days on end. "I'm alive. We're alive."

He merely held her closer, as if he were afraid she would disappear into thin air if he let her go. Penélope herself felt as though the entire storm had been a dream, since the massive wave had borne their ship aloft, and she fell, sliding across the deck and swallowed up by the sea, her last image Zeb's wide eyes.

Penélope pulled away, her heart pounding in her chest. "Leandros, where is Zeb?"

"He's here."

She whipped her head around, though the movement made her dizzy. "Zeb!"

Leandros reluctantly released her, and she stood up, grateful for the small dress covering her body. Zeb stood before her, leaning against Owen, who looked equally exhausted. Behind them, Mono and King Leon supported a pale-faced, shivering Nausicala, while Dora nervously attended to her. Penélope looked out upon the sea and saw the remains of the splintered ship scattered across the waves.

"How did you survive?" she asked, turning to Nausicala and Dora in wonder.

Nausicala and Dora glanced at Owen, who blushed. "If it were not for your friend here," Nausicala said, "we would not have jumped, and it would have been too late."

Zeb looked at Owen in surprise. King Leon nodded his head approvingly.

"We are in your debt, son of Godfrey," King Leon said, bowing his head. "If there is anything you desire, you need simply ask."

"Well, there may be a thing or two—" Owen began.

"Where is everyone else?" Penélope interrupted, craning her head but not seeing any of the crew nearby.

Mono grimaced. "Half the crew has succumbed to the waves, my Lady. The others have washed ashore and began foraging the woods to make camp." He paused. "We thought you had come to the same fate as those taken by the sea."

"I almost did." Penélope scanned the woods clinging to the coastline, as if she might spot the sorceress walking among the trees. "What island is this?"

"Hard to say for certain," Leandros said, eyeing the sky where the sun had already begun inching closer to the horizon. "We have traveled much farther north, in the opposite direction from Helena. The Sea God did not wish us to return home."

"We should scout the area," Penélope said, recalling the goddess Leucothea's advice. "Make sure no giants or violent tribes live nearby."

Leandros looked like he wanted to protest, but then nodded. "Once the crew returns and builds our camp, we shall draw lots as to who joins our scout. Monopous, seeing as you cannot walk, you shall remain to oversee the camp with the Queen Nausicala and ensure that she remains safe."

Mono bowed. "I shall protect her with my life."

Once they returned to where the other crew members had begun setting up camp, Penélope asked if she could borrow a crew member's vest to wear over her white slip. Mono immediately offered his, considering he would have to remain back by the camp anyway. Then Leandros arranged the lots for the crew members to draw. Of the twenty or so men who remained, six of them drew the short sticks, and while they groaned and lamented their ill luck, the men dutifully followed Penélope and Leandros into the woods.

Along the way, they found a wide, clear stream, and all of them stooped to drink from it eagerly, having no stores of water and parched from the salty sea and their long trek in the woods. Leandros eyed the currents flowing from somewhere inland out to sea, then suggested that if the island were inhabited, they would most likely dwell near a river, and so they continued hiking by the banks as the sunset glowed to their left.

"If we do encounter giants," Owen asked from the rear of the group, "with what weapons will we defend ourselves?"

"My crew and I always carry weapons," Leandros called back as he walked beside Penélope, his hand gripping the handle of the sword still strapped to his waist. "Not even a storm shall easily find us unmanned."

"Ah, I see I've missed that memo," Owen responded dryly.

Leandros took something out of the inside of his vest, then turned and threw it in Owen's direction, who jumped out of the way as it sailed to the ground. He then stooped to pick up the object, which Penélope saw in surprise was a dagger sheathed in leather.

Owen slid out the blade, which glinted menacingly in the glow of the waning sun, looking at Leandros in disbelief. "Was I supposed to *catch* that?"

Penélope raised a brow. "Weapon at the ready, Owen. This island might be crawling with giants, and soon it will be dark."

The other crew members hid their laughs under their arms or with a cough. Owen scowled, but held the knife anyway, peering around the trees as if at any moment a giant might appear and attack them.

"You should not make light of such things," King Leon said, looking around the woods warily. "The last uncharted island I came across, a clan of violent giants sold me to the Phaeacians, and on the one before that, I was held captive against my will."

"By Calypso, right?" Penélope asked without thinking, then nearly winced when she caught Leandros tense up beside her.

Leon's face hardened. "Yes. How do you know of this?"

"We also landed on the shores of Ogygia," Leandros said coldly. "The goddess told us of your journey and how you remained on the island with her."

"Here we go," muttered Owen.

"You did not mention your stay with the goddess," King Leon said in surprise.

"Well, I supposed you already knew much about her, given your past intimacy."

"Leandros," Penélope whispered, but he ignored her, his hands flexing into fists by his sides.

King Leon forced the group to a stop, eyeing Leandros warily. "Is there something you wish to tell me, son?"

"Me?" Leandros turned around, facing the King with a clenched jaw. "There is nothing *I* wish to say. I never betrayed my wife, nor my family. You ought to be ashamed, *Father.*"

Leon stepped close to his son. He glanced at Penélope, then lowered his voice to a harsh whisper. "You are quick to throw stones at your father, who has only ever been loyal to his people and has sacrificed much for his family. What, after all, do you know of marriage? Of family? Of loyalty and sacrifice?"

"More than you know," Leandros shot back.

King Leon laughed humorlessly. "There is much you do not know, my son. And I hope you never have to learn it."

They remained facing each other before Leandros lowered his eyes, turning away and heading off along the river, trudging deeper into the island. Penélope sighed and followed after him, the others hesitantly trailing behind her. Up ahead, Leandros wove through the woodland with long strides until Penélope breathed hard to keep up with his pace. The forest thickened the deeper into the island they hiked, and the ground steadily climbed, as if they were nearing a mountain, the river disappearing beside them in a steep ravine.

Suddenly, Penélope broke out of the woods and entered a small dell, less lush and flowered than Calypso's vale, but still pleasant and sheltered from an offshore wind that had whistled across the beaches and through the woodland.

Leandros stood still a few paces away, staring up at a crag jutting further down in the dell like the rocks in the sea that the ship had crashed against. Atop the rocky foundation, built out of the same polished stone so that it blended in with the surroundings, was a house, smoke rising from its lofty roof.

Circe.

The Witch of Aeaea

"Now dropp'd our anchors in the Ææan bay,
Where Circe dwelt, the daughter of the Day!
Her mother Perse, of old Ocean's strain,
Thus from the Sun descended, and the Main
(From the same lineage stern Aeaetes came,
The far-famed brother of the enchantress dame);
Goddess, the queen, to whom the powers belong
Of dreadful magic and commanding song.
Some god directing to this peaceful bay
Silent we came, and melancholy lay,
Spent and o'erwatch'd. Two days and nights roll'd on,
And now the third succeeding morning shone.
I climb'd a cliff, with spear and sword in hand,
Whose ridge o'erlook'd a shady length of land;
To learn if aught of mortal works appear,
Or cheerful voice of mortal strike the ear?
From the high point I mark'd, in distant view,
A stream of curling smoke ascending blue,
And spiry tops, the tufted trees above,
Of Circe's palace bosom'd in the grove.

—*Odyssey,* Book 5.135-150, translation by Alexander Pope

37

STONE STEPS HAD BEEN cut into the rocky outcropping, leading up to a porch where mountain wolves and lions lounged about yawning or sleeping, some even on their back and pawing the air like house cats.

The others had caught up to them and looked at the house and the wild predators in alarm. A faint melody in the air could be heard floating from the open doorway. Penélope's heart pounded painfully in her chest, knowing that inside lived the dangerous sorceress she had been warned about. Owen squinted at the mountain wolves and lions, his face blanching. He tightened his hands on his dagger.

"Who lives up there?" Owen asked.

Zeb exchanged fearful glances with Penélope, as if he were recalling the same story of Odysseus approaching a house of polished stone, where a goddess had enchanted wild animals around her home with drugs. But Penélope could not tell them what she knew, so she remained silent.

The singing voice grew louder, reciting what sounded like the creation of the world, beginning with Chaos and the birth of Gaia, Mother of the Gods and Creator of the World, though Penélope could not catch all of the words. Somehow, the voice did not sound as lovely as Calypso's, which had been truly divine, like how Penélope would imagine the warmth of sunlight would sound. Instead, this voice held an imperfect grit, a tenor in its depths like the grinding of stone against stone, which Penélope could only describe as human.

"I have heard of a sorceress who sings with a mortal voice," King Leon said darkly, noticing the imperfections in the voice as well. "We ought to be careful in our approach, for they say she has the power to kill men at sight."

Penélope allowed the others to walk ahead of her, remaining with Zeb and Owen near the rear of the group. The men silently withdrew their swords, daggers, and arrows, holding them at the ready. They climbed up the winding stairs, passing the mountain wolves and lions who did not growl or attack but rather strolled up to them, rubbing their snouts affectionately against their legs, others with tails wagging excitedly, jumping and licking their faces.

"Something's not right about this," murmured Owen, glancing around nervously and reluctantly petting the shaggy mane of a lion that pranced up to him with a happy grin, his pink tongue panting like a dog.

Once they reached the porch, King Leon held up a hand, then tiptoed up the steps to the open doorway. A sweet smell of meat and mulled, spiced wine wafted toward them, making their stomachs growl and their mouths dry in anticipation. Leon gripped his sword with both hands, the knuckles white.

"Hail, my Lady!" he called into the house. "We come in peace and in dire need of aid! Come forth and reveal yourself!"

The singing stopped. For a moment, all was silent as they waited impatiently for a response. Then footsteps echoed softly on stone, and suddenly the figure of a woman stood in the doorway, but before King Leon could speak, she lifted her arm, holding a long wand carved of wood, and the gem inset in a hollow at the top of the wand sent forth a blast of light.

Penélope automatically shielded her eyes with her arms, but after nothing happened, she lowered them and gasped. Where just before the others had been standing around her, now they had disappeared and were replaced by pigs snorting frantically—not *replaced*, Penélope realized with her heart in her throat, but *transformed*, each and every one of them.

The woman's eyes widened as they fell on Penélope and saw that she had not been affected by the spell. Penélope herself stood dumbstruck when she had the time to look more carefully at the goddess. Despite her mortal voice, she was beautiful as no mortal could be, tall and proud in height, her thick, dark hair braided upon her head and falling in loose ringlets around her shoulders. Her eyes were the color of liquid gold set in a pale, angular face, and her lips were tinted blood red.

"Please," Penélope whispered hoarsely. "I mean no harm."

"You are a woman," the goddess said in surprise, approaching her cautiously. Penélope nodded hurriedly. "How have you escaped my magic?"

Penélope held very still as the goddess stopped before her. "You are Circe."

Circe raised a brow. "Yes. No mortal besides the famed Odysseus has ever escaped my spells. Yet you still stand, despite having drunk from the river which I enchanted with drugs."

"I was protected." Penélope undid Mono's vest around her chest and revealed the thin slip beneath.

"The veil of Leucothea," Circe said in wonder. Her hands brushed the fabric along Penélope's waist, and Penélope nearly shivered. "The gods have devised our meeting. You must be Penélope, then, whom the Argus Slayer prophesied would come to me."

"Hermes?"

Circe paused. "You are clever, as your namesake suggests, though I am sure not to be the first to tell you so."

Penélope almost smiled, then remembered her friends, and panic seized her once more. "Can you turn them back?"

"Come," Circe said, beckoning her inside. "Let us speak over some food and drink."

She hesitated, glancing back at the pigs now chewing grass, narrowing her eyes at one pale white pig that she had a suspicion was Zeb. If the circumstances had been different, Penélope would've laughed. Instead, she swallowed nervously and followed Circe inside the house. Four handmaids were walking about the house, though they did not seem human, strong scents of fresh grass, mossy brooks, and flowery springs trailing behind them. One wove at a tall wooden loom against the wall, another stoked a great fire burning in the hearth at the far end of the room, while the two others ground grain and stirred wine.

When they saw Circe and Penélope, they rushed forth and greeted their mistress, who ordered them to set a table and prepare food and drink for them. One placed two chairs by the fire and covered them with thick, purple blankets while another placed small tables of silver before them, set with golden baskets filled with flat bread and fruit. Penélope took a seat on one of the chairs, Circe sitting beside her, where she laid her wand on the back of the chair. The other two handmaids mixed wine and water in a silver bowl, pouring the mixture into two golden cups they placed before them.

Circe motioned for Penélope to drink, so she picked up her cup and took a wary sip. The wine was sweet but refreshing, lightly spiced, and spread a warmth through her limbs, which she did not notice were shivering. One of the handmaidens draped a fur blanket over her body, then pushed forward the bread and fruit, while another handmaid carried over steaming stew in a cauldron that had been cooking over the hearth. She ate some of the stew with the flatbread, marveling silently at the burst of flavor and subtle heat of the meat.

"Now that you have eaten, let us converse privately," Circe said once Penélope finished her meal. She waved her handmaidens away, who disappeared inside the house down the side corridors. "How did you come by my humble abode?"

"Our ship was caught in a storm and crashed into the rocks around your island," Penélope said after taking a sip of wine. "The storm was sent by Poseidon, who doesn't wish us to return home. He has cursed the line of King Philoxenos since he kidnapped Nausicala from the Phaeacians. Leucothea saved me from the sea and told me you lived here, but not to tell my companions anything. I think I understand why now."

Circe eyed her sadly, reaching out and brushing back Penélope's hair from her face. "You have faced such terror, and felt such deep sorrow, with still more to come. How will you return home when the gods are against you?"

"I was hoping you could help me," Penélope said hesitantly.

The goddess pondered for a moment. "You have angered the Lord of the Sea, Earth-Shaker Poseidon. If you wish to cool his wrath, you must heed me, for there is only one way you shall be able to appease him. I may not tell you directly, for I am sworn against helping the line of King Philoxenos return home, but there is nothing to prevent me from singing a song that has long been sung since the days Odysseus still wandered these waters."

Then she softly chanted the following rhyme, as though it were some kind of riddle:

> *"To cross the wine-dark sea back home*
> *and quell the wrath of Ocean King*
> *both far and wide then must you roam*
> *but first beguiling maids who sing*
> *must one aboard your ship endure*
> *then seek the Pillars of the Sea*
> *where daughter his may grant succor*
> *and from his curse shall set you free."*

Penélope tried to understand the words, but she could only think of what she didn't know. *Beguiling maids who sing? The Pillars of the Sea? Whose daughter?* For the first, she had an educated guess, but the others she had never heard of, and wanted to ask the goddess if her guesses were correct. But before she could ask more questions, Circe held out her hand and led her away from the tables and chairs. Her throat ran dry as the goddess guided her down one of the side corridors lit with golden lamps to a room fitted with rich rugs, candles, a plush couch, and a roaring fire in a hearth, before which a bronze tub filled with water stood upon bronze sculpted lion feet.

"Here, Lady Penélope," Circe said. "You must be so weary from your travels."

Without another word, Circe helped Penélope out of her vest, then began lifting her slip, before Penélope stopped her, worried that if she took off Leucothea's veil, she would lose her protection from the goddess' spells. Circe raised a brow as if she read her thoughts.

"I swear on the dreaded waters of the Styx, Lady Penélope, that I will not bring harm to you nor your comrades."

Then Circe helped Penélope out of the slip and held her hand as she lowered her into the bath. Her feet touched the water first, which was hot and soothing, and Penélope couldn't help sighing as next her body sank inside the bath.

"You poor thing," Circe murmured, dipping a silver pitcher into the water and pouring it over Penélope's head, gently cleaning her hair and shoulders with her hands. She then poured aromatic oil on her head that glimmered as it dripped down her skin, not unlike the ambrosia Calypso had washed her with.

Once Penélope finished bathing, Circe dried her by the fire herself, though Penélope felt abashed to allow a goddess the menial task, a protest Circe sternly brushed aside. The goddess dressed her in soft, rich robes of purple and gold, then she took Leucothea's veil—once more in its original shape—and draped it over her bare shoulders.

Circe paused, gazing upon her. She touched her knuckles beneath Penélope's chin, studying her face and shaking her head with a small smile. "Though mortal you are, indeed, you are beautiful."

Then she leaned in and kissed her, as if it were the most natural thing in the world to do. Penélope stood frozen as the goddess' lips touched hers, as warm and sweet as the mulled wine they had drunk earlier. She felt Circe's hands curl around her waist, which drew her closer to the goddess helplessly, Penélope's mind hazy with mingling shock and pleasure. All thoughts of the riddle and her current plight melted from her mind, fading in the face of the gentle caresses on her body, the heat that burned from the inside out, and the possibility of always feeling this way forever.

Why would I lie with the goddess? I told you once before, I shall never seek the arms of another woman unless that woman is you. I swore an oath, Πηνελόπη.

The memory of his voice brought her back to reality. She recalled the argument between King Leon and Leandros like a slap in the face. *I never betrayed my wife, nor my family.*

Penélope staggered back, held in place only by the goddess' hands on her hips. "I-I can't. I'm sorry."

Circe cocked her head, her golden eyes undeniably seductive as they lingered on Penélope's face. "You refuse the pleasure of a goddess?"

"I am married," Penélope said, holding out her left hand where the ring of sapphire still rested on her ring finger. "I cannot betray my husband."

"Betray?" She laughed. "But he is a man, my love! And none are more shifty and fickle than mortal men."

"He did not betray me when we were on the island of Calypso. He did not lie with her, even though we were only betrothed. He owed me less at that time than I owe him now."

"Very well," Circe said with a careless shrug of her richly robed shoulders. "It is your choice, Lady Penélope. I have already counseled you as best I can. All I can provide you now is food and shelter until you choose to depart from my halls."

Penélope curtsied low. "Thank you, my Lady. You are very kind."

Circe escorted them back to the main hall. Night had already descended, and through the small opening above the hearth, Penélope glimpsed a sky full of stars. The handmaidens lit torches about the room and then went about setting another table of an even greater abundance of food and drink, this time surrounded by linen-covered couches.

"As long as you are a guest in my home," Circe said, motioning toward the feast with an elegant arm, "you shall lack for nothing. But if you require something, all you need is ask."

"There is one thing."

Circe turned to her in surprise, and Penélope blushed. "Oh?"

"My comrades," Penélope said awkwardly. "They are still transformed into–into pigs. I was wondering if you could turn them back. You *can* turn them back, right?"

This time Circe smiled, a blinding, full-lipped smile like the reddening sun as it sets below the sea's glowing horizon, so that for a brief moment Penélope wondered if she had indeed made a mistake in refusing her. "That, my love, I can do."

38

Circe stood over the pigs scurrying around her front porch and held out her wand. Penélope could now see the purple crystal inset inside the carved wooden head. The goddess closed her eyes.

"Now rise," she murmured, as light flooded from the crystal, bathing all before them.

When the light receded, all the men stood in the same place as before, lowering their weapons in confusion, looking at Penélope and Circe. King Leon quickly realized what had happened and rushed toward the goddess with his sword, but before Circe could utter another spell, Penélope stood between them.

"Don't hurt her," Penélope said, holding out her hand until King Leon lowered his sword.

Leandros stepped forward, glancing between Circe and Penélope. "What is the meaning of this?"

"Any friend of Lady Penélope is a friend of mine," Circe said, smiling and bowing her head with an air of coyness. "Please, enter my halls, good lords. Already a feast has been prepared."

At the mention of food and the warmth of a fire, the men did not protest anymore, following Circe inside. Penélope could feel Leandros' gaze burning in the back of her head as she took the place of honor on the couch beside Circe. She had half a mind to make Leandros wonder what had happened, just as she had to wonder when he stayed behind with Calypso.

"Goddess," King Leon said once they were all reclined and the crew began eating with barely concealed hunger. "For a goddess you must be, despite your voice, which sounded human to our ears. Why did you use your wand against us when we came in peace?"

"Peace?" Circe repeated with a derisive laugh. "No man holding weapons at my door has come in *peace*, my Lord. You had drunk from my river, potent with a mixture of magical herbs I had made. A precaution, you see, against armed men who come knocking at my door."

King Leon nodded slowly, his face flushed. "I had a terrible dream of being transformed into swine, though I suppose it was not a dream at all."

Penélope had a hard time not laughing, made worse by Owen nearly spitting his drink out and coughing, and Zeb slapping his back with unnecessary force. She glanced at Leandros, whose face remained still and serious as though carved from stone, though she swore the corner of his mouth twitched. Circe merely waved her hand, and one of the handmaidens refilled their cups with more wine.

"A precaution, as I have said."

"Our ship drowned in a storm, crashing against the rocks near your island," Leandros said tersely. "We lost half our crew. The others remain camped by the beach, with no shelter or food, and rely on *your* river for water, which has been all but poisoned. Please, my Lady, tell me how we shall ever leave your island?"

Circe and Penélope shared a glance, at which Leandros narrowed his eyes.

"The goddess has promised to aid us while we are guests in her home," Penélope said hesitantly, wincing internally at Leandros' raised brow.

"It certainly seems she has aided one of us," Leandros replied, nodding his head toward Penélope's new dress and fragrant, brushed curls.

The interaction seemed to amuse Circe, who glanced between them, her gold eyes glittering like a bed of coins. "By an oath I swore, I may not aid in your return home, but my handmaids may provide you with tools to fell trees and build a new ship, fitted with all the supplies you may desire. Until the ship is ready, you all may reside in my halls and take comfort in my hospitality. Rooms have already been fitted for those who wish them."

She had risen from the couches as she spoke, the dinner having finished. The others followed suit, glancing around the cozy hall for the first time and taking in the luxurious furs draped across the floor, the silver chairs before the roaring fire in the hearth, and the handmaidens attending quietly to the loom and the boiling water over the fire.

"To what do we owe your generous hospitality?" Leandros asked before anyone could leave the couches. "For it is known to men that a goddess such as yourself does not give to mortals freely."

Circe glanced at Penélope knowingly, who blushed when all eyes turned to her. "You need not worry, young lord. Any debt to me will be paid by your company in my halls."

Then with a swish of her purple and gold robes, she glided down the corridor and led them deeper inside the house, where each was provided a bedroom, small in size but fitted for royalty. Owen and Zeb gratefully disappeared inside their rooms, closing their doors without so much as a weary nod of their heads. One by one, her friends were escorted inside their rooms until only King Leon, Leandros, and Penélope were left in the last corridor, where three doors remained.

"For you, King Leon," Circe said, gesturing to the first door, before bowing her head to Leandros and Penélope, where she swore the goddess hid a smirk. "We shall discuss more on the morrow, when you are all rested."

With one last lingering look, she crossed the hall to the third door, which she swung wide as she entered, revealing the same plush couch and roaring fire where Penélope had bathed, and Circe had kissed her. The memory caused the blood to rush to her face, even as the door closed gently behind her retreating figure. She caught King Leon gazing after her with a hint of regret, as if he wished the goddess might ask for his company. For the first time, Penélope thought she understood him.

After King Leon disappeared inside his room with a murmured goodnight, Leandros opened the second door, which could only have been prepared for them. They entered a spacious room with its own fire and a wide, cushioned couch inviting with its soft furs and blankets. Once the door closed behind them, Leandros turned his hardened face on her.

"What happened between you and the goddess?" he asked.

Penélope arched a brow and pretended to walk towards the couch. "Wouldn't you like to know."

Leandros caught her wrist in his hand, and she looked back at him in surprise. His eyes were dark and dangerous. "Tell me, Penélope."

She wrenched her hand out of his grip, which did not try to hold her. "Do you seriously think I would betray you the first chance I got?"

"Goddesses are cunning," Leandros said harshly. "She may have—she may have drugged you, as she had us, and then seduced you."

"She bathed me, Leandros, and I was never drugged or enchanted because a god gave me protection." Penélope lifted the veil of Leucothea, which glinted like silver armor in the firelight. Leandros gazed at the veil in mingled awe and fear. She hesitated, debating whether she should even mention it. "Then she kissed me."

"Ah, then I was right!" He laughed in disbelief, though his voice was bitter.

"She kissed me," Penélope repeated, grabbing his arm when he turned away, "but I refused her!"

"Surely!"

She forced him to look her way, holding his arms in place before her. "Yes, I refused! I said I was loyal to you, that we were married, and I wouldn't betray you. Then I asked her to turn you all back into men. What more could you want from me?"

Leandros stared at her with a wild, pained look, then grabbed her waist and pulled her close, kissing her with the force of a soldier attacking an enemy, as if all this time he had been holding his true strength back. Her eyes fluttered shut, and she allowed herself to be lifted off her feet, pressed flush against him. Leandros broke away only to trail kisses in her hair and down her neck.

"You," he whispered hotly against the base of her throat, "are dangerous, Πηνελόπη, more than any goddess."

Then he gathered her up in his arms, kissing her fully, and her legs automatically wrapped around his waist. He brought her to the bed, where he laid her down gently, though he kissed her with even more passion than before, so that any thought of Circe and their kiss instantly fled from Penélope's mind, burned up in the real desire that had sparked like a flame between them the moment they had seen each other that day on the ship.

Penélope splayed back against the pillows as Leandros kissed her neck, her shoulders, her arms, until the heat blossoming inside was too much, and she threw her veil to the ground, unpinning her dress with trembling hands. Leandros steadied her hands and helped her unpin the golden fibulae until the purple robes slipped down her body, pooling around her waist, before she shrugged them off.

Leandros gazed upon her bare skin with half-lidded eyes, still breathing hard, his legs straddling her waist. She tugged at his leather vest, which he shrugged off easily. Then Penélope reached out and touched his chest where his tunic had torn, revealing the rest of the white scar that traveled across his face, splitting his lips, and snaking like lightning down his chest. She lifted the tunic from his body, Leandros reluctantly helping her slide it over his head and casting it to the ground where her clothes were already piled beside the bed.

With a fingertip, she traced the scar down his chest, where it roped thick and white along his breastbone, splitting his muscled stomach and disappearing beneath a thin cloth tied around his hips. Leandros' eyes fluttered shut when she skimmed the hem of the loincloth, the sharp indents of his hips shifting.

"Have you ever?" Penélope asked quietly, looking up at him.

He nodded absently, his hands sliding up her waist, which prickled where his touch passed. "Before I met you, yes, but with none have I felt what I feel for you."

"I have too," she said, wanting to see his reaction. But Leandros only raised his brows. "Once. He was kind, but it wasn't..."

"Me?" Leandros asked with a devilish smirk, his hands gripping her hips and bringing them close. His eyes grew serious as their mouths brushed. "You do want this, do you not?"

Penélope nodded.

"I need to hear you say it," he said in a near whisper, his gaze passing over the bruise that surely still ringed her eye and nose. "Never again shall you suffer a man against your will."

She slowly wrapped her arms around his neck, pulling him close with a small smile. "Yes, Leandros, I want this."

Before he could speak, she kissed him, threading her fingers through his hair. How long had she imagined this moment? How many times had she secretly undressed Leandros in her mind, wondering where that scar ended?

Impulsively, she kissed a trail down his chest, following the scar as it sliced his stomach, which quivered under her touch. She stopped when she reached the cloth around his hips, then undid the tie until it fell away. The scar continued down the side of his groin and along his inner thigh, where it stopped in a deep, mangled indent, as if a long fang had torn through both skin and muscle. Penélope touched the scar on his thigh, and Leandros sucked in a quiet breath.

"Scylla did this, right?" she asked softly.

He nodded, looking away, his face red, embarrassed but not ashamed. "I was lucky to survive."

A rush of fierce protectiveness, unlike any she had ever felt, filled her heart. She kissed his chest, on the scar, then his cheek, his mouth, cradling his face between her hands.

"God, you're so beautiful," she said, looking into his brown eyes.

"God?"

"You know what I mean, Leandros."

"Well, by *my* gods, you are the most beautiful woman on this earth."

"Enough talking."

She kissed him again, silencing any response, and Leandros kissed her back as his arms slid around her waist, one hand tangled in her hair while the other cupped the back of her thigh, lifting her legs around his hips. Penélope arced her back against the soft bed as Leandros held her close and gave herself up to that burning fire.

39

A warm touch brushed the length of her body, pulling her out of a pleasant dream, which faded from memory as Penélope fluttered her eyes open. Beside her, Leandros kissed her bare shoulder, murmuring her name.

"Sleep well?" he asked.

She turned around and curled her body inside his arms, his skin wonderfully hot. "I *was*."

Leandros shifted against her, kissing the top of her head, his fingers lazily twisting locks of her hair. "We should rise and break our fast, though I have half a mind to stay here with you all day."

"Your crew wouldn't miss you too much, I think."

"Perhaps I *should* get up," Leandros said, moving to leave. To stop him, Penélope sat up and climbed on top of his waist, nearly laughing when his eyes widened slightly in real fear. She could hardly believe what had happened last night, but at the same time, nothing in her life had felt so natural before.

"Not so fast, captain," she said, grabbing his wrists and pinning them at his sides. "You have other duties to attend to first."

He looked at her in all seriousness. "I'm yours to command, my Lady."

She lowered her face until their lips brushed. "Here's your first order." Then she whispered the words into his ear until he broke free of her grip and wrapped his arms tight around her waist.

When they did finally leave their room, hastily bathed in the bronze tub by their fire and dressed in fresh linen, everyone else was already gathered in the main hall, where a low fire burned in the hearth, a cauldron hung above it, cooking something that smelled sweet.

Leandros breathed in deeply and brightened. "Honeyed oatmeal."

"That always was your favorite as a boy," King Leon said with an air of reminiscence. It seemed for now the argument between them had been set aside. "You have just missed the goddess, who departed to collect herbs in the forest. She has left us with food and supplies to bring back to the camp."

Leandros nodded, reclining on the couch beside the King. "We shall need all hands at work building the ship if we wish to depart as soon as possible."

When Penélope took her seat beside Leandros, Owen leaned across Zeb's couch toward her. "Late night, eh?"

Zeb rolled his eyes, pushing Owen away, who grinned when Penélope did not respond, hoping her face was not as red as it felt. Leandros glanced at her, and seeing the flush on her cheeks grew red himself.

"Speaking of departing," Penélope said, clearing her throat, "there's something we need to discuss. While you were all...under her enchantment, I was able to speak privately with her, and she told me a kind of riddle about how to quell the wrath of Poseidon, which we have to do if we want to return home."

"She couldn't just tell us herself?" Owen asked dryly.

"Apparently, she swore not to help us directly."

"Surprise, surprise." Owen shook his head. "Out with it then."

Penélope nodded, then repeated the verses Circe had told her yesterday, as if they had been seared in her memory by magic:

> *"To cross the wine-dark sea back home*
> *and quell the wrath of Ocean King*
> *both far and wide then must you roam*
> *but first beguiling maids who sing*
> *must one aboard your ship endure*
> *then seek the pillars of the sea*
> *where daughter his may grant succor*
> *and from his curse shall set you free."*

Everyone sat silent as they pondered over the lines. No one seemed eager to offer solutions. Penélope herself, who would usually jump at the possibility of solving a riddle like this, had been rather occupied since she heard it, and hadn't spent much time on picking it apart.

"Well, let's start with the obvious," Owen drawled. "The *Ocean King* must be

Poseidon."

Zeb gave him a sidelong glance. "Tell us something we don't know."

"Beguiling maids who sing must one aboard your ship endure," Leandros murmured. "That can only mean one thing. But why?"

King Leon nodded grimly. "Sirens. Perhaps Poseidon shall be easier to calm if he knows we have suffered beforehand."

"So first, one of us has to hear the sirens," Penélope reiterated, confirming her initial suspicions, "then we seek someone's daughter at the Pillars of the Sea. Is that Poseidon's daughter? Or someone else's?"

"Poseidon has many offspring," Leandros said. "It may be impossible to know of whom it speaks."

"The Pillars of the Sea," Penélope repeated the phrase under her breath, closing her eyes. "Where have I heard that before?"

"Atlas," King Leon murmured. "That is one of his names."

Penélope's head snapped up. "That's it! Atlas! The Atlas Mountains!"

"It said the Pillars of the *Sea,* not *Earth,*" Owen said pointedly.

"The Atlas Mountains are said to be the Pillars of the Sea because they are at the edge of the known world—the edge of the entire world, really," Penélope explained, quickly adding her correction of Emmeson's geography as far as she remembered it from glimpsing Leandros' maps in his cabin. "The mountains have roots at the edge of the Middle Sea. That's why they are called the Atlas Mountains, because Atlas holds up the pillars that separate heaven and earth, just like the actual mountain range."

Leandros nodded. *"As above, so below."*

Owen and Zeb stared at her dubiously, but King Leon was smiling. "The Atlas Mountains, where dwells the Sibyl of Apollo. It seems I shall fulfill my original quest after all."

"The Sibyl of Apollo must be the daughter!" Penélope exclaimed, only to pause. "She *is* the daughter of Poseidon, right?"

"Yes, she is."

They all turned. Circe stood in the doorway, a large woven basket hanging from her arm, filled with a variety of herbs tied with string, as well as flowers and roots. She strode inside, handing the basket to one of the handmaids, while another removed her brown cloak, revealing the radiance of her skin, robed in rich red cloth, the same color as her blood red lips. Penélope tore her gaze away, only to see King Leon staring helplessly after her. Leandros clenched his jaw, his eyes fixed firmly on the floor before him.

Circe joined them in the space between Owen and King Leon, both of whom marveled at the goddess with unabashed desire. She poured herself a glass of wine, apparently not bothered by the silent attention she now received as she sipped her golden chalice.

"Since the god Apollo established his oracle in the mountains," Circe said at last, "there dwelt a priestess in the caverns at the mouth of the sacred spring deep inside the Pillars of the Sea."

"The Sibyl," Penélope murmured.

Circe nodded her head. "So she is called, once Apollo has chosen her."

"Then the Sibyl is a daughter of Poseidon?" Zeb asked doubtfully.

"They say that long ago, at the time when Apollo needed to choose his next Sibyl, he fell in love with a Nereid, Amphitrite, and took her to be his priestess."

"They say?" Owen echoed. "Who says?"

Circe leveled him with a look, and Owen blushed. "As the story goes, Amphitrite had been promised to wed Poseidon. Some say she had fled to Atlas, the Titan god, in refusal of the marriage, but others say after falling in love with her, Apollo took her to the Atlas Mountains to be his new Sibyl."

"I thought it was supposed to be the daughter of Poseidon," Penélope said in confusion, "not his wife."

"Amphitrite was returned to Poseidon," King Leon interjected, then, catching Circe's raised brow, added, "At least, as we tell the tale, the Sea God sent many to retrieve her. Only the daemon Delphin was able to bring her back, and thereafter Poseidon raised the dolphin among the stars in gratitude."

"Well, there is another story told in other parts of the world," Circe said with a small, amused smile. "After the Earth Shaker heard of Amphitrite's betrayal with Apollo, he grew angry and threatened to crush the Atlas Mountains with a wave, for his love of the Nereid was great. In fear of Poseidon's wrath, Apollo returned Amphitrite to the King of the Sea, in exchange for a daughter of Poseidon to be named his new Sibyl. Poseidon gave his daughter, Aethusa, whose mother was the daughter of Atlas, and therefore bore the separation, to dwell with her mother and kin. But she is still held dear by her father, who listens to her appeals."

"Then we must sail to her immediately," Leandros said, standing up as if he were ready to leave now.

Circe laughed. "Are you so eager to leave my halls, Leandros, son of Leon? I do not suppose they lack for any comfort."

Her eyes slid imperceptibly toward Penélope. Leandros blushed. "No, they do not, my Lady, and we shall be forever grateful for your hospitality when we needed it most. But we cannot linger here for long. Our city needs us now more than ever."

Penélope touched Leandros' arm. "We still need to build the ship first, and that doesn't happen overnight. Why don't we eat breakfast and then visit the camp?"

Leandros' eyes softened on her. She ignored Zeb, who rolled his eyes, and Owen who snidely commented something about newlyweds. "I suppose we can afford to stay a few more days."

After a breakfast of rich, honeyed oatmeal, which Penélope savored with fresh fruit, they hiked down to the beach, where the rest of the crew that had remained behind were at work. Already axes and other sharpening tools had been sent ahead by Circe, so the men had begun chopping down trees in the woods and arranging the long planks for building the ship. Nausicala oversaw the construction with her usual unbending authority and reserve, only revealing her true emotions when she saw her son and grandson ambling down to the beach. She rushed over to them, hugging and kissing them, until she ascertained that all was well.

King Leon and Leandros, with the help of Owen's enthusiastic remarks, relayed the events of the last day since they left, including being spelled into pigs, the strange riddle, and staying the night. Many of the men complained loudly that they were not able to return home yet, but Leandros quelled them by warning that if they didn't do as the goddess suggested, then they would encounter another storm by Poseidon like the one that had brought them to this island in the first place. That silenced most of them, though many still showed their frustration, a few even regretful that they had rescued King Leon at all.

She understood how they felt. The thought of traveling to yet more uncharted waters and lands caused her to shiver. What monsters might they encounter on their journey? Who else might die before they reached home?

Nausicala joined her by the water's edge, where Penélope had stepped away while the others assisted the men in sawing tree trunks and sanding planks.

"How are you feeling, my Lady?" Penélope asked.

"Better, after a day of rest." Nausicala nodded at Mono, who stood nearby, tying two planks together with rope the goddess had provided them, assisted by a fussy Dora, who helped tie the rope with surprising strength. "A first-rate sailor, Monopous is. He did not let me out of his sight until I could walk on my own."

"Mono is a true gentleman, at least for a pirate."

Nausicala laughed. "A pirate with the heart of a gentleman." He glanced at Leandros keenly. "And a prince with the heart of a wanderer. They make the perfect pair."

Penélope shielded her eyes from the sun, which glared in the sky, watching Leandros carry a long plank with Owen over to a growing pile of wooden beams ready to be sanded and fitted together. The muscles in Leandros' arms strained as he lifted the heavy plank and set it down with a labored exhale. Even Zeb helped with the less physically intense work of drilling smaller holes into planks and wrapping rope around intersecting joints.

"Leandros is a wanderer at heart," Penélope said finally, "but I know a part of him longs for home."

"Perhaps he merely needed to *find* his home," Nausicala said, softly nudging her arm with a knowing look.

Penélope blushed, that same fierce protectiveness rising in her. Her eyes burned with tears despite how strangely content she felt. "I guess he's my home now too."

"You left much behind, then? In coming here?"

She nodded. "My entire life. My education. All of my family. Parents, siblings, my dog." Penélope shook her head with a small, sad laugh. "But it's more than that. It's all I know, the world I left behind. My country, California, and my town, Tierra del Sol. In your language, it means *Land of the Sun.*"

"Your home is who you love," Nausicala said, her voice tinged with sadness. "I know that well."

"And now I'm the wife of a prince," Penélope said quietly. "One day, if we survive this war, I might even be...I might be—"

"Queen," Nausicala finished. "Yes, you will be queen one day, Penélope."

She closed her eyes, forcing the tears away that gathered so easily behind her eyes these days. "I don't know how to be queen."

"Being queen is not something to learn, but someone to *become*. In time, you shall adjust to life in the palace by your husband's side. My only regret is that the oath you swore to my father will bring such sorrow to you both."

"This was never supposed to happen. None of it." Penélope shook her head. "Sometimes I imagine getting back to the city and leaving all of this, returning to my family, pretending I never came here. Pretending I had never…never fallen in love." She could barely speak the last word without a tremor, and the tears that had begun welling in her eyes finally fell down her cheeks, which she hurried to wipe away, hoping no one would see them.

"You cannot pretend, no more than I can pretend that my husband still lives, or my son, Alexander." Nausicala took her arm in hers, and her emerald eyes shone a hard steeliness in their depths. "The gods deal out our fate, but it must be *we* who face it, for running away shall only tighten the noose, and cause us to fall into utter madness, as Oedipus, willfully blind to his fate, gouges out his eyes once he learns it."

"Then I suppose my fate is to love," Penélope said, only half-jokingly. "At least, that is what the goddess Calypso told me."

Nausicala squeezed her arm. "Your fate, Penélope, is like any story. Who else shall tell it but you?"

40

THEY SPENT THE REST of the day on the beach, but when the sun began to crawl closer to the horizon, one of Circe's handmaidens came to the camp and summoned them all up to her halls, where she had prepared them a huge feast.

Some of the men were wary of trusting the goddess, but once Leandros and the others began describing last night's meal, the rest of them relented and hiked eagerly to Circe's home, where smoke continued to waft pleasantly from the roof. Her humming voice could be heard inside, and the men all walked into the hall in a daze.

Large wooden tables long enough to seat thirty people were surrounded by linen-covered couches. Upon the tables were crowded plates of freshly caught and cooked fish, roasted duck, hot stew, bread, fruit, cakes, and mulled wine. The men gleefully reclined on the couches, thanking the goddess profusely, many of them gazing at her longingly. Only Nausicala spoke to Circe with an air of reserve, and Penélope wondered if King Philoxenos had ever been caught astray on the island before.

Once the feast concluded, everyone filed off to bed. Two handmaidens led the rest of the crew to the guest bedrooms down the other side corridor. Penélope and Leandros returned to their bedroom to find their bronze tub had been filled with clean, warm water.

"The goddess has certainly not forgotten a single comfort," Leandros joked, but he grew serious when Penélope slipped out of her dress, slowly dipping a foot inside the bath.

"Well?" she asked. "Are you not going to join me?"

By the time they curled up in bed with Leandros' arm draped protectively over her waist, Penélope fell asleep swiftly. The following day, the men went down to the beach to continue building the ship, while Penélope, Nausicala, and Dora remained behind with Circe and her handmaidens to start weaving the sails. It was a difficult task, requiring four massive looms made of wooden poles as tall as the ceiling, set up in a warehouse attached to the back of the house. While the loom and shuttle with which Korinna had taught Penélope how to weave could be worked sitting down, this loom had a shuttle the size of Penélope's arm, and had to be worked by two or even three women at the same time, passing the shuttle between them as they crossed the threads, and using both their strength to move the heavy log that separated each singular taut thread pulled down by a huge stone weight.

Another five days passed in this way, the men building the ship, the women weaving the sails, ending each day with a massive, merry feast filled with sailors' drinking songs and jaunty dances. Penélope and Leandros would return to their rooms still laughing and half-drunk on wine, kissing the moment the doors closed behind them.

A week passed as if in paradise, even with all the work they had to do. Nausicala taught Penélope weaving songs to pass the time, which she picked up easily thanks to Hermes' gift of language. Her favorite was called 'The Golden Shuttle,' which they chanted like a hymn, lightly knocking their shuttles against the loom's beams to create a rhythm:

> *The Golden Shuttle wove in dread*
> *all fates of mortals trapped by thread*
> *like flies in spider's net ensnared*
> *no soul once caught in web be spared.*
>
> *By Morai spun the threads of Fate*
> *allotted each on loom a weight*
> *and woven back and forth by one*
> *thus may the will of Zeus be done.*
>
> *Until the last with hated shear*
> *when cursèd day of death draws near*
> *the thread of life untimely snipped*
> *not when nor how may man predict.*

So weaves the Golden Shuttle still
up till the loom divine they fill
whose cloth shall godly halls adorn
when all the cosmos be reborn!

But not everything was perfect. A new tension had sprung between her and Zeb, made worse by the fact that she and Leandros had become more intimate together. Nights in bed with him were a solace to the hurt she felt when Zeb turned his face away from her coldly at dinner, as if she had chosen Leandros over their friendship and now wanted to punish her. Even Owen made his own cutting remarks about how they were on their honeymoon now, but Penélope chalked that up to his jealousy that Zeb was also giving *him* the cold shoulder.

The next night, while lying back against Leandros' bare chest, their hands lacing and unlacing by their sides, she asked if Zeb seemed strange to him as of late.

"Your pale friend has always been strange."

Penélope rolled her eyes. "Yes, but recently. Does he seem different? Stranger than normal?"

"Perhaps," Leandros said slowly. "Or perhaps it is you who is different."

Her heart twisted inside her chest at the thought. "Different how?"

"You are married, for one." He held her left hand up where her wedding ring now graced her ring finger, his thumb and forefinger twisting it gently so that the stone caught the firelight and glowed. "And you can understand our language now and speak it."

"I didn't exactly choose any of that," Penélope muttered. "But he's choosing to ignore me now."

"Did you not choose it?" Leandros asked. "Did the Queen of Death not ask if you accepted your fate?"

Penélope was silent. He was right, after all. During the long nights awake side by side, or curled up together in fur blankets by the fire, she had told Leandros all of what had happened to them since Alexandria showed up in Tierra del Sol, and arriving in the city of Helena. She only omitted detailed descriptions of her home and how her old life was, save for the New Academy and Sister Stella.

Leandros had listened carefully, responding with thoughtful observations and questions that revealed glaring mistakes or clues that Penélope and her friends had missed in their chaotic descent into Helena. Then he would describe some of his own life, how it was to be a prince at the palace, the pressure to live up to his family name, even his mother, Queen Cleopatra, who was a famed alchemist in her own right and worked closely with the Seven Sages in her research.

While he loved his parents and Helena, as a child he had often felt suffocated, forced to learn princely manners and customs, shadowing his father in councils and learning to play every sport and use various kinds of weapons. Writing poetry and songs had been more of a pastime, as he only had scant lessons with his tutor on the subject, spending more time on memorizing epic lays and histories for recitation, learning several other languages, along with geography, cartography, and city planning. All of his upbringing had been to prepare him to be King one day.

"Yet I fear, despite all of my studies, I shall never learn to be half the King my father and his father have been," Leandros had said one night, murmuring his doubts in the darkness of their room, lying side by side in bed, the fire having dimmed to embers.

"Being king is not something to learn, but someone to *become*," Penélope had said, repeating the words Nausicala had told her, taking his left hand and kissing the twin sapphire ring resting there.

He had looked at her in surprise and then longing, as if for a moment he had forgotten that this was not just a dream, before he rolled on top of her without another word, snaking his arms around her waist and pulling her in close.

Leandros wrapped his arms around her now when she still did not respond, kissing the top of her hair. "Do not worry about your friend, my love. There are greater cares on your mind as it is."

"I have to worry about him," Penélope said, feeling the tears press close behind her eyes. "I'm the only friend he has." *And he's mine,* were the words she almost spoke, but with a pang in her chest, she knew they were no longer true.

"What about your other friend? The son of Godfrey?" Leandros asked, gently wiping the tears from her face. "Surely he considers Zeb a friend, and will watch over him when you cannot."

Penélope went still, wondering how much Leandros knew, but from the tone of his voice, he appeared not to have picked up on their romantic relationship. She shook her head with a sigh. "I'm not sure they're friends at all."

"The customs of your people are strange. Two people may risk their lives for one another, but hardly consider each other friends. Two friends who are more akin to family will ignore each other without reason. And a man and a woman who love each other may not declare their love openly, but must court in disguise and deception until one takes a knee, yet even then their loyalty may be cut short."

She laughed despite her tears. "When you put it like that, we do sound strange. But I could say the same for your people. A father and son will risk their lives to save each other, but can barely speak to each other honestly. Women may be queens and command an army of men, and goddesses may sleep with any man they choose, but otherwise, they can't even wear a pair of pants while sailing. And a man will declare his love for a woman whom he had only just a few hours before held captive on his pirate ship!"

"I thought I had already apologized for that," Leandros muttered childishly. "Besides, you ought not to judge us so harshly. My people are now your people, after all."

Penélope twisted around with a wince. "You're right. I'm sorry."

Leandros shook his head in disbelief, his hands coming to rest on her hips, his eyelids half-closing as his gaze swept over her body in a subtle wonder. "If one of us ought to be sorry, it is I. And yet, with you here in my arms, I find it difficult to feel sorry at all."

By the time Dawn's rosy fingers gently woke her up, Leandros had long left her bed, and she heard voices in the main hall. She washed herself quickly, rubbed scented oil over her skin, and slipped on her robes, then joined the others for breakfast. She found Zeb and Owen speaking in low voices by the fire away from the rest of the crew, and instead of avoiding them, she plopped herself on a chair beside them.

"What are you two whispering about?" Penélope asked teasingly, as she used to do when she found Zeb and Ari in the library speaking in murmurs, though usually it was only about some esoteric subject or another.

"Coffee," Owen said with a groan. "I miss it desperately."

Zeb agreed with a solemn nod of his head. "Me too."

"I miss showers more," Penélope said.

Owen sighed, then ruffled his hair, which had grown out in tight curls, now only maintained with oil and thin silver combs provided by Circe. "And barbers."

"And razors," Zeb said, scratching at the stubble on his chin and cheeks.

"You know Mono could shave it for you," Penélope said pointedly.

Zeb crossed his arms. "And let that pirate near my throat with a knife? No thanks."

Owen cocked his head. "I quite like you with a bit of scruff, you know." Zeb blushed, staying resolutely silent. "Makes you look older." The blush deepened. "More rugged."

"Okay, that's enough, son of Godfrey," Penélope said dryly, using Leandros' nickname for him. "Zeb doesn't need another reason to make your life Hell...or should I say, *Hades?*"

Owen burst into laughter with Penélope when they caught each other's eye, and Zeb tried to school a reluctant smile into a frown. "That was bad even for you, Pepa," Zeb had murmured reluctantly.

"So, how are the sails coming?" Owen asked once they stopped laughing.

"Almost done," Penélope said, stretching out her hands and forearms, which had been sore the first two days from weaving all day long. "And the ship?"

Owen raised a brow. "Almost done."

"When do you think we'll leave?" Zeb asked, glancing at Penélope as if to gauge her reaction.

She forced a smile, pretending it was what she wanted, though the drop of her stomach and the dread that filled her heart told her otherwise. Every day here felt like a paradise—a honeymoon, even if she'd never admit that to Owen—and a respite from the real world, the upcoming war, and the dangers they still had to face before then. The thought of leaving was terrifying, and a part of her wanted to force Leandros to stay with her here and never leave, just like Calypso had with Odysseus.

Across the room, Leandros was already looking at her, as if he had heard her thoughts. She turned away uneasily. Was that why King Leon had stayed with Calypso? Was that why Odysseus had been unable to leave her all those years long? Had a part of them—the part most hurt by the ghosts of the past—longed for peace, for unthinking, blissful peace, even if it meant giving up all that was good in their old lives?

But was that not simply running away? Nausicala had warned Penélope of running away from her fate. All this time, she had assumed it was about marrying Leandros and becoming queen of Helena one day. Now she wondered if accepting her fate had more to do with herself, facing the good *and* the bad in her life, just as she had faced the wrath of Demeter, unflinching.

For to eat the fruit of Love is to eat the fruit of Death. None may return once the first bite is taken.

Perhaps Persephone had not meant her love for Leandros at all, but merely another name for Life and Death, like two sides of the same coin. *As above, so below.* She had never considered it before, but now it seemed obvious. Love encompassed both Life and Death, as it was told in the Hymn to Demeter, when Persephone, snatched by Death, is the reason that Earth cycles around in seasons, a continual rhythmic circle of endings and beginnings, like planets circling the sun, like a story that repeats itself over and over again. First Helen, then Elena, and now Alexandria. First Odysseus, then King Leon, and now Leandros. Was it merely chance that had brought Penélope to this realm between worlds? Or did the gods truly keep their own counsel, weaving the threads of their fate into one single tapestry?

Either way, one thing was certain. They could not while away their time on this island. She would have to face her fate, or like the Queen Nausicala had said, risk falling into madness. That was the only thing she *could* do.

"We will leave when the ship is ready," Penélope said firmly. Zeb's brows hitched in surprise, but he did not contradict her. "Then we find the Sibyl of Apollo. It's time to go home."

41

A CLEAR SKY UNFURLED above the ship, which stood tall and grand on the beach. Zeb watched Penélope, Nausicala, and Dora help the handmaidens attach the sails to the wooden masts, Mono and Leandros, along with other sailors, hauling the thick cloth up by ropes.

A hand lay on his shoulder. Zeb saw Owen standing beside him out of the corner of his eye. His pulse quickened at the proximity, but he took a step away until Owen's hand slipped off his shoulder.

Owen eyed him warily. "No need to be so skittish."

Zeb ignored him, turning angrily toward the large wooden desk scattered with wood, and grabbing a knife he had been using to carve the long-handled oars.

"You ignore me now," Owen said in a low voice, coming close to him again, "but will you ignore me tonight?"

He glared at Owen's smirk, though there was no triumph in his eyes, only a cold certainty. It was true, after all. Ever since their stolen kiss in the hull before the storm, Zeb had found his way into Owen's room every single night. But just because he succumbed to his weakness in the darkness of the night did not mean he needed to acknowledge it during the light of day.

Zeb picked up the end of the oar where a block of wood remained at the bottom of the long, carved handle. He began slicing wood away from it, following the dark lines drawn to guide his strokes.

"What are you so afraid of anyway?" Owen asked. When Zeb didn't answer, Owen grasped the handle of the oar close to where Zeb's knife had just swiped, shaving the bottom of the oar's head. "Look at me, Zeb."

"Don't distract me," Zeb said icily, "or my knife might accidentally slip."

Instead of taking him seriously, as many would, and growing scared, Owen only gave a short laugh, his hand flexing around the oar handle challengingly, the muscles of his forearm corded from weeks of rowing, distracting Zeb more than anything Owen could say.

"Take a break, *mate*. No one would notice if we just slipped away..."

Zeb briefly closed his eyes, breathing deeply to calm the sudden pounding of his heart at the thought. "Too dangerous."

Owen released the oar with a frustrated sigh. "No one would even care. Half the crew have probably slept with a man at some point or another. How do you think they survive year-long journeys at sea with no women about? It isn't like it was back home."

"I won't even ask how you know that," Zeb muttered, barely hiding his jealousy. "And it *is* always like that, no matter where you are or what they say. They might have slept with a fellow sailor if they were desperate enough, but it's different with us."

"Different how?" Owen repeated incredulously. "And I know it because I *talk* with them. Or I try to, at least, with what little Greek I speak." He paused, then catching Zeb's glare, rolled his eyes. "Alright, I also know because they flirt with me. Happy?"

Zeb could hardly think from the blinding jealousy and anger. He grabbed his knife, and Owen took an instinctive step back. When Zeb merely continued shaving away at the oar, Owen shook his head.

"I can never understand you, Zeb. One minute you want me, another you hardly look me in the eye. If you plan to leave the city when we return, why do you care so much about what the crew thinks, anyway?"

Zeb's knife clattered to the table, and the oar dropped to the ground, startling some of the men nearby. Zeb took a menacing step toward Owen. "This has nothing to do with them. This is about *us,* and what the hell we're doing here. All I want is for you to admit that this means nothing to you, that I'm just a friend—or less—and that I'm a distraction, someone you're using until we get back home and you have better options."

Owen stared at him, his jaw clenched, but he remained silent.

"See? You talk a big game, Owen Godfrey, but when it comes down to it, you're just as scared of this as I am. You don't care if the whole crew knows that you're sleeping with a man, but God forbid you might feel something more than lust!"

"Then you want to be in a relationship?" Owen asked, throwing up his hands. "Is that all it is? Because I can be your boyfriend if it's about the labels."

Zeb laughed without humor, shaking his head. "I don't know why I even bother with you. From the start, I knew how this would go."

He turned to leave, but Owen grabbed his arm. "Wait, Zeb—"

"For the record," Zeb said, wrenching his arm from his grasp, "it's about love, not labels. But you've never loved anyone in your life." He nodded toward the wooden table. "Finish carving the oar. And don't wait up for me tonight."

Then he turned and walked away, though he had no idea where he was planning to go. As he walked blindly from the shore, he heard his name, then walked faster. Penélope followed him, calling his name again. He ignored her.

"Zeb Hades, stop now!"

He reluctantly slowed, turning around to see Penélope standing there in pale yellow robes, her short braids pinned back like Nausicala wore her hair, as if she had truly become Helene royalty. She crossed her arms, reminding him painfully of all the times she had told him off back home. Would they ever see each other again once he went back?

"You can't keep ignoring me, Zeb," Penélope said, sounding stern, though he detected the telltale sign of a tremor in her voice. "We have to talk."

"About what?" Zeb asked harshly.

She flinched, but did not back down from him, all too used to his harshness. "About how I'm married now, for starters. Did you ever consider that this situation hurts me just as much as you? Did you ever stop to think that I am also mourning for what I've lost in accepting my fate? My family and my home?"

"At least you have a family. You were the last of mine, but I guess it's *my* fate for all of them to abandon me."

Penélope stuttered in disbelief, tears jumping to her eyes. "Zeb, that's not fair—"

"Well, life isn't fair," he interrupted. "I learned that lesson a long time ago."

Then he left before he said anything more damaging. He felt a twinge of regret at pushing away both Owen and Penélope in the same moment—who were the only friends he still had in his life besides Ari—but decided it was probably only a matter of time before all of them decided he wasn't worth the effort anyway. He had never been a kind person, after all, but he had foolishly prided himself on his loyalty, only for that to be thrown back in his face.

In his escape from the beach, he had blindly stumbled into the woods, as if he were returning to the goddess' home inside the island. Nearby, he heard the bubbling of the river that Circe had enchanted, and cut through the sparse woods until he came upon its banks. He sat down by the water's edge, where the soft grass rolled down the hillside and brushed the gently moving currents, then lay back, closing his eyes before the tears could fall. He had never felt so alone, so very unloved.

As he lay there, a heavy exhaustion weighed on him, as if a wave of sleep washed over his mind, and he slept, aware that he slept, but as if from a distance, as darkness overtook him.

From the darkness he blinked, looking up from where he was sleeping in a white wooden crib. A familiar face hovered over him, before hands reached inside the crib and pulled him out, lifting him into a lovely warmth. The man kissed the top of his head.

"I love you, Zeb," a voice murmured from above. "I love you so much."

Another voice spoke behind them, and the man turned, Zeb turning with him. "Babe, what do—oh, there's our sweet boy! Look who woke up from his nap..."

Zeb sat up with a gasp, as if he had been underwater. Across the river, a basket filled with herbs under one arm, Circe stood watching him, cloaked in brown robes. Her red lips lifted into a smile, her golden eyes glowing when she turned, and the light caught her face, shining through the tops of the trees.

"That was my dad, wasn't it?" Zeb asked, knowing somehow that the goddess had caused the strange dream. "Why?"

The goddess studied him for a long time, so long that Zeb heard the breeze whistling between the trees and the birds chirping their songs. Then she turned away and began walking slowly down the riverbank, stopping only to stoop low and pull out a tangled, mossy plant clinging to the water's edge, half-submerged in the river.

Zeb scrambled to his feet and followed after her. "I only had dreams like that in the Underworld. Is there something in the water that made me see all that?"

Circe's laugh floated down the river like tinkling bells. "I have indeed enchanted those waters, but you have seen nothing that you did not wish to see."

"My parents," Zeb whispered. "My parents were happy. I never got to see them like that. Was it real? Or was I imagining it?"

"Memory is a strange thing," Circe said, dipping low again, but this time her hand scooped some water from the river, then, lifting her hand, allowed the water to run down her fingers and drip back into the water, though for a split second Zeb swore the water turned into silver. "Who is to say what is real or imagined?"

Zeb's head spun with her words, said in her quiet, murmuring voice like a spell. "Then everything I saw in the Underworld was memory."

"Not everything, for Death, as Life, is like a circle that never ends, neither begun nor ended, but eternal, like the gods above."

"Then I also saw...the future?"

He recalled the vision he had once while in the Asphodel Fields, of a ship rocking beneath him, blue waves crashing against the hull. He remembered turning to see the roaring, fanged mouth of a terrifying monster above him, just before he heard Penélope's voice screaming.

Zeb—!

Then he blinked, and the memory—or was it a vision?—faded. Perhaps when he was dead, even the future felt like memory, because time no longer worked in a straight line, but more like a circle, as the goddess had said.

Circe smirked as if she could read his thoughts, then crossed the stream, lifting her dress so her bare ankles waded in the river, climbing up her pale calves until she forded the currents to the other side. She continued meandering inside the woods, pausing here and there by the base of trees where mushrooms and roots grew in knotted, gnarled clumps.

"Who are you?" The question fled from his mouth without his thinking as he followed her into denser woodland.

She glanced back at him with a raised brow. "I am many things."

"What should I do?" Zeb asked, the utter loneliness he had felt when he had collapsed on the riverbank returning in one fell swoop, choking the very breath from his lungs. "Help me, please. I have no one else."

Circe stood and placed a long flower with a black stem and white flower petals into her basket, then lifted the hood of her cloak over her head, shrouding her face in shadow. "Strange you mortals are, surrounded by love yet blind to it, while immortals see all, and therefore stand alone."

Then Zeb blinked and she was gone, disappearing behind a tree trunk, as if she had disappeared into thin air. He took in a deep breath, wiped the tears from his face, and then made his way back to her home. Food already awaited them on large tables, though everyone was still by the beach putting the finishing touches on the ship. Zeb took his share and returned to his room, wishing to be alone, Circe's words still ringing in his mind.

He dozed off to sleep as the crew's merry voices and chatter floated down the corridor from the main hall. His dreams circled round and round the same memories of drowning in different places, always alone, always abandoned by those he most loved. Suddenly, he was wrenched from the depths of darkness, his head hazy, realizing it was night streaming in through the window, the moon's light deceptively bright. A knock softly sounded once more.

Zeb stood and crept toward the door, listening through the wood. But his heart already beat faster, knowing who it was. He slowly opened the door a crack, peering outside. Owen stood on the other side, his forehead resting where the door opened a sliver.

"What do you want?" Zeb asked, though he knew the answer.

Owen sighed, looking up at him through his lashes, subtly green and pleading. "Forgive me?"

Zeb hesitated, but he thought of his encounter with the goddess by the river, wondering if it was by chance, or if he had needed to be reminded of the love he had been given freely, even by those he now shunned, judging his parents and friends for all their faults. Hadn't Elena denounced that very judgment, calling him out for his blatant ignorance and hypocrisy?

You do not know of what you speak. You do not know love, nor sacrifice, nor motherhood. Your words are merely a child's insecurities.

"I do like you," Owen whispered, his eyes shut tight as if it pained him to say. "More than you know. It's just–difficult. For me. I'm don't–I'm not used to trusting people. But please, Zeb, don't shut me out."

You drown still, with no help from your mother.

Zeb opened the door wider. Owen straightened up in surprise, then followed Zeb inside without another word. Before Zeb could walk away, Owen grabbed his wrist and reeled him back until their lips met, all anger melting like ice when it thaws in the sun, Owen's hands uncharacteristically tender as they slid down his sides.

And just like the day he had nearly drowned to death, Zeb didn't fight it, giving himself up to the currents that had always been stronger than him.

42

Their last day on the island of Aeaea passed quickly now that the ship was built, fitted with sails, rowboats, and oars, and no longer in need of their day-long labor building it. Instead, they spent the day leisurely transferring stores of food and water to the ship before the crew boarded and hauled the ship out to sea, anchoring it amidst the waves.

Circe spared no luxury for their parting feast, providing an array of rare fish, squid, octopus, clams, oysters, crab, lobster, and other creatures Penélope had never seen before; she was hesitant to try the more colorful, strange-smelling dishes. Besides the seafood were platters of roasted and smoked meats, seasoned and drenched in spicy, creamy sauces. The usual oven-baked flatbread, honey, sesame dip, and fruit accompanied the extravagant dinner, ending with various desserts such as small cakes of sesame honey, poppy lemon, and olive ginger, as well as candy made from hardened honey and sesame, a honey-sweet custard, a rose-flavored flour paste, and a thin, flaky sheet baked with almonds and walnuts.

Of course, wine was served in copious amounts with their meal, and after all the plates were cleared, the handmaidens brought out hot, mulled wine in silver chalices. After that, a thick, highly fermented wine with a syrupy texture was passed around in smaller gold bowls, so that all of them were quite drunk by the late evening.

It was a feast worthy of kings and queens, which Penélope supposed was partly why they had such a feast to begin with, King Leon and the former Queen Nausicala reclining in the seats of honor on either side of the goddess.

"Ah, the final hour approaches!" King Leon exclaimed as another round of the strong, syrupy wine was poured, holding up his bowl. "Loth I am to depart the shores of such an enchanting isle, much less the homely halls of our host."

Circe inclined her head toward the King. "It has been my pleasure, King Leon, son of Philoxenos. And if I had a say—though goddesses like I seldom do in the affairs of greater powers—you all would remain here longer, until all your troubles melted away and were forgotten."

Some of the men glanced around with flushed cheeks, including King Leon, the idea of remaining with the goddess all too appealing. Penélope herself resisted the hazy enchantment of those golden eyes, knowing in her heart that she had to leave. Zeb, however, looked down at the ground with a hardened face, while Queen Nausicala appeared unaffected, lying stiffly beside Circe.

"I fear our troubles shall only end when we return home and finish what has already been set in motion by those greater powers you speak of," Nausicala said, her voice chilly.

The goddess raised a brow. "Then you plan to seek the Sibyl?"

"Yes, my Lady. We plan to sail to the Mountains of Atlas, but only after passing the sirens, where one of us shall hear their treacherous song."

"And who shall undertake this burden?" Circe asked.

Leandros spoke when no one else did. "I shall."

Everyone turned to him, many with protests at their lips, King Leon's brows furrowing, and Nausicala's face paling. Penélope looked at him in surprise, since he had not told her his intention of hearing the sirens' song, assuming that King Leon would offer himself.

"Son, you do not know of what you speak," King Leon urged. "I am older and wiser. Allow me to take this burden."

Nausicala nodded in agreement. "My dear boy, listen to your father—"

"I am not a child," Leandros interrupted. "I am captain of my ship, and therefore it is my duty to bear this burden, as Odysseus himself, my forefather, once did. Shall you dishonor me further by refusing me this charge?"

Penélope placed a hesitant hand on his arm. He glanced at her, his eyes steeled and ready for her dissuasion. The words were near to escaping her lips. *Do not risk your life so carelessly. We need you more than anyone. I need you.* Then she recalled all the times she had also walked fearlessly, even recklessly, into danger, no matter if Leandros wished her not to. She heard the Queen of Death's cold, merciless voice once more. *Who else? Who shall you condemn to your fate?*

If this was Leandros' fate, then so be it.

"I'll listen with you," was all Penélope said, and Leandros' eyes softened.

"No!" Circe sat upright, her eyes wide and her face filled with terror. "No, Lady Penélope, you may not! Only one aboard the ship may listen and pass unscathed, so long as he is bound tight to the mast. The rest aboard must plug their ears with beeswax and thus render their songs powerless. If any other than the chosen sacrifice should hear their song, none will be suffered to pass."

"I sacrifice myself," Leandros said firmly, squeezing Penélope's hand. "I shall listen to their song. Alone." No one argued with him after that.

Once the last round of wine was drunk, they left one after another to bed, all of them save Nausicala reluctant to put the night's festivities to rest, who had retired to her quarters early. Even Zeb, who had wished to leave more than anyone, lingered to hear Mono chant a slow, tender sailor's ballad dedicated to Amphitrite, the Queen of the Sea and Wife of Poseidon, in a surprisingly pleasant tenor of voice, which Penélope was thankful to understand in her own tongue, though she longed to hear the rolling, rich syllables of the Greek as she once had, sounding more like musical notes the less she understood:

> *The Nereids on Naxos danced*
> *when King of Ocean there advanced*
> *among the lovely nymphs who twirled*
> *with liquid feet, their braids unfurled,*
> *and saw the august, ox-eyed maid,*
> *fair Amphitrite, whom he bade*
> *to run away as lovers do,*
> *so wedding wreath to him she threw.*
>
> *Now down in ocean's deep they dwell*
> *unless you heed the tales they tell*
> *on Naxos heavenly they say*
> *when Lord Poseidon came that day*
> *how Nereus' daughter fled*
> *to mountains tall where none dare tread,*
> *the Titan pillars of the sea,*
> *where virgin still she might roam free.*
>
> *For long he sought her far and wide*

so King might have his ocean bride
and sent out creatures everywhere
to lure the nymph back to his lair,
but one by one returned alone
and wept the King atop his throne
until one dolphin swam the seas
and found her hid by Titan's knees.

Then pleaded long for her return
and not Poseidon's love to spurn.
Endeared by thoughts of lover dear,
on Delphin's back as steed to steer
and swiftly rode to Ocean's floor
where shiny shells and pearls they wore.
In golden palace ruled the King,
Poseidon, Dark-Haired, Earth-Quaking

His trident gold commands the sea
for none there be so strong as he.
To kingly throne did Delphin swim,
then Amphitrite sat by him,
the Queen of Aegae, fish and seals,
of dolphins, whales, sting rays, and eels,
who rules the moaning breakers loud
on open sea where fishes crowd.

The eldest Nereid of all,
with august ox-eyes did enthrall
Poseidon, Shaker of the Earth,
whom Tritan by his wife gave birth.
To honor Delphin, Lord of Steeds,
immortalizing his good deeds,
the King of Ocean raised him high
and cast the daemon in the sky.

There now Delphinus shines so bright,

his stars like shells and pearls gleam white,
reflected in the wine-dark sea,
when summer skies from winter flee,
before he dives beyond the edge
as once he swam to rocky ledge,
the Atlas Mountains, Titan's bane,
where by his knees the nymph had lain.

Fulfilling Lord's behest he bore
the maid, as wife forever more
of Ocean, Earth-encircling,
now Queen beside Olympian King,
a marriage born among the waves
where ill-lucked sailors find their graves.

"Did you know Mono could sing like that?" Penélope asked Leandros with a laugh once they returned to their room, her body still warm and humming from the wine and the beautiful performance Mono had given. Everyone had loved his rendition so much that at their request he sang it again, this time accompanied by the handmaidens and a few sailors who knew how to play the lyre, drums, and aulos, the rest of them clapping along to keep the rhythm.

Leandros smiled fondly. "I did. When I was still exiled, he once sang to all our crew a song of a prince sailing the seas—no doubt a sly reference to me, though the rest of the crew did not know my royal lineage. The tale told of a prince who was enchanted by a siren, one of Ocean's daughters, and after crossing the endless seas in search of her, he was granted the tail of the mermen and lived the rest of his days in the depths of the sea with her. I cannot remember all of it, but this is how it began." Then he took Penélope's hands and tugged her closer to him as his voice began chanting in a low murmur:

"Beware the seas, said captain old,
to handsome Prince a tale he told
of monsters dread beneath the deep
where siren songs send men to sleep
but worst of all by far is she
the princess of the Middle Sea

a mermaid graced with lovely-hair
whose deadly voice must men beware
lest hearing song so soft and sweet
will jump the sailor down to meet
the Ocean's daughter, Sirena,
her crown adorned with nymphaea..."

As he sang, his hands had brushed aside Penélope's hair, leaving her neck bare. He leaned down as he finished singing, humming the tune against her neck, then kissing the sensitive skin there. Penélope hooked her arms around his neck and pulled him into her embrace.

"Promise me you won't jump to meet her," Penélope whispered, shutting her eyes tightly against a fresh flood of tears aided in part by the wine, threading her fingers into his soft hair. "When you hear the sirens singing, promise me you'll stay on the ship."

Leandros pulled away, then kissed her cheeks where the tears had fallen unwillingly. "Do not forget, I shall be chained to the mast." She laughed thickly through the tears, and he kissed the top of her head. "But with you by my side, Πηνελόπη, I can survive any torment, for you alone have saved me from exile forevermore, even if I never return home."

She bit her lip, wishing the tears would stop, but something about this night felt different, his arms winding around her waist a bit tighter than the nights before, his kisses lingering longer, reluctant to be separated from her touch, as if Leandros himself did not know if they would survive the journey, and this night could be their last alone together.

As if sensing her thoughts, Leandros slowly lifted her into his arms and kissed her with all the tenderness and sorrow of a true goodbye. Then he led her to their bed, where they lay together in love until Dawn rose into the sky.

43

A CRISP MORNING AWAITED them by the beach as they prepared to set sail. Much of the crew had already boarded, fitting the ship and the sails and running last minute surveys of the ship's safety. Owen, Zeb, King Leon, Nausicala, and Dora had taken the previous rowboat to the ship, leaving her, Leandros, and Mono to oversee the transfer of the last supplies from Circe's generous stores.

Leandros came up to Penélope and brushed the back of his hand against hers. In public, they abstained from open affection, however much it irked Penélope. But she didn't wish to offend the crew or King Leon and Nausicala, so she merely smiled at him, recalling the night before with a blush, earning her a scarred smirk.

"We are nearly ready to set sail. I shall board the ship with Monopous now," Leandros said, nodding his head in Mono's direction, who stood waiting by a rowboat, a new silver peg fashioned by Circe's wand attached to his leg. Only a few men were left to pack up the camp. "Are you ready?"

"I'll take the last boat," Penélope said, turning away from the ship and gazing back at the island. Leandros followed her gaze briefly before nodding, then he joined Mono, and together they pushed the boat out into the tide.

Penélope stood staring at the woods by the beach, gentle fingers of a morning fog threading their silver-gray trunks. Beyond the woods, she could just make out a smudge of smoke atop the trees, where Circe's home was nestled in her enchanted vale. She did not know why now she was reluctant to leave, but her feet remained stuck in the sand, heavy like lead. Peering at the line of trees, she swore a shadow flitted between the trunks.

Without thinking, Penélope took off towards the woods. She heard her name called by one of the sailors uncertainly, but she ignored him. Soon she reached the tree line, slightly out of breath, the tall lengths of their trunks casting shadows over the grassy ground sprinkled with small flowers. Ahead of her, she saw a figure wandering, cloaked and hooded, holding a basket filled with herbs. She followed until the figure paused, though she must have sensed Penélope's presence from the start.

"Circe."

The goddess turned to her slowly, her face obscured but her golden eyes still visible, flashing like the dawn against a dark night. "Why do you linger, Penélope, daughter of Estela? Have you a change of heart after all?"

Penélope stood there dumbly, a battle in her heart. One part of her longed to stay, to allow Circe's elegant, purple-robed arms to embrace her, for the pleasure to melt away all her troubles and sorrows. Another part of her recalled the burning kisses Leandros had left across her skin and wondered why she had run after the goddess at all.

"Nay, my Lady," Circe said at last with a sad smile, "your fate lies not on this isle."

She sighed, relief flooding through her, as if she had needed the goddess to speak the words, thus releasing her from her spell.

"I just came to say thank you," Penélope said. "We are forever in your debt."

Then Penélope turned to go, but paused when she heard her name, facing the goddess once more, her heart in her throat.

Circe came to stand before her, the hood of her cloak drawn back so that the light of the sun glowed warmly on her rosy face. In that moment, Penélope recalled she was the daughter of the Sun and glimpsed the true power of the divine in that light. She held up a hand to Penélope's face, gently cupping her cheek, and Penélope held her breath.

"I have only one request of you, Lady Penélope," the goddess said, "which is that you name your firstborn daughter Aeaegona, in honor of me. Do this, and any debt to me shall be repaid in full, for all eternity."

Before Penélope could speak, Circe leaned forward and kissed her. Penélope's eyes fluttered shut automatically as a gentle warmth pressed against her lips, before the touch faded and she opened her eyes.

Circe was gone.

With a deep, weary sigh, Penélope turned and walked back to the beach. Two sailors awaited her anxiously by the last rowboat ready to leave, the camp already packed up and the sails of the ship unfurled. Once she stepped foot on the deck, a weight lifted from her mind, as if the enchantment had ended at last, and she looked around the ocean with new eyes, feeling sharper and clearer as she took in the bustling deck, the rowers at their oars, the sailors pulling on the ropes, and Mono and Leandros shouting orders.

It was as though their ship had never crashed and drowned in the storm, as if they had never stepped foot upon the island of Aeaea nor slept in the halls of the sorceress. She looked back at the island, swallowed up in the sea as the ship surged ahead, then recalled her promise. She slipped the veil of Leucothea off her shoulders and allowed the wind to carry it down to sea, where she swore a white arm lifted to catch it, though it could have merely been the sun glancing off the waves.

Then Penélope turned her back on the island and eagerly took her place by Mono's side, who flashed his yellow-toothed grin, the sunlight flashing on the metal teeth. He was always happier when they were on the open sea.

"Nice leg," she said with her own grin.

"The lady teases," Mono said, then leaned close in with a conspiratorial air, "but I daresay one kick from my here leg could kill a wild boar."

"Oh, I don't doubt it," Penélope answered in mock seriousness. "But be careful what you wish for, because you might just need to use it in my defense if we run across any more murderous giants."

"Oh, there are far worse than murderous giants in the unknown parts of the sea, Lady Penélope." But Mono paused, thinking, then motioned with his hand for her to follow. He led her to the captain's cabin, built with more room than the old one, where he rummaged inside a metal chest and pulled out a long leather scabbard.

"What's that?" Penélope asked, startled, though she knew exactly what it was.

"A sword, my Lady," Mono said, coming out of the cabin and unsheathing the sword halfway, the sunlight dancing across its bronze edge. "It is time the lady wore one, for there is nothing more perilous in this world than to be alone and unarmed. This one Circe claimed was forged in the very flames of the Sun by her father, Helios. It is worthy of the Lady Penélope, wielder of the Golden Blade and Dragon-Slayer, and will not fail her if the time comes."

Penélope took the sword hesitantly, the burning of the Golden Blade flashing through her mind, how the heat had melted her skin, leaving ugly white scars.

Leandros had never seemed to care that her palms were marred, perhaps because he himself had scars enough for both of them. Her right hand wrapped around the handle of the sword, lightly at first, then with more confidence.

She slid the sword out of its sheath, the naked blade appearing longer when she held it at the ready in front of her. "I barely know how to wield a sword, you know."

Mono shook his head in amusement. "Nor *should* the lady. But gods and monsters make little difference between mortal men and women. If the lady has cause to use it, only courage shall strike true."

"Let's hope it never comes to that."

Before she could slide the sword back into its scabbard, a familiar, icy voice spoke from behind her.

"You're not planning on actually *fighting*, are you?"

Penélope turned around, surprised to find Zeb standing there, his arms crossed, looking at the sword in her hands with disdain. He had ignored her attempts to reconcile, so his snarky comment angered her too much to consider talking sense into him. "Maybe."

"The only person you'll hurt with that is yourself," he muttered, then made as if to leave.

"Why do you care?" she asked loudly, forcing him to a stop. He glanced at her in annoyance, as if it had been *her* approaching him and not the other way around.

"I care for my own safety."

"Oh, do you?" She took a step in his direction, and his eyes widened, his feet stumbling backwards automatically. "Then if I were you, I wouldn't come near me with your rude comments and utter lack of sympathy when I have a sword in my hand."

Zeb's face hardened at her words, though he no longer backed away. "I only want what's best for you, Penélope. *You're* the one who insists on risking your life for people that you haven't known for six months, let alone practically your whole life!"

The hurt and anger that she had bottled up inside now welled to the surface. She walked close to him and pointed a finger at his chest. "No, Zeb. You don't want what's best for me. You want what's best for *you*. You want me to go back home for *you*."

"Well, maybe because you're all I have!"

She flinched at the raw pain in his voice.

"Fine! Maybe I do need you," Zeb continued, then grimaced, as if he were trying with all his might to hold the words back but could no longer help himself. "Maybe I can't live without you, Penélope. Have you ever thought of that? Or do you just care about Leandros now? Is your mind so clouded from how often you and Leandros—"

Penélope's palm struck his face before she knew what had happened, her sword lowering at her side. Zeb stared at her with wide eyes. She had not laid a finger on him since they were younger and would get into stupid arguments. Her cheeks burned when all the nearby crew glanced at them in surprise, before Mono and Leandros hurriedly gave them new orders, turning their attention away.

"How dare you," Penélope said in a low, threatening voice, sheathing her sword with trembling hands. "How dare you try to embarrass me in front of Leandros' family."

He stepped forward and said almost pleadingly, "Who cares about them, Pepa. This isn't our world. This isn't your *life.*"

"No, Zeb. This isn't *your* world. But my fate is already decided. Can't you see? I've made my choice. It's time you made yours."

Zeb's face fell, and some resolve in him broke, so that his body sagged, like removing the foundation stone of a tower and watching its grand defenses come crumbling down. "I can't win, can I? You'll always choose him now. You'll always take Leandros' side."

"Win? Side?" Penélope echoed. She felt more exhausted than angry at this point. "Zeb, listen to yourself. I haven't chosen any side. If anything, I've chosen the side of a war, the side of Gaia, and you'd better hope we win."

He was silent, his eyes lowered in defeat, though Penélope didn't feel as though she had won anything. The crew continued manning the ship as if nothing had happened, bustling around them like a river's current around a jutting rock.

"You have a choice too, Zeb," she said softly. "More than one choice, I think. Will you stand and fight with me? You know I wouldn't judge you if you left."

Just then Owen came up to them, rubbing the sleep from his eyes. He had been off shift napping in the hull and would start rowing again soon. Their ship had made swift progress across the sea, and by the next early Dawn, they would approach the dangerous territory of the sirens.

Owen stretched his arms with a yawn, one hand coming down on Zeb's shoulder, who stiffened at the contact. "What's all this about?"

Penélope raised a brow at Zeb meaningfully, but he only shouldered his way past Owen, muttering, "Nothing."

Once he left, Owen tore his gaze away from his retreating figure down the hull, looking at Penélope with a sympathetic smile. "He'll come around, don't worry. He just needs time."

"That's the problem," she said grimly, her hand tightening around the hilt of the sword. "Time is exactly what we don't have."

44

Even though no supernatural storm had yet assailed them, the wind struggled against their ship all that day, then suddenly stopped the moment the sun sank beneath the sea. Penélope stood by the prow, gazing ahead into the swelling black waves. She could hear the grunts of effort from the crew rowing into the still night as their ship crawled blindly ahead.

The belt on her waist was heavy with the sword strapped to it. She placed a hand over the hilt, finding the cool weight of it comforting, though she doubted it could save her from a dolphin, let alone a massive, bloodthirsty sea monster. After Zeb had argued over her accepting the sword, he had retreated to the hull and had not resurfaced.

As she watched the mingling black of ocean and sky, the half-moon rose blood-orange and sat large over the horizon, outshining all the stars so that many faded into the moon's hazy glow.

"A red moon rises."

Her pulse rose and fell at the sound of his voice. Leandros came to stand beside her, his eyes scanning the horizon as if he might already catch a glimpse of those sirens circling the waters ahead.

"Is the red moon a bad omen?" Penélope asked.

Leandros softly chanted:

"Black is moon to start anew,
White is moon for spells,
Gold and red is moon if one
Against the gods rebels."

Penélope raised a brow. "That's a real saying?"

"No." Leandros laughed at her expression. "Well, partly. I altered the last two lines to fit our current plight."

"They sound like the prophecy—first is black, second white, third is gold, and last is red," Penélope murmured.

"Perhaps they are not unrelated," Leandros mused. "Our people have long studied alchemy and its relations to the heavens. My mother herself has studied it all her life under the supervision of the Seven Sages."

Somehow, Penélope knew it could not be a mere coincidence. "What were the original lines?"

Leandros paused, then, in a near whisper as if afraid the gods would hear them, he chanted:

> *"Black is moon to start anew,*
> *White is moon for spells,*
> *Gold and red is moon at sea*
> *If soon come stormy swells."*

The memory of the wave lifting their ship into the air flashed through her mind, and she shivered. "Then it's a bad omen."

"It's just a sailor's superstition," he said with a shrug, though he eyed the moon warily. "We are not returning home anymore. Not at least until we ask the Sibyl to intercede on our behalf. The King of the Sea has no reason to assail our journey. The most danger we shall face will be the song of the Ocean's daughters."

"Are you ready to face the sirens?" Penélope asked, her stomach flipping nervously at the thought.

Leandros smiled wryly. "With you at my side, I am."

She took his hand without thinking. "I won't leave your side. No matter what."

His gaze lowered to their joined hands. The innocent touch felt strange, as they had scarcely touched each other in the days since leaving Aeaea. After the string of nights wrapped in each other's arms, it was unsettling to have him so close and yet not be able to kiss him in public.

Leandros' neck flushed as if he were thinking the same. He cleared his throat. "Come. I have something important I must show you. In the cabin."

"What is it?" she asked, startled at the change in subject.

He didn't answer, walking back to the cabin's room. She followed quickly, wondering what it could be. Perhaps to show where they were on one of his maps? Or another clue to how they were going to actually find the Sibyl in the Atlas Mountains?

"Leandros," she said as they entered the cabin, closing the door behind her. "What are you—"

He lifted her in his arms, silencing her with a kiss. She was so surprised, all she could do was sink into his arms, her hands automatically finding his curls, pulling at the soft strands as she loved to do. Leandros groaned into the kiss, setting her down against the desk, where she unstrapped her sword, the heavy metal landing with a loud thud on the wooden floor.

At the sound, he pulled away, his face painfully ghosting her neck, his breath warm on her skin. Her chest rose and fell heavily against him. "I cannot bear not touching you."

"Then touch me," Penélope said with a sly smile, her hands climbing up his arms that framed her legs. He grew still at her touch, his hands flexing on the desk. "No one can hear us over the sounds of the waves."

Leandros spoke roughly. "We should not."

"Oh, I know." She placed a kiss on his bicep, then his jaw, her hands lightly raking his chest. "We'll have to be *really* quiet."

Without another word, he took her by the waist, and she gasped involuntarily just before his mouth found hers, hungry and firm, while his hands lowered on the back of her thighs. She pulled him closer, until their bodies were flush and she could feel every muscle tensed and shifting against her.

"You," he said between kisses, moving down her bare, flushed neck, "are," the dip between her breasts, "my," her belly, his lips sparking desire down her navel, "weakness."

He grasped her knees and then slid up her dress, but all of a sudden Penélope went cold all over, her head spinning, the image of Leandros' mouth softly kissing her belly reminding her of Circe's request, which she had hardly understood in the moment or thought much of after in the excitement of leaving and her argument with Zeb.

I have only one request of you, Lady Penélope, which is that you name your firstborn daughter Aeaegona, in honor of me. Do this, and any debt to me shall be repaid in full, for all eternity.

How had Penélope not seen it? Aeaegona, or Αἰαίγονα in Greek, which literally meant *Aeaea-born.* If Circe had wanted her to name her first daughter *Aeaea-born,* that could only mean—

"Penélope?"

Leandros was kneeling between her legs. She stared at him in silence, for the first time unable to think of anything to tell him. All her limbs felt frozen, numb, as if she had drowned to the very coldest, darkest depths of the ocean.

"Penélope, what's wrong?" he asked worriedly.

Her mouth fell slightly open, but nothing came out save her struggling breath, a wave of panic clawing up her chest, the cabin swaying dangerously before her eyes, only to realize they were filled with tears.

"Captain!"

Mono's shout and hard knocks on the door drew her back to reality. Penélope snapped her gaze to the door, then back to Leandros, who met her eyes in widening fear. She quickly stood up and shoved her dress down at the same moment Leandros adjusted his tunic and belt, combing down his unruly curls.

"Yes, Monopous?"

"Captain, we are nearing the daughters of Ocean!"

Leandros closed his eyes briefly, then nodded to himself before calling out. "Give me–I will be there in a moment! Prepare the crew with beeswax!"

"You have to be chained before you hear them," Penélope said, forcing the words out, though her heart still pounded fiercely in her chest. "We can't waste any time."

With a stumbling step, she shakily latched onto the door handle and shoved herself outside. Leandros followed behind her silently. She was shocked to see that no wind billowed the sails and no waves beat against the hull. Everything was still and eerily quiet, even the rowers had ceased their grunts while they filled their ears with warmed-up beeswax that Circe had given them, cut in chunks from a round, hard block the color of a pale yellow morning.

Penélope walked with Leandros to the main mast, where Monopous met them with large, thick ropes in his hands. King Leon and Nausicala had come to join them, their ears already plugged with wax, hovering near Leandros worriedly. Zeb stood beside Owen's rowing bench, the two of them carefully sticking the wax in their ears and cringing at the same time at the sensation.

King Leon helped Mono strap the ropes around Leandros' chest, his arms tied behind his back, and his feet bound for good measure. To see him tied helplessly to the mast, knowing what she knew now, it took all her strength not to sink to her knees beside Leandros.

"Lady Penélope," Mono said. She looked at him, then down at his hands where a clump of wax rested, but she hesitated in grabbing it. Mono eyed her critically. "My Lady?"

"My sword," she stammered. "I-I left it."

Mono shook his head. "The lady shall not need her sword tonight."

She ignored everyone's stares as she swallowed down another wave of panic and grabbed the wax, surprised to find it was warm and soft, and faintly smelling of honey. The sweet scent seemed to revive her senses. With trembling hands, she tore the wax in two and plugged her ears, wincing at the coolness of the wax that seemed to melt against her eardrums, sealing up even the sound of her choppy breaths.

Mono was the last to fill his ears with wax. Everyone glanced at each other in uneasy apprehension once he was done. Penélope looked out at the sea, though the moon had long climbed high in the sky, smaller and whiter than when it had first risen above the horizon, shedding little light on the glinting black waves.

King Leon led Nausicala back to her cabin, where Dora awaited her after one last regretful glance at Leandros, who merely nodded, his jaw hardened in determination. Mono left them alone at the mast, using his arms and hands to order the rowers back into motion.

Penélope stood by Leandros' side, her hand resting on his arm automatically, though she hardly knew if it was to comfort him or herself. His mouth moved, shaping a word she couldn't hear, though she didn't have to hear to know what he said.

Πηνελόπη.

She took his face in her hands, scanning the now familiar features, the brown eyes, the dark curls, the scarred nose and mouth, the last of which she kissed. Then she spoke, though she could not hear herself say the words.

"I'm here."

45

THE SHIP SURGED AHEAD into the dark, the arms of the rowers working in unison to pull and push the long oars, plunging them into the water repeatedly. Out of the corner of her eye, she could see Mono's limping figure sternly point at rowers and clapping his hands to indicate their pace.

Beside her, Leandros stiffened. She tried to listen for some faint melody, but all was silent and muffled by the wax. His face scanned the horizon anxiously, all of his muscles tensed. Penélope's hand tightened on his arm.

Suddenly he jerked out from under her touch. He strained against the ropes, his body twisting as if he wished to come loose. Even though she could not hear anything, her head grew hazy and warm, as if the sun had broken through the night and shone its fiery heat directly on her.

Leandros moved again, shuddering, a gleam of sweat on his forehead, his cheeks flushed. His eyes roved around until they landed on her. Then he began shouting, though she couldn't hear what he said. But she didn't need to hear, because she already knew; he wanted her to set him free.

"No," Penélope said, shaking her head.

His eyes narrowed in rage, and he began twisting and yanking at the ropes with all his might, forcing Penélope to take a hasty step back, tears filling her eyes. King Leon rushed towards them, along with Mono, and the two of them wordlessly wrapped yet another rope around him, pulling him back to the mast with such force Leandros hit his head against the wood, causing him to groan and look up at the sky, his mouth moving as if he were praying to the gods.

She saw the crew falter in their strokes at the clear anguish of their captain, but Mono and King Leon quickly passed among the benches, encouraging them to keep rowing. Ahead in the darkness, Penélope could just make out towering, jagged rocks, much like the ones by Circe's island, but taller, sharper, and angled too close together, creating a maze of dangerous corridors that the ship had to sail narrowly through without crashing.

Leandros continued to strain against the ropes, his face flushed and the veins of his neck raised as he continued to shout at her to let him go. Instead, she came toward him and placed her hands on his chest. He tried to shrug her off, but she held fast, repeating his name over and over.

"Please, Leandros," she would say, softly at first and then louder, though it was strange not to hear her own voice spoken. "Look at me!"

Then he would stare at her wildly, frozen, and she would kiss him. When he would begin crying out again, she would run her hands down his chest and touch his face in an attempt to distract him. Still, he would fight against her, shouting, almost in pain, and the craze in his eyes brought more tears to her eyes.

"Leandros, it's me," she said thickly through the tears. "Just keep fighting it."

He didn't seem to understand her, closing his eyes tightly and turning his face toward the sky, his jaw clenched. Penélope curled herself up against him, even when he struggled against her touch, refusing to be shoved away.

She wrapped her arms around his neck when his movements grew weaker, their ship passing the last jagged rocks, murmuring into his ear. "If you go with them, you'll lose me forever. You'll never get to meet your daughter."

He didn't seem to understand, still shuddering against the ropes like he was fighting something in his mind, his head hanging forward until his lips brushed her shoulder. So she held on, saying his name over and over until he sagged against the net of ropes. They had to be nearly past the sirens, for Circe told them their power only reached as far as their voices could be heard.

Penélope nearly stepped back when a commotion caught her attention across the ship. Owen and Zeb were locked in an embrace—no, she realized in confusion, they were *fighting*—Zeb struggling to hold back Owen, whose strong arms fiercely shoved him away until he tripped and fell on the deck. She could see that the wax which used to be in Owen's ears had vanished. Zeb shouted, though she could not hear it, his face streaming with tears when Owen turned and ran to the bulwarks before anyone could hold him down, diving headfirst into the water and disappearing over the side of the ship. Penélope gasped, then saw Zeb take three long strides and jump after him.

Penélope ran.

She nearly reached the bulwark when hands wrapped around her. Mono held her back. She stumbled as if she had been pushed forward. But it wasn't Mono. The ship itself was rocking, the waves around them moving choppily, where before it had been calm. Clouds broiled overhead and rolled across the sky, extinguishing the stars until even the moon's light weakened. A storm was about to begin, and it was not a natural one.

Without a second thought, she took the beeswax out of her ears—and immediately regretted it. Bloodcurdling, monstrous screams tore through the air. She shared a fearful look with Mono, who had also taken his wax out.

"Are those the sirens?" Penélope asked, horrified, raising her voice over the noise and wishing she could cover up her ears again.

Mono nodded grimly. "They are angry! Only one was supposed to hear their song!"

Penélope looked out at the water where she glimpsed the white face of Zeb, clutching what looked like a lifeless Owen floating face-up on the surface. "I have to save him!"

She started as if to run, but Mono grabbed her again, holding her back. "It is too late, my Lady!"

"No!" She cried out, struggling to free herself.

"I will not allow the lady to die!"

A blur of movement passed her side. She glanced and saw Leandros jumping overboard, a rope still bound around his waist. A terrible shout left her mouth, scratching her throat, but Mono held her back.

"Leandros, no!" she sobbed. "You promised me!"

"My Lady, look!" Mono pointed at the swimming figure of Leandros, hidden and reappearing with each dip and swell of the waves as he cut across the water directly towards Zeb. "He is trying to save them!"

Penélope held her breath. While Mono was distracted, she managed to free herself from his grip and ran to the bulwark, though she didn't jump, anxiously scanning the tumultuous waves for a sign of them. The rope that had tied Leandros to the mast was pulled so taut that Penélope feared it would snap. Rain had begun pouring in frigid sheets from the sky, hitting her skin like needles, and wind swirled the afore calm night sky. Soon, the ship would lose command of the waves, and they would have to lower their sails.

"Captain, the clouds cover the stars!" Mono shouted even louder behind her as the pitch of the sirens' screams grew to an impossible, ear-bleeding cry. "I shall try to steer with the moon!"

Penélope looked back at him in surprise, wondering who he could be talking to if Leandros had not returned. Then she realized in horror that if Leandros were no longer captain, she had been assigned next in command as his wife. She nodded numbly, wincing at the continual screams, wondering distantly if her ears were bleeding. "Do what you can to keep us steady! Call King Leon to me! And six strong men!"

Mono quickly saluted and ran across the deck, which was already slick from the mingling rain and seawater. She turned back towards the ocean, where she caught a glimpse of white flashing in the dark, but saw that it was only the reflection of lightning from above.

King Leon rushed to her side. "Where is my son?"

She pointed in the direction of the rope, unable to speak.

"Men! To me!" he shouted, then ran off, before quickly coming back with another coil of thick rope and a group of their strongest sailors. He scanned the ocean waves rapidly, which climbed ever higher with the quickening wind, tossing the ship side to side like a seesaw. "There!"

Penélope squinted but saw nothing. King Leon unraveled the rope and with a loud grunt cast it out to sea. A hand emerged from the sea and grasped the rope, followed by Leandros' gasping face, who handed the rope to a wide-eyed Zeb, an unconscious Owen towed behind him.

"You three, take the other rope!" King Leon shouted, and though his words died in the wind, the men seemed to understand, splitting in half, one group pulling on Leandros' rope and the other helping King Leon drag Zeb closer, who clung to Owen's chest.

Thunder clapped above, and vicious, cold voices rang out, piercing her eardrums like knives, and they all groaned aloud.

"NONE WHO HEAR OUR SONG SHALL BE SUFFERED TO PASS!"

The ship listed to the right in the direction of Leandros, Zeb, and Owen, as if the very ocean were pulling them down to its depths. The wind blew against the ship, whose wooden planks creaked in protest, threatening to be drowned or torn apart. It seemed that if they did not release the ropes and allow them to drown, the ship would sink, and they would all perish. Was the fate of Helena worth losing the people she loved most? Why had the gods helped her this far only to abandon her now?

Have faith, Penélope.

Penélope clasped her hands together, praying silently to the sky above. *Please, Hermes, if you can hear me, spare them. I have already given up my daughter. Do not take their lives too.*

Nothing happened, then—

"Pull!" King Leon shouted. The ropes had slackened slightly, as if they had swum closer to the ship. "Harder!"

With cries of effort, the men heaved the ropes back until Penélope gasped, seeing Leandros emerge from the water once more, still grasping the rope with his hands. Beside him, Zeb was also holding on to his rope in one hand and Owen with the other. Seeing their captain alive encouraged the crew, who all shouted triumphantly, and a few more sailors left their rowing posts to join them at the ropes.

Soon, Leandros threw an arm around the ship's bulwark and hauled himself over the side, rolling across the deck, drenched and coughing up water. Owen was helped over the side by the other sailors, standing shakily on his feet, conscious again.

Once Zeb stood on the deck, Penélope rushed forward, pausing a step away uncertainly. They both stared at each other before Penélope threw her arms around him, hugging him tightly as the sobs racked her chest, and she vowed never to let go again.

46

"I'm alive, Penélope," Zeb said with an uncharacteristic laugh. "But if you don't let go—"

Penélope laughed, releasing him from her grip, yet not before she caught a golden streak on the sea behind him. She squinted and swore she saw the wings of golden sandals running across the waves, but it was gone before she could blink.

The waves had calmed once Zeb stepped foot on the deck, though the clouds still blocked all the stars above save the moon, which glimmered weakly through the thick gray. Even the wind had calmed to a gentle breeze, filling the sails so that the crew would not have to row as hard.

"I'm sorry, Zeb," Penélope said, squeezing his hand.

His eyes softened. "No, *I'm* sorry. I was being selfish. I only want what's best for you, even if that means you staying in the city and me going back home. I'll miss you like hell though."

"Zeb, I—"

A violent retching sound interrupted her. She turned. Leandros was leaning over the side of the ship, his body shuddering as he vomited. Mono and King Leon hovered nearby. Penélope wanted to go to him, but hesitated.

"Go," Zeb said, nodding his head with a knowing look. "I have my own to worry about."

She followed his gaze to Owen, who was swaying dangerously, held up by two of the crewmen. Zeb squeezed her shoulder, then walked over to Owen, relieving one of the men from holding him up. Then together they walked toward the ladder, disappearing beneath the deck down to the hull below.

Penélope wasted no more time, hurriedly joining King Leon and Mono by

Leandros, who hung his head over the side, coughing and spitting out seawater and bile. She rubbed his back in soothing circles until he finished coughing. Mono gave him his flask of liquor to drink.

Leandros turned around and took the flask, still shuddering as he drank, though Penélope realized it was from the cold, his tunic clinging wetly to his skin.

"He needs to change into dry clothes," Penélope said firmly, grabbing Leandros' hand. "Come on."

No one contradicted her as she led him to the captain's cabin. Mono and King Leon quickly went around the crew to make sure everyone was alright.

Once they were behind closed doors, Penélope helped Leandros out of his soaked leather vest and dirtied tunic, dropping them on the floor. She rummaged in the chest and found a rag she used to dry his torso. Her fingers brushed the scar running down his chest, then looked up and met his eyes, brown and pained.

"What happened?" she asked.

He closed his eyes. "The sirens. I heard them sing. At first, it was so beautiful... but to hear it and not follow after them felt like burning alive from the inside." His hand covered hers on his chest. "Then the singing turned into screams, and the enchantment lifted. I saw your friends jump."

"Thank you," Penélope said, hardly whispering, afraid she might begin crying again. "For saving them."

Leandros brushed a knuckle beneath her chin, his face grave. *"You* saved *me."*

Then he kissed the top of her head tenderly. Her hand nearly reached up to cradle his face and kiss him before she remembered the panic she had felt earlier in this very cabin at her recent revelation. She pulled away reluctantly. He was silent as she used the rag to dry him. Then he fished out a clean tunic and vest from his small pile of clothes and changed. As he stooped down to grab his wet clothes, he saw her sword still discarded on the floor.

He lifted it up. Penélope avoided his searching gaze. She took the sword wordlessly and strapped it around her waist, though her heart thudded clumsily at the thought of telling him. Should she tell him?

"When we left the island of Aeaea," Leandros said slowly, "you spoke with the goddess once more, did you not?"

Penélope nodded, and he stiffened, as if surprised it was true. She could not form the words, unable or unwilling to describe the vision of Circe approaching, her golden-laced eyes, and that warm kiss, sealing her promise for eternity.

"What did she say?"

She shook her head, cheeks burning. "Nothing important."

His jaw clenched. "You did not wish to leave."

This time she looked up and met his eyes, surprised to find them filled with anger, and the part of her that had wanted to tell him what she knew retreated in annoyance. "The goddess had a strong enchantment. You of all people should know now how hard it is to fight divine spells."

"This was different," he protested. "The song of the sirens was real enchantment."

"Oh, and Circe's was not?" Penélope drew a line with her finger down his chest, slowing as she passed his abdomen, his eyes reluctantly lowering heatedly. "There is no wile in the world that can defeat the charms of a woman."

Leandros narrowed his eyes, holding her hand still at the wrist. "Who told you that?"

She smirked. "Take a guess."

"I saw my mother suffer day and night when my father left," he said in a low voice. "And all the while he was languishing on the isle of a goddess, laden in luxury and pleasure. I will not suffer the same fate."

"Whose fate?" Penélope asked innocently, while her other hand curled around his neck. "Your mother's...or your father's?"

He went still under her touch, his storming brown eyes fixed on hers, as if he were battling between kissing her and arguing with her. She herself didn't know which way the scales would tip, nor which side she wished to tip them towards.

Suddenly, she recalled what she had told Leandros at the mast, and wondered if he was pretending not to remember, waiting instead for her to tell him. Once she considered it, she couldn't shake her superstition.

"You don't remember anything I told you at the mast, do you?" Penélope asked, looking deeply into his eyes to see if she caught a hint of his thoughts.

But Leandros' brows only furrowed, suspicion creeping into his gaze. "Unfortunately, I could hear nothing save the voices of the sirens. Why do you ask?"

Before she could speak, there was a soft knock at the door. Mono's muffled voice filtered through a second later. "Captain, there is a problem."

Leandros released her wrist and reluctantly stepped away. "Come in."

Mono hesitantly opened the door, then seeing that all were decently dressed and physically well, came inside and shut the door behind him. "The stars are covered by the clouds, Captain, and even the moon has disappeared from view.

It is nigh impossible to ascertain our direction."

"Can you find where we were before when the clouds were still visible?" Leandros asked, taking out scrolls of hand-drawn maps that Circe had helped them make. He unraveled one on the desk, pointing to a small island off the coast of the Cimmerians. "First, we left Aeaea and traveled almost due south."

"Yes, and we successfully sailed through the Islands of the Sirens," Mono said.

Penélope scoffed, recalling those jagged rocks jutting out of the water. "Islands? Those were more like mountain peaks!"

"The song of the sirens lures men closer to the rocks, before they crash their ship against them," Leandros said grimly. "We were lucky to pass through unscathed."

"Not lucky," Penélope murmured, recalling the glimpse of gold on the surface of the waves. They all looked at her questioningly, but she just shook her head. "It doesn't matter now. What are we going to do next?"

"We shall sail south as best we can." Mono traced a line down from the Islands of the Sirens to the Atlas Mountains bordering the southwestern edge of Emmeson. "As long as we do not encounter any...dangers, we shall make the journey in roughly two weeks. We cannot risk landing for supplies on the way, but we have enough stores to last us."

Penélope held up a hand. "Hold on. What dangers?"

Mono and Leandros shared an apprehensive glance. She waited for an explanation, but Mono only half-smiled at her. "There are many dangers on the open sea, my Lady."

She saw Leandros absently touch his chest, where she knew his scar roped down from his face, knitting together where his skin had split apart under sharp teeth and claws. "You mean Scylla, don't you?"

They said nothing. Mono saluted quietly in response as if to give them space and left the cabin. Leandros sighed when the door shut behind him. Penélope stared at the desk, her mind racing through every possible horrific scenario if they should encounter that monster, only realizing after a long silence that her hands were resting subconsciously on her belly.

"Penélope."

She jumped, swearing to herself, then turned to him, her hands falling at her sides.

Leandros reached out and took her hands in his. "I will not let any harm befall you."

"I know," she said, forcing a smile, before standing on her tiptoes and kissing his cheek. "You should get some rest while you can. I'm going to check on Zeb and Owen."

Then she squeezed his hands, turned, and left, the tears that had welled in her eyes only falling once she was out the door.

47

ZEB STARED AT OWEN'S sleeping figure in the hammock, drugged from the herbs Circe had given them. The hull was strangely quiet, the rest of the crew busy at work rowing. Even Nausicala, who had administered the drugs, had returned to her cabin above deck.

Owen's hand hung limply outside of the hammock. Zeb held it loosely, closing his eyes against a wave of burning tears. He would not cry. He refused to cry.

"What are you so afraid of?" Owen asked softly.

"I can't–I don't—"

Owen took his hand. Zeb looked down at the strong brown hand in his pale one. "We do it together."

Zeb's heart beat faster, though because of what they were about to do or Owen's hand in his, Zeb didn't know. Owen took one step forward, then another, waiting as Zeb took a hesitant step, then another, until they walked in unison toward the crashing waves.

"I won't let go," Owen said firmly once the water climbed up their chests. His blue-green eyes, the same color as the sea around them, were unusually serious. "I promise."

Then he pulled them underneath the next wave before Zeb could stop him.

Water submerged his head instantly, the weight of his backpack and clothes sinking him to the sandy bed below, helpless to swim against the current. But even as he drowned, the feeling as familiar in its raw panic as the water clawed into his throat, he still felt Owen's hand tight around his.

He opened his mouth and—

"Zeb?"

"You're awake," Zeb said quickly, the memory fading when he opened his eyes to see Owen staring at him under heavy, drugged eyelids. "Sorry." He tried to move his hand, but Owen tightened his grip, keeping their hands locked.

Owen's voice was groggy and almost slurred when he spoke. "You saved me."

Zeb wanted to snap back some witty reply, but all that came out was, "Technically, it was Leandros."

Owen didn't seem to hear him. "But you can't swim."

"It's like you said," Zeb said jokingly, though he sounded all too serious, "I just used my legs."

"Sometimes," Owen said with a delirious chuckle and shake of his head. "Sometimes I wish I could say I love you."

Zeb was silent, frozen at his words. He had no idea what to say in response, but it didn't matter. Owen was already asleep once more, pulled into a dream by the powerful drugs. His heart still beat painfully in his chest, and his mind refused to believe he had heard the words.

The creaking of the ladder sounded behind him. Zeb turned and saw the familiar strapped sandals of Penélope as she nimbly jumped the last two rungs.

She smiled at Zeb, coming over to hug him tightly. He was secretly pleased they had made up, since there was so much he wanted to talk with her about. They had never gone this long in an argument, but given the severity of what was at stake, he supposed it took two near-death experiences to bring them both around.

"How is he?" she asked, gesturing to Owen.

"Sleeping." He paused. "Definitely drugged."

She raised a brow, knowing him too well, even though he tried to force away the blush rising to his cheeks. "Did he say something?"

"Maybe. But he probably won't remember when he wakes up."

"I see." She nodded absentmindedly, her hands fiddling in front of her. "I'm surprised you jumped after him."

Zeb huffed a laugh. "I have no idea why I did. I hate the bloke half the time."

"Bloke? You two spend more time together than you let on," Penélope said teasingly, lightly shoving his arm. "But that was really reckless of you. You can't—"

"I can't swim, yeah, I know," he interrupted, unable not to sound childish. "But I couldn't just let him drown. Plus, I knew you would make Leandros save him if I were there too."

Penélope's mouth fell open, half-laughing. "You psychopath! And for the record, I didn't tell Leandros to save you. I tried to jump in myself, but Mono held me back. Then I saw Leandros jump in after you two. If it wasn't for him, you'd both be dead."

Zeb was stunned into silence, staring at the ground in slight shame. He had been so sure Leandros did not really care for him or Owen, putting up with them because they were Penélope's friends. Now a rush of gratitude swelled in his chest, and he wished he could take back every mean thought and snide comment he had made about the scarred prince.

"There's something I have to tell you," Penélope said quietly, interrupting his thoughts.

He glanced up, and his heart dropped to the floor. Tears welled in her eyes. The last time Penélope had spoken words like that, with the same look, had been when she told him that Ari and Alexandria had kissed. Of course, he had long seen the tension between them and assumed that would happen, even if she claimed to have some rich boyfriend back home.

He himself had ceased to care so much about it once he and Owen started things up, but hearing that the first person he had ever truly loved had kissed someone else had still stung. Penélope had also told him the news while they were fighting for their lives in Helena, so the pain of betrayal was forgotten amid the chaos, and certainly was the last thing on his mind in the Underworld. He wondered if this time she was going to tell him that *Owen* had kissed another man among the crew.

"You can tell me anything, Pepa," he said softly, bracing himself.

She nodded, wiping at her eyes with a sniffle. Her hands settled on the front of her stomach. "I think I'm—Circe told me—I haven't told Leandros—"

Zeb's breath was nearly stolen from his lungs. "Oh shit, Penélope. You're pregnant, aren't you?"

"Shhh!" Penélope glanced back at the ladder to check if anyone was coming down. "I'm not one hundred percent sure."

"You're pregnant. I can't believe it," Zeb repeated quietly, unable to comprehend the words. "How long have you known?"

"Zeb, listen to me," she snapped, then sighed, rubbing at her eyes. "I'm sorry. This is just overwhelming. Before I left the island of Aeaea, I spoke to Circe again. She asked that I name my firstborn daughter Aeaegona."

"That's a horrible name," he said automatically.

"Zeb! That's not the point. It's what it *means.*"

He thought for a moment before the meaning of the name dawned on him. "Born of Aeaea. You think she was trying to tell you that your daughter was... conceived...on Aeaea?"

Penélope nodded, biting her lip.

"And you haven't told Leandros yet?" he asked. She shook her head. "Why? And why tell me?"

"You're my best friend," she said, a waver in her voice. "I couldn't tell him yet. I needed to think about it first. The idea of having a child...I've always wanted to be a mom, but I'm still so young, and I thought I would go to graduate school first, and travel abroad, and–and now—"

She had never seemed so young and helpless as she did to him then. For the first time, he understood why Penélope had chosen this fate, even if it meant they would have to live apart forever. Why had he ever judged her for marrying Leandros when the decision had always meant so much more, even if she had loved him all along? She was just trying to do what she could to survive, to make sure they *both* survived, even if that meant sacrificing her previous life for a new one.

Zeb strode over and hugged her, allowing her to cry into his chest. "It will be okay. You can still–you can still study. Sister Stella will help you. Leandros told me that Queen Cleopatra studied in the Great Library. And Ari can teach you at the Academy. You'll be rich too, now that you've married a prince, and you can travel all over Emmeson, and maybe even our world too. I'm sure the gold and jewels here are worth a lot back home."

Penélope laughed through her tears, squeezing him tighter. "It won't be the same, though. I won't have you with me all the time. I'll have a child, even though I'm sure we'll have people to help take care of her. But I won't be just–just *Penélope* anymore. I'll be a princess, a mother, and a wife, and then one day maybe even a queen."

"You'll always be just plain old Penélope to me," Zeb said, forcing himself to say the words calmly. He knew the tears would rise if he let them, so he pushed them down. "I'll come visit, you know, and I'm sure Owen will too. Ari and Chloe will also be there, remember? It's not just you who has chosen a different fate."

"Maybe it was always our fate," she murmured absently.

"You think?"

Penélope stepped away now that the tears had subsided, her face thoughtful. "When I spoke with Persephone in her Grove, she told me that when Demeter gave me her Golden Blade, she had set in motion a war that would shake the foundations of the cosmos. She also said my descent into the Land of the Dead was no mere chance, not even our meeting, though it did seem that way to me. Then she said the Fates had brought me to her so that she could have her revenge."

Zeb shivered, the voice of Elena echoing in his mind as though from a distant dream. *Much has been set in motion that cannot now be undone. The gods keep their own counsel, after all.*

"And during the sirens' storm," Penélope added, "I prayed to Hermes to save your lives. At first, I thought he didn't hear it or care to help, but then, as the storm calmed, I swear I saw him running on the waves." She paused. "But even if some gods are on our side, there are many that aren't. This war has the very order of the universe at stake."

"We have to get to the Atlas Mountains," Zeb said finally, trying to sound more sure than he felt. "If the Fates have been leading us in the right direction, then we'll find more answers there."

A shadow passed over Penélope's eyes before she smiled, brightening her face. "Let's hope so. Mono says it should take us two weeks if we're where he thinks we are, though it's hard to be sure without the stars." She took his hand and squeezed. "I should get back on deck to help Mono with the sails, but you should stay here and look after Owen." Before she took the ladder up, she turned. "And thank you for always being there when I need you most."

He nodded, the words stuck in his throat. She smiled knowingly, then without another word, left the hull up the ladder. He hardly had a second to compose himself when another pair of strapped sandals climbed down, this time slowly and carefully. Nausicala had returned with more medicine.

While Nausicala still had most of her raven black hair and her face barely lined with wrinkles, Zeb knew she was old enough to be his mother. They had only a few sparse conversations, but he found the former Queen to be more reserved than either her son or grandson, perhaps in part due to her captivity under the roof of her father, King Kleomachus. She preferred to remain in her cabin, where she slept in a cushioned hammock alongside Penélope and Dora.

Nausicala approached quietly, her green eyes sweeping across Owen's figure. "Has he been asleep?"

"Yes," he said, then flushed all over again, remembering Owen's brief time awake. "Once, he spoke, but it wasn't lucid."

"Very well," Nausicala said in her thick accent, which was much stronger than the King and Queen of Helena or Leandros and had a slightly different lilt. "He should be recovered by morning, though I will keep a close eye on him tonight. You need not remain here if you do not wish to."

"I wish to," Zeb said quickly, then fought a blush at her raised brow. "I mean, I don't have anything to do on the deck. It's better if I stay out of everyone's way."

"I see." She nodded slowly. "You two were friends, were you not? Where you all come from?"

Zeb scoffed and muttered, "Barely." He caught her stare and cleared his throat. "Well, yes, we were friends. We all were. Though I'm closer to Penélope. I've known her since I was five years old."

"That is a long time indeed, though you are both so young," Nausicala mused. "Shall you return home when all this is over? Or shall you remain with the Lady Penélope in Helena? I am sure my son, King Leon, would agree to admit you into the royal guard, for instance."

He hesitated, glancing at Owen. Her eyes followed his gaze, and she seemed to understand too much of his thoughts. "I want to stay with Penélope. She's the only family I've really known. But at the same time, back home..."

Nausicala placed a gentle hand on his arm, her eyes heavy with sorrow. "I understand. You have your life back home, which you cannot live here." Her hand dropped, her brows creased with memory. "Once long ago, I made the decision to leave my family for a life of my own choosing. Despite the pain that has caused me to suffer, I do not regret it. My father never understood that, refusing to believe I could be happy without him, even if that happiness was mingled with sadness at our parting. He never forgave me for that happiness, until it was too late. And up until very recently, I never forgave him for taking it away."

He stared at her, shocked that she was telling him any of this. Penélope had always been the one to speak most with Nausicala, since she could speak in her native tongue thanks to the gift Hermes had bestowed upon her. Zeb, not speaking any real Greek, let alone the language of the Phaeacians, had hardly spoken with anyone at all.

Nausicala shook her head, as if she were lost in her own thoughts. "If you truly care for the Lady Penélope, and she cares for you, then forgive each other for being happier apart. Do not make the same mistake my father and I did."

Then she left, leaving Zeb alone with Owen once more.

48

Nearly a week passed with no sightings of land or monsters, though they now knew they had sailed too far west despite going south, and were passing uncharted waters to correct their position. Penélope had taken over the job of directing the sails while Mono and Leandros kept a close watch on the horizon and their maps, discussing their route in low, urgent whispers in the cabin.

Penélope knew they feared encountering Scylla again, and that even though they did not know where she was precisely, they were nearing the area that sailors avoided and were debating whether they should take a circuitous route and delay their journey or risk sailing directly. Since their night surviving the sirens, Leandros had needed more rest to recover his full strength. King Leon had stepped in to fulfill some of his duties, and even Nausicala had emerged from her cabin to help in any way she could.

Despite the gravity of their journey and the possibility of danger on every horizon, the sea unfurled about them in blue-green waves, warm and inviting. It was hard to imagine monsters like Scylla lurking in the glittering waters, but Penélope had seen firsthand how the sea had a mind of its own when a storm hit or night fell, casting the earth into utter darkness.

As the afternoon came on, the winds suddenly picked up. She had very little notion of what day it was, but she didn't need a calendar to know that summer was ending as she shivered in her cloak. From her perch near the prow she saw Leandros emerge from the captain's cabin. He spotted her across the deck and paused, just looking at her. She raised a brow. Nearby, Mono called him over, and Penélope turned her attention back to the sailors who pulled the ropes of the sails, since the wind now faced them and would require more technical maneuvering to make any forward progress.

By the time Leandros came to see her, the wind had begun throwing strong gusts at them, forcing them to sail at steep, zigzagging lengths. They had not really spoken since the night of the sirens. A strange tension had grown between them after their argument, as if both of them were holding on to their pride and unwilling to submit to the other.

Penélope knew she should apologize for the incidents with Circe, especially given his feelings for his father's past. But now that she knew she was pregnant with their child, a resolute defensiveness rose in her at the mere thought of apologizing.

"Mono reckoned we were eight nights away," Leandros said in greeting. "Now that the wind blows against us, he is not so sure." He gave her a sideways glance. "We have already been delayed once and cannot afford another one."

"All that matters is getting to the Atlas Mountains safely," Penélope said in a firm voice.

They fell into an uneasy silence. She could hear Mono shouting orders behind her. That now familiar awkwardness rose between them, a pregnant silence that they both knew meant more than they were letting on. Now would be the perfect time to tell him, but something held her back.

"You really don't remember hearing anything else besides the sirens' song?" Penélope asked, then immediately regretted it.

Leandros narrowed his eyes at her. "This is the second time you've asked me this, yet you have failed to tell me why."

Her cheeks burned. Leandros was too smart to be deceived so easily. But she supposed a part of her wanted him to press and prod until she was all but forced to say something. Zeb did not understand her unwillingness to tell him, urging her to trust that Leandros would support her. But that wasn't what she was worried about exactly. Of course he would support her as the father of their child. Maybe what she was really worried about was that, given the oath she swore, he would eventually come to resent her. Or even worse, he would stop loving her and leave her in the city by herself, wandering the seas in search of enchanted isles, if only out of spite.

"You can tell me anything, you know," Leandros said softly. Her heart stirred. It was as close to an olive branch as she would get.

Before she could answer, her attention was pulled away by angry shouting across the deck. She turned to see Owen walking across, Zeb trailing after him with fury twitching his pale face. After nearly drowning from the sirens' song, Owen had taken much longer to fully recover than expected, with Nausicala prescribing him a potent drought for sleep and as much rest as he could take. It seemed he was finally fed up with it.

"...can row if I want to," Owen said, stalking down to his rowing bench, despite still being dressed in a simple white tunic that jerked around his body like a flag in the wind. He seemed to ignore the fact that the bench was now occupied by another crew member.

"You aren't well enough to row," Zeb said angrily. "Don't come crawling back to the hull when you don't feel well. You won't find any sympathy from me!"

Owen shook his head in mock amusement, though Penélope thought she had never seen him so upset before. "You cannot keep me locked up in the hull like some princess in her tower!"

"That's a nice thing to say to someone who *saved* you from drowning! I was only trying to help—"

"Well, I don't need your help anymore," Owen shot back. "I never asked for you to jump in after me, so you cannot use that against me. I don't owe you anything now. And we're not married like Penélope and Leandros, last I checked."

"I wasn't the one who said *I love you* while half-asleep but conveniently doesn't remember it anymore," Zeb said coldly. Owen stared at him in shocked silence. "But you're right, you don't *owe* me anything. You can row yourself to death for all I care."

Then Zeb turned on his heel and stalked off toward the ladder descending into the hull. Owen shook his head, covering his face with his hands. The rest of the crew continued to row, a few of them glancing at Owen curiously. None of them could understand what they had been saying, but you didn't need to speak the same language to know when two people were fighting.

"Your friends certainly know how to cause a scene," Leandros said from beside Penélope with a shake of his head, having witnessed the entire argument.

She sighed. "They've always been like this, but it's gotten worse recently."

"Is it true what they say? That they are...involved with one another?"

Penélope paused, her heart beating faster. She wondered if she should lie and try to explain the argument another way. But Leandros did not seem fazed by the idea, and she loathed the thought of lying about anything more. "Yes. Is that a problem?"

Leandros shrugged, watching as Owen was given his spot on the rowing bench, as well as a leather vest, which was customarily worn over a tunic for protection. "Amongst my people, it is not uncommon between men of certain rank, but I have never seen it between two people that hate each other so."

"I'm not sure it's hate," Penélope said wryly.

He glanced at her keenly. "Then it is love?"

She felt her heart in her throat. "Fear of loving, maybe."

"Why should they fear it?" he asked. They didn't seem to be talking about Zeb and Owen anymore.

"Maybe they fear not being loved in return." She hesitated, her face lowered, not able to look him in the eyes as she spoke. "Or maybe fear of that love being lost."

"Ah," Leandros said. "I see." Then she felt his knuckles beneath her chin, lifting her face up. His brown eyes were warm and full of undeniable love. "Do you really not know what I feel for you? Have you not seen the signs?"

She took an automatic step forward, the weight of her body drawn to his, before she remembered that they could hardly touch in public, let alone embrace. "Leandros, there is something I have to tell you."

His eyes widened.

"All hands to their positions!" Mono shouted. He was running across the deck from behind the cabins. "Rowers to their benches! Lower the sails!"

As he shouted, violent gusts of wind suddenly stormed against the ship from all sides, flattening the sails backward and jerking the ship as it trembled against the stormy gales. Leandros and Penélope turned around wildly, her heartbeat leaping into her throat. On the horizon, the once bright blue sky was now teeming with dark, threatening clouds as far as the eye could see. Afternoon had long waned, and soon night would be upon them.

Mono rushed toward them out of breath. "There is no way around it, I fear, lest we turn back and try to outrun it."

Penélope groaned. "Did the gods send this storm too?"

"No, my Lady," Mono said with a grin, his metal teeth glinting in the fast-fading light of evening. "No, this is like to any storm you may encounter on the open sea. But 'tis a storm nonetheless!"

Leandros nodded grimly. "It is a storm, indeed, and we must face it undaunted. As they say at sea, the heart of a sailor lieth closest to a storm, for there also may lie his grave."

49

THE SEA BEFORE A storm and during a storm were two very different beasts. After half a day battling the monstrous waves and icy, pouring rain, Penélope forgot what it felt like to sail without a storm howling and beating against their ship. All of her energy was focused on walking the slippery deck without falling in order to help Mono and Leandros wherever an extra hand was needed.

Penélope crossed the deck to the mast, cowering against the swirling wind beating the rain into her face. She held onto a rope that was tied to the ship and her waist, securing her as they rode the roller-coasting waves, rising high when it crested and speeding low as it tumbled back down.

"The lady should remain in the cabin with Queen Nausicala!" Mono shouted as he passed her, pausing to yell instructions to one of the sailors who would report to the steersman at the back of the boat.

"I want to help!" Penélope shouted back, scarcely louder than the howling wind.

Mono shook his head with a chuckle. "The lady might just be more reckless than her husband!"

She turned around and saw Leandros near the prow, tied by a rope around his waist in case the ship pitched him overboard, watching ahead to see the patterns of the waves and prepare the crew for impact.

Leandros caught them looking and smiled, saluting them from afar. He glanced at the waves and his eyes widened, before he shouted, "Row, my comrades! A big one comes!"

Penélope's heart dropped into her stomach as the ship dipped low into the sea, a rearing wave building before them, threatening to drown them. "Leandros!"

"Hold the rope!" Mono shouted to Penélope, eyeing the wave with a determined glint in his eyes. "Steady, men!"

She held her breath as the wave rushed over them, the weight of the water crashing her to the deck, her knees hitting the wood hard before she was swept up by the force of it, skidding back into the mast, her hands burning against the rope she clutched. The water suddenly receded, and she gasped, standing up shakily on her feet, shivering and drenched to the bone. She felt as if she had died and come back to life.

Mono shook out his wet hair, grinning. "The lady is indeed braver than many men!"

"Is sailing always like this?" Penélope asked, her teeth chattering, wrapping the rope more tightly around her waist.

"Aye, my Lady!" Mono said with a laugh, spreading his arms wide, a look of pure bliss on his face as he gazed at the storming sky. "Welcome to the life of a pirate!"

She could not help but laugh, a smile on her face too. Her nerves were completely shot, so that she felt equally numb from fear and exhilarated at the thought of surviving dangers across the sea.

Beneath them, the ship groaned and creaked from the assault, though thanks to the light but sturdy wood of Circe's forest, the ship nimbly followed the rise and fall of the waves without even a crack in her hull or deck. Leandros remained perched on her nose, bracing himself as the waves crashed against the prow, rushing in cold tendrils across the deck. Penélope watched him standing there, sword strapped to his waist, his tunic wet and clinging to his strong, broad chest, and felt as though she had slipped through a crack in time, a pathway between worlds, but one which allowed for no return. This was her world now, and she knew with a damning certainty she would live and die in it.

"My Lady, look!"

Penélope followed Mono's fearful gaze, expecting another towering wave ready to engulf them, but instead saw that they were careening into a thick fog, white tongues of its smoky mist already curling around their ship, swiftly obscuring the sea before and behind them. She squinted, trying to see the choppy horizon separating sky and sea, but only saw a murky gloom of fog, rain, and foaming salt sprays from waves crashing against the hull.

"How will we know which way we're going?" Penélope asked anxiously.

Mono shook his head, his face grim. "We won't!"

She looked back towards the prow and gasped. Leandros was gone, the front of the ship ensconced in fog. "Leandros!"

"I'm here!"

He stepped out of the fog, joining her at the mast with Mono. They looked around them in panic, gripping their ropes tightly as the ship continued to ride the waves, shuddering as it hit the low swell before it rushed high with the next crest. Rain pelted in their faces. Penélope wiped at her face and eyes, struggling now to see the rowers at their benches, the white fog growing thicker around them.

"Is *this* a normal fog?" Penélope asked, wincing when thunder clapped above and a fork of lightning splayed across the sky, only further illuminating the fog instead of the sea around them.

Leandros and Mono shared an apprehensive glance.

Penélope grasped Leandros' arm. "If this is a god's doing, we need to turn back!"

"It is too late!" Mono said, shaking his head. "We cannot fight a storm blind!"

"We'll drown if we don't!" Penélope said, grasping for her rope as a wave slammed into the ship and she nearly stumbled to the side, only saved from falling to her feet by Leandros' strong arms holding her up.

"That is not what I fear," Leandros replied with a grunt as the ship leaned to the side, all of them skidding to a stop on the slippery wood, then righting themselves as the ship found her balance once more. "We run too close to graver dangers."

Suddenly, a loud screeching sound split the air. They all ducked as the left side of the mast splintered against something it hit in the fog, falling in sharp pieces around them and into the sea. Their ship cried out in protest, flailing about with the loss of half its top weight.

"Steady, boys!" Leandros shouted, looking about to see what hit the mast, though they could not see through the fog. He turned to her and Mono. "I fear the worst has come."

Mono paled, but his hands made fists at his side. "Aye, captain. So do I."

Penélope noticed with a strange dread that the wind and waves had calmed in the commotion, as if the storm had let up, only rain falling straight down a sign that the storm still surrounded them. The fog was thick and impenetrable as their ship floated in the water, the crew having ceased to row in case they were in danger of hitting something else, lifting their oars close to the ship.

Leandros had his eyes closed. She thought he was praying, then realized he was listening intently, waiting for something. Mono was still, one hand on the hilt of his sword. She strained her ears, though she had no clue what she should be hearing.

"The wind is behind us," Leandros said, though he sounded wary.

"Isn't that a good thing?" Penélope asked hesitantly.

Mono looked around them as if he could see something in the fog that she could not. "It is as though we have entered...a channel, sheltered from the wind on both sides."

As if his words had been a spell, the fog had lifted as he spoke, dissipating into the sheets of rain. Penélope gazed ahead, her mouth dry at the sight before her. Towering on either side of the ship were sheer, black cliffs, glinting like swords in the sea, or like dark, blood-stained teeth under a half-moon which had since been obscured by the storm. But the storm clouds had parted above them as if they had entered the heart of the storm, leaving them battered and bruised but calmly sailing in the narrow channel.

Mono had been right. The channel formed between the cliffs sheltered them from the waves beyond and forced the wind to blow between the tall rocks. While it now allowed them to raise their sails, the wind filling the tattered canvases, it meant they could not turn around, entrapping them in the narrow path with only one way out.

"Where are we, Leandros?" Penélope asked, her voice trembling.

Leandros closed his eyes with a soft sigh. "Never did I think I would face her again."

She felt faint. "Is it Sc—"

"Don't speak her name," Leandros said coldly, and she flinched. "The men must not know."

Mono stepped closer, his voice a low growl. "I am ready, Captain. Long have I waited for my revenge."

"Steady, friend." But Leandros' eyes also glinted in anger. She recalled what he had told her of the story all those weeks ago. *We lost many a comrade that day.* "There is only one way to survive such a daemon, and it is not by the sword. We made that mistake last time, and it cost us dearly."

"Then what do you suggest, captain?" Mono asked dutifully, though he sounded disappointed.

Leandros turned to her. "You must remain in the hull with Queen Nausicala and your friends, no matter what. If any of you wish to remain above deck, I cannot answer for your safety. We shall sail as close as we dare to Charybdis, but I fear that to escape such a whirlpool is impossible, and so the daemon shall have her kill."

Penélope's heart stuttered inside her chest at the thought of anything happening to Leandros or the crew, but she nodded, silent and terrified, unable to argue against his command. She suddenly regretted every angry word she had spoken to him, their time together seeming as fleeting as a dream, and she wished she had not wasted so much time since that very day he declared his love for her.

At her agreement, Leandros' shoulders relaxed ever so slightly, then he took her face in his hands and kissed her as if it might be the last, not caring that the entire crew witnessed it. The kiss was over far too quickly, and before she could call after him, he had turned away.

"Go!" he called behind him.

She turned and ran.

50

PENÉLOPE PACED THE HULL, her pulse racing like wings of a bird trapped in her chest. Zeb watched her warily, silent and pale. Owen's knee bounced where he sat on a small wooden stool, always preferring to be in the action rather than waiting around for it to end.

Queen Nausicala stood by the ladder that led out of the hull beside Dora, her head tilted intently as if she were trying to hear what was happening. But all was oddly calm and quiet, the ship gliding smoothly across the water. Even the oars had ceased their splashing, only gently pushing the ship further, the rudder steering them clear of the cliffs.

"Your pacing is loud enough to alert every bloody monster of the sea within five leagues of here," Owen said, looking at Penélope pointedly.

She stopped in her tracks, the loud creaking from her footsteps ceasing too. "Sorry. I'm scared, okay? Someone should tell the crew what's coming."

"No," Nausicala said sternly, shaking her head. "If they knew what was coming, their courage would fail them. Besides, many of them already know."

Mono had escorted the others down into the hull and ordered Nausicala's armed guard to remain above deck for added protection, having no inkling of the horror to come. Penélope had immediately told them where they were headed and Leandros' plan. Instead of arguing or panicking, the rest of them had nodded gravely, accepting their fate with mingled dread and relief that they were not expected to be on the deck when they faced her. But Nausicala's steadfast serenity now annoyed her.

"How can you be okay with this?" Penélope asked. "Your son and grandson are up there. They could *die*. It's like you don't even care."

Nausicala bristled, her chin lifting as her hard glare fell upon Penélope. "Do not preach to me of death, child. This is not the first time I have remained behind while my family fought on the battlefield, though it may be yours."

She immediately regretted having spoken, remembering the song about Nausicala which described the war against Helena, and how her husband and firstborn son had perished in the fight. Zeb and Owen glanced nervously at the two of them.

"I'm sorry," Penélope said, her face burning under Nausicala's unwavering gaze. "I just hate feeling helpless."

Nausicala raised a dark brow. "Are we not all helpless against the will of the gods?"

"I'm sure Leandros knows what he's doing," Owen said with his usual drawling confidence, though his tense face and glances at every noise told otherwise. "Perhaps we won't face Scylla at all."

As if her name had invoked it, a wild, painful yell tore through the air, right before chaos erupted on the deck. Footsteps pounded, men shouted, and the oars crashed into the water on either side. Far off, Penélope could hear a loud roaring of water, as if they were nearing a waterfall.

"Charybdis," Zeb whispered, standing up.

"The fight has begun," Nausicala said, her voice laden with sorrow. Owen offered her his seat, and she took it with a sigh. "It won't be long now."

Another wail rose and faded, as though something had snatched one of the crewmen and borne him up and away. Penélope's hand tightened on her sword, every muscle in her body tense. Then she heard Leandros' voice call out to the men to stand their ground and keep rowing.

"I can hear him," she said, running toward the ladder to listen better.

A beastly roar drowned out all noise, then she heard the sound of cloth ripping, and realized Scylla must've torn through the sails with her claws. Her heart jumped to her throat when her roar ceased, and she heard Leandros once more.

"Row! Row as if your lives depend upon it! Keep rowing, we're almost—"

His voice was cut off in a strangled shout of pain. Penélope's mind went blank. She unsheathed her sword with one hand, the other already reaching for the ladder rungs, when something pulled her dress from behind, stopping her with one foot off the ground.

Zeb stood behind her, holding her back. "Penélope, you can't—"

She brandished her sword, and Zeb backed away with stumbling steps, his eyes wide and fearful. Nausicala and Owen could only stare at her dumbly. "Don't follow me."

Then she climbed the ladder, her sword at the ready, emerging onto the deck into what felt like another storm, but this time of a different kind. Half the crew had left their posts at the benches, some running around screaming, others hiding with chattering teeth, only a few standing with their swords held out shakily in front of them. She crouched by the opening, but there was no monster in sight.

Her eyes quickly scanned the deck and saw Leandros splayed out by the prow, his eyes closed, one arm cut open down the bicep and spilling with blood. Without their captain, the crew had descended into chaos, terror in all their shouts and blubbering cries, praying to the gods for help. She saw Mono and King Leon hiding behind the thick wooden mast, their swords in front of their chests and their legs bent as if ready to spring and attack.

Penélope looked around at the black cliffs, but could hardly make out anything in the night besides their looming masses, the half-moon already gone from the sky where stars shone weakly, as though they too were terrified of the monsters lurking beneath the waves. The sound of water being sucked into a whirlpool had only grown louder, as if they would soon be swallowed by it. Up ahead, she glimpsed a small gap in the cliffs where the channel spilled back out to open sea.

With one last trembling breath, she ran across the deck towards Leandros. She passed Mono, who saw her out of the corner of his eye and called out her name in protest, but she ignored him. Once she reached him, she collapsed at his side, her sword dropping to the floor so that she could bunch up her dress and press the fabric against his open wound with her hands.

At her touch, Leandros stirred, his eyes fluttering open. His gaze landed on hers, and the corners of his mouth lifted. "My love..."

"Don't speak," she said, her eyes filling with tears. "I need to bring you down to the hull."

His eyes struggled to focus on her, roving around feverishly and then up, before closing once more. "Πηνελόπη..."

"My Lady, run!"

She sprang to her feet at Mono's voice, her hand fumbling for her sword, but when she stood at the ready, her legs nearly gave way beneath her. Crouched over the prow of the ship, its twisting, black tentacles gripping the bulwarks, was a hideous, enormous monster, with six long, slithering necks of six serpent heads protruding from a thick, bulbous mass. In each head opened a jaw of bloodied, sharp teeth, framed by round, filmy-gray eyes that seemed to look everywhere and nowhere at the same time.

Penélope stared at it, frozen in shock. It was uglier, more terrifying, and more awful than any description, each head as big as a bull, and its farthest, inky tentacles stretching wide enough to hoist itself up both cliff sides.

She took one step back. Scylla hissed, its mountainous body inching upward from its hiding place below the hull. Penélope stopped moving, glancing at Leandros, worried that if she took another step away that Scylla would pounce on his helpless body. Before she could decide to take another step, to Penélope's horror, a deep, almost feminine voice purred in her mind, just as the monster growled, and she knew it was the voice of Scylla.

Never before have we tasted the flesh of womankind. Is it sweeter? How she squirms! Do we eat her companion, make her watch as we devour him whole—?

"No!" She raised her sword higher between them.

Scylla screeched in response, rising as if on her hind legs, the ship groaning as it tilted forward with the weight of the monster. *She hears us! She hears us! Curse the god who has gifted you so! But you shall rue the day such a gift was given, as we grind your lover to the bone, his delicious, tender meat filling—*

"Monster!" Penélope's voice shook as she leaped over Leandros, waving her sword in front of her, and for a moment, Scylla flinched backward. "I will die before you touch him!"

One of Scylla's tentacles arced and came crashing down on the deck, the scaly arm tearing through the wood and through the hull. *Stupid girl! Foolish to cling to love! You shall watch every comrade of yours die until you beg for death!*

Before she could move, three of the serpent heads shot forth and clamped their jaws on two of the crewmen each, their screams fading as they were swallowed whole, followed by the sickening sound of crunching bones and slurping of her serpent tongues.

Scylla's eerie laugh cackled in her head. Penélope gripped the sword more tightly in both hands, her legs heavy as lead, her breath held. All she could think about was Leandros. Leandros could not die. She would not let Scylla take him and devour him as she had seen her do with the others. Not Leandros.

He shall be next!

Suddenly a shout came from behind Penélope, then someone moved in front of her. King Leon stood there with his sword bared and glinting. "Be gone, Scylla!"

One of her serpent heads shot out and latched onto his side, tossing King Leon out of the way and sending him flying across the deck covered in blood, his head hitting a rowing bench and rendering him unconscious. Penélope knew that they would be next. There was nothing standing between them and the bloodthirsty jaws of Scylla.

One of the serpent heads reared back, ready to strike. Penélope held out the sword helplessly. The jaws came down—

A whimper of pain came from the monster, the head halting and swinging away. Mono had jumped out from the side and kicked the serpent head with his leg's silver peg, the weight of it momentarily befuddling the monster. He hacked his sword into the neck of the hesitating serpent head, which howled terribly in pain, faltering low to the deck, until Mono sliced clean through it.

Scylla roared louder than she had ever before, a guttural, screeching sound like tectonic plates shifting beneath the earth, her tentacles flailing about the ship, knocking a sailor into the water, who cried out before crashing into the jutting rocks beside the cliff.

"No lady dies on my watch!" Mono shouted, shoving the beheaded serpent away with his silver peg-leg. He turned to Penélope. "Get back inside the hull!"

Penélope opened her mouth to thank him when another serpent head flew suddenly across the deck, its jaws clamping around Mono's waist. He grunted in pain, his eyes wide.

A scream left her mouth, scratching her throat raw, but she heard it distantly to the ringing in her ears as she watched Mono's limp body swing high into the air and disappear inside one of Scylla's fanged mouths, the slimy throat working before the serpent head faced Penélope once more.

Tears fell down her cheeks as she gasped for breath, choking on her sobs. She heard a groan beneath her. Leandros had woken up again, struggling to sit up. He turned and saw Scylla, his eyes wide, before he turned to Penélope in mingled confusion and dawning terror.

"Penélope, get back in the—"

Something slammed into her side, and she crashed to the deck with a scream, a knife-like pain hitting her chest at the same time as she felt a dull crack of a bone. Her lungs ached for breath, the wind knocked out of her. When she tried to sit up, the ship somersaulted before her with a wave of dizzying pain, but she could still make out Leandros hobbling to his feet.

She tried to move, and a knife seemed to lance through her chest, piercing her lung. It was too late. No word came out as she watched another serpent head strike at him.

But the bite never came.

Leandros had blocked the attack with his sword, now sprayed with black blood, his muscles straining against the force of the monster, and his teeth gritted together. Scylla, enraged, towered higher, preparing to pounce again. But then she heard a shout. Zeb had climbed out of the hull and seen Penélope on the ground before rushing over to her. Now he leaned over her in panic, cursing and saying her name over and over again.

Behind his trembling shoulders, Penélope saw Scylla turn all her fanged serpent heads towards them with horrible hisses. *Fresh meat!*

"Zeb—!"

He turned and gazed in horror at the monster rearing over the prow of the ship as though caught in a nightmare come to life. Then he picked up Penélope's sword that had fallen to the ground, holding it clumsily before him.

Ah, the monster purred in its guttural voice. *This one cares for you, does he?*

One of Scylla's tentacles flicked out before Penélope had time to scream, knocking the sword clean from Zeb's hand while he stumbled back. The sword flew across the deck with such force that it landed by the prow, near her other tentacle buried deep in the ship, which had caused them to stop moving, caught in Scylla's trap like a fly in a spider's web.

An idea popped into her head as she stared at the sword near the tentacle, glinting and sharp, still untainted by blood. She had been too terrified to use it when it counted the most, and now it was too late. *If the lady has cause to use it, only courage shall strike true.*

No. It was not too late for those living, and she had more than one life to protect now. Mono had not sacrificed himself for nothing, and it would be over her dead body that Zeb returned to the Underworld.

Penélope heaved herself to her feet and ran in four bounding steps to the sword, picking it up and with a hoarse cry swinging with all her might at the tentacle. To her surprise, the blade sank clean through the flesh, encountering no bone, and split the tentacle in two.

With a pitiful screech, Scylla wobbled, and the tentacles latched onto the cliffs slipped off as the weight of her massive body tilted back toward the sea, her two bloody stumps unable to catch a grip. She tumbled into the churning, spiraling waters of Charybdis, who eagerly sucked her down into the whirlpool. The ship pitched forward with the momentum from Scylla's fall, then sprang upright once it was free from the monster's clutches, the wind in its sails speeding it forward effortlessly.

King Leon had woken up and with a limp stood and ordered the crew back to their posts. The remaining men scrambled to their oars, rowing furiously as the steersmen maneuvered them around the lip of the whirlpool at the end of the channel until they flew back out onto the clear open sea.

Suddenly Leandros was there, his arms enveloping her in their familiar warmth and strength. Her knees gave out as the tears returned, and she let him hold her as the sobs shuddered through her, the sword in her hand clattering to the ground.

51

A COLD WIND BLEW *through the opening of the cave, winding through the many narrow corridors cut deep into the mountain, following the steep, twisting paths to damp caves trickling with stalagmites. In one cave, carved with high, smooth walls, a black spring flowed out of the rock beside an altar, still burning with the calf thigh bones piled over olive wood, the smoke clouding the ceiling, carved with the patterns of constellations.*

She walked across the stone floor, her feet bare on the cold rock, pale and youthful. Long had the cold ceased to afflict her, having dwelt in this mountain for countless ages. A breeze from outside swept through the cave, rustling the leaves she had sprinkled on the ground, etched with prophecies, some fulfilled, some that would not be fulfilled for another thousand years, when she was no longer bound by oath within these cavernous walls, cast aside for the next Sibyl to come.

The fire was no more than embers, pinpricks of glowing orange amid the wood, which one meager exhale could put out. She reached out her hand and prodded the thigh bones, still covered in melted fat. It was hot to the touch, oily and smooth, though in some places the fire had cut through the fat and charred the bone black. Was it a good omen? Or a bad one?

Footsteps tore her attention away from the sacrifice. She turned with her heart beating despite herself. He appeared as she had always seen him, since the very first day, a tall young man with night black curls, a handsome smile, though it was not exactly kind, his bow and arrows slung effortlessly over one shoulder.

She bowed silently, careful not to look into his eyes. "To what do I owe the honor of your visit, my Lord?"

"Oh, Aethusa, my dear, you already know why I have come."

"Then you mean to carry on with your plan, my Lord?"

He did not answer, his footsteps softly echoing on the polished stone. She felt his fingertips run down her bare arm, and the touch alone was like fire itself, like the light of the sun searing her skin.

She recalled the first time he had touched her as though it were branded in her memory, and she nearly shivered, though not from the cold. "What have you seen, my Lord?"

"Look at me, Aethusa."

His knuckles forced her chin up, and she looked into his dark eyes before light exploded in her vision and she fainted with the pain, as his voice whispered in her ear.

"They are coming."

Penélope opened her eyes with a gasp. She was back in her hammock, rocking with the movement of the ship. The blinding light of morning assaulted her vision from the open door of the cabin. Nausicala entered, carefully shutting the door behind her and returning the cabin to darkness.

"Awake?" Nausicala asked. "I thought I heard you speaking."

She ran a hand over her eyes. "In my sleep, maybe."

"Oh?"

"My dream was very..."

"Real?"

"Yes!" Then Penélope paused. "How did you know?"

Nausicala revealed a flask of Circe's herb potion, which was brown and filled with crushed leaves and petals. "This healing tonic is particularly potent and can very well cause visions."

She felt her left ribcage, where she had sprained two of them in her fall and fractured one when Scylla attacked her, wincing at the soreness. But more than any bodily pain, her very heart hurt at the mere memory of that night and the death of Mono. More than a week had passed since then, but she could not rid herself of that image of Scylla's jaws clamping around Mono's side. Tears sprang to her eyes before she could stop them.

Nausicala sighed. "You ought to rest. We shall be arriving any day now."

"No land in sight yet?" Penélope asked, wiping the tears away.

"Your friend, Lord Godfrey, swears he does every day, but alas, his eyes must be deceived by some spell."

Penélope laughed, though it hurt to do so, both at Owen's antics and

Nausicala's name for him. "Owen is very...optimistic."

"Well, some optimism is needed among the crew," Nausicala said. "I fear their spirits are quite broken."

As is mine, Penélope thought, but didn't say. She only nodded, accepting the flask of healing tonic and taking a sip. It was smooth besides the flecks of crushed herbs, with a strong, bitter taste that made her wince. But after a few moments, the drug began working its magic, warming her from the inside out and numbing any aches and pains. She could breathe easier, as though she no longer had any injuries.

Nausicala took the flask and turned to leave. "I will let you be, but soon I will bring some food from the stores."

"Thank you," Penélope said, her voice laden with emotion. "For taking care of me."

"It is I who should be thanking you, Lady Penélope," Nausicala replied with a tender smile. "You had the courage to face what even some of the bravest soldiers would flee from."

Penélope could only stare as Nausicala nodded and left the cabin. But she didn't feel any gratitude, just guilt. Zeb and Owen had both visited her multiple times to thank her for saving their lives—which she told them had not been the case at all, and it was more thanks to Zeb's bravery that she was still here—and to tell her that the crew was all indebted to her for her supposedly heroic deeds.

"Why the Hell did you come out of the hull?" Penélope had asked after hugging Zeb the first time they saw each other since the battle. "I told you to stay there. If you had sacrificed your life for me again, I would've killed you."

Zeb had laughed, but his eyes were surprisingly tender. "It was just something you said to me a while ago, about choosing to stand and fight. I don't know if I'll fight in any war, but I couldn't let you fight Scylla alone. There are some things worth fighting for, and to me, you're one of them."

But no matter how much they told her she had done the right thing fighting against Scylla, Penélope could not shake the feeling that she was responsible for Mono's death. It had been Mono who shielded her from the monster's first attack, after she had foolishly come on deck and tried to defend Leandros. If only she had listened to him and remained below in the hull, safe from Scylla, then maybe Mono would still be alive.

Or maybe Leandros would be dead instead, sneered an unhelpful voice in her head that sounded suspiciously like Zeb, though she had never voiced her guilt aloud to him. They wouldn't understand. Her reckless behavior had finally reaped consequences, but this time it hadn't been her own life that paid for it, and somehow that made it all the worse.

Another knock at the door sounded, and she weakly asked who it was.

"Leandros," said the muffled voice.

Penélope sighed. He had been in a worse state of injury than her and had been recovering in the hull with King Leon and the other severely injured crew for the first few days since the battle. When he had tried to come visit her yesterday, she had refused, claiming she was not well enough. But the truth was that she didn't know if she could face him, knowing how Mono, his helmsman and closest friend, had sacrificed himself for her.

"Penélope," Leandros said, and she heard his forehead rest on the door. "Penélope, my love, please."

She swallowed hard against the rising tears. "Come in."

There was a pause, as if Leandros was surprised she had agreed. Then the door opened and Leandros walked in, fitted in a fresh, clean tunic, his right bicep bandaged with strips of linen, and his skin peppered with blackening bruises and scabbing cuts. She herself had a bandage wrapped around her chest to compress the sprains and fracture in her ribs, as well as many small bandages covering scratches where Scylla's sharp claws or flying pieces of wood and rock had grazed close enough to draw blood.

Leandros closed the door behind him and looked at her, his eyes heavy with sorrow. She lowered her face, biting her lip to try and prevent the tears from coming before they had even spoken a word. Knuckles brushed her chin and lifted her face.

"Look at me," he whispered, his voice hoarse.

She looked at him, her heart full of guilt and pain, but she only saw love in his eyes, not the anger or judgment she had expected. Then he kissed her, and she swung her legs out of the hammock, ignoring the slight pulsing soreness in her side, wrapping her arms tightly around his neck.

Leandros kissed her like they hadn't seen each other for an eternity, cradling her face in his hands. She automatically ran her hands down his arms but sprang back when he winced.

"I'm sorry!" she exclaimed hurriedly.

But he only laughed, smiling wryly and glancing at his bandaged bicep. "I suppose I will have another scar for you to kiss."

She gently brushed her fingertips over his lips, where his other scar spliced the skin in a jagged white line, nearly shuddering at the thought of what he had gone through the first time he faced Scylla, now knowing what it was like to face her and the grief afterward.

"I am sorry," she said quietly. "About everything."

He nodded, his eyes closing. "Me too."

"If I had just stayed in the hull—Mono, he'd—"

"—be dead," Leandros finished firmly, his eyes opening and revealing the same steely strength she had seen in Nausicala before the battle, a strength generations in the making, since Odysseus had left Troy and weathered ten years wandering the open seas. "We would all be dead. You saved my life, Penélope, and the lives of my crew."

"Mono saved my life," she protested, the tears falling swiftly now. "Scylla would've killed me. And you. She wanted me to watch as she ate all of you one by one—"

"She spoke to you?"

Penélope nodded her head with a wince at the mere thought of her deep, purring voice in her head. "I think the gift of language Hermes had given me also allowed me to understand Scylla. It felt more like a curse than a gift though."

Leandros shook his head, tucking a strand of her hair behind her ear. "You are a marvel, Penélope."

"Don't," she said thickly, fearing his words would only make her cry more.

"I am the luckiest man alive to have you as my wife." He took her hand and kissed the ring still safely resting on her finger.

She tried to shake off his hand, but he held fast to it, taking her other hand too. "I'm the reason Mono is dead."

"Monopous might have sacrificed himself to save you, but I know he would have it no other way," Leandros said firmly. "He owed you his life, remember? There is no greater honor than fulfilling a life debt in a valiant feat of bravery. That is the pirate's code, as well as the soldier's code. And he did not just sacrifice his life for you. He gave his life for the safety of the crew and also for me, to whom he owed another life debt. For it was I who saved him from death after Scylla had grabbed him by the leg, and the reason why I bear these scars."

Penélope wiped her tears, nodding. Though his words alleviated some of the guilt, they did not take away the grief at Mono's death, who had always been more of a gentleman than a pirate.

"How is your father?" she asked, recalling how King Leon had jumped in front of them before Scylla tossed him aside like a ragged doll, his leg badly injured from the fall.

Leandros nodded, his eyes lowering to hide some passing thought. "He is recovering, but he shall not be well enough to travel on foot for some time. We will brave the Atlas Mountains without him."

She squeezed his hands. "I'm not asking you to forgive him, at least not now, but he did risk his life to protect us from Scylla when you were unconscious."

He looked up at her in surprise. "He did?"

"Maybe he is not so selfish after all," she said, kissing his cheek.

"Maybe," he relented, the corners of his mouth lifting in a reluctant smile. "Or maybe you simply see the best in others, believing them to be like you."

Penélope leaned in close, but stopped short of kissing him. "Or maybe, you have more of the vengeful pirate in you than the pampered prince, *Wanderer.*"

He smirked, leaning in to kiss her, when shouts were heard from outside. They both froze, Penélope's heart galloping in her chest. Was there another monster? Had they survived all that only to die when they least expected it, so close to their goal and yet still so far?

But this time it was good news.

"Land ahoy!" Owen was shouting the words over and over as loudly as his lungs allowed. Penélope could just hear Zeb telling him to calm down. "Χέρσον εὑρίσκω! Land ahoy, ladies and gents! We've reached the Atlas Mountains!"

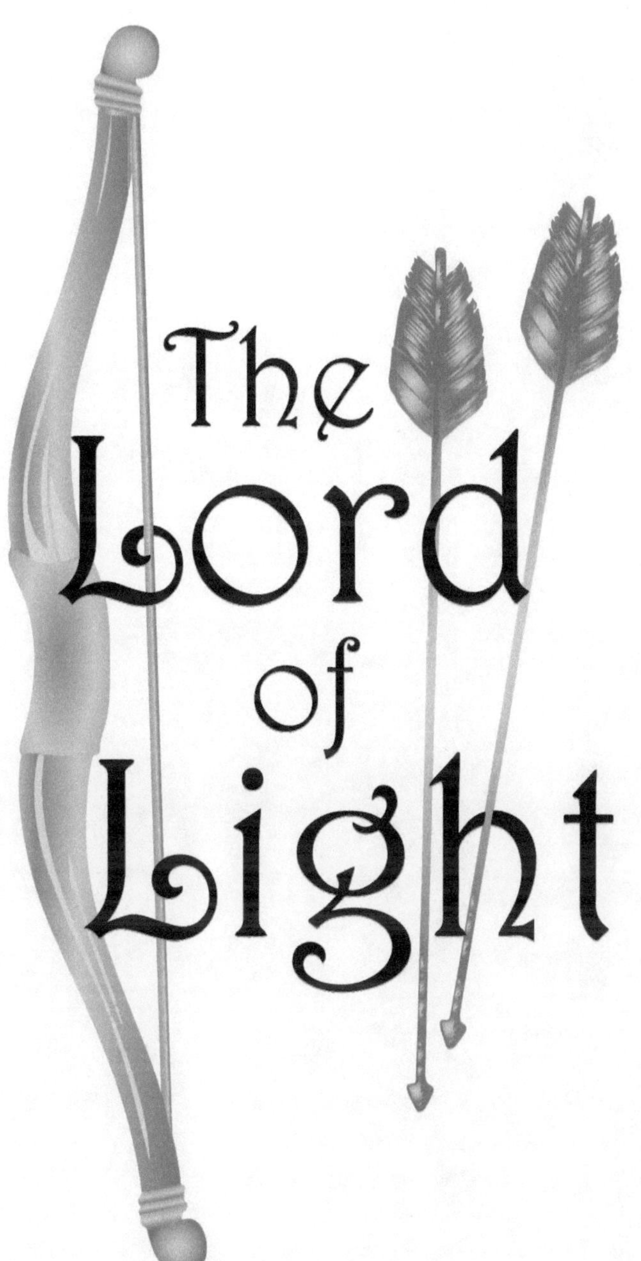

The Lord of Light

And by his side the mad divining dame,
The priestess of the god, Deiphobe her name.
"Time suffers not," she said, "to feed your eyes
With empty pleasures; haste the sacrifice.
Sev'n bullocks, yet unyok'd, for Phoebus choose,
And for Diana sev'n unspotted ewes."
This said, the servants urge the sacred rites,
While to the temple she the prince invites.
A spacious cave, within its farmost part,
Was hew'd and fashion'd by laborious art
Thro' the hill's hollow sides: before the place,
A hundred doors a hundred entries grace;
As many voices issue, and the sound
Of Sybil's words as many times rebound.
Now to the mouth they come. Aloud she cries:
"This is the time; enquire your destinies.
He comes; behold the god!" Thus while she said,
(And shiv'ring at the sacred entry stay'd,)
Her color chang'd; her face was not the same,
And hollow groans from her deep spirit came.
Her hair stood up; convulsive rage possess'd
Her trembling limbs, and heav'd her lab'ring breast.
Greater than humankind she seem'd to look,
And with an accent more than mortal spoke.
Her staring eyes with sparkling fury roll;
When all the god came rushing on her soul.
Swiftly she turn'd, and, foaming as she spoke:
"Why this delay?" she cried, "the pow'rs invoke!
Thy pray'rs alone can open this abode;
Else vain are my demands, and dumb the god."

—*Aeneid,* Book 6.35-53, translation by John Dryden

52

THE ATLAS MOUNTAINS LOOMED tall and menacing over the horizon, wrapped in white snow on the higher slopes, their peaks disappearing into the cloudy sky so that they looked like thick white pillars jutting out of the ocean, holding both the heavens and the earth apart.

For days, the mountains remained just so, hovering out of reach like phantoms bordering the sea. Penélope now took slow walks on the deck to breathe the fresh air and return some strength to her limbs. Surprisingly, Zeb began helping the crew row after they lost so many sailors to Scylla.

King Leon had also begun walking once more, though at a much slower pace. When Nausicala wished to rest or had to attend to other injured soldiers, Penélope would offer to help King Leon walk up and down the deck, holding his arm to keep him steady. On those walks, he would describe to her the many places he had seen in his travels, the tribes of men he had met, both hospitable and violent, and the beauties of the realm of Emmeson.

As he spoke, in his eyes she saw the same eager glint that Leandros had when they sailed swiftly across the sea under a hot noonday sun, the ocean unfurling around them uncharted and limitless. She knew that what they both loved most about the sea was the feeling of being unmoored, of wandering without being lost. For some inexplicable reason, it also reminded her of Alexandria, and she wondered if Elena and Helen before her had not had the same glint in their eyes.

Occasionally, King Leon asked her what home was like where she came from, and without giving too many details, she would describe the desert, the mountains, the New Academy, Tierra del Sol, and her family. He was shocked that women studied alongside men, and that they survived in the middle of a desert without a large river or lake nearby, and had many questions about their customs that she tried her best to answer vaguely.

Today, he was curious to learn how she and Leandros met. At first she did not answer, wondering how she could begin to explain all their exploits in the city, or Alexandria's search for her mother, or their descent into the Underworld and back. Not in the time they had, at least.

"It's a long story," Penélope said finally, recalling the night they were kidnapped on the Necropolis Island and chained to the mast. "But Leandros says he fell in love with me the first time he saw me."

She said it jokingly, but King Leon only shook his head with a small smile. "He takes after his father, then, and mine. From the first moment my eyes fell upon the beautiful face of my wife, Cleopatra, I loved her. That happened to be our wedding day, when we met at the crossroads of Helena as is our custom, dressed as Horus and Hathor."

"Like the Feast of the Beautiful Meeting," Penélope murmured, though her smile fell as she remembered the smoke and fires in the South Quarter that day and fleeing for their lives.

"You shall make a great lady of Helena, indeed," King Leon said, then glanced at his son with a mingling look of love and regret. "Leandros is lucky to have met you in such unlikely circumstances. One cannot help but wonder if it was not Fate after all."

Nay, not even our crossing here was left up to chance, though it may seem that way to you.

"He will come around, you know," Penélope said quietly, her heart aching for the two of them, filled with so much love but both unwilling to lower their pride.

King Leon nodded with a deep breath, wincing with his next step. "He was much stronger than I."

She knew that he was speaking of Leandros' night with the goddess Calypso. *There is no wile in the world that can defeat the charms of a woman.* But then she thought of Circe, the night Penélope refused her advances. Had it even been her choice? What if the goddess had been toying with her, simply to make her question what she felt for Leandros?

Gods may lie to us mortals if they are not bound by a dread oath to tell the truth.

"I think if the goddess had truly wished to entrap Leandros as she had you," Penélope replied slowly, "it would have been in her power to do so."

"Lady Penélope," King Leon said, looking upon her in admiration. "Slayer of Monsters and Wielder of the Golden Blade, since the day I met you, you have never ceased to surprise me."

She did not know what to say. But she didn't have the chance to speak anyway. Leandros called out from the prow of the ship that they were close enough to cast anchor and row the rest of the way to shore. King Leon bowed to her before Nausicala and Dora came to escort him to their cabin, his new resting quarters. None of the crew seemed very eager to row off the ship, wary of encountering more dangers. But they complied with their captain's orders, whom they honored above all, and were more complacent knowing they would not go any further than the beach.

Only Zeb and Owen would accompany her and Leandros on the journey to find the Sibyl of Apollo. Nausicala and Dora would remain on the ship to tend to the wounded, while King Leon was still too weak to travel on foot. Most of the crew were too disheartened by the death of so many of their comrades anyway, many were injured. Ultimately the fewer who ventured into the foreign land, the more easily they could slip past any tribes or monsters they might encounter on the way, and more swiftly they could find the Sibyl.

Penélope said her last goodbyes to Nausicala, King Leon, and the crew, her heart aching as she scanned their faces and did not see Mono's familiar metal-toothed grin among them. The boat was quiet as they rowed to the beach. Even Zeb and Owen did not bicker as they dutifully picked up their oars.

Once on the beach, they filled large sacks with supplies that they would carry on their backs, brought from the ship by the other sailors who began pitching a small camp on the shore.

She looked up at the mountains, whose feet yearned for the sea, while their peaks disappeared in the clouds above, making it seem as though they reached up into the heavens. Unlike the islands they had visited, no trees or shrubbery were shielding the mountains, their bare, sandy-gray rock exposed and sheer, so that she could not see a single path traced on its surface. Penélope had a hard time imagining them hiking up the mountain, and wondered how they would find the Sibyl of Apollo, who, Circe had told them, presided over the caverns at the mouth of the sacred spring, deep inside the Atlas Mountains.

Leandros did not seem worried, however, only pensive, strapping his sack of supplies around his shoulders and chest, which seemed as if it weighed a hundred pounds. He caught Penélope's eye and grinned. "Do not worry, my love, this will only grow lighter with the passing days."

"Days?" she asked, realizing they would have to camp along their route. She had assumed they would find the Sibyl today and leave the following morning.

"Days *and* nights," Leandros murmured suggestively.

Owen stalked past them, his supplies already strapped to his back. "Enough flirting. We haven't all day before the sun sets."

"That's rich coming from you," Penélope shot back, but Owen had already continued walking towards the mountains, where the ground began steeply inclining as soon as the sand turned into hard rock.

Zeb shrugged only semi-apologetically, then followed after Owen. Penélope sighed watching them, then strapped her pack tighter around her shoulders.

"How long do you give those two before they fight?" Leandros asked wryly.

"Not even two hours," Penélope answered.

He shook his head with a small laugh, then nodded after them. "We may as well make sure they do not run into any trouble without us."

So they took off towards the mountain with only one last look behind them at their ship. She swore the small, elegant robed figure of Nausicala waved at them from the prow, though she couldn't be sure. Penélope had the fleeting thought that she may never see the ship or Nausicala or King Leon again, but pushed it away. All they had to do was find the Sibyl, ask her to intercede on their behalf, and then leave. What could go wrong?

Penélope quickly learned that, in fact, much could go wrong when they first stopped after hiking all day up the steep, rocky terrain and pitched their camps for the night in absolute darkness, unprotected and exposed to the elements and any wild animals prowling nearby. She heard a distant howl and shuddered.

"Wolves," Owen said in mock fear, raising a brow as they piled on wood to start a fire between their tents.

"I would not use their name lightly, for they say that beasts of the night can smell their prey ten times ten leagues away," Leandros replied gravely, and Owen stared at him in real fear this time.

"Well, I'm tired," Zeb said, huddled next to Penélope by the flames. "We've hiked with no rest for eight hours straight. If we don't sleep before dawn, I won't make another day."

Leandros nodded, standing up. "You are right. We must rest, for tomorrow the path grows more arduous, and we need all of our strength to continue."

They allowed the flames of the fire to burn to embers, hoping the lingering light would still ward off any lurking predators without alerting any tribes of men. Zeb claimed a tent for himself and Penélope, but to their surprise, Leandros interceded.

"Penélope shall sleep with me, as she is my wife," he said, causing Penélope to blush, though her heart warmed at his protectiveness.

Owen raised a hand. "And I, personally, would prefer not to share such a small tent with a man that size, especially if he snores. No offense."

Leandros narrowed his eyes at him. "None taken."

Penélope waited, watching Zeb battle internally, not willing to fight against Leandros' wrath, who could so easily defeat him physically, but also not keen on sharing a tent with Owen, with whom he was always arguing. But she knew deep down Zeb would be secretly thrilled at the prospect of sleeping in close proximity to Owen, even if they were currently on less than good terms.

"Fine," Zeb said, then turned to Owen in contempt. "But if you snore even once, I'm out."

Owen laughed. "Oh, darling, you know I don't snore." Zeb blanched, then flushed, speechless for what felt like the first time. Owen draped an arm around his shoulders, and Zeb surprisingly did not resist. "Come on, off to bed. I'm sure we'll be quieter than *those* two, after all."

Now Zeb was not the only one who was flushed. Leandros stood with his cheeks red, before he looked at Penélope. She merely raised a brow and gestured for him to enter their tent first.

Once they were inside the tent and Leandros began preparing his thin mat, Penélope crawled on top of him, straddling his hips. His eyes widened, though he did not push her off, his arms wrapping automatically around her waist.

"They will hear us, my love," he whispered, though his eyes betrayed him, filled with a burning desire.

Penélope curled her arms around his neck, brushing their lips together. "Oh, I don't think they'll hear us at all..."

Then she kissed him, forgetting momentarily that she was camped on the steep slope of foreign mountains, losing herself to the warmth of Leandros' embrace until they fell asleep for the night, her head resting upon his chest, listening to his heart beat steady with his breaths.

53

Zᴇʙ ᴄᴏᴜʟᴅ ɴᴏᴛ ꜰᴇᴇʟ his legs by the time the sun neared the highest point in the sky. All of his muscles were sore from their first day of hiking and carrying his pack of supplies, and he doubted he would be able to make it the rest of the way. They weren't even sure where the cave of the Sibyl was, only that it was deep inside the mountains at some sacred spring.

Owen and Leandros, annoyingly enough, seemed to be doing just fine, despite the fact that Leandros had been badly injured only a few weeks ago. Penélope occasionally demanded a break, out of breath and clutching the side of her chest, but then, after a quick rest and bite of their rations, they were on the move again, their different paces naturally bringing them into single file.

As the morning bled into afternoon, Owen lagged to fall into step beside Zeb, who scowled immediately, even if he was secretly pleased by the attention, something he would *never* admit to Owen's smirking face, and hardly admitted to himself, hating how much he wanted it.

"You can't ignore me the whole day," Owen said, raising a brow.

Zeb huffed a laugh. "I could if I wanted to."

"But you don't."

He was silent, partly to test him, and partly because he didn't have a good enough argument against it.

Owen grinned. "Just admit it, you wanted to kiss me last night."

This time Zeb glared at him, though this only made Owen's grin wider. But a small part of Zeb was disappointed. He had, in fact, desperately wanted to kiss him, yet the moment they entered the tent, Owen had rolled over and slept. Zeb had remained awake, almost positive that he heard noises from the other tent and staring at the ceiling, wondering if Owen was even interested in him anymore. He was always so flippant, so casual about their strange relationship, and it terrified Zeb more than anything, save perhaps the possibility of wolves attacking them while they slept.

His weighty thoughts had eventually lulled him into a fitful sleep, in which he dreamed a weird, confusing dream, reliving some of his memories in the Underworld, turning and seeing the fanged faces of Scylla rearing overhead, Penélope shouting his name. Then Owen was kissing him in the hull—but no, he was *watching* Owen kiss him, except it wasn't him but Chloe, both of them seeing him and laughing at him, before Chloe morphed into Calypso, dragging Owen to bed in her cave, while all Zeb could do was watch helplessly. Before he woke up, Calypso had changed into Ari—not Ari, Zeb had realized in confusion, but a god that looked like him, or rather like the one they had seen after the revelry, yet colder in his power. He was handsome, dark-haired, and naked save a slender gold crown on his head that looked like the rays of the sun. His hands wound tight around Owen's waist as he looked knowingly over his shoulder at Zeb, but the moment their eyes had met, a painful, blinding light struck him, exploding all around him, and he had opened his eyes, having woken with the dawn.

Owen looked at him now in mild concern. "Is anyone in there? I asked you a question."

"What? Sorry, I was just..."

"Are you alright?" Owen asked, genuinely worried now. "You look pale." He paused. "Paler than usual, at least."

Zeb shook his head, too exhausted to even glare at him. "I just had a weird dream, that's all."

Owen grinned. "Was I in it?"

"Yes."

Instead of triumph, suspicion crept into Owen's voice. "Really?"

Thankfully, he didn't have to explain. Penélope was calling them over excitedly, a huge smile on her face. They rushed over to her, Zeb's heart racing faster, not knowing what to expect.

"What is it?" he asked, out of breath from their sprint.

Penélope pointed below, where the rocks fell off into a steep crevice. Zeb could just hear the telltale bubbling of a river. "See!"

"What does it mean?" Zeb asked doubtfully.

"If we follow it, Leandros thinks we'll reach the sacred spring and find the Sibyl!"

"Well, to me," Owen drawled, "this means I can finally bathe."

So it was decided that they would follow the river until it surfaced and they could all bathe before heading onward. They had spent weeks on the ship without making landfall, after all, though at the time bathing was the least of their concerns. At last, the river turned, climbing steadily up and out onto a wide, flowing stream, from where it continued winding higher and deeper into the heart of the mountains.

Leandros led them to a level stretch of the river, where they split into two groups, Leandros going with Penélope since he refused to leave her as he had on the island of Scheria.

"Five minutes," Leandros warned them before following after Penélope toward the riverbank. "Then we are on our way."

Owen and Zeb agreed and trudged further upstream, where Owen quickly undressed and plunged into the water. Zeb hesitantly removed his tunic and underclothes, then dipped a foot into the river, letting out a yelp at the freezing current.

"Like hell I'm going in that!" he shouted.

Owen laughed, though he was careful not to look at Zeb directly. "You don't have a choice, unless you want to smell rancid for the rest of the hike."

Zeb rolled his eyes, then took one step further in, then another, until the water reached his upper thighs. His feet were numb, clinging to the small rocks on the riverbed. By the time Zeb had lowered himself so that the water covered most of his torso, Owen had already swum a few laps in the deeper part of the stream, washed his curly hair, and scrubbed his face clean of the dirt and grime from weeks at sea.

Owen looked at Zeb and gave him a subdued smile. "Can you believe where we are right now?"

Zeb shuddered against the cold stream. "This is worse than the Underworld."

Owen waded over to him and ran his hands down Zeb's arms, spreading some warmth into his skin. "Better?"

His teeth chattered in response, though possibly more from the sudden contact with Owen's hands than the temperature of the river.

"The water is probably coming from the snow on the mountains," Owen said, rubbing his own arms. "We'd be warmer if we swam."

Then without a word, he dove under the waves, resurfacing in the deeper end of the river, then backstroking a few paces before turning and swimming the other way. Zeb watched him half-terrified, half-longingly. Owen paused, looked at him strangely, then beckoned him over.

"Come here," he said. "I'll teach you how."

Zeb stood frozen, though not from the cold. His heart beat haphazardly in his chest at the mere thought of his feet leaving the ground. But another part of him wanted to brave his fear, to allow Owen's strong arms to guide him, just as he had that night they almost drowned in the shipwreck.

He nodded, as if his body no longer belonged to him, then waded closer. Owen met him halfway, then with his hands firmly holding his, brought them to the deep end.

"Don't worry," Owen murmured. "You can still stand here."

The water reached the top of Zeb's chest, fully standing. He clutched at Owen's hands, not caring if this made him look ridiculous. But there was no mocking smile or laughter in Owen's eyes, just encouragement.

"First, you'll lie on your back and I'll hold you up. Then you'll practice kicking and stroking with my help."

Zeb nodded, unable to speak. Owen moved him closer, almost as if he were going to kiss him, then gently turned Zeb around and lowered him backwards. His stomach in knots, Zeb allowed himself to be positioned on Owen's hand, which rested beneath his lower back.

"Now let your body float a little," Owen said gently. "Lift your legs up. I promise I won't let go."

With his teeth gritted together, Zeb lifted his legs, allowing them to float in the water. Owen's hand remained firm on his lower back, the other helping to lift his legs. He shivered as his body floated on the surface, though he still felt the weight of his body yearning towards the bottom if Owen were to let go of him.

"Now kick with your legs. I'll still guide you."

He kicked as best he could despite the numbness in his muscles, and was surprised to find that he moved smoothly across the water, remaining level with the surface.

"Now your arms too, like I was."

Zeb hesitantly lifted one arm backward, then another, until he got the hang of timing it with his kicks.

"Good!" Owen said. "There you go. See?"

His confidence grew, and he kicked a little faster, finding that his body already felt warmer and the cold water almost refreshing.

Suddenly he noticed that Owen's hand was barely touching his lower back, and he gasped, trying to stand, failing, his body sinking, but before Owen even reached out to him, his feet touched the ground, and he stood, still gasping for air. Owen grabbed his waist to steady him, but Zeb shoved him away.

"You said you wouldn't let go!"

"You were swimming before you noticed," Owen said pointedly. "And I was still holding you up. Nothing would've happened."

He shoved Owen away when he tried to come close again. "I could've drowned!"

"Zeb, look at me!"

He looked up wildly. Owen held his face and kissed him, forcing his head to be still. Zeb instantly relaxed, all thoughts of protest flying from his mind. Because Owen was right. Zeb *had* wanted to kiss him last night, and it had taken all of his willpower not to reach over and pull Owen closer.

"God, you're a prick," Zeb said, leaning back. He was out of breath, but not from the swimming.

Owen laughed. "You'd make a good little English boy, you know." He looked around them, tightening his hold on Zeb's waist. "Do you think five minutes are up?"

"A *looong* time ago," Zeb said with a smirk.

After a beat of silence, Owen said, "You never told me your dream."

"It was...strange." Zeb hesitated. "I saw you kissing Chloe. You were both laughing at me. Then it was Calypso. And then I thought she changed into Ari, but it was actually some god, though I don't know who it was."

Instead of the snide comment Zeb was expecting, Owen looked at him in confusion. "That is strange."

"What do you think it means?" Zeb asked.

"I'm not sure," Owen said honestly. "Chloe and I have made amends, but we will never be what we once were. I never felt for her what I feel for you."

Hope fluttered in his chest. "And Ari?"

Owen huffed a laugh. "Are you sure it wasn't you kissing him?" He rolled his eyes at Zeb's glare. "Joking, mate."

"Calypso?"

"I wanted her only as much as the next bloke, but once we left her cave, I no longer thought twice of her." He paused. "But the god...What did he look like?"

"Handsome," Zeb murmured. "Dark-haired."

Owen raised a skeptical brow.

This time Zeb rolled his eyes. "There was a gold crown on his head, like the sun."

"You know, I had a strange dream myself," Owen said, suddenly pensive once more. "Not of any gods, but of my father. We were in London. I was talking with him about—"

A sharp whistle interrupted them, coming from downstream, and they quickly moved apart. They saw Leandros and Penélope hiking up, her hair still wet and curling around her neck, a small, pleased smile on her face.

"Oi! No more delay!" Leandros called out, then he turned to the side, and they disappeared from view.

Zeb and Owen shared a dry look before they both got out of the river, dressed, and hurriedly joined Leandros and Penélope once more.

54

The path they picked along the river up into the mountain turned steep and dangerous as Leandros led them single file in switchbacks as narrow as one footstep. Penélope's heart would pound every time her foot slipped and rocks crumbled down the mountainside, foreshadowing what would happen if she lost her balance and fell. Occasionally, Leandros would help her climb up a particularly slippery incline, grabbing her arms and lifting her. But she tried to avoid it, noticing his wince at the pain in his right bicep where Scylla's poisonous claws had dug deep.

When they finally reached a flatter clearing naturally built against the steep mountainside, they would camp for a few hours and rest before waking once more and continuing on. They found little rest in sleep by the river anyway, whose constant gurgling and hissing had a strange way of weaving itself in their dreams and putting them all on edge.

The weather was as extreme and testing as the climb. During the day, the sun beat down upon them mercilessly, and with no shade of trees or even shrubs in sight, they would sweat and overheat easily. But the moment the sun slipped past the horizon, night bore a bone-deep chill, as if a breeze carried the cold from the snow on the slopes above and exhaled on them. It was best to keep moving at night for fear of freezing to death, but if they had to camp, she would sleep close to Leandros, their mingling heat warm enough to give them a few hours respite.

But even though they followed the river, they could not be sure they were headed in the right direction. Owen often complained of this, but Leandros would send one withering glare his way that would silence him. If there was one person Owen truly respected, if out of slight fear, it was him, which secretly pleased Penélope as much as it annoyed her, wishing she, too, had that respect from him.

Tonight was their fifth night hiking when they began to pass small clumps of frost and snow. Penélope could see her breath puff white in front of her face. When they camped, they begged Leandros for a fire, though they only had meager supplies left of it. Seeing the blue tinge of Penélope's fingernails, he relented.

As they sat around the fire, Zeb asked Leandros who, exactly, was the Sibyl, and what did she do for Apollo. Leandros stared into the flickering flames in silence before responding.

"They say when Apollo chooses the next Sibyl, he grants her immortality if she lies with him, but if not, she is permitted an abnormally long life of a thousand years, only felled by the sword or disease, before the next Sibyl must be chosen. As his Sibyl, she is responsible for interpreting omens in the stars and in sacrifices, having been gifted with the sight of what has been, what is, and what shall be. Many have pilgrimaged to her oracle seeking answers, but few ever return to tell the tale, and if they do, never return quite as themselves."

Penélope shivered, and even Owen was silent. She caught Zeb's eye across the fire, whose face was pale and tense, reminding her of how he had been after returning from the Underworld, as if a part of him had remained in the Land of the Dead. Had he returned as himself? Or would he always be changed, marked, as it were, by Death?

"We should sleep," Penélope said with a sigh, not wishing to linger on dark subjects while the night was still waxing and the river slithered ominously nearby, hidden from sight by night's utter blackness.

Everyone agreed and made their tents, which took up all the space on the small shelf. Penélope curled up beside Leandros, who brought her even closer to his chest, and she relaxed against the heat radiating from his skin.

"I wish the river were wide enough to bathe in," Penélope said. "It's been days since the last time."

Leandros glanced down at her with a raised brow, and she blushed, recalling how he had wanted to bathe quickly, telling her it was time to go after five minutes, but instead she had lured him back in the water.

"The others will be waiting for us," Leandros had whispered between kisses, lifting her out of the water and into his arms.

"Let them wait," was all Penélope had the patience to say before she had kissed him again, gripping his arms and not caring if they both bruised their injuries again.

Now Penélope prodded her left ribcage, wincing with a smile. "I think I'm still sore from that."

Leandros leaned down and kissed her there. "You were not so gentle either, as I recall."

She threaded her fingers into his hair and tugged. "But you liked that, didn't you?"

Before she could lean in and kiss him, they heard muffled shouts from the other tent. They both hurriedly stepped out into the cold night air and saw Zeb and Owen conversing heatedly outside of their tent, looking to be on the verge of an argument.

"I know what I heard," Zeb said harshly, his chest rising and falling as if he had just run a sprint. "And no, it wasn't just a dream." He glanced at Penélope, and relief melted his tense features. "Oh, thank God. Pepa, you have to believe me. I heard the voices. I know I did."

"What voices?" she asked in alarm.

Owen crossed his arms, his jaw clenching. "He thinks he's hearing the voices of the dead. I told him it was just a dream. We're all having weird dreams."

Penélope knew Owen had a point, but she also knew Zeb would never lie about something like that. "I believe you, Zeb. But what does it mean?"

"I want to follow them," Zeb said firmly.

"See?" Owen said, pointing at Zeb. "That's what I didn't like. Nothing good ever happens when you start following the voices of the dead."

"The son of Godfrey is right," Leandros said gravely. "To follow the voices of the dead is to risk becoming one of them."

Zeb turned away angrily. "We have no idea where we're going. Just admit it! This is the first clue to finding the Sibyl. I know it. You guys have to trust me."

"Maybe a part of you wants to follow the voices," Owen shot back. "Maybe a part of you *wants* to see where it leads."

Penélope hated that she agreed with Owen, but when she saw the hurt flash across Zeb's face, she regretted it. Zeb had trusted her so far without a clue about what had happened since being trapped in the Underworld. Maybe it was time she trusted him in return.

"I say we follow them," Penélope said, and all eyes turned to her in surprise. "It can't be a coincidence that the moment we started hiking these mountains, we started having strange dreams. Maybe there's a reason he's hearing these voices."

"Yeah, maybe because he was the only one of us who's already died," Owen deadpanned. He closed his eyes briefly, then opened them with a sigh. "But if you truly think this will put an end to these miserable nights, I am willing to set aside my doubts and follow the voices."

Everyone waited for Leandros, who stroked his beard thoughtfully, his eyes dark and wary. "We follow the voices for one day. If we do not find the Sibyl by then, we stop and continue following the river."

They packed up their camp in silence, then waited for Zeb to lead the way. He closed his eyes, though they flickered behind his eyelids as if he could see the dead as well as hear them. Then he took off, climbing with a sure step in the opposite direction from the river.

Penélope's stomach filled with dread the further they walked away from their only source of water, but she equally dreaded any more nights camped out on the edge of a cliff, shivering and restless. But even as she reassured herself that they could always turn back, a part of her knew Owen and Leandros were right.

There was no turning back once they followed the dead.

Dawn rose in the east and lightened the dark. Still, Zeb continued, only pausing briefly to listen, then marching on. Penélope noticed their path took them around the mountain instead of further up, as if they were heading deeper inland. This intuition proved true by late afternoon, when they lost sight of the sea which had always accompanied them, so alike to the blue sky that sometimes Penélope had imagined they were looking over the edge of the world.

Owen became restless by evening, muttering about the coming night and not having any water. Even Penélope sensed that they were running out of time. But his words became even more ominous when the sun sank behind the ridge of the mountains, and they suddenly came upon a wide, sluggish river as black as the night sky flowing down the mountainside like ink spilled from the bottle.

Zeb stopped suddenly, staring at the water in a daze, his voice a hoarse whisper. "This is it. The voices are across the river."

He took a step toward it, but Owen grabbed his arm, pulling him back. Penélope half-expected them to fight, but Owen merely pointed over to their right, where along the river snaked a path built into the rock, polished and gleaming in the last glowing light of the sun.

"I do not think it wise to cross the river," Leandros said to Zeb carefully, who glanced anxiously across the currents as if he could see something there that they couldn't. "Let us follow the path. The Sibyl must be close."

With effort, Zeb nodded and allowed Owen to lead him along the river to the pathway, which solemnly followed the black water as it bent around a ridge and suddenly disappeared between massive boulders into the mountains, from which it poured out bubbling and thick.

And carved above the boulders like the face of a ten-story building yawned a hundred caves cut into the rock, their black openings like the eyes of a terrible monster staring down upon them. They all stopped, beholding the caves in awe and terror when a voice shook from within the mountain, echoing from every cave:

"WHO DARES TO ENTER THE CAVE OF THE SIBYL?"

55

At the voice that rang out in the stillness of the night, they all stood frozen in shock. Then Leandros stepped forward, his hand on the hilt of his sword.

"I am Leandros, son of Leon, descended from King Helenus, son of Priam, offspring of Zeus! My companions and I demand an audience with the Sibyl, but shall give no further explanation until we have come face to face with the priestess herself!"

No response was given by the voice, but they heard a loud grinding noise come from the path ahead, where the stone walkway suddenly stopped against the mountainside next to the massive boulders where the river had its source. The grinding came from the wall of rock blocking the path, which opened as if by magic to reveal a dark tunnel, disappearing into the mountain.

All of them shared fearful looks before Leandros took the lead, following the pathway into the tunnel, carved deep and endless. Once they were inside the mountain, the stone door ground shut behind them with a horrible, resounding *boom*, burying them in pitch black darkness, until a moment later a sconce lit up a few paces ahead of them.

Penélope let out a breath, then took Leandros' hand in hers as they continued down the tunnel, finding comfort in his strong grip. He held her hand with one, but kept the other on the hilt of his sword, just in case they encountered any nasty surprises lurking in this damp tunnel.

"Look," Owen whispered, pointing ahead to where the tunnel branched off into different directions.

They stopped at the intersection, unsure. Zeb took a step forward, his eyes closed. Then he pointed to the left tunnel. "It's that way. I can hear them again."

Owen began protesting that following the voices was a bad idea when the left tunnel lit up with sconces, as if signaling them to enter it. Penélope caught Owen's wide-eyed gaze, which reluctantly turned defeated. They had no other choice.

"Follow me," Zeb said coldly, shouldering past Owen and down the tunnel glowing with the red-orange light of the sconces.

Penélope briefly rested a hand on Owen's shoulder before following after Zeb with Leandros. As the tunnel descended more steeply and narrowly, they had to walk single file, Zeb's blond head lit ghostly white ahead of her. She hated how stuffy and cold the air became as they delved lower, as if they were heading toward the heart of the mountain.

After a while, they came upon another intersection, this time of five tunnels, where from one of them could be heard the faint growling of an animal and from another the thick stench of some bog. Just as before, they took one of the other tunnels, soon lit by sconces, Zeb confirming that the voices also came from there. They passed several intersections this way for what felt like an eternity, her breath shallow and sweat clinging to her neck despite the ever-present chill in the air, longing for the fresh air outside even if it froze the very blood in her veins.

Suddenly the tunnel they tread opened upon a lofty hall, its smooth walls interspersed with carved pillars, the high ceiling engraved with constellations and other patterns and symbols Penélope did not recognize. On the far side of the hall, behind a stone altar, trickled black water, which flowed out to the right in thicker streams and disappeared once more behind large rocks on the other end of the hall.

And standing barefoot before the altar, surrounded on the stone floor by scattered, browning leaves, and dressed in white robes, her hair long and black as the flowing currents of the river, was a young woman. She was eerily beautiful, with round, dark eyes set a hair's breadth too wide in a pale white face the color of moonlight, as though the sun had ceased to kiss her skin for a thousand years.

She opened her arms wide. "Welcome to the Oracle of the Lord of Light!"

As she spoke, a shaft of light—whiter than sunlight, but harsher than moonlight—pierced the air from somewhere above, briefly shining upon the altar and the trickling water behind it before the light faded back into darkness.

"Step forth and be welcomed, weary pilgrims, for you must be weary after such an arduous climb and descent to seek my humble abode."

After hesitating at the mouth of the tunnel, they entered the hall, following the path directly to the priestess. Their footsteps echoed along the cold stone, but Penélope found she could breathe easier in the wide open space, as if a draft of air had entered from where the light had just shined.

"I can understand you," Owen said in surprise, looking at the priestess in slight confusion.

The Sibyl smiled, and for the first time Penélope saw how young she seemed, hardly older than them, though there was something in the glint of her dark eyes that was older than the very roots of the mountain. "My gift of prophecy allows me to speak all the tongues of mortals."

"Then you are immortal," Penélope said, near breathless. "You are Aethusa, daughter of Poseidon, granddaughter of Atlas. You are the Sibyl of Apollo."

Aethusa inclined her head. "And you must be Penélope, daughter of Estela, who has slayed the Serpent of Osiris with the Golden Blade." At her shocked face, the Sibyl laughed, a rich sound that echoed in the lofty hall around them. "Ah, yes, your name has reached even my ears, for the gods have been watching you, have they not?"

Penélope did not respond, a chill running down her spine. Leandros tightened his grip on her hand.

"Enough pleasantries, my Lady," Leandros said coldly. "We have come to seek your aid."

"Is that so?" Aethusa asked, though she did not sound surprised in the least. "And what aid might you require from me?"

"Long ago, a curse was cast upon my grandfather, Philoxenos, by your father, Poseidon, Lord of the Sea, after he was denied hospitality by the Phaeacians and he bore Nausicala, the daughter of King Kleomachus, back to the city of Helena. We have since then made amends with the King of Scheria, but the Earth-Shaker in his unquenchable wrath besets our homeward journey. We have been told to seek the Sibyl of Apollo, that as the daughter of Poseidon you may intercede on our behalf and end his curse upon my family, so that we may return home at last."

The Sibyl began walking around them, staring at each of them in turn, before she spoke again, the stone around them carrying her whispering voice to their ears. "Long has your father, King Leon, wandered the waters wide in search of me. He is not the first. Many men have come seeking answers, though few ever like what they learn. For to know is to suffer, while ignorance is a gift that cannot be bestowed again once it is taken away."

"We do not ask for your knowledge," Penélope said firmly, ignoring the flush on her face when the priestess' eyes fastened on her. "Only that you supplicate your father on our behalf."

"Do you not ask for knowledge, Lady Penélope?" Aethusa asked, stepping toward her. "You, who has ever sought knowledge, dares to lie to the priestess who sees all? You bring terrible knowledge with you that shall alter the very order of the cosmos!"

Penélope was suddenly fearful, sharing a glance with Zeb. "How do you know that?"

The Sibyl lifted her arms high, her eyes rolling to the whites as she shouted in a voice so deep and powerful it no longer sounded human: *"I am the Oracle of Apollo! Through my eyes shines the light that pierces both shadow and flesh! All that He sees, I see! All that He knows, I know! Nothing escapes my knowledge, for I see All!"*

They stumbled away from her as she trembled with the very force of her words. Then suddenly she ceased, her body sagging, as if some energy that had coursed through her had been stoppered up, like rocks covering a spring. She lowered her face, her voice now returned to normal.

"I shall do what I can to appease my father, though his wrath be hot and unending as the eternal flame." She paused, then flourished a hand. "But sleep, first, my dear guests, for you are weary, and the temple is ever a sanctuary welcoming to those who need rest."

"Do we sleep on the ground?" Owen asked doubtfully, eyeing the cold, hard rock where the priestess had pointed.

"You shall find that it is quite comfortable," Aethusa replied, "and sleep swift and restful."

Then the priestess turned with a swish of her robes, disappearing back through the tunnel they had come in from, her retreating figure swallowed up in the darkness. They watched her leave and then turned to each other, visibly shaken, but also exhausted, as seen in the dark circles lining their eyes and their haggard faces.

"I say we sleep," Owen said first. "I don't care if my back hurts. At least we're not out in the cold."

Leandros nodded stiffly, taking out their supplies. Owen followed suit, and they laid out their mats on the unyielding stone floor side by side. Penélope lay between Zeb and Leandros, her eyes open to the impossibly high ceilings, tracing the constellations etched into the stone, wondering how this marvel of a cave came to be, and had trouble believing it to be made by the hands of mere mortals.

Penélope glanced to her left and right and saw that all of the others had fallen asleep. But she suddenly did not feel tired, alert and watchful of every trickling, echoing sound in the hall. With a sigh, she forced her eyes closed.

56

It was impossible. She could not sleep.

Penélope opened her eyes once more, looking around the cavernous temple. Then she blinked at the altar, where she saw the slithering, scaled body of a massive serpent, much like the one she killed in the Underworld, though this one's scales glinted emerald green, and its eyes were dark as the black soil of the earth. She blinked again, but it did not disappear. *Where had it come from?*

She watched, paralyzed, as the serpent effortlessly slid over the altar, its heavy body gliding down on the stone floor, moving directly toward her. But she could not scream, wondering why the others remained asleep peacefully, unaware of the danger headed their way. What could she do? She no longer had her golden sword, and her hands remained at her sides like lead, unwilling to move and defend herself.

The serpent coiled before her mat, reared its head and flashed its fangs, then pounced on her, its jaw wide and ready to snap as she opened her mouth to scream—

An arrow sang past Penélope's face and buried itself deep into the serpent's neck, who screeched suddenly and terribly, tossing its wounded neck back and flailing about in pain. Her companions still did not wake. She turned her head sluggishly, as if she were underwater, to see a man emerge from the tunnel, bow pulled taut with another arrow set to fly. He released it, and the arrow sank clean into the serpent's left eye, spurting red blood that turned bright, liquid gold as it fell to the floor.

She watched the god approach—for he could only be a god, Penélope knew—the same that she had dreamed of once before in this very hall, with dark, curling hair and a handsome smile. He strapped the bow to his back then took out a gleaming sword, and in one stroke beheaded the serpent, its blood gushing out like a stream, dripping past Penélope and down to where the black river had been just moments before, filling the shallow, dried up creek in the ground with its blood.

Look at me, Penélope.

When she looked back at the god, he was looking straight at her, when suddenly a blinding light exploded painfully in her vision, but this time, within the light, she saw visions flash lightning-fast before her eyes. She glimpsed a palace room, Leandros beside her, and cradled in her arms—

Penélope gasped as her eyes opened.

She stared at the ceiling, lying flat on her back. When she forced herself to sit up, she felt simultaneously as though she had slept for an eternity and like no time had passed. Standing by the altar was the Sibyl, piling the stone slab with wood. Gone were the snake and the god, and the blood that had stained the ground and filled up the empty ground where the river now shone, still black and sluggish. Beside her, the others remained asleep.

"I thought I saw..." Penélope said hoarsely.

The Sibyl glanced behind her knowingly. "My lord does not reveal himself to all mortals who sleep in his temple. Consider yourself honored."

Penélope did not feel honored, but rather threatened, as if she had been shown that vision to scare her or send her a message. If there was any message hidden in the terrible murder of the serpent, Penélope could not find it, though it did not take much pondering to know what she had seen.

"He showed me the slaying of Python."

Aethusa said nothing.

"Then he told me to look at him," Penélope whispered, not caring if the priestess could hear, since she surely already knew. "And I saw myself, in the future, holding—"

But she never finished, interrupted by a shout beside her.

"Penélope!" Leandros cried as he awoke, sitting up with his chest rising and falling rapidly. He blinked as he looked around, and then when he saw her, his shoulders sagged. "I apologize. In my dream...I thought you—"

"There shall be time to discuss later all that you have seen," the Sibyl interrupted, almost impatiently. "Awaken your comrades. It is time for the sacrifice."

Penélope gently shook Zeb awake, whose eyes flew open to show the terror within, before he looked around and saw that he was still in the temple. But he avoided her gaze, instead turning to Owen, who woke up only after Zeb shoved his shoulder.

He sat up with a yawn. "Blimey, if that crazy lady wasn't right! I had the best sleep of my life."

Zeb signaled with his eyes behind Owen, but he didn't seem to notice, looking at each of them in growing worry.

"Why do you all look as though you've seen a ghost?"

Penélope cleared her throat, looking behind Owen at the Sibyl. He finally caught on and turned around, smiling sheepishly when Aethusa raised a brow at him.

"Not to all does the Lord of Light reveal himself," the Sibyl said, "though some may consider that more of a blessing than not."

She had to agree with the priestess, but there were more pressing matters to discuss. "You said it was time for the sacrifice. Does that mean you've agreed to help us? You'll appease Poseidon's wrath?"

The Sibyl lifted her head proudly. "I shall do what I can." She turned and walked purposefully toward the altar.

They hesitated, then scrambled to their feet to follow her. She had already piled thin branches of olive wood atop the altar, its stone blackened with soot. Once they were gathered before her, she turned, a thin, silver dagger held out on her open palms.

"I may intercede on your behalf, but to appease my father's anger, first a just sacrifice must be made to set the scales in balance once more."

"What kind of sacrifice?" Leandros asked suspiciously.

"Blood," the Sibyl replied, and they all flinched. She turned to Penélope. "You once swore to give your firstborn daughter freely to the Phaeacians as payment for the theft of Nausicala, firstborn daughter of King Kleomachus. Now must your oath be bound by blood."

"But I already swore on the dread waters of the Styx," Penélope protested, fearing the thought of drawing her own blood and what that might entail.

"To mortals, words may be enough, but for the gods, an oath must be sealed in blood for the mortal soul to be fatally bound with the words."

Leandros stepped forward, shielding Penélope. "No more blood shall be spilled on account of this curse."

"Do not worry, Leandros," the priestess said slyly. "Only a few drops will do, not only of hers, but of yours as well, for the child shall be of *both* your blood."

He paled at her words, glancing at Penélope hesitantly. It was up to her. She did not wish to spill any blood, even more so of Leandros. But if she didn't, then they would never be able to return home, and all that they had been through would be for nothing. They would be risking more than their own lives then.

"It is the only way to appease my father's wrath and end the curse once and for all," Aethusa said quietly.

Penélope squeezed Leandros' hands and nodded. "We will do it."

"Penélope—" Zeb protested, but she silenced him with a look.

"This is my choice, remember?" she asked.

Zeb stared after her miserably, but did not try to stop her again. Owen looked on in equal measures worried and sad, nodding at Penélope before she turned to face the priestess. The Sibyl handed Zeb and Owen each a long strip of gauzy, white linen for them to use after the blood was drawn, then led Penélope and Leandros before the altar.

"Hold your left hands together," the Sibyl said.

Leandros took Penélope's left hand with his, their arms crossed between them, their wedding rings glinting in the hazy darkness of the cave. She could not help but feel as though this were some perverted form of a wedding, their vows not of love but of the sacrifice of their firstborn child, Zeb and Owen standing as their witnesses.

The priestess hovered over the pile of wood and struck two stones together until a spark caught on the branches, igniting a flame that slowly flickered small and red inside the wood. As the branches blackened and crackled from the growing fire, the Sibyl held out the knife, along with a small silver bowl, and beckoned for their hands.

Penélope swallowed against the rising panic in her throat, holding out her right hand. Leandros did the same. Then the priestess placed their hands side by side, aligning their palms. Before Penélope could blink, the priestess sliced the dagger across their palms, a stinging pain instantly following.

Blood welled in their palms like a spring dug up from the ground. The Sibyl turned Leandros' hand first, allowing the droplets of blood to spill into the silver bowl, then did the same to Penélope, who shivered when she saw her bright red blood mingling with his.

Zeb and Owen immediately came forward and began wrapping their palms in the strips of linen. Penélope's palm was warm from the blood, pulsing as Zeb tightened the strip with a knot on the back of her hand. Once they were both properly bandaged, they turned their attention to the priestess, who had taken the silver bowl of blood and circled the altar, standing behind it and facing them.

The fire now roared with large, hungry flames, crumbling the wood to ash. With her eyes looking skyward, the Sibyl cried out in her loud, echoing voice.

"Let the Earth be my witness," she called out, raising the bowl, "and the broad heaven above, that by the dread waters of the Styx, this mingled blood shall bind the oath sworn, promising to the King of the Phaeacians the firstborn daughter of Lord Leandros, son of Leon, and Lady Penélope, daughter of Estela, thereby absolving the curse set upon King Philoxenos' lineage by my father Poseidon, King of the Sea and Earth-Shaker, lest they break their oath and be punished with Death!"

Then she cast the blood upon the fire, which hissed and spurted in response, glowing even hotter than before. The ground began to tremble, and then the walls shook, until all around them the mountain seemed to groan and heave with the force of a thousand earthquakes, threatening to bury them alive beneath the weight of the Pillars of the Sea.

All of a sudden the earth ceased shaking, the fire sputtering its last flames, exhaling smoke. The wood crumbled weakly, scattered with embers and stained red from the blood. All was calm once more, as if nothing had happened, the silence like a fog blanketing the hall.

The Sibyl did not seem alarmed, merely peering over the burnt wood as though she were reading something written there. Penélope held her breath as the moment seemed to last an eternity. Then Aethusa looked up with a smile.

"Your oath has been fulfilled, and the King of the Sea has accepted your sacrifice," the Sibyl proclaimed. "You may return home."

57

Penélope stood in disbelief before she threw her arms around Leandros, laughing at the same time as the tears came. Leandros laughed too, lifting her up on her tiptoes. She hugged Zeb and Owen too, who both looked relieved at the good news.

"Before you leave," the Sibyl said, her firm voice cutting through their excitement, "there is one thing I must ask of you to do."

"But I thought we could go home," Penélope said in confusion, her heart sinking to her stomach at the thought of any more sacrifices. "We performed the oath and gave our blood. What more can we do?"

Aethusa inclined her head in agreement. "And you may return home, but if you wish to return to victory, then you must heed my instruction."

"Victory?" Leandros echoed. "As in the war to come?"

But Penélope had always known this journey would reveal more than they had bargained for. She had known since crossing paths with the Queen of Death that the gods had been keeping their own counsel, moving mortals like pawns on a chessboard.

The Sibyl met her gaze, a gleam in her dark eyes. "You know of what I speak, Lady Penélope."

"You said before that I brought terrible knowledge with me," Penélope said slowly. "You're right. I've been told of the war to come, the unbalance in the universe. But I was told that we needed to save King Leon to succeed, which we have already done."

"The gods have a way with words to bend the truth," the priestess replied with a smirk. "Rescuing the King of Helena brought you to the island of Scheria, where you were fated to restore the Queen Nausicala from the shadows and set to right a century of wrong. But it is no mere chance that you have come to my halls. Since the King of the Gods has been overthrown, Chaos has reigned freely, as the Kosmos is caught in the midst of a war not even Mother Earth can end on her own. Not only the city of Helena, but all the worlds of Men will be at stake."

"But why did we have to come here?" Penélope demanded. "What is it that we are supposed to learn?"

"Not learn," Aethusa said, "but *find*."

"Find?" Owen repeated. "Like an object? Please tell me it's not the Emerald Stone."

The Sibyl shook her head. "No, not the Stone. But like the Stone, this power has already been wielded by a mortal, gifted by the Goddess of Grain, and left behind in the Halls of Death. With this weapon, the war may be won. Without it, all will surely be doomed."

"The Golden Blade," Penélope whispered.

"But if it was left behind in the Underworld..." Owen started, faltering.

"Then one of you must return to the Land of the Dead to retrieve it," the Sibyl finished gravely.

"Absolutely not." Penélope looked at the others, but they were all silent and pensive. "No! No one is returning to the Underworld. We barely escaped with our lives the last time. I'm not risking it."

The Sibyl raised a brow. "Then the war may be lost."

"What side are you even on?" Penélope asked angrily, the depths of despair she felt after such elation at the prospect of going home felt like Hell itself. "How do we know this isn't some trick to kill one of us?"

"I am on no *side,* as you say," the Sibyl responded haughtily. "I serve the Lord of Light until my charge has ended. He has foreseen your arrival as an opportune moment that hangs in the balance, but the choice has been left undecided, with either choice demanding its own consequences. I, however, have played my part, and shall not sway your decision any further."

Penélope turned to Leandros, who looked back at her grimly, but did not speak. Neither Zeb nor Owen would look her in the eye. The choice was hers, and after all, who else would she condemn to her fate?

"If I choose to retrieve the Golden Blade, how do I get there?"

This time Zeb answered. "The river."

Penélope's heart skipped a beat. "What?"

"The river," he said, louder this time, pointing at the black flowing waters that trickled down behind the altar, gathering in a slow, wide current, and slithering along one side of the room. "If you cross that river, you will go to the Land of the Dead."

"Yes," the Sibyl said, looking at Zeb curiously. "You hear them, do you not?"

Zeb nodded, but stared at the ground with a closed-off expression.

"This river flows from the heart of this mountain and joins the Acheron and the Styx in the Land of the Dead. If one of you chooses to retrieve the sword, all they must do is cross."

"But those who wander willingly into the Halls of the Dead," Leandros said darkly, "are not allowed to return to the world of the living."

"Not without payment," the Sibyl replied, glancing knowingly among them.

They were silent. The words tingled some since-forgotten memory, and she struggled to recall it, like grasping the wind with her hands. Penélope closed her eyes.

She was back in the Grove, the Queen of Death towering over her, queenly and terrifying. Behind the goddess stood the Elm of False Dreams, where memory and truth were warped by secret desires and hidden fears.

In the goddess' hand was a long leather leash holding back the three-headed Cerberus, who appeared as docile as a dog beside the goddess' heels. She smiled knowingly, then Penélope heard her voice chant inside her head, like a spell cast, or a song sung, more deadly than any blade or arrow.

> *Golden bough on Elm of Dreams*
> *Falsely sent by iv'ry means.*
> *If the dead can claim its coin,*
> *May he cross the Acheron.*

Penélope opened her eyes. All of them were staring at her. She had spoken the words aloud, unknowingly, as if she had truly been under a spell. The Sibyl did not move, standing still and patient as the stone pillars around them, waiting for their decision. Then Penélope saw a movement out of the corner of her eye and her stomach dropped in dread, knowing before he spoke what the words would be.

"I will go."

Zeb had stepped forward, holding something in his hand. She looked closer and realized it was the golden bough he had taken from the Elm of Dreams, still faded to brown but unmistakably unreal, as if it did not belong to this world and was merely a ghost of itself.

"You kept that?" Penélope asked in disbelief.

He nodded, staring at the bough in his hands. "It always felt like a part of me had stayed behind in the Land of the Dead, so I kept it as a reminder. Now it seems I know why."

"No," Penélope said firmly. "You're not going back. Not after we saved you. If anyone's going, it's me."

Zeb looked at her, oddly calm. "But you can't."

Her heart pounded. "Why not?"

"Didn't you hear what Leandros said?" Zeb asked, still in that strange, eerily calm manner. "Those who enter the Halls of the Dead are not allowed to return to the world of the living. But what if I never truly left? What if half of me returned, but the other half stayed behind?"

"You don't know that, Zeb," Penélope argued. "We have the payment. This is my choice. I won't let you sacrifice yourself for me again."

"This isn't your choice, Penélope. It's mine. *I* was trapped in the Underworld. *I* found the Golden Bough. *I* can hear the voices. *I* led us to the Sibyl." Zeb paused, then a small, wry smile appeared on his face. "Mother knew all along. She told me I lived with one foot in the dark and one foot in the light. At the time, I thought I knew what she meant." He glanced briefly at Owen with a flush, who raised an incredulous brow. "But maybe she knew it would come down to this moment. Maybe she knew it was my fate to leave half of me in the world below, and that it was my fate to bring the sword back."

By the time he finished speaking, Penélope could not stop the tears from falling. She had just saved him, and now it felt like all that striving and grieving and hoping was for nothing. He was always going to die anyway.

Zeb placed his hand on her arm in a rare display of affection. "I can come back, remember? I have the payment. All I need to do is find the Golden Blade." He paused, then looked at the Sibyl. "Where *do* I find the Golden Blade?"

"You must seek the Death Bringer," the Sibyl said. "Only she has the power to give away her mother's sword to those deserving."

Penélope shivered, recalling the cold, deathless power radiating from the goddess. "And how does he return?"

The Sibyl motioned toward the black river. "Cross back over the river with your payment, and your life shall be restored."

Zeb took a deep breath and nodded. "I'm ready."

"You don't have to do this," Penélope whispered, her voice thick from the tears.

"I was wrong, you know," he said in reply, half-wistfully. "This war *is* going to affect our world. All the *worlds* of Men are at stake. That's what the Sibyl said. If you need the Golden Blade to fight this war, it's only right that I get it for you. This is me fighting, Penélope, not just for us, but for our home. Let me do this for them too."

Penélope looked into his familiar blue eyes, but all she could see was an earnest hope, something she had not seen in his eyes in a long time. She could not say the words, worried they would be the last. Instead, she hugged him, struggling to keep back the tears. When she stepped away, Zeb faced Owen, who looked at him with a blank face, as if he could hardly comprehend what was happening. They nodded briefly at each other before Zeb walked past him, meeting the Sibyl by the river.

"You will find the crossing to be quite dry," she said, then bowed and stepped away to let him cross by himself.

Zeb glanced back at Penélope. She wished she could smile, but all she could do was watch anxiously. He took a deep breath in, clutched the bough tighter, and then walked into the water. It only took five strides for him to reach the other side.

When he stepped on the other bank, he was gone.

58

THE MOMENT ZEB DISAPPEARED, Penélope gasped, her heart thudding painfully in shock. A part of her had not truly believed it would work, that Zeb would cross the river and stand on the other side, and they would all laugh at the Sibyl's trick.

But he was truly gone.

Owen also looked at the river in disbelief. He did not speak, but his shoulders sagged when he realized that Zeb had really crossed to the Land of the Dead. She wanted to comfort him, but there was nothing left to say.

Leandros came and hugged her, and she sank into his chest, exhausted. She did not cry anymore, as if all the tears had been dried up over the past months at sea. How would she carry on now if Zeb *didn't* come back? What would she tell Ari? Sister Stella? Her family? *His* family?

"It was his choice," Leandros murmured, kissing the top of her head. "You are not to blame."

Still, the guilt did not fade. Penélope should've fought harder to go in his stead, or to convince them that their lives mattered more even than a cosmic imbalance. But the rational part of her knew that if they didn't retrieve the Golden Blade, if they didn't try to win this war, then everything she knew and loved would be lost. Then it wouldn't matter if she saved their lives now, just to lose them all later anyway.

"Lady Penélope."

She turned in surprise. The Sibyl stood before the altar, waiting.

"Come with me. There is something I wish to show you."

Leandros stepped away and nodded for her to go. She hesitated, glancing at the Sibyl and and then Leandros, torn between the burden of learning more and the bliss of ignorance, until her curiosity won out. With one last look at Leandros and Owen's forlorn faces, Penélope walked after the Sibyl, who led her around the altar. Hidden to the left, away from the spring, was a dark opening that looked like a well. Penélope saw spiraling stone steps winding down and down into darkness.

"What's down there?" she asked fearfully.

"Many things," the Sibyl murmured. She gestured for Penélope to go first.

She glanced back, but could not see Leandros or Owen from behind the altar. The Sibyl did not move. She was left with no choice. After a deep breath, Penélope began walking down the spiral steps, the Sibyl behind her. With each step, her heart pounded, wondering what could be waiting for her at the bottom. She was reminded of the room in the Great Library that hid the Emerald Stone, where Zeus had found them, and she shivered.

There were no sconces to light the way, but a pale light glimmered from somewhere below, faintly illuminating the staircase. Her feet hit solid ground after several winding turns, leaving her dizzy and blinking her eyes to regain her balance as she took in her surroundings.

Around her, the mountain rock had been roughly hacked away, leaving a low-ceilinged room more akin to a primitive cave. At the center of the floor was a stone basin carved from a thick pillar jutting out of the ground. The basin was filled with water, glowing with an inner, iridescent light, bathing the room in an eerie, half-shadowed haze.

"What's in the water?" Penélope asked, approaching the basin cautiously.

The priestess joined her at the basin, flourishing a small glass flask from her robes. She carefully filled the flask with water from the basin, then stoppered it.

"This water comes from the Lake of Memory," the Sibyl said, handing Penélope the flask of water. "Your friend shall need it if he returns."

Penélope grasped the flask, her thoughts jumbled with dread and hope. "Do you think he will come back?"

"That is still to be seen."

"I don't understand," Penélope said in frustration. "One minute you seem to be helping us, the other you're not. If a war is really coming, then there *are* sides. You have to choose one."

Aethusa arched a brow. "The Lord of Light chose me as the Sibyl. My only duty is to proclaim his oracle, nothing more."

Penélope studied the priestess' face, her youthful, high cheeks and dark, steady eyes, the flush that bloomed across her face every time she spoke of Apollo. "You're his lover, aren't you? That's why you were chosen as the Sibyl."

Unexpectedly, the priestess laughed, an odd, careless sound in the damp, cold cave and the gravity of the situation. She shook her head in amusement. "Love is a dangerous word, Lady Penélope. The Lord of Light has favored me, that is all. But when the time comes, he shall choose another Sibyl, and I shall return to my father as Aethusa once more."

The vision of Apollo slaying the Python in her wakeful dream crossed Penélope's mind. "Why did I dream of him? What did it mean?"

"A dream could mean many things," the Sibyl said. She brushed her fingertips over the surface of the water, and in the rippling liquid, Penélope glimpsed the fanged serpent, Apollo's arrow sinking into its neck, before the water calmed and the image was gone. "Or it could mean nothing at all."

Penélope shook her head. "When I looked into his eyes, I saw myself holding a baby. Was that the future? Or just what *could* be?"

The Sibyl did not show that she knew this was what Penélope had seen, merely staring at her with those steady, dark eyes. "Only the gods know what has been, what is, and what shall be."

She sighed. There was no way to get a straight answer from the Sibyl, though she supposed that was how it went with seers. Maybe she wasn't meant to know the answer, only glimpse the possibilities. In some ways, it was comforting not to know her fate for certain. Would she have chosen to accept her path and rescue King Leon if she knew it would end in a marriage with someone she hardly knew and a firstborn daughter she would lose as soon as she came of age?

But it didn't matter now. She had chosen the path she was on, treading blindly with dangers on either side. If she did not walk carefully, there would be a risk of death—or worse.

"Do not dwell on dreams," the Sibyl murmured as she moved away from the basin toward the staircase. "For even true dreams harbor false omens, while false dreams most easily twist the truth."

Penélope had no choice but to follow her up the stairs and back to where Leandros and Owen had stayed behind, conversing in low voices. When they saw her return, Leandros visibly relaxed and came to her side.

"What did the Sibyl show you?" he asked.

She held out the flask of water, still faintly luminescent in the glass phial.

"Water from the Lake of Memory. I have to give it to Zeb if he comes back."

"He will return," Leandros said with more confidence than she felt. "It is only a matter of when."

Penélope looked down at where Leandros held her hand loosely in his. "What did you dream about last night?"

Leandros glanced away from her gaze. "It was nothing."

"You woke up saying my name," she said. "Sounding afraid. Were you shown a vision of the future?"

He paled at her question, hesitating on whether to tell her or not. "We were in Helena. There was a battle. I was fighting at the ramparts, defending the city walls from enemy ships. But you...you were there too, fighting alongside me, armed with the Golden Blade. I saw an arrow pierce your stomach, then I watched as you fell into the sea, drowning to death."

When he finished, Leandros had his eyes closed, his hands tight on hers. She could only wrap her arms around his neck, kissing him gently.

"Don't read too much into dreams," Penélope whispered, fighting against the sickening feeling that rose inside. "They're just dreams after all."

But deep down, she knew that whether their dreams were true or false, they could mean nothing good.

59

Zᴇʙ sᴛᴇᴘᴘᴇᴅ ᴏᴜᴛ ᴏɴ the other side of the river, only to stand on the banks of an eerily familiar shore. The murmuring of the dead had grown louder, and he saw shifting shades all around him, no more than fleeting shadows. He glanced behind him and saw a wide stretch of black water as far as the eye could see, rippling and deadly. Long gone were the Sibyl's temple or Penélope looking after him longingly, or even Owen's shocked face or Leandros' grim frown.

He was alone.

Before him rose the tall, dark trees of the grove they had escaped from, where he had climbed the Elm of False Dreams and torn the Golden Bough from her branches. That alone was enough to make him shudder, but there was something—or someone—else that prowled the grove that made him dread to enter it.

But he knew it was where he was meant to go. *You must seek the Death Bringer. Only she has the power to give away her mother's sword to those deserving.*

Zeb took one step forward, then another, until he began walking towards the grove, his footsteps reluctant, his feet dragging like lead. As he looked around the Land of the Dead, he felt as though he had fallen back into a familiar dream, but one that always ended the same, terrible and lonely. He struggled to recall why he had ever left in the first place, snatches of memory fading with every step closer he took to the grove.

As he entered the thick line of trees, shadows stole over him, deeper and blacker than the darkness already looming in the sky. Gnarled tree roots and branches weighed down with ancient, evergreen leaves encumbered his path. He tripped suddenly and his body pitched to the ground.

His knees hit the soft grass.

"You okay, buddy?"

Zeb looked up. His dad was there, baseball cap on backwards and a grin on his face. The sun was shining as it always did, hot and shimmering on the desert mountains around them. He carefully got to his feet, taking the bat in his hand and preparing for another hit.

"Ready!" Zeb said excitedly.

"You got this, baby!" his mom shouted from the bleachers, where she had a book held loosely in her hand, though she wasn't reading from it, snapping pictures of them with her camera.

His dad laughed and took a few steps back, a soft baseball in his hand ready to throw.

"Three...two...one...swing!"

Zeb swung, and the bat connected with the ball, sending it skidding across the grassy baseball field that had long been neglected by the town, patches of dirt among the dried-up grass. But it didn't matter. His dad cheered, and Zeb pretended to run around and slide on home base, rolling about on the grass as both his parents celebrated—

He stood up, gasping, the forest rising up around him between one blink and the next. Zeb was dizzy and disorientated, wondering if that was a memory, but knowing in his heart that it had never happened. His dad had rarely been around at that age, even if Zeb had desperately wished it.

Across from him, someone moved out of the shadows, coming to stand before him. Zeb stared, his heart pounding, rooted to the ground where he stood. A massive dog nearly the same height as him, with three heads bulging from its neck, stood crouched and growling. But that was not the strangest thing.

Standing beside Cerberus and looking at Zeb with the same icy blue eyes and pale hair was none other than himself.

"Who are you?" Zeb asked, his voice shaking.

"You already know that, don't you," said his other self, low and sarcastic. "But go ahead. Ask another stupid question."

Zeb could hardly comprehend what he was seeing, like looking into the mirror and seeing your own face make different expressions. "Are you the half of me that was left behind in the Underworld?"

"That's one way to put it." His other self smirked, looking him up and down.

"I am everything you could have been."

"Everything I could have been?" Zeb echoed, starting to feel anger mingling with his horror. "If what?"

"If you had never drowned that day. If Dad hadn't gotten himself locked up. If Mom hadn't started drinking to cope. If you didn't always fall in love with the wrong people—"

"I get it," Zeb interrupted coldly, crossing his arms. His body shivered, the temperature having dropped all of a sudden. He looked down at his arms and saw that his skin was pale and translucent, as if he were fading into air. "What's happening to me?"

"Don't you see?" His other self took a step forward, then another, his voice velvet smooth and persuasive. "I am who you always *wanted* to be. The Fates dealt you one card, but I am your chance at drawing another. If you trade your life for mine, you will never hurt again."

"If I trade my life…" Zeb shook his head, the cold and dizziness making it hard to think. He could barely speak now, his tongue heavy in his mouth. "Then I would have my dad back? And my mom? I'd have a normal family?"

"Yes, that memory you saw would be yours," urged his other self. "You would never know what it meant to be alone in this world. You would love your parents, and they would love you. You would never have people like Penélope taking pity on you. You would never need Ari's approval. Boys like Owen would fall at your feet, begging to be loved by you."

Zeb felt faint. His other self was in front of him now, the three-headed dog behind him, standing guard like a sentinel. "What do I have to do?"

"All you have to do," said his other self, drawing from behind him a flashing light—no, a golden sword—and holding it upright between them, "is draw the sword upon yourself, thus trading one life for another. It's as simple as that."

He reached out as if in a dream and grasped the hilt of the sword. The gold was hot to the touch and brimming with power. All he would have to do was tip the sword against his chest, and everything wrong in his life would be made aright. It seemed so easy, his gaze dragging down the golden blade as if all of his desires were hidden on the sharp edge.

"I would never need Penélope?" Zeb asked, his voice sounding far away. "I would never fall in love with Ari? Or meet Owen?"

His other self's dark eyes glittered with amusement. "All of your problems would cease to exist."

Zeb gripped the sword tightly. "Then I don't think that's a life worth living."

He thrust the sword forward, sinking the blade into his other self's chest, blood bursting from the wound that gaped before him, the edge eating away at the skin like flames burning paper. The strange, dark eyes widened in momentary shock before his other self staggered back, then fell, hitting the ground dead.

Zeb stared at the body, breathing hard. Warmth flooded through his veins, as if his other self had been sucking the very lifeblood from his soul. It was strange to see himself dead, but even as he looked, the body shriveled up into smoke and floated away. He glanced up instinctively and saw another figure standing beside the three-headed dog, her hands grasping the leash bound to his thick neck. She was tall, terrible, and deadly, her dark eyes knowing and cold as they rested on him.

"*Death Bringer*," he whispered, his voice hoarse.

The Queen of Death—for that was who the goddess was—towered over him in height and pure, radiating power, cloaked in a blood-red dress, her dark locks adorned with a gold disk encircled by two horns. Her hands held tight on the leash of Cerberus, and her gaze was keen and unflinching as it rested upon him. Then she spoke, her voice cold and velvet in his mind.

Much strength does it take for a mortal to resist the seduction of Regret.

"Would it have worked?" Zeb asked, a small seed of doubt still in his heart that he had chosen right. "Would I have traded my life for...his?"

No. The single word fell cold, clanging in his ears like the swing of an ax upon metal. *The daemon would have drained your life, and you would have remained imprisoned in the Land of the Dead, neither alive nor dead, but a wraith, leeching off the misery and regret of other souls.*

Zeb looked at the Golden Blade in wonder, the hilt still warm in his palm. "It was a test."

It was a choice. You chose to forgive.

"Why?"

But a part of him knew why, even if he couldn't explain it in words.

Forgiveness cuts through grief as the scythe fells the stalk. Without forgiveness, there would be no Spring after Winter, nor Life after Death. Only a mortal who can seek forgiveness in the face of Regret is worthy of the Golden Blade.

"Then I can go back? I can return to the world of the living?" Zeb asked.

At his words, Cerberus growled low and threatening, but Persephone held the leash with her unforgiving, unmoving strength. Then she chanted familiar verses:

Golden bough on Elm of Dreams
Falsely sent by iv'ry means.
If the dead can claim its coin,
May he cross the Acheron.
But if the living choose to stay
Never will they see the day.

Zeb heard the last two lines with a shudder. "Then I have the choice to stay in the Land of the Dead, or return to the world of the living?"

The goddess merely bowed her head, even as Cerberus growled, sensing the decision Zeb was about to make. He wondered if he turned, whether the leash would slip out of the goddess' hands and the terrible jaws would come snapping down on him.

Slowly, Zeb held up the bough in front of him. As he did so, the bark glowed from within, returning the bough entirely golden as it had when he first wrenched it from the Elm of False Dreams. At the sight of the Golden Bough, Cerberus began to whine, his jaws closing as he lay down fully, resting his massive, obedient heads on his paws.

"I have the payment," Zeb said, trying to keep his voice from shaking. "I wish to return to the world of the living."

Then all you must do is cross.

Before he could change his mind, Zeb turned and retraced his steps back to the shore of the Acheron. He could still feel the eyes of the goddess fixed on him as he broke past the tree line and stopped at the black, calm waters lapping the dark sand.

Zeb held the bough in one hand, the Golden Blade in the other. He knew, now, what Mother had meant all those months ago, that a part of him *had* died and remained in the Underworld. But it was the part of him that had held onto a life that did not exist, kept alive by regret, and only killed with forgiveness. Only now was he ready to live fully in the light.

He took a step into the water and left the shores of shadow behind.

60

Penélope held onto Leandros, not wanting to let go and face the real world. In his arms, she could imagine that they were the only two people in existence and that none of this nightmarish journey on the sea had ever happened.

"Penélope," Owen said hurriedly from somewhere to her right. "He's back."

They both turned. Penélope ran blindly to the edge of the river where Zeb had appeared, stepping onto the bank with the Golden Blade in his hand. But she didn't care that he had succeeded, only that he was alive, and so she hugged him with all her strength.

He stood stiffly in her arms. She stepped back. Zeb's blue eyes wandered over her and the others in that familiar, hazy confusion. They all hesitated, worried that he had come back only to die in the temple.

"Thirsty," Zeb whispered, his voice hoarse.

Suddenly Penélope remembered, scrambling to take out her flask of water from the Lake of Memory, popping off the stopper and lifting it towards Zeb's mouth.

"Drink this," she said gently.

He drank eagerly from the flask, and then he gasped, dropping the phial on the stone floor, the glass crashing and splintering into a thousand pieces. But he didn't seem to care, his eyes focused and roving around with a newfound energy. His cheeks were now flushed, as if all the blood that had frozen while in the Land of the Dead had begun pumping once more in his veins, rushing beneath his pale skin.

Before any of them could ask how he felt, Zeb laughed—a full-chested, exhilarated laugh, accompanied by a grin as he tipped his head back. Penélope and Owen shared an alarmed look that only made Zeb laugh harder.

"Are you alright, mate?" Owen asked with a hesitant smile.

Zeb only laughed again, leaning down on his knees. "Oh, mate, I'm more than alright. I'm *alive.*"

Penélope's cheeks hurt from smiling so much. Zeb stood up and looked at each of them with an uncharacteristically fond gaze. Then he hugged Penélope again, his arms familiarly tight and wiry around her. She stepped back, wiping the tears from her eyes, though this time they were from pure happiness.

"I'm so glad you're alive," Penélope said. She glanced at the sword. "How did you find it?"

He raised a brow and held out the sword to her. "I didn't."

She took the Golden Blade with some hesitation, but was surprised to find the hot hilt strangely comforting in her palm, despite the damage it had once done her.

"It found me," Zeb said, his eyes clouding with a passing memory which he shook off with a smile. "It doesn't matter how. What matters is that it's yours now, and it gives us a fighting chance in this war."

Penélope wondered if she were to wield it, whether the flames would burn her again. She looked at the Sibyl, knowing somehow that she would read her thoughts.

"Never more shall the blade burn," the priestess said. "For its fire already burns inside of you."

Her hands automatically flexed around the hilt, a surge of confidence flooding through her chest. For the first time, Penélope had hope for the future. Zeb met her gaze and nodded, as if he understood how she felt.

She looked at the Sibyl. "Thank you."

Aethusa inclined her head. "May the Fates watch over your return home."

"Only if they make it safe!" quipped Owen, earning laughs from everyone save the Sibyl, who merely bowed, though Penélope swore she hid a slight smirk.

After everyone hugged in relief and joy, Leandros led them back through the tunnels with new directions from the Sibyl, who remained in the temple room, watching them leave in her usual stoic stillness.

Penélope breathed in deeply when they stepped out of the tunnel's mouth and into the open air, this time finding that their path had left them much further down the mountain slope, the hundred cave opening not visible from their vantage point, and the black river nowhere in sight.

From there, Leandros easily picked a path back down to level ground, where they stumbled across the same river. Penélope dragged Leandros away with a smirk, Zeb and Owen hiding their laughs at Leandros' bright red face. She knew they would appreciate the privacy and would soon forget about them anyway.

Leandros did not protest as Penélope kissed him hard on the bank of the river, threading her fingers in his hair with abandon. She stepped away and undressed, running into the water before he could speak, not caring that her skin instantly went numb beneath the icy currents. Leandros quickly followed suit, grinning as he chased her in the deep end and finally caught her, lifting her half out of the water as he kissed her again, just as hard as she had.

Once they had dried, they stretched out on the riverbank, unwilling to return to Zeb and Owen so soon. Penélope watched their hands lace and unlace between them, the sky purpling above as the sun had already set in a glow of orange and red. Leandros' hand was larger and scarred around hers, though she now had her fair share of imperfections to match his. Somehow, it was a comforting thought.

"The dream I had in the temple showed me something else," Leandros said quietly. She turned to look at him, and he did the same. "Before the arrow struck you, my father had been fighting by our side and sacrificed his life to save you."

"Maybe that was a reminder of the past," Penélope said pointedly. "He had already saved my life when we fought Scylla. And yours."

Leandros nodded, his eyes softening on her. "I know. Since that night, I have thought that perhaps if I wish to pass judgment upon him, I ought to weigh his virtues as much as his faults. He is my only father after all."

Penélope kissed him. "Let the gods weigh our souls when we die. All we owe to the living is our forgiveness and love."

He shook his head with a small smile. "I would be a lesser man without you." Then he pulled her closer, kissing her again, and Penélope sank into the bliss of his touch, the heat of his bare chest, wishing they could stay here for an eternity.

But the stars soon shone in the night sky, and Leandros led her back to Owen and Zeb, where they had already set up their tent, a fire roaring in front of it. They did not comment on their long absence, merely handing them some dried meat from their rations and water that they had boiled and cooled.

For the first time, Penélope slept easily, without any strange dreams plaguing her subconscious, wrapped in the safety of Leandros' arms. She woke only when the sun pierced the sky with bright rays and Leandros left her side with a light kiss on her shoulder, beginning to pack up the camp. Once they were ready to leave, they continued their hike down the mountainside.

Today they made much more progress, invigorated with new energy and higher hopes from the preceding events and spurred on by the gentle decline that made the distance feel shorter. Soon the ocean came back into view, where they gleefully spotted a dark ship anchored near the shore.

After camping for only two more nights, they reached the camp of sailors. Nausicala was ordering the men about with her usual stern command, but hearing the shouts of the crew, turned and saw them. With a gasp, she rushed toward them, throwing her arms around Leandros and kissing his cheeks and his hair as if he were a child and not a full-grown man. Then she hugged Penélope with the same force and feeling. Penélope had the urge to cry, a profound love filling her chest at the affection.

"Oh, I'm so glad you all have returned safely," Nausicala said, clasping her hands in front of her, her emerald green eyes shining with tears.

"Me too," Penélope said with a shaky laugh.

King Leon approached them from the opposite side of the camp, having heard the commotion. He came to stand in front of Leandros, a smile already on his face, but he hesitated to move closer.

"Well?" he asked.

Leandros nodded his head. "The curse has been broken."

King Leon's shoulders drooped in relief, and he passed a hand over his face where the exhaustion of wandering had already left its mark. He met Leandros' gaze with a look of longing and tender affection. Then Leandros stepped forward and closed the distance, embracing his father firmly, and murmuring something that made King Leon close his eyes and nod his head, as if he were holding back tears.

Penélope's heart warmed at the sight, knowing how difficult it had been for Leandros to reach a place of forgiveness, and how much King Leon had suffered from it. Zeb and Owen made their rounds among the crew, and Penélope was surprised to see Zeb greet the other men with an open smile, his usual coldness and reserve replaced by a cautious but welcoming air.

She felt Leandros stand beside her once the others were gone. He took her left hand in his, a grand gesture for him to make before his crew. Then he kissed the sapphire ring, his lips brushing her knuckles, holding her gaze meaningfully.

"Ready to return home?" he asked, raising a brow.

Penélope smiled. "If I'm with you, I'll go anywhere."

61

THEY SET SAIL THE following morning, a swift breeze behind their sails, a peaceful blue sky unfurled above and below them. Penélope stood at the prow of the ship, her hand resting on the hilt of the Golden Blade, which was now strapped to her waist. From the corner of her eye, she could see her old sword hanging from Zeb's waist, where he helped keep the time of the rowers.

He caught her looking and winked at her. She shook her head, wondering if Owen wasn't rubbing off on him after all. Owen himself was near Zeb at his rowing bench, his shirt off to soak up the bright sun, his toned muscles gleaming with each stroke of his oar. Penélope wondered if they had ever resolved what was happening between them, then decided that Zeb could take care of himself.

Thanks to the stores they had kept from Circe's island and their careful rationing, as well as some successful hunts by the foothills of the Atlas Mountains, they did not need to stop on the way back to the city, rowing both in the day and through the night, the crew taking shifts at the benches. Even though they had fewer men after all the battles they endured, it was enough to keep the ship flying across the water at the same speed as the wind.

Though they did not land for the night, they hugged the shore due east, hoping they would soon see the familiar desert landscape. As their ship skipped across the waves, Leandros came to meet her by the prow, having called a council meeting to discuss what they had learned from the Sibyl.

Nausicala, King Leon, Zeb, and even Owen gathered near the prow, waiting to hear what Leandros had to say. He took a deep breath in before he explained all that had occurred since they began hiking, describing the voices that Zeb had heard and their strange dreams, the one-hundred-cave entrance and the tunnel that delved deep into the mountains, and then meeting the Sibyl in the temple of the Lord of Light. But he omitted the prophetic dreams they had that night in the temple, instead narrating the blood sacrifice and Zeb's crossing to the Underworld and return with the Golden Blade. Once he finished, both Nausicala and King Leon were stunned to silence.

After a long moment, Nausicala bowed low to Penélope. "I did not know the Lady Penélope had been bestowed such an honorable gift."

Penélope glanced down at the Golden Blade with a wry smile. "A gift is equally a curse. But I give Zeb all the credit for retrieving it from the Land of the Dead."

Nausicala turned to Zeb in surprise, then bowed her head. "I see you have chosen well." Penélope watched in fascination as Zeb and Nausicala shared a small knowing smile.

"And this war," King Leon said slowly. "Did the Sibyl say who would attack first or when it would occur?"

Leandros shook his head. "She only said that this weapon would give us a chance of success. Without it, we would have all been doomed."

An uneasy silence settled over them that was interrupted by Owen, who clapped his hands together. "Then it's a good thing we have the sword, eh?"

"What's the plan when we return to the city?" Zeb asked, voicing the question all of them surely had been contemplating in the following silence.

Leandros raised a brow. "I thought you would be returning to your homeland after our journey concluded."

Zeb flushed, fixing his eyes on the ground and refusing to look at either Owen or Penélope. "I am. But I was just wondering what you guys were all planning to do. My best friend will be living there now, remember?"

"We plan to raise walls along the coast," Penélope said, saving Leandros from answering and only annoying Zeb further. "If anyone attacks us from the sea, we'll be ready."

They all nodded in agreement, though no one looked too confident. If the gods were truly bent on war, no fortified walls—no matter how high and well-built—would keep out their wrath.

"But first we have to speak with the Seven Sages," Penélope added. "They are on our side, after all. Maybe they know more about the future war than they've let on."

"The Seven Sages may advise," King Leon said, "but they are bound by oath against any act of violence. I fear if war comes, we shall stand alone."

The words were dark, but they did not sound so ominous on such a beautiful day as today. Penélope knew a storm of a very different kind was brewing on the horizon, but for now, she was content simply enjoying the sea breeze and the miracle that she had survived the harrowing dangers of their journey.

So much had changed since she had stepped foot on the ship and sailed away from Helena. Penélope wondered what Ari and Chloe would think of her marriage to Leandros, and whether they would want to stay in the city knowing that a war was coming. She wouldn't blame them if they left.

Nausicala sighed. "At the very least, we may hearten ourselves with the celebrations to come. For there is much to celebrate, is there not?"

She looked meaningfully at Penélope, who froze under that knowing look. Had she guessed the truth? How did she find out? Had Zeb let it slip without realizing it?

"What are we celebrating?" Penélope managed to ask.

Nausicala laughed. "Your marriage, of course! Or did you forget? You must have a wedding according to the customs of the Helenes too, not only of the Phaeacians."

Penélope relaxed, though she could not shake the feeling that something was glaringly missing from all this, and it was not only the fact that her family would be absent from both weddings. She forced a smile so that the others would not see her discomfort, though she avoided Leandros' eyes, not wishing to dampen his spirits.

Only Zeb seemed to sense her thoughts, reaching out and squeezing her arm. The others brightened at the thought of celebration and feasting in the comfort of the royal palace, and even the crew seemed to row faster at the prospect.

At long last, after eight days and nine nights, the Dawn rose behind the mountains surrounding the city of Helena, standing proudly at the lip of the vast desert, which glowed like a golden sea beneath the rising sun. The tall, stone lighthouse of the Necropolis Island surveyed the seas, as elegant and imposing as Penélope remembered.

Nausicala stood beside Penélope as they approached the city, her eyes gleaming with tears. "Never did I think I would live to see that lighthouse welcome me home again."

Penélope looped her arm in Nausicala's. "At times, neither did I."

They glanced at each other before they both began laughing quietly. It was hard to believe when Penélope had left Helena that she had no clue of Nausicala's existence, but now considered her like family. She supposed the same could be said for most of the crew, including Mono. It was a joyful thought amid the still-cutting grief.

As the city rose tall and familiar on the horizon, Penélope could see the Gate of the Moon glinting under the sun, and beyond it Priam Boulevard, which she was shocked to see was filled with crowds of people, as if they were welcoming them home. Their ship sailed effortlessly toward the docks, where they cast their anchor and began unloading the ship.

Penélope, Zeb, and Owen shared nervous smiles when they stood on the docks, their sea legs shaky as they followed Leandros, King Leon, and Nausicala to the crowds of people waiting for them, already cheering and singing songs about the might of the city of Helena. And before the crowds, safely protected by her royal guards, was the Queen of Helena, Cleopatra the Alchemist, who stood still and impassive as her son and husband approached, her face veiled.

First, Leandros came to her and embraced her. The Queen held him close, stroking his head, and though the veil obscured her face, Penélope saw tears running down her cheeks. Once Leandros had stepped away, King Leon came forward.

The King stood before the Queen, and the entire city seemed to hold its breath. Husband and wife faced each other after his long absence. Then he lowered himself to his knees, resting his hands on the folds of her dress, his head hanging down and his shoulders shaking with tears. The Queen stooped and helped her husband back on his feet. She turned to the crowd, then lifted one of his arms into the air as her voice rang out loud and clear.

"Honorable citizens of Helena," she exclaimed. "Your King has returned!"

The crowds erupted into deafening cheers, shouting his name over and over again. King Leon bowed low to the crowds, then leaned over to his wife and whispered something in her ears. She looked at him in surprise, then craned her neck and scanned the crew until she saw Nausicala, robed in gray and similarly veiled, standing quietly beside Dora, who gazed upon the city of Helena in unconcealed awe.

Penélope waited apprehensively, wondering how two queens of Helena would address each other, especially when they both held claims to the King—one being his mother, the other his wife—who had yet to meet each other.

Nausicala separated herself from the crew and came before her daughter-in-law, both of them assessing the other. Then Queen Cleopatra curtsied low, her head bowed, and when this happened, all of the city followed suit, as if they knew who Nausicala was simply by this gesture alone.

To Penélope's surprise, Nausicala took Queen Cleopatra's hands and lifted her up, before bowing low herself, as if to show her own submission to the new Queen of Helena. The city burst into applause, whistling and clapping at the happy meeting, and perhaps a little relieved that both queens would join each other in peace as one family.

Suddenly Zeb nudged her hard, and she looked at him in confusion. "What was that for?"

"Look," he said, nodding towards the crowds where one figure had stepped forward, wearing all white and veiled like the two queens. "It's Sister Stella."

Sure enough, the figure removed her veil to reveal the smiling, creased face and snow-white curls of Sister Stella, her blue eyes bright as she gazed upon Penélope and Zeb. Penélope ran over to her and hugged her, laughing at the surprise on Sister Stella's face.

"It is very good to see you again, my dear," Sister Stella said warmly, and hearing her familiar Irish accent nearly brought tears to Penélope's eyes. "And I am so glad you have returned to us, Zeb."

Penélope stepped back to let Zeb hug her. Sister Stella patted Zeb's head and back as if he were her son, which in many ways was not far from the truth.

"I have so much to tell you, Sister," Penélope said excitedly once Zeb returned to her side, discreetly wiping at her tears.

Sister Stella nodded. "And I would love to hear about all of your adventures in Emmeson. But first, there are two people who would very much like to see you both."

Penélope glanced around, then saw Ari and Chloe pushing their way out of the crowd, their eyes frantically roaming the docks. She and Zeb bolted towards Ari without a second thought, both of them colliding with him as they brought him into a group hug like they did the summer when Ari came back from Harvard.

Ari groaned as he struggled to keep himself upright, but he was laughing too, bringing them closer. "I've missed you two so much."

Out of the corner of her eye, she saw Owen and Chloe hugging too, all bitterness gone. Penélope let herself relax, sighing into the familiarity of Ari and Zeb as if she had never left Tierra del Sol.

She had finally come home.

62

"I can't believe you visited the Phaeacians," Ari said with a shake of his head, smiling at Penélope and Zeb, who reclined beside him. Next to Zeb, Owen and Chloe reclined, deep in their own conversation. Even though Zeb didn't look over once, she knew he was thinking about it.

Since returning to the city of Helena, Penélope, Zeb, and Owen had been given plush, luxurious rooms at the palace, but as Chloe and Ari were so busy, they hardly saw them except at the extravagant feasts they held at the palace each night in celebration of their successful return. Today was their third night, and still, it felt like they had so much to catch up on.

"The palace was beautiful, Ari," Penélope said with a sigh, recalling the towering bronze walls glinting under the sun and the vast swathes of fruit trees. "It was more beautiful than Homer even described."

"Yeah, the dungeons were *really* beautiful," Zeb added sarcastically.

Ari laughed. "Glad to see Zeb hasn't changed one bit."

"Oh, he has," Penélope said, patting Zeb's head until he shook her off, rolling his eyes. "In more ways than one, maybe."

"Really?" Ari looked between Zeb and Penélope curiously. "I guess both of you seem different. Is there something you haven't told me?"

Zeb and Penélope shared a brief look, surely thinking of the same thing. But Penélope wasn't about to say anything, at least not until she told Leandros first. So she played it off with a smile and held up her left hand, where the sapphire wedding ring still glinted.

"You mean that I'm married now?" she asked.

Ari took her hand and gazed at the ring. "I guess I did miss that." He sounded rather saddened by it, which surprised her, though she supposed he had always been like a brother to her in that small town. "Will you have another wedding ceremony here?"

Penélope nodded, the thought of it at once exciting and sad. She glanced across the room and saw Leandros seated next to the King and Queen at the couches of honor. Nausicala reclined beside them, her smile a sign of happiness, though her eyes still held that ever-present glimmer of sorrow that Penélope was beginning to know well and she herself understand.

"Enough about me," Penélope said, forcing a smile. "How has the Academy been?"

"It's been amazing," Ari said with a smile. "I've really improved my Ancient Greek, though it seems I'll never reach your level of fluency now. But I love teaching and walking around the grounds of the Academy. Everyone is so kind and welcoming. The library is a treasure trove in of itself, though the Seven Sages keep the most valuable texts under lock and key in the Great Library. Chloe could probably tell you more about that."

At her name, Chloe turned her head. "What can I tell you more about?"

"The Great Library," Zeb repeated, looking in her direction—and therefore Owen's—for the first time since sitting down.

Chloe arched a brow. "Actually, I'm not allowed to speak about that."

Owen nudged her shoulder playfully. "What secrets are you ladies hiding in that library, eh?"

She narrowed her eyes. "Wouldn't you like to know."

"Well, how has it been with the Seven Sages?" Penélope asked just to put an end to their banter, catching Zeb's stony face as he took a long drag of his wine.

"It's been interesting," Chloe replied with a disconcerted shrug. "I have to learn Ancient Greek, so Ari's been teaching me that. We have to wear these ridiculous outfits too." She lifted her thick white robes in disdain.

"I thought you swore a vow of celibacy anyway?" Owen asked pointedly.

Chloe glared at him. "First of all, I haven't sworn anything yet. And second, it wouldn't change the fact that I actually *care* about fashion, unlike you."

Owen placed a hand over his heart. "Hey! I'm always fashionable."

"I guess some things never change," Ari said dryly to Penélope, watching the two of them bicker as if no time had passed at all. Zeb looked increasingly annoyed, refilling his cup with more wine.

"Have you been back home since we left?" Penélope asked.

Ari nodded carefully. "Once, though Sister Stella doesn't encourage it. I have enough to keep me busy here anyway, and few people I still speak to back home." He paused. "Sister Stella has spoken with your parents. They're doing well, and happy you're studying abroad."

Penélope nodded, swallowing against the lump in her throat. She couldn't speak. They had decided to tell her parents that she would stay a full semester in Greece in the study abroad program.

He placed a comforting hand on her shoulder. "You'll see them soon. I know they'll understand. They love you, Penélope."

The tears began to well in her eyes when suddenly she heard her name being spoken behind her. Penélope turned and saw Queen Cleopatra standing there, her face no longer covered by a veil since King Leon's return. She had a radiant smile on her face as she observed the room.

"Queen Cleopatra," Penélope said, hurriedly getting to her feet and inclining her head.

"Please, Lady Penélope, there is no need for such pretense," the Queen said gently. "We are family now, after all." She held out her arm for Penélope to take. "Come. Let us take a turn about the palace."

They walked off arm in arm, Penélope sneaking a glance back at Zeb and Ari, who watched her leave in mild concern. Once they left the lofty, festive hall where most of the guests were gathered and entered the maze-like, marble-floored hallways, the Queen began to speak.

"Lady Penélope, I am most impressed with all that I have heard of your courage and honor at sea. But most of all, I am indebted to you for rescuing my husband, King Leon, and ending the curse upon his family name, even if it came at the dearest cost to yourself."

"I think I should be apologizing," Penélope confessed. "It also came at the dearest cost to your son."

The Queen led her to the inner courtyard, where a massive fountain flowed in the center with clear, glittering water, and tall, painted statues circled the perimeter with their eternal gazes. She came to a stop where the moonlight fell upon the gleaming marble tiles and took both of Penélope's hands, facing her with dark eyes, both happy and sad. Never before had the Queen looked so young, young enough to be her older sister, married to King Leon before she was sixteen.

"My son loves you," the Queen said firmly. "While the pain of losing your firstborn daughter shall never leave, you will find solace in each other. Despite your…unconventionality as a lady, there is no other woman in the world I would rather give to my son, nor any other I would most love to be Queen one day, when I am no more."

Penélope felt the tears return to her eyes. She wanted to protest, to tell her that she didn't deserve it, that she didn't know how to be a wife, let alone a queen, but then she recalled Nausicala's words to her. *Being queen is not something to learn, but someone to become.*

"I love Leandros more than I can even say," Penélope whispered.

"I know," Cleopatra said, smiling with her own tears. "But why don't you tell him that yourself?"

Then she looked knowingly over Penélope's shoulder. Penélope turned around, her heart in her throat. Leandros stood there with his hands held behind his back, his beard and hair neatly groomed and curled, and dressed in rich blue robes to match hers. She glanced back at the Queen, but she had already left, her dress swishing behind the corner as she walked back inside and down the hall, leaving the two of them alone in the courtyard.

Penélope turned back to him. "Leandros, what—"

Leandros came to stand before her and then knelt on one knee, looking up at her with those familiar dark eyes. "I know that you wished for a proposal of marriage according to the customs of your people. While I cannot pretend that this erases any regrets you may have in choosing to begin a new life here, I do sincerely hope it shows how much you mean to me." He held out a gold band between his fingers, carved as a snake swallowing its own tail, the two eyes inset with small rubies. "This ring belonged to my grandfather, King Philoxenos, given to Nausicala in marriage, who has since kept it and given it to me, a sign that love not only crosses oceans, but time as well. And I know I love you the same way. Penélope Reyes, daughter of Estela, will you marry me?"

This time, the tears in her eyes fell as she nodded, hardly able to say the word. "Yes!"

He smiled as he slid the band beside her other ring of sapphire, both their hands trembling. Then she threw her arms around his neck and kissed him as he lifted her and spun her around.

"Was that good?" he murmured, kissing her cheek.

"It was perfect." She kissed him again, then hugged him, whispering the words she had wanted to say for some time now, but hadn't had the courage to say them, knowing just how powerful they were. "I love you, Leandros, and I always will."

63

Penélope stared at herself in the shiny bronze mirror. Her yellow veil obscured her face, but she could just see the kohl lining her eyes and the red tint on her cheeks and lips, as well as the fading bruises from when Lord Iason had slammed her against the door.

She sighed and lifted her veil. This wasn't the first wedding ceremony she had been in, but now it felt different.

When she turned around, she saw three other women wearing the same yellow veils and white dresses. It was custom for the female guests of the wedding to wear the same clothes as the bride, and so Penélope had gotten ready with Nausicala, Cleopatra, and Chloe. Although the Seven Sages were exempt from this tradition, Chloe had not yet been initiated and therefore could participate.

More than just the height and the long black hair peeking out from the veil, it was obvious which one of the three women was Chloe, who stood with one hand on her hip, her nails still sporting sharp red acrylics. Penélope wondered how she kept up with all her cosmetics, then recalled what Ari had said about returning home occasionally. Her stomach flipped at the thought, even though Sister Stella had already told her she ought to wait until Thanksgiving break and attend to her duties as the wife of Prince Leandros in the meantime.

"I never liked weddings," Chloe said to break the silence, at the same time as Cleopatra said, "You look beautiful, Lady Penélope."

Both Nausicala and Cleopatra glanced in momentary confusion at Chloe, but Penélope only laughed it off. "Thank you, my Lady."

"Please, call me Cleopatra now," the Queen said, inclining her head.

Penélope knew it would take her a while to warm up to such an intimate address, but she nodded anyway. Nausicala came forward, grasping her hands affectionately.

"Are you ready?" she asked.

"Nervous," Penélope replied honestly.

"Isn't this your second time?" Chloe asked, raising a brow. Penélope knew she was trying to be supportive in her own way, but it was impossible to shake the nerves that threatened to eject the meal she had earlier.

"Yes, but this time is different." Penélope glanced down at her left hand, where both rings rested perfectly on her finger. "This time I said yes."

Chloe shrugged. "This is what you always wanted, remember? Just enjoy it, because married life doesn't get any easier."

Cleopatra cut Chloe an exasperated look. "It is normal to be nervous on your wedding night. But Lady Chloe is right. Marriage is not without its trials. Yet a wise man once said that there is nothing mightier and nobler than when man and wife are of one heart and mind at home."

"A grief to their foes, but a great joy to their friends," Penélope added, continuing the quote, much to Cleopatra's surprise and respect.

"But their own hearts know it best," concluded Nausicala, squeezing Penélope's hands. "Come, the guests shall be waiting for us."

They exited Penélope's bedroom and followed Nausicala and Cleopatra down the corridors to the great hall, where all of the guests had already found their seats, the women sitting on one side, dressed in the same white robes and yellow veils. Leandros sat on the other side of the couches with the men, beside King Leon, Zeb, and Owen. While a traditional wedding would include the engagement ceremony where the betrothed would dress as Horus and Hathor and meet at the crossroads, Leandros had thought it only right that getting down on one knee had replaced one half of Helena's traditions, symbolically resembling the union of their two cultures as well.

Leandros saw her come into the room and carefully hid a smile behind a sip of his wine. Once they all sat down on the empty couches reserved for them, the official festivities began, with musicians and singers walking around, singing marriage songs and reciting verses about gods and famous heroes. After the food was served and everyone ate their fill, the guests stood up and milled about, though remaining on their side of the hall.

Sister Stella approached Penélope and Chloe a little while later, after most of the female guests had come up to her to introduce themselves and congratulate her on the marriage. There were many distant relatives of Leandros or women from important noble families she had never met. Some of the women clearly harbored jealousy at Penélope for securing the prince of Helena, remarking that they wished Leandros had a younger brother for their own daughters. Penélope merely thanked them warmly with a pleasant smile, much to their chagrin.

"It has been many years since this palace last celebrated a marriage," Sister Stella said, bowing her head towards Penélope as Chloe silently slunk away to give them privacy, joining the other Seven Sages nearby.

"Please, Sister," Penélope said, her cheeks warming at the sign of respect. "You've known me my whole life."

"I have always known you were destined for great things, Penélope, but never could I have dreamed that we would find ourselves here now."

"Neither did I," she tried to joke, though it came out quite serious. She had still not mentioned anything to Sister Stella about what she had learned of the war to come. "Sister, I'm not sure if you heard, but something horrible is going to happen to the city, and maybe even the whole world."

Sister Stella nodded her head. "Ah, yes, Queen Cleopatra may have mentioned that you had been warned by the gods of a war."

"A terrible war against old enemies and new ones. The Queen of Death gave me the Golden Blade so that I could fight against Him. But if the war is coming soon…I don't know…" Penélope trailed off, biting her lip. Her hands had moved down to her belly, a movement Sister Stella eyed with sudden understanding. "I don't know if I'll be able to fight."

"I see," Sister Stella said carefully, her eyes full of tenderness. "Yes, my dear, we must prepare for war, but it will not come quite yet, nor in the way we think. There is much we do not know, save that the gods keep their own counsel. The retribution of the fallen King of the Gods will be great, for he does not like to be challenged, much less to lose. However, we hold powers that he little understands." Then she smiled forcibly, one old, wrinkled hand resting gently on Penélope's shoulder, the other covering the hand on her belly. "But enough of that! This is your wedding, and there will be time for more serious discussion later. Now more than ever, we must celebrate such joys. Thus I say congratulations, Penélope, and may the gods shower your union with many *more* blessings."

"Thank you, Sister," Penélope said, blushing, then watched as she returned to the group of Seven Sages, Chloe looking young and at odds amidst such an old crowd, especially with her yellow veil.

Across the aisle, Penélope saw Zeb standing next to Ari and half-sulking while Ari spoke in animated conversation with the other guests. Owen was elsewhere chatting up a youthful, wealthy-looking lord in his broken Greek, though Penélope caught his subtle glance back to look at Zeb. She sighed, wondering if their relationship was simply hopeless.

As she returned to her couch, Penélope saw Leandros stand at the front of the room, where the bard and musicians took their place beside him. He caught her eye with a small smile as the room grew quiet and waited for their prince to address them.

"Thank you all for joining in this important celebration of marriage," Leandros said. "In honor of my wife, Penélope Reyes, I have composed a song about her namesake, Penelope, daughter of Icarius and wife of Odysseus, the hero who wandered the seas for ten years before returning home."

Everyone applauded in hesitant surprise as Leandros stepped forward with a kithara at the ready, his fingers plucking at the strings with his plectrum, the sweet, twangy notes piercing the air. Penélope stared, her heart filled with love at the sight of those scarred hands deftly strumming the kithara. Their eyes met, then he took a deep breath and began to chant in his deep, melodic voice:

> *In rocky Ithaca she stayed,*
> *Her husband by the gods delayed,*
> *By day she wove in silent dread,*
> *Of suitors cruel in her halls fed,*
> *To stall their greedy appetite,*
> *Unraveled in deceit by night,*
> *A shroud for poor old Laërtes,*
> *His son still lost to wine-dark seas.*
>
> *For twenty years his labors long,*
> *Immortalized in ancient song,*
> *Kept far the arms of loving wife*
> *and tossed about the waves in Strife,*
> *Odysseus who sailed the sea*
> *and longed for dear Penelope*

but by Poseidon's wrath invoked
his Fate bound tight as oxen's yoke.

Across the ocean wide to roam
the hero must to come back home
but sirens, beasts, and Cyclopes
enough to shake a soldier's knees
he fought and lost his comrades dear
but never lost himself to fear
and goddesses both cunningly
entrapped on isles enchanting he
whom nymph Calypso, Circe fair
for eight long years held captive there.

When gods immortal him returned
the Argive hero homeward yearned
and after greedy suitors killed
their blood in homely halls he spilled.
Then asked his wife a question sly
to move their bed but in reply
her husband swore no god could move
their marriage bed and so did prove
his love like roots of tree trunk deep
where bed he carved for them to sleep
and so she led him to their room
like once they did as bride and groom.

64

ONCE LEANDROS FINISHED HIS song, everyone applauded and cheered in delighted shock at his abilities, crying out for him to sing again. He smiled and thanked everyone, but returned to his couch, while the musicians at the edge of the room struck up another tune, this time more festive.

Zeb stuck to Ari's side the entire celebration, since he wasn't allowed to cross over to the women's side where Penélope was seated. He soon considered it a blessing after he saw the other women flock to her in congratulations, and she had to speak with each and every one of them. Ari, unfortunately, was not much better, since as headmaster of the Academy he was considered in high honor among the court, and his conversational Ancient Greek had so much improved that he could carry on fluent conversations with ease, leaving Zeb to stand awkwardly by his side in silence.

Over the past few days, Zeb had spent most of his time with Penélope in the palace. They both sensed that their time together was coming to an end. In fact, a week from now, he was supposed to be escorted to the New Academy, where he would integrate back into school life and finish his college degree, sworn to secrecy from ever revealing Emmeson's existence to another soul. Even the thought of going back to school alone was strange and slightly terrifying, let alone leaving all of this behind, including his two closest friends, Penélope and Ari.

After one more proud lord introduced himself to Ari and put in a favorable word for his son who studied there, Ari sighed and leaned over to Zeb, lowering his voice. "It turns out there are some downsides to the whole headmaster thing."

"You're almost as popular as the royal family," Zeb muttered, nodding his head toward King Leon and Leandros, who had not ceased entertaining audiences of the other guests.

Ari studied him carefully. "Are you sure you don't want to study at the Academy?"

Zeb looked down at his feet. A part of him wondered why he clung so much to his old life when he had nothing keeping him there. No strong ties to family, no friends, no major career prospects. But that was half a lie. He looked up and his gaze automatically found Owen expertly weaving through the crowds, his charming smile making Zeb's heart pound.

"This city isn't my home, no matter how much I might want it to be," Zeb said. "I don't belong here like you and Penélope. Even Chloe's found her place."

"I see." And he did seem to see, too much at times, looking into Zeb's eyes and then nodding in Owen's direction. "How is it going with him?"

"With who?" Zeb asked immediately, hating how his face burned.

Ari raised a brow. "Did you think I wouldn't know? I caught you two in the alleyway the first night we were in the city."

Zeb's blood ran cold as if he had set foot in the Underworld. "What's it to you? You've never even asked about…if I even swung that way."

"I'm only looking out for you," Ari said carefully, sensing the delicate nature of the topic. "You're like a brother to me."

"A brother," Zeb echoed, nodding his head. He hated to admit that it still stung. Perhaps that was why the words came out so easily, full of bitterness. "If you knew what I was this whole time, then you knew I was in love with you too, didn't you?"

Ari looked down into his wine cup with a small sigh before raising his gaze and looking Zeb in the eyes, a sad smile on his face. "Yes, I knew. But I understood. You were young and we were close. It never changed how I felt about you."

Zeb fought down a wave of revulsion mingled with anger. "It was pity."

"No," Ari said adamantly, shaking his head. "No, I never pitied you, Zeb. You're my family, remember? All we have is each other."

The instant he spoke the words, Zeb's anger melted away, leaving only a faint sadness, but it was overpowered by the love he felt. Because Ari was right. They were each other's only family in the end.

"Owen fancied you too, for the record," Zeb said defensively.

Ari rolled his eyes. "He's a flirt, that's for sure. But you know he's only had eyes for you."

Zeb saw that Owen was coming towards them, perhaps noticing that they were on their own for once, and any response died in his throat. Owen grinned, looking between the two of them, but now Zeb swore he glimpsed a hint of jealousy in those green eyes.

"Speak of the devil," Ari muttered, earning him a glare from Zeb.

Owen cocked his head. "Talking about me, are you?"

"Wouldn't you like to know," Zeb taunted, repeating the same line Chloe had said the other day when they were so obviously flirting with each other. It had taken everything in him not to scream at them or storm off. Owen narrowed his eyes at him as if he sensed the accusation.

In the subsequent silence, Ari quickly excused himself on the pretense of making another round among the guests, but Zeb knew he merely wished to give them privacy. After all, besides the royal family and Ari, no one else among the men knew their language, so they could speak freely together.

"Are you upset with me?" Owen asked seriously, all teasing from a minute ago gone. "You know if you just said the word, I would kiss you in front of all these people. I wouldn't care."

Zeb knew his defenses were up after his conversation with Ari, but despite Owen's innocence in that, he felt annoyed at the apparent ease with which Owen moved in any situation he was put in, whereas Zeb struggled to even smile at another person.

"You were flirting with Chloe yesterday," Zeb said, his voice more resigned than angry. "Don't deny it."

"I talk like that with everyone," Owen argued. It was true, but it didn't make Zeb feel any better, and besides, they had already argued this particular point to death. "Chloe is different now. She has no interest in me, nor I in her. In a few months, she'll have taken a vow of celibacy, and I'll be off in another world. Literally."

Zeb let out a reluctant laugh.

Owen placed a hand on Zeb's arm, subtly squeezing, before letting it drop. "All of that is fake. The flirting, the banter, the winks. I would flirt Sister Stella's habit off if it meant I'd get a laugh out of her. But with you, it's not like that. It's not just banter. With you, it means something. It means something real. *You* are real to me, Zeb."

"What happens when we go back to our world?" Zeb asked pointedly. "When things actually get *real?*"

Instead of growing defensive as Zeb half-expected, Owen asked, "Remember that dream I had in the mountains? On the way to the Sibyl?"

Zeb racked his brain for any memory of Owen's dream, but he could only recall their argument after Zeb had seen the terrifying faces of the dead calling to him from across the river. Then he remembered their day swimming on the way up the mountain.

"You never ended up telling me," Zeb said. "It was of your father, right?"

Owen nodded. "I never had the chance to finish, and then we found the Sibyl, and you returned to the Land of the Dead. I had never felt so much regret in my entire life that I had not told you it before then."

"What did you see?"

"I was in London with my father in one of his fancy hotels. But I wasn't alone. *You* were with me and you were shaking hands with my father," Owen said with a growing smile on his face. When Zeb didn't react, he continued eagerly, "I was introducing you. Don't you see? That was a vision of the future!"

"Or a false dream sent from false gates below," Zeb muttered, not willing to believe it to be true when he had already been so disappointed in the past.

Owen shook his head as if Zeb was still not getting it. "It doesn't matter, Zeb. Whether it's the future or a false dream, the moment I saw it, I knew it was possible, that it was something I wanted, and that it was up to me to make it happen."

"What are you trying to say, Owen?"

"I'm trying to tell you that I want you to be in my future," Owen said slowly, each word measured and clear. "The question is, do you want that to be your future too?"

Zeb stared at him, then nodded, unable to say the words. They had already said everything there was to be said, after all, and words only held so much weight after dying twice and realizing that life was so much more than any words could describe.

Then Owen took a deep breath in. "Will you come with me?

"Where?"

"Everywhere." Owen grinned. "I want to see the world with you."

Zeb couldn't hold back a smile, though he still had his doubts. "What about Harvard? And the New Academy?"

Owen waved them away. "We can take this year off. I'm sure Sister Stella will understand after everything you've been through, and Harvard already thinks I'm taking a gap year. It's perfect."

"I can't afford it."

"You don't have to pay a dime, and you know that," Owen countered. "Come on, mate, you already died twice. Live a little. Consider it a thank you for sacrificing yourself for us."

"And then what?" Zeb asked after a pause, unable to disguise the slight tremor in his voice.

"What?"

"After we travel the world, what happens next? Do we return to *real* life then?"

"I don't know," Owen said honestly.

Zeb grimaced. "And that's exactly what I'm scared of."

Owen didn't hesitate. "So am I! But I'm less scared doing it all with you."

"God, I really want to kiss you right now," Zeb muttered reluctantly, lightly shoving Owen back when he pretended to lean in. He looked around the room cautiously, but no one was even looking their way.

For a moment, he met eyes with Penélope as she scanned the room as well, and she gave him a small smile that he managed to return. While he felt a slight guilt for leaving her here in the city, Zeb could no longer deny the happiness he felt at the prospect of being with Owen. At long last, it felt as though he had finally stepped into the light.

Slowly, the guests began migrating back towards their couches, as if someone had given a signal. Zeb looked around, but merely noticed that the dawn had begun shining from the eastward-facing windows high on the walls, rosy and golden. He had not noticed how late it was, the wine and conversation with Ari and Owen keeping him awake through the early hours of the morning.

Across the room he heard a squeal and excited mutterings, and looked up to see Chloe reclining beside Penélope, playfully poking her, a bright smile beneath her yellow veil. Suddenly Zeb was struck with a memory—no, not a memory, but a dream—the one he had while sleeping in the temple.

"Owen," he whispered as they sat down on their couches, "I have to tell you something. My dream in the temple—it was about Chloe."

Owen turned to him in worry. "Was it bad?"

"I'm not sure." Zeb saw the vision of the temple under the mountain, the figure standing before the altar, at once Chloe and yet not her at all, like staring at the stars in the sky and knowing they were light and fire and yet sensing they were more at the same time, eternal and far away, too far away to name. "We were in the temple, and the priestess was there, but when she turned—"

"Shhh!"

The room grew very quiet all of a sudden. Zeb's voice failed him as he looked around. Everyone's gaze had fallen upon Penélope, who reclined still and silent on her couch, like an etched drawing of a goddess on ancient vases that Zeb had only seen in museums before coming here. Then Leandros stepped in front of the room, and Zeb understood, his heart dropping at the same time as it filled with love.

Penélope had finally found home.

Zeb shared a glance with Owen, and this time he knew what those green eyes were telling him without needing to hear the words to believe it, and he knew his own reflected them.

Me too.

65

Leandros stood at the front of the hall, surveying the room like a lion atop his kingdom of grass. Penélope's heart pounded as he prowled around the couches on the women's side, nearing her seat. She knew how this part of the ceremony was meant to go, but experiencing it firsthand was entirely different, more wonderful and terrifying than anything she had felt before.

Penélope watched as he pretended to grab some of the other women, who laughed nervously and squealed before his hands returned to his sides and he moved on to the next. Even Sister Stella chuckled at the scene, while the men cheered and shouted him on encouragingly. She looked around the room, spotting Zeb and Owen amid the couches, smiles on their faces. Her heart panged at the obvious gaps of people she would've had at a normal wedding back home, not only her parents and brothers, but all of her extended family, with rambunctious party music for the dance floor, tequila, and her favorite Mexican dishes.

The only thing that consoled her was that she would return to Tierra del Sol soon and see her parents. She would have to lie, say that she met someone while abroad in Greece, that they were getting married and quickly because she was pregnant. Sister Stella told her they would carefully craft a believable story that would excuse her long absences from the city. The thought of lying to her parents was heartbreaking, but it was the only way to ensure the secret of the Seven Sages from being revealed to too many people. Penélope was just grateful she would still be able to see them, even if she could no longer share her life with them.

Suddenly the rays of Dawn pierced above the mountains and shone through the windows, directly upon Penélope's couch as if they had planned it that way, illuminating her figure in gold sunlight amid the dark, dusky room. Leandros came to her and lifted her easily into his arms, so quickly and without warning that Penélope could not help but cry out, even though she was supposed to do that anyway.

Leandros grinned down at her, and she wrapped her arms around his neck as he carried her out of the feasting hall. The guests rose from their seats and followed them while the musicians struck a tune, and everyone joined in a jaunty wedding song:

> *A song for bride and groom we sing!*
> *O Hymen, honor them in bed!*
> *As marriage bells so loudly ring*
> *a song for bride and groom we sing*
> *and pray the gods their blessings bring*
> *to those whom Love today has wed!*
> *A song for bride and groom we sing!*
> *O Hymen, honor them in bed!*

Penélope laughed at the suggestive lines—suddenly cut off into a terrified shout when Leandros threw her in the air and caught her, much to the amusement of the guests, who cheered and continued the song with more enthusiasm.

> *Today the bliss of Love draws near*
> *between a man and his wife dear!*
> *There stands the bridegroom tall and proud*
> *as marriage songs are sung aloud,*
> *like heroes tall and strong of old*
> *with handsome face and heart so bold—*
> *Behold! the bride is no less fair*
> *a nymph-like smile and braided hair*
> *beneath her yellow bridal veil*
> *her cheeks a-flush, so lovely pale*
> *as rays upon a flower shine*
> *its petals soft as wings divine*
> *of Eros flying down on high*
> *and with his bow his arrows fly!*

A song for bride and groom we sing!
O Hymen, honor them in bed!
As seeds upon the couple fling
a song for bride and groom we sing
as Hymen sang on lyre string
the day that Bacchus Ariadne wed:
A song for bride and groom we sing!
O Hymen, honor them in bed!

At last, they reached their new room. Young boys and girls of the household opened the door for them as they showered handfuls of seeds upon them with blessings of fertility. Before they crossed the threshold, Leandros lifted her veil, then the guests quieted. He leaned down and kissed her softly. She threaded her fingers in his hair, pulling him closer as the guests broke out into rowdy cheers. Then, without breaking the kiss, Leandros carried them across the threshold.

Their voices faded once the door to their room was shut behind them. He carried her quietly to the wide, cushioned couch where newly woven blankets displayed a tapestry of the familiar scene when Odysseus and Penelope reunite in their marriage bed carved within a tree. She blushed once he set her down on the couch. Despite how many times they had been intimate with one another, this time it felt different.

Leandros knelt before her, his hands resting on her knees. He kissed her again, slowly and tenderly, then her neck, then her chest, where her white dress had already begun to slip in the commotion. She placed a hand on his arm, stopping him.

He looked up, a sliver of worry in his eyes. "What is it?"

She took an uneasy breath in. "There's something I need to tell you."

Fear shone in his brown eyes, but he nodded, taking her hands in his. "You can tell me anything."

"Before we left Aeaea, I spoke with the goddess one last time, remember?"

Leandros nodded in confusion. "You said nothing had happened."

"And nothing did," she said firmly. "But the goddess asked me for a favor in return for her hospitality, clearing us of any debt to her. She asked me to name our firstborn daughter…Aeaegona."

Then Penélope led Leandros' hand to her belly as his eyes widened with understanding. She was so nervous she couldn't speak anymore, her heart stuck in her throat and her breath shallow.

"Αἰαίγονα," Leandros repeated hoarsely. "*Aeaean-born.* Then this means—?"

She nodded her head, the tears that had unwillingly risen to her eyes falling fast down her cheeks. "I'm sorry I didn't tell you sooner. I wanted to be absolutely sure. And I know it's only a reminder of our future sorrow."

Leandros shook his head as if in a daze, then smiled slowly, before he picked her up again and spun her around in his arms. He kissed her as he lowered her onto the couch once more, leaving feverish, reverent kisses down her body, pausing at her stomach. He closed his eyes briefly, as though he could hardly believe it, then gently kissed her navel. She held his face in her hands, gazing down at him, her heart heavy in her chest as though it were full of the very life-force of the universe, the gravity of love that spun the sun and stars around the earth.

"Through both the sorrows and joys," Leandros murmured, kissing each of her scarred palms, "I shall never stop loving you, nor our daughter."

Then he leaned forward and kissed her once more, sweetly and tenderly, losing herself in the familiar heat of Leandros' touch as the singing voices of the guests crowding around their door were heard muffled in the air, the verses of the marriage song fading into the distance...

His eyes alight when bride he sees
and from his arms she screaming flees
like Daphne fair from God of Sun
across the fields and vales did run
afraid to lose her maidenhood
Apollo's love she long withstood.
Just so the bride cries out in fright
and struggles him with all her might
but when he carries wife away
on blissful blessed wedding day
then never more she mourned for her
dear maidenhood, so sweet and pure,
for lay in love the bride and groom
on nuptial couch in marriage room!

A song for bride and groom we sing!

O Hymen, honor them in bed!
An oath they swore with golden ring
a song for bride and groom we sing
with Hymen, godly marriage king
as Dawn shines forth in gold and red!
A song for bride and groom we sing!
O Hymen, honor them in bed!

66

ON THE LAST DAY of October, roughly one week after Penélope's wedding, the King and Queen of Helena hosted a farewell feast for Owen and Zeb, who were to leave the city on the first day of November.

Penélope pretended to be as happy as can be—and really, she *was* happy—reclining beside Leandros, chatting with the other guests, laughing and joking around with Zeb and Owen as if nothing had changed already, or more to the point, as if nothing were about to change forever.

Leandros gave her space to spend time with Zeb, knowing how much she dreaded his departure. After their wedding night, he had spared no luxury for her, making sure she was comfortable at all hours of the day, convinced that even one small inconvenience would upset both her and their child. Penélope had yet to feel any differently in that regard, but knew soon enough that would change, which was both a terrifying and exciting thought.

They had also yet to tell the King and Queen, wishing to wait until it was impossible to hide any longer. In a private meeting with Sister Stella, she had assured Penélope that any modern medicine and care would be provided to her, though most likely she would have to give birth in the palace, as was tradition, which always made her shudder when she imagined it. Leandros, however, had reminded her that Dora would be there to attend to her and that their housewives were the very best in all of Emmeson. He then added that his own mother had given birth to him in little over four hours and screamed very little.

"That's comforting, thank you," Penélope had said dryly at this last comment. "I'll be sure to remember that when I'm screaming my head off!"

Leandros' eyes had widened as he laughed and apologized, kissing her until she forgave him.

Thankfully, in comparison to their wedding celebration, this feast had only a small number of guests, limited to those who knew Owen and Zeb, including Leandros' crew at Owen's special request. Sister Stella conversed mainly with Queen Cleopatra and Nausicala, while Chloe and Ari hung around Zeb, Owen, and Penélope. Everyone seemed to be doing their best to keep cheerful, passing around the wine and giving each other hefty pours. The sailors even sang some drinking songs, along with one more sorrowful mourning song in honor of Mono, to which Penélope shed a few tears.

By the time the dead of night had passed, Penélope found herself huddled on a couch between Ari and Chloe, Zeb and Owen sitting across from them and holding hands. No one dared comment, not even in congratulations, all of them pleased for once that peace had settled between them.

"So what countries are you guys thinking of visiting first?" Ari asked Zeb and Owen after they poured out another round of wine.

"First, we'll visit London and meet my friends and family there," Owen said, slinging an arm around Zeb's shoulders. "Then I'll take him to see where I grew up in South Africa."

"I can't believe you two are leaving us here to fight this war on our own," Chloe said to Zeb and Owen, crossing her arms, but she had a look of fondness hidden in her dark, critical eyes that Penélope had become skilled enough to detect.

"They've already done enough, don't you think?" Ari asked wryly. "Owen rowed the entire Middle Sea, and Zeb died twice. What have *you* done again?"

Chloe muttered an indecent phrase at Ari that Penélope knew from Zeb's blank face and Owen's delighted one that she had said it in Ancient Greek.

Ari held up his hands defensively. "I did not teach her that."

"No," Owen said with a wicked grin on his face. "But I did."

Penélope and Ari laughed while Zeb rolled his eyes, a reluctant smile on his face. Chloe soon smiled as well, hugging Penélope in a rare display of affection.

"Well, I'm glad you're staying," Chloe said. "I couldn't survive here without you."

She hugged Chloe back, surprised to find her heart go out to her, though she had never had close female friends before her and Alexandria. "Do you know when you'll have your initiation?"

Chloe sighed. "When I'm ready, apparently. Sister Stella is very secretive about it."

"But you're sure you want to go through with it?" Owen asked, raising a brow. "You know, given the whole celibacy vow…"

"I'm sure," Chloe said, leveling him with a look. "But who cares about me? Penélope just got *married*. To a prince. Do you guys realize what that means?"

"That she's almost as rich as you?" Owen joked, earning him one of Chloe's ruthless glares.

"No, though she's now richer than all of us combined from what I've heard." Chloe rolled her eyes when no one offered an answer to her question. "What it means is that she's going to be Queen of Helena one day! Do you guys even know how much power she will hold? She'll rule this entire kingdom!"

Although Penélope had already realized this, to hear it from the mouth of someone like Chloe struck her to the core. Her reality as a wife and mother had hardly sunk in, let alone her future responsibilities to an entire people. The others looked at her in slight awe, though Penélope detected a glimmer of pride in Zeb's gaze, which she was warmed to see.

"All that would mean nothing if I didn't have you guys as friends," Penélope said honestly, looking around at each of them. "No matter what happens with this war, I'm just so grateful that this place brought us all together."

They all nodded in agreement, falling into a deep silence. It seemed the night was winding down to the final hours before dawn, and soon they would all go to bed and wake up to say their final goodbye. Fear clutched at her heart, followed by a deep wave of sadness. She wished this night would last forever, that Zeb and Owen had any reason to stay even one more night before returning home.

As if in answer, the doors to the hall opened with a loud *bang,* and everyone turned in surprise. Even the band of musicians abruptly ceased playing their music. No one was supposed to join their party this late or disturb them save for emergencies. But none of them were thinking about that as they stared at the figure half-obscured in shadow.

Ari stood up, his shoulders tense, staring wordlessly as the figure crossed the threshold into the hazy glow of the lamps lining the room, revealing familiar shoulder-length brown hair and a serious face.

Penélope gasped. Chloe's hand flew to her mouth. Zeb and Owen both turned and froze in shock. Alexandria saw them and nodded her head, awkwardly standing with a duffel bag at her feet, a backpack carelessly hanging from one shoulder. She looked exactly how Penélope remembered, in the same emerald green dress she and Chloe had made for her, though now in the face of their royal robes it seemed haphazard and cheap.

"What on earth is she doing here?" Owen muttered under his breath.

This seemed to rouse them from their shock. Ari started forward at the same moment as Chloe sprang to her feet, but before they could reach her, another voice spoke loudly in the quiet.

"*You.*"

Penélope turned to see King Leon standing up and staring straight at Alexandria, his face pale and his eyes wide, as if he were seeing a ghost.

"But it can't be," King Leon said, his eyes filled with fear, and Penélope suddenly understood. "You're dead!"

Then Ari stepped forward. "That is not Elena, my King," he said gravely. He paused and met Alexandria's eyes, one of which Penélope clearly saw glimmered green like the Emerald Stone. "That is Alexandria. Her daughter."

Epilogue

The pitted, burning battlefield *below the city walls stretched before her eyes like the very Land of the Dead on Earth. By the curved shore, the slim Greek ships were moored next to their military camp. Long had her people fought against their invasion, but the end was nearing.*

She sighed. How could she stand by and watch the destruction of her home, her city, without warning them? When she knew the death and destruction to come?

But she also knew no one would ever believe her. How many times had she warned Priam of the consequences that Alexandros' love for Helen would incur? How many times had she prophesied the ten years of war? How often had she told her people of the generosity that would in truth be their downfall?

No one ever listened to her. It was her fate to stand at the ramparts and watch as Hector and Achilles faced one another. It was her fate to watch when the Trojan heroes all fell or fled one by one, including Priam himself. And there was nothing she could do about it.

"Mourning already?"

She swiveled around, her heart beating fast in her chest. No one was nearby, not one guard or lamenting wife peering over the walls at the battle below. Only him, dark-haired and handsome, but ruthless and cruel as only the gods could be. His dark eyes sought hers, but she glanced away, her body flushed and tense under his gaze, as if it were the sun's harsh light striking her.

"My Lord," she said obediently, bowing her head. "I was merely observing the battle."

He approached slowly, leisurely, his limbs strong and corded with muscle, his bow slung over one shoulder, appearing at ease, but she knew in a flash quicker than lightning he could let loose destruction. When he came to stand before her, she shivered. He raised his hand and brushed his knuckles against her neck, lifting back the thick locks that flowed around her shoulders in the style of mourning.

"You have the power to stop this war," he murmured. "Don't you, Cassandra?"

She held her breath as he traced a fingertip down her arm, pure, burning power radiating from that touch alone. But she had long ago sworn her vow of chastity and would not stray from it, even if it meant angering a god.

He sighed, gently turning her around, then pointing at the battlefield below. "You know what will happen to the race of Trojans. You know Hector shall die, dragged impiously by bold-hearted Achilles in grief for the slain Patroclus. You know that wily Odysseus shall devise the Gift-Horse to slip past Troy's defenses. Yet you would rather watch them all suffer, doomed to their fate."

Cassandra lifted her chin proudly. "As mortals, we are all doomed to the same fate. One day, I shall be slain by the same sword that fells the great son of Atreus, despite my warnings. After all, it was not my gift of prophecy that has led men astray, but their denial of it."

"By denying me," the Lord of Light said coldly, "you deny your own gifts."

She turned around, heated and ready to fight, when suddenly she was no longer at the walls of Troy, but in the stone-carved temple at the heart of the pillars of the sea. He stood before her, too close for comfort. Her mind still spun with the vision of Cassandra.

"Why have you shown me this, my Lord?" she asked.

He smiled slowly. "I believe you already know the answer to that, Aethusa."

She went still, her heart beating faster. "You wished to be her lover. She denied you. That is why you cursed her gift of prophecy, is it not?"

"Clever girl."

"Then you want the same of me?" she asked, standing tall, undaunted by all of him save the eyes alone, whose blinding vision was too powerful to behold straight on, like gazing directly at the sun.

But while Cassandra had been a mortal and vowed chastity, Aethusa was a goddess, daughter of the Sea King, and had taken no such oath. She had been chosen as the next Sibyl of Apollo according to her father's will, and she would not now go against him.

"If you do not wish to share the same fate," he murmured. "Then yes."

Aethusa nodded, sealing her fate. "So be it."

The handsome god did not wait to be told twice, wrapping her in his arms and kissing her. His very touch was burning hot, like fire, like the light of the sun glowing under her skin. She gasped when he pinned her to the floor with his unforgiving strength, their legs entangled on the cold stone, pleasure coursing through her veins like molten flame.

As she threw her head back, their eyes met briefly, and her vision exploded in white, but within that painful burst of light she glimpsed all—the broad heavens and the wide-skirted earth, the realms of gods and mortals and Death, all that was and all that will be mirrored above and below like light glancing off the wine-dark sea—just before she saw her two sons born by Apollo, her lover for all the days allotted to her before he chose his next Sibyl, whom she could see now as clear as if she were lying down beneath her, as if she were seeing her from his eyes as they embraced, a young woman with black hair, high cheekbones, pale, shapely limbs, whose name was—

"Ἔγειρε, Χλόη!"

Chloe opened her eyes with a gasp.

Appendix of Untranslated Ancient Greek

Ἴθι! *"Come!"*

Ἴθι, κόρη. *"Come, girl."*

Καλῶς. *"Well said."*

Πέος. *Penis.*

Πηνελόπη Ἅιδόσδε ἦλθε καὶ δράκων Ὀσείριδος ἔκτανε! Ἡ ἐν θανάτῳ οὐ μόνον ἔβησεν ἀλλὰ νεομένη κόσμον ἀρχαῖον ἀνένεικε! Σὺν ᾗ τὸν βασιλῆα Λέοντα σώσομεν!"

"Penelope went to Hades and slayed the dragon of Osiris! She not only walked through death but she returned home and restored the Old Order! With her [help] we will find/rescue King Leon!"

Κύκλωψ. *Cyclops.*

Τίς ἐνταῦθά που ἔρχεται? *"Who goes there?"*

Τίς εἶς? *"Who are you?"*

Οὐ ἀνήρ. *"No man."*

ἡ γυνή? *"A woman?"*

Μούνη? *"Alone?"*

Οἶνος? *"Wine?"*

Ἱμείρεαι οἴνου? *"You want wine?"*

Βάλλετε! *"Strike!"*

Κλέπται! Φονῆς! Ἀρκεῖτε! *"Thieves! Murderers! Help!"*

Ἐμή ἥρως. Τὸν ἐμόν βίον σοί ὀφέλλω. *"My hero. I owe you my life."*

Χαῖρε, Μονόπους. *"Thank you, One-Foot."*

βασιλεύς Λέων. *"King Leon."*

Μηρία καίεσθε. *"Burn the sacrifices."*
Αἷμα ἐμοὶ δίδωθι. *"Give me the blood."*
Ποῦ Τειρεσίας ἐστι? *"Where is Tiresias?"*
Ἄξεσθε Τειρεσίαν! *"Bring forth Tiresias!"*
Τειρεσίη. *"Tiresias."*
Ποῦ πατὴρ ἐμός ἐστι? *"Where is my father?"*
Κέρβερος. *"Cerberus."*
Φεύγετε! *"Flee!"*
Καλυψώ. *"Calypso."*
Ἕλκεσθε ἱστία! Πλέεσθε κώπαισι! *"Raise the sails! Take to the oars!"*
Χέρσον εὑρίσκω! *"I spot (dry) land!"*
Ὠγυγία. *"Ogygia."*
Ἄναξ Λέανδρος. *"Prince Leandros."*
Μονόπους, Ἀκάκιος, Νικόστρατος, ἴτε! *"One-Foot, Akakios, Nikostratos, come!"*

ἄνδρα μοι ἔννεπε, μοῦσα, πολύτροπον, ὃς μάλα πολλὰ
πλάγχθη, ἐπεὶ Τροίης ἱερὸν πτολίεθρον ἔπερσεν...

*"Tell me about a man, Muse, of twists and turns, who wandered
very much, after he had sacked the holy citadel of Troy..."*
—*Odyssey*, Book 1.1-2

Ἢν σὺν σοὶ μένω, σῖτον καὶ οἶνον ἑταίροις πέμψεις. Αὐτίκα ἔργον λεγώμεθα. *"If I stay
with you, then you will send food and wine to my comrades. Then let us talk business."*
Εἰ δοκεῖ, ἐμοὶ ξεῖνοι, λαμβάνετε ὅσον σῖτον βούλει. *"Please, my friends, take as much
food as you wish."*
Γύναι ἐμή. Ξεῖνε. Πίετε! *"My Lady. Guest-friend. Drink!"*
Εὖγε, παῖδε. *"Well done, kid."*
Οὐ τὸν σεαυτοῦ πατέρα γιγνώσκεις, Λέανδρε? *"Do you not recognize your own
father, Leandros?"*
Πάτερ? *"Father?"*
Χαῖρε βασιλεῦ Λέον. *"Hail, King Leon."*
Ἔγειρε, Χλόη! *"Wake up, Chloe!"*

Acknowledgements

The making of a sequel, even one that feels as distinct and whole as this one, requires a different kind of self-belief than the first book in the series. Thankfully, I had the support of my amazing family, who have nonstop encouraged me in my writing journey. That belief would not be as strong without you.

A big thank you to my friend and fellow Classicist, Grace, who read my first draft and gave me such positive and constructive feedback. Her close attention to the Ancient Greek dialogue and poetry is unparalleled, and I am forever in her debt for correcting my at times wishful Greek constructions and free-spirited attitude toward accent marks. Thanks also to our intellectual discussions and our travels in the ancient world, from which many of the descriptions of Emmeson and the philosophical themes explored took their inspiration.

As always, thank you to my extremely talented cousin, Alexis, who has designed all my covers, and yet each time manages to blow me away with her artistic genius. If it wasn't for you, I would struggle to publish more than my first novel, and I certainly wouldn't like seeing my books half as much on my shelves. Here's to many more collaborations kept in the family!

Finally, I want to acknowledge the role that poets like Alexander Pope and J.R.R. Tolkien had in my creation of the poems—or really, songs—that occur in this novel. In part, I wanted to evoke the world of Homer more realistically, in which song and dance were a primary, if not *the* primary, form of entertainment and communal living. Rituals would have had songs, and any form of dinner party, especially among the elites, had bards (like Homer, if a bard by that name indeed once existed) who would sing songs for them.

Poets like Pope and Tolkien, who translate ancient material in creative, poetic ways, and with the latter inventing poetry that feels equally archaic and meaningful for a world harkening back to that murky age in prehistory, have certainly inspired me to try my hand at various styles of poetry to explore daily life in a similarly ancient—and often magical—world.

398

About the Author

Zoë Tavares Bennett is a writer based in Los Angeles, California. She is also the author of the Ancient Roman historical novel *The Sun of God* and the mythology-inspired poetry book *Sofia Before Love*. She has a degree in Classics from Williams College, specializing in Ancient Greek and Latin, and is currently a graduate student at UCLA's Proto-Indo-European Studies program.